Across the Dead Line

The Complete Legend Series

To Mary–
Enjoy!
6/17/2017

J.L. Fredrick

Lovstad Publishing
www.Lovstadpublishing.com

ACROSS THE DEAD LINE
THE COMPLETE LEGEND SERIES VOL. 1

First Edition

ISBN: 0692390839
ISBN-13: 978-0692390832

Printed in the United States of America

Cover design by Lovstad Publishing
Cover photo by Joel Lovstad

Dedicated to all my loyal readers

Novels by J.L. Fredrick

Across the Dead Line
Across the Second Dead Line
The Private Journal of Clancy Crane
Unfinished Business
Piano Man
The Other End of the Tunnel
Another Shade of Gray
The Gaslight Knights
Thunder in the Night
The Great Train Robbery of Monroe County
Mad City Bust
September Ten
Aftermath
Cursed by the Wind
Dance With a Tornado

Non-Fiction
Rivers, Roads, & Rails
Ghostville

Across the Dead Line

Part 1

Across the Dead Line

ONE

Only the slight whisper of a breeze rustled the leaves. A few birds chirped back and forth in coded messages only they could understand. Cory faced the old two-story brick building that stood among scattered remains of decaying, crumbling structures. Faint piano music seemed to be coming from within it, although there was no evidence that anyone had entered the premises recently, perhaps years. No wonder its existence didn't appear on the map – it looked as if it had been forgotten generations ago, left to endure the elements on its own. Shaded by towering, arching oaks and maples that suggested a cathedral, the drab walls reflected just enough of the mid-afternoon sun to reveal the faded remnants of a sign painted above the front verandah: *Tanglewood Lodge.*

The name certainly seemed appropriate. It was difficult to imagine how such a picturesque setting could have been abandoned and left to crumble away. But the more he thought about it, Cory remembered what a remote location this was, and he reminded himself that he was stranded there. His four-wheel-drive Ford Bronco was out of gas, and he was at least five miles – maybe more – from the highway, across several ridges and valleys.

Wading through the waist-high grass and weeds toward the verandah he could still hear the piano, and now there were voices and laughter. That meant people – and a ride back to town.

Barely supporting his weight, the deck planks sagged and creaked under his feet. He pulled on the door. The rusty hinges screamed an eerie screech that reverberated through the big empty room – empty except for the remains of several broken tables and chairs and an upright piano, one end partially submerged into a rotted floor.

He stood there a few moments in the dead silence. Now there was no piano music. There was no laughter. There were no voices. Just silence. Dead silence.

"HELLO?" he called out. "HELLO? IS ANYBODY HERE?"

There was no answer.

"HELLO?" he called out again. He was certain he had seen some movement at the back of the room when he came in, but now there seemed to be nothing but dust and cobwebs.

He walked cautiously toward the staircase leading to a second floor balcony listening for the least bit of noise, but all he heard was the squeaking floorboards with each step he took. The stairs shuddered and moaned and the banister wobbled under the slightest pressure. At the top he peered down a long, narrow corridor. "IS ANYBODY HERE?" he called out once more, and again there was no response. He opened every door along the hallway – at least twenty rooms, some closet-sized and some quite large – but all empty. There was nothing.

Somewhat perplexed with the situation, Cory returned to the outside verandah, listening carefully again, but now all he could hear was the chirping birds and the wind stirring the leaves. Thoroughly convinced the building was void of any living creatures and the sounds he had heard earlier were just a product of his imagination, he sat on the edge of the porch contemplating the four-hour hike back to Wellington. There were probably more important things he should have been doing on a Saturday afternoon, but right now he had no choice. And exploring the reaches of this new and unfamiliar wilderness, and the opportunity to step into the shadows of yesteryear and to fill his eyes with this grand utopia was worth every minute he would have to make up when he returned to the new apartment that was in total disarray.

By the time he reached the highway, the sun was just a red glow on the horizon. He thought about sticking his thumb out to the passing cars and hitching a ride the rest of the way into town, but it was only another mile, give or take, and the walk would help him get more familiar with the new surroundings.

His tiny apartment over the garage of the big old house on Harrison Street was a welcomed sight, even though he had just arrived there that morning, and all his belongings were merely heaped in the middle of the living room floor. It was home for the next ten months. The Wellington College campus where he was enrolled was less than a mile away, and a gas station, a neighborhood grocer, and a laundromat were just a few blocks down the street. Several restaurants were just minutes away, should his cooking skills prove to be less-than-desirable. What more could he possibly need?

Somewhere under that disorganized stack of boxes and bags existed a Styrofoam cooler containing a few essentials he had packed: pork and beans, a loaf of bread, and a package of hot dogs. Although it didn't sound like the most appealing fare for his first night of independence in a new home, it was his only choice, and it would have to suffice.

He located the temporarily lost cooler and hoisted it onto the small kitchen table. There came a knock on the door. He wasn't expecting anyone -- he didn't know anyone here.

"Who is it?" he said peering toward the door.

"Mrs. Higgins, the landlady."

Cory opened the door. The gray-haired Clair Higgins was the only familiar face so far, and he had met her only once this morning when she handed over the key and introduced him to the apartment.

"I heard someone come in, but I didn't see your car in the driveway... thought I'd better check."

"Oh, it's just me. My car ran out of gas out in the country. I'll have to get it tomorrow."

"Well...okay. My husband's car is in the garage, but it hasn't been out in years...since he passed away. And I don't drive, you know, so I can't be of much help I'm afraid."

"That's okay. I wouldn't think of bothering you, anyway."

The old woman glanced around at the chaotic disarray scattered about the room. "Looks like you have quite a mess."

"Yeah," Cory replied. "It'll keep me busy for a while." He had seen her living quarters downstairs, and one would be hard-pressed to find a single knick-knack out of place or a speck of dust anywhere.

"All right, then," Mrs. Higgins said. "If you need anything, I'll be downstairs." She turned her stooped body away from the door and slowly made her way down the steps. Cory wasn't sure if she was truly concerned about an intruder, or if she was just a busybody.

TWO

Silver Spring was no longer just a little mining camp. For years it had remained no more than a supply base for prospectors in search of that lucky strike that everyone was sure existed somewhere in these hills. Its business district consisted of a log cabin housing the General Store, a simple shack serving as a saloon, and a livery stable where the stagecoach stopped for a fresh team. The rest was a hodgepodge of shanties and tents dotting the hillsides. There was no railroad then. People and supplies arrived by wagon over a trail that could scarcely be called a road.

It was commonly known as "Dog Patch" then, and it wasn't until an old prospector, Samuel Benson struck the richest vein of silver ever found in this part of the country, that the citizens became self-conscious. With the future of their town assured, they renamed it "Silver Spring" in honor of Sam Benson's discovery.

To Silver Spring then men and women began pouring in by stage and covered wagon. Desperate miners and dreamers, alike, arrived on foot carrying with them nothing more than blankets. Wagon trains came in with loads of lumber and other building materials. Great wains drawn by sixteen-mule teams rumbled down its single dusty street loaded with ore destined for the mills.

From the handful of fortune hunters huddling in tents, wagons, and ramshackle huts, Silver Spring leaped upon the map as a full-fledged town. Within months the population was estimated at three hundred; two years later that figure tripled. The railroad arrived, and the town sprouted and grew.

Those meager beginnings were only memories to those few pioneers who still remained, and history to the thousand residents who flocked here after that old prospector, Samuel Benson, changed the course of destiny for this quiet little corner of the world.

Now there were streets and stores, hotels and saloons, blacksmiths and barbers, wagon works and billiard halls, clothiers and a bakery, butcher shop, brewery, sawmill, a school, churches, a newspaper and a Post Office. Sam Benson's claim, along with many others, had long since been sold to Hayden and Smith Mining Company, who wasted no time to construct the silver reduction mill, and smelter furnaces. The Wilson Stage Line had contracted to carry away the bullion, cast in bars weighing two or three hundred pounds each. The silver production process was complete, and so was the town it now controlled.

It was the mining element – those men who made the strikes and squandered their fortunes in traditional free spending – that set the standard of Silver Spring life. But it was the average citizen who maintained the steadiness. He filtered in, looking toward this successful new place to give him his due in life. Out of the hundreds and thousands, he might be the one to strike it rich, but more often he would settle for a meager living at his trade. Or he might discover some unclaimed plot of fertile valley soil ideal for a crop of corn, wheat and alfalfa. He rose early and worked hard, and eventually, toughened himself to an attitude of devil-may-care, and convinced himself that he really didn't need all the luxuries he left behind in another time.

THREE

"There's a ten dollar deposit on the can," the gas station attendant said. "And I'm alone on Sunday mornings so I can't give you a ride back to your car, either."

"That's okay," Cory said, embarrassed by his mistake. "Maybe next time it'll remind me to look at my gas gauge before I leave town. I'll bring your can back this afternoon...it's a long walk."

About a half mile out of town, a pickup truck stopped beside him. The driver leaned across the seat, rolled down the passenger window and asked, "Run out of gas? How far do you have to go?"

"Just up the road a ways...but my Bronco is way out in the woods."

"Hop in. I'll give you a ride."

Cory lifted the gas can into the bed of the four-wheel-drive truck and climbed into the cab. The driver looked about twenty-five, friendly, and eager to help. Perhaps he *wouldn't* have to carry the forty-pound burden all that way.

"I really appreciate your help." Cory said, as the truck got up to speed.

"No problem. My name is Milton Sinclair...but everybody calls me "Slinky."

"Glad to meet you, Slinky. I'm Cory Brockway ...but everybody calls me "Cory.""

Slinky chuckled at the response. "Never saw you around here before...you just visiting?"

"No. I start college at Wellington in two weeks. Just got into town yesterday."

"College boy, eh? Well, you'll like it here. Lots of good bars and plenty of girls too."

Cory had always placed his college education in a more serious light than frequenting bars and chasing wild women, but this conversation seemed to be leaning toward a friendship, and it certainly wouldn't hurt to make a few friends.

"Now where's that Bronco of yours?"

"It's quite a ways off the highway...down that dirt road up on the right."

"How far off the road?" Slinky seemed a bit disturbed when he saw where Cory was directing him.

"Long way. About five miles, I think."

Slinky stepped hard on the brake. A cloud of dust engulfed the truck as it came to an abrupt stop on the dirt road. "You mean you're way out in Silver Spring Hills?"

"Is that what it's called?" Cory detected a certain amount of terror in Slinky's voice.

"This is as far as I go. Sorry."

"Well, that's okay...I didn't expect anyone to go all the way out there. Thanks for the ride."

Cory jumped out of the truck and retrieved the gas can, then waved as Slinky backed up to the highway and drove off. What had started out as his salvation from a long walk ended in an act of abandonment. Obviously Slinky had no interest in going any farther on this dirt road, much less beyond where it ended.

And what a strange way of cutting off the conversation: as soon as Slinky had spoken the words "Silver Spring Hills" it was as if he had flipped a switch on his personality control panel.

"Oh well," he thought as he picked up the gas can and started walking. "I planned on this... might as well get on with it."

His feet had been hurting for quite a while by the time he got to the stream. Taking his shoes and socks off and submerging his bare feet into the cool water turned out to be the perfect therapy. Almost immediately the burning sensation dissipated. He sat on the creek bank for a few minutes enjoying the instant relief. From there he couldn't see the Bronco yet, but he could see the top of the hill and part of Tanglewood Lodge. Wondering if other people knew of this place he began to recall the strange experience he had there yesterday. Certainly the noises he thought he heard then were just his imagination -- there was no better explanation.

He looked at his watch – 2:15. It had taken a little more than four hours to get here from the highway, and it was four hours he was glad were behind him. With shoes and socks in one hand and the gas can in the other, he waded across the thirty-feet-wide stream, eager to feed the Bronco and start the easier journey home.

As he poured the gasoline into the tank, he felt a peculiar urge to climb the hill to Tanglewood again, to take one more look. He didn't know why, exactly, but he'd developed a certain fascination with the old building, and not so strange, he rather enjoyed the serenity this obscure hilltop offered. It was like no other place he'd ever been.

The Bronco came back to life with a little coaxing, but Cory wasn't going to waste a single drop of the precious fuel climbing the grade to Tanglewood. He wasn't taking another chance on running out before Wellington was in sight.

The scene at the top of the hill hadn't changed. The birds still sang their cheerful peeps, and the breeze still whistled through the trees. Tanglewood Lodge still sat poised as the appointed sentry overlooking the valley.

Cory stomped through the weeds in the small clearing toward the other side of the ridge. Only the foundation rocks remained of the ruins of several smaller buildings. Further down the hillside, he could see a ribbon of land that looked as though it had been cut into the hill.

"A road?" he thought. He had to investigate. He stepped onto the narrow strip of level ground and tripped on something quite solid hidden from view under the weeds. Railroad tracks. This was a railroad bed. The rails were rusted and the ties were all but rotted away. He scanned the grade in both directions. It seemed to disappear around the hillside a hundred yards to the west, and maybe twice that far to the east. With all the timber covering these hills it was impossible to pick up any sign of it continuing on anywhere else. Now his curiosity had reached a point somewhere beyond his imagination. He began walking, following the tracks to the west. Just past the bend the tracks ended at the edge of a deep gulch. On the other side he could see the remnants of the trestle that had once spanned across, and apparently its footings had been washed away by floodwaters. He found much the same sight two hundred yards in the other direction. Time and the elements had isolated Tanglewood from the rest of the world.

Cory started back to the Lodge. He was relishing the beauty and breathing in the freshness of this forgotten paradise when an intermittent whistling sound pierced through the tranquility. A strange bird species? An airplane? No, it wasn't any of those. It sounded more like... no, it was just his imagination playing tricks again. But then he heard it again. He stopped to listen. This time he identified the sound, and it wasn't his imagination. It sounded like a train whistle. An old-fashioned steam locomotive whistle. High-pitched, shrill, and coming nearer. He turned to look behind him up the tracks from the east where he had just gazed at the crumbled trestle. For just an instant, his eyes fixed on the front of the locomotive, thick, black smoke bellowing from its stack, white steam hissing from the sides, and so close he could feel the heat. He dove off the tracks, tumbling, crashing through the tall weeds.

Only a moment later as he lay there in the weeds, he heard nothing but the birds and the wind. He looked up, relieved that he had narrowly escaped the crushing blow of a speeding locomotive. But now there *was no locomotive.* He looked down the tracks to the west. Nothing. Not even a trace of the black smoke. Not a single weed disturbed.

"That's it," he said to himself. "I'm going home before I lose my mind completely."

As he passed by the Lodge, he thought he'd stop to remove the pesky pebble that had gotten into his shoe. He sat on the edge of the verandah taking off his sneaker, trying desperately to ignore the piano music and the laughter coming from inside. Surely his imagination was getting the best of him, just as the phantom locomotive had. Suddenly, two gunshots rang out and the sound of shattering glass quieted the voices, but the piano kept playing.

"Okay!" he said, as if answering someone's call. "I'll look in there *one more time."*

He pulled the door open. Silence. His vision blurred for a moment, but he had seen a movement. He walked slowly toward the far end of the room where a broken-down bar sat among the rubble of dozens of shattered bottles and glasses. On the wall behind the bar were a few remaining shards of the mirror that once hung there. Cory realized then that it had been his own reflection in the bits of mirror that created the illusion.

He climbed the rickety stairs, pushed open the squeaky doors of each room, and just as yesterday, the rooms were all empty.

Cory looked at his watch. It was 3:15. He could get the borrowed gas can back to the station before it closed at five o'clock.

FOUR

Jeremiah and Daniel Crane were two rugged, ambitious young men ready to meet the challenges of their chosen new surroundings. Bravely determined to establish a new life, their wagons rolled into Silver Spring heavily laden with everything they and their wives owned, a substantial bankroll, big dreams, and their ten-year-old brother. A late family arrival and now orphaned, Clancy had become more like a son to Jeremiah, the oldest of the Cranes. Spirited and adventurous, he too was eager to discover the excitement of this new place they would call home.

A spiritually strong woman, Millie, Jeremiah's wife, remained loyal to her husband, and with great confidence in their future, she would support and encourage Jeremiah's ambitions and was willing to make the best of whatever came their way in this strange new land.

Kate, though, was already sick of the daily hardships that made life miserable to one who did not harden to them. She kept plaguing Daniel to go back to Ohio where there were bathtubs, wallpaper, neighbors and flat acres of rich soil to plow and plant. But her protests could not persuade Daniel to turn their wagon back.

To add to the misery, available housing in Silver Spring seemed almost non-existent. Several days went by while the only roof over their heads was the canvas of their wagons, and meals were prepared over a campfire on the banks along Silver Creek just outside of town. The days seemed long and the nights treacherous, especially to Kate, as she, Millie and Clancy sat huddled next to the fire, staring off into the darkness and wondering when Jeremiah and Daniel would finally bring some good news.

All this time, the Crane brothers were rubbing elbows with society. The saloons and gambling halls attracted even the prominent businessmen during the nighttime hours, and Jeremiah was quickly gaining the interest and support of several influential men of the community.

Oliver Grumby took a liking to Jeremiah right from the start. He owned the controlling interest in *The Striker*, Silver Spring's only newspaper, and he held title to most of the vacant land left within the town. Some considered him less-than-honorable, as he had been the "boomer" – the town promoter who had seductively convinced many a businessman in the East to buy building lots and set up shop in Silver Spring with highly exaggerated reports of development. But as time went on, the prosperity of the mining region around Silver Spring allowed Grumby to make good his promises of a thriving community.

William Hayden, the banker and co-owner of Smith and Hayden Mining Company, had earned the respect and admiration of the working class. He had established and operated the first banking house in a rented room at the rear of the hardware store until his own building could be erected on Main Street. Considered by most as straight as a wagon tongue, he readily extended generous credit to the miners for building homes, and had financed many of the structures housing entrepreneurships that comprised Silver Spring's prosperous business district.

Jeremiah's wagon was hitched to a star, and he impressed both men with his plans to build and operate a large, luxury hotel in Silver Spring. But he needed the land, and the sale of a much lesser Inn back in Ohio wouldn't cover the expense of his proposal here. He would need some additional financial backing. And now he had both.

"You know," Grumby said, "I have a piece of ground on Connor Street, right at the end of Main that would be perfect for your hotel."

"And as long as Silver Spring needs an establishment like you're proposing," Mr. Hayden added, "I'm sure my bank can assist you with the finances."

The plan was in motion. Jeremiah was now committed to a much larger scale operation than he had anticipated, but in order to make anything at all happen, it had to be that way.

"But we need a place to live in the meantime," Jeremiah said, "and my brother and his wife need a place, too."

Oliver rubbed his chin. "Stop in at my office tomorrow. I have a couple of empty houses over on South Street. They're small and they're nothin' fancy, but you can probably move in tomorrow."

And with that, Jeremiah rounded up Daniel from the faro table and headed back to the wagons and their lonely wives to deliver the good news. This was the last night they would sleep by the creek. Millie and Kate had cooked their last pot of stew over a campfire. By tomorrow night, they would be gazing through real windows to view the smoke blue horizon tuning to a flushing red sunset.

As it turned out, there was only one house, and just like Grumby had told them, it wasn't much of a house. Poised in a neighborhood of many just like it, its paintless form faced South Street, the last street on that side of town. Beyond there – across the "dead line" – lay that part of town where seemed to collect the less desirable class of people – panhandlers, freeloaders, thugs, winos, and mostly those too lazy to take full-time work to afford better. The streetless hillside was a crowded mass of tarpaper and tin shanties and wooden shacks that probably did little more than keep the rain out – the abandoned temporary dwellings of the first prospectors to settle here, and now host to society's outcasts.

The move into that house was not entirely satisfactory to Kate. She had hoped for something better, and if it hadn't been for Millie calming her down, she might have started walking back to Ohio. There were advantages to sharing the house: they could share the cooking and cleaning chores as well, and they would have each other's companionship in a town where they did not yet have any friends, and in a neighborhood where they weren't too sure if they *wanted* any.

From the first time Millie peered onto the half acre of gnarly, tangled trees and brush, she didn't question Jeremiah's intentions. She pictured a quaint little Inn with a half-dozen rooms to rent, perhaps a small pub and a lunch counter – something like the one they had left in Ohio. And perhaps that's what she thought was being built at first sight of the coach house and livery stables at the far side of the lot. But then Jeremiah informed her this would be their next temporary home until the completion of the hotel – *Tanglewood Lodge,* as it would be named after the tangled wood lot it was replacing. Millie still didn't question any of this. It seemed logical to her that they would need a stable for their horses, and a carriage house wasn't unreasonable either, as long as it meant moving away from the "dead line."

The carriage house seemed a palace in comparison to that dilapidated old shack they had occupied on South Street, and although it was large enough to accommodate Daniel and Kate in its upstairs rooms, Jeremiah, Millie and Clancy would have it all to themselves. Daniel had taken a job with the Wilson Stage Line as a shotgun messenger – he would ride as the armed guard beside the driver atop the Concord carrying the silver bars to Red Hawk, thirty-five miles away, three times a week. Now, he and Kate were moving into their own house in a picture-postcard neighborhood across town. Everything seemed to be working out quite well.

It was late fall when the outer shell of Tanglewood was up and the roof going on when Millie could no longer hold back her comments. She had made a vow not to interfere in Jeremiah's business, but now, three months pregnant with their first child, she was getting a little concerned.

"My goodness!" she said to Jeremiah. "This certainly seems a lot bigger than I expected."

"Well, I made a deal with Mr. Hayden at the bank: If I built a bigger hotel, and made it the nicest place in town, he would loan me as much as it would take."

Millie didn't dare ask how much that would amount to. She knew better.

"And our guests will dine on rosewood tables with Aubusson carpeting underfoot, and six of the rooms upstairs will have big brass beds –"

"Sounds like you're expecting just rich folks to stay here," Millie interrupted.

"Oh, but there will be fourteen regular rooms, too."

"Twenty rooms! And just who do you think is going to take care of all those rooms? I'll have a baby to look after!"

"Don't worry, Millie. This won't be like our little Inn back in Ohio. We'll have maids hired to do all that."

Somehow, Millie suspected there was going to be more than hotel rooms and dining. Since they arrived in Silver Spring, Jeremiah had spent a lot of time in the other saloons and gambling halls, and now it seemed logical that similar facilities would adorn Tanglewood as well.

Now that they had their own stable and corral, Clancy would miss the daily visits with old Brook, the stable proprietor. It had become Clancy's responsibility to look after their horses boarded at old man Brook's Livery. Brook was a gruff old man, but somehow Clancy could charm him into hours of conversation. Besides the rig of high stepping horses and fancy carriage that could be rented by the hour, day or week, he was an excellent storyteller with a never-ending supply of tales of when he served with the U.S. Cavalry, or when he was a wagon master on the high plains. He'd spin yarns with the details of harrowing escapes from Indians, run-ins and gunfights with bandits, and rides through raging floods and blinding blizzards.

It wasn't surprising that his stable had soon become Clancy's favorite spot, and whenever he couldn't be found, Millie always knew exactly where to look.

FIVE

Cory pulled the Bronco up to the gas pump. He had been holding his breath for the last couple of miles, as the gas gauge was reading almost empty again.

This time, instead of the middle-aged gentleman who he had seen there before, a younger fellow in his early twenties strolled out to the gas island.

"Fill 'er up," Cory instructed the attendant. He stepped out of the truck, walked to the back, opened the tailgate, and retrieved the empty gas can. "I gave the guy who was here this morning a ten-dollar deposit on this can."

"That was my Dad. He said someone borrowed it, but by three o'clock he didn't think he'd ever see it again."

"Sorry it took so long. I was about five or six miles out in the woods where I ran out. Took a long time to get back out there."

"Six miles! Why didn't you get someone to give you a ride?"

"Well, I'm new in town -- don't know anyone yet."

"Going to school here?"

"Yes, as a matter of fact, I am."

"Kind of early to be moving into the dorms."

"Oh, I'm not in the dorm. I rent an apartment just down the street."

"Well, you've got a couple weeks to get acquainted. Been downtown to any of the bars yet?"

"No...I just got here yesterday. Didn't have any wheels last night, so I just stayed home."

"Well, you'll have to come down to the "Academy" on Third Street tonight. That's where a lot of the college crowd hangs out on weekends.

Cory paid for his gas, and the attendant returned the ten- dollar deposit.

"My name's Jimmy. I'll be at the Academy tonight about eight. Come on down... I'll buy you a beer and you can meet some of the gang."

"Okay... I might just do that. Maybe I'll see you there."

It kind of went against his better judgment to start hanging out in the bars. His apartment still looked like the aftermath of an earthquake; a mountain of dirty laundry awaited attention; there was no food in the cupboards; no less than twenty letters to friends needed writing. But an evening at the local hangout could prove to be beneficial. So far, he'd had minimal contact with anyone here, and this would be a good opportunity to meet some new friends. Organizing the apartment could wait another day.

The Academy was a typical, dimly-lit bar with black lights making the checkerboard black-and-white tiled floor to appear as if it were only half there, and all the white shirts to move around with a brilliant, ghostly glow. Otherwise, there didn't seem to be any particular theme to the decor.

Sunday night didn't appear to be the night for the largest crowd, although it wasn't quiet by any means, either. A substantial gathering was certainly enjoying the last remnants of the weekend as a blaring jukebox pounded out a lively cadence for two dozen energetic dancers.

"Hey! There's the Bronco Boy!"

Cory heard the distinctive voice slice through the noisy atmosphere. It sounded familiar. He searched the room of strangers until he saw the face that matched the voice. Slinky Sinclair stood at the end of the bar, hoisting a long-necked brown bottle to his lips. He apparently had been here a while.

"How ya' doin' Bronco Boy?"

"Hi, Slinky. I came to check out the local establishment."

"Well you came to the right place. What are you drinking? I'll buy you one."

"Thanks. I'll have a *Bud*."

Slinky turned to the bartender and requested "A *Bud* for the Bronco Boy... on me." Cory scanned the crowd some more. He took a sip and set the bottle on the bar.

"Thanks, Slinky. I'm sure glad I ran into at least *one* familiar face. You're the only person I've met here so far, except for Jimmy at the gas station. Do you know Jimmy?"

"Sure. We went to school together and we still hang out together a lot."

"Have you seen him here tonight?"

"Yeah, I saw him earlier... he's here somewhere. And you should feel damned lucky to be here at all!"

"Why is that?"

"Because *nobody* goes out to Silver Spring Hills and comes back alive. *That's why.*"

There was that name again: Silver Spring Hills. Cory wondered if it was going to end this conversation the way it had that morning, but he was willing to take a chance that it wouldn't. A significant reason for the fear of that area was quite evident – at least to Slinky – and now it sounded as if Slinky was indicating others feared it as well. He had to pry loose some further comment.

"So, what is Silver Spring Hills and what's so terrible about it?" Cory asked.

"Mack." Slinky replied.

"Who's Mack?"

"Oh, yeah. You're new here... you probably don't know about Mack... but anybody who lives in Wellington can tell you about Mack."

"So, who's Mack?" Cory was persistent.

Slinky pulled up a barstool and sat down. "Mack is the ghost out in Silver Spring Hills."

"Ghost? Did you say *ghost?"* Cory pulled up a stool and sat.

"Yeah! There was a whole town out there a long time ago, but I guess the only thing left is an old hotel. Mack is still out there, and he kills anyone who tries to find his treasure that's buried out there."

"Treasure? There's *treasure* buried at Tanglewood?"

Slinky looked curiously at Cory. "Tanglewood! What's Tanglewood?"

"The name on the front of the old hotel."

"Well, I don't know what it was called. Just how close *were* you to Silver Spring?"

"Close enough to see the name on the front of the hotel." Cory thought best not to tell Slinky that he'd actually been inside it. He wanted to be the one to keep asking the questions.

"Well, anyway..." Slinky continued. "...When everyone moved out, Mack burned down the rest of the town, all except for the hotel, and he got killed in the fires, and now his ghost is there guarding the treasure."

"How do you know all this?" Cory asked.

"My Grandpa told me. He said when he was younger, back in the Twenties, there were people who went hunting for the treasure, but none of them ever came back alive. Evil Mack killed them all!"

"Who's your Grandfather? I'd like to talk to him."

"Elmer Dickens. But you can't talk to him – he died ten years ago."

A hand fell on Cory's shoulder. "Well, I see you made it, and you found somebody to talk to," Jimmy said. He sat down on a stool beside Cory.

"Hi, Jimmy," Slinky said. "Tell Bronco Boy, here, about Silver Spring and Mack. I don't think he believes me."

Jimmy took on a peculiar grin. "Nobody goes out to Silver Spring Hills and lives to tell about it. But how did you get on *that* subject?"

"Bronco Boy, here, ran out of gas. And guess where. Silver Spring Hills."

Jimmy looked at Cory with surprise. *"That's* where you ran out of gas?"

"I guess so. From what Slinky told me—"

"Well," Jimmy said, "You must be pretty damned lucky. Just last fall, the Sheriff found a hunter not too far from there – dead. They said he died of a heart attack, but everybody knows that Mack probably scared him to death."

Cory let out a little laugh. "Come on. You guys are pulling my leg."

"No!" Jimmy insisted. "Ask anybody. They'll tell you the same thing. There have been a lot of people found dead out there. Mack doesn't let anybody out of there alive."

"But I got out of there alive."

"You're just lucky."

It was only a matter of time on Monday morning that all forward progress of apartment organization ceased. Cory couldn't stop thinking about Tanglewood and Mack, its resident ghost.

"There's got to be more to this story," he thought. "Some people here certainly believe that Silver Spring Hills is haunted, but none of them have ever been there. They've never seen it. They don't even know the name of the hotel."

He began accumulating in his head all the elements he had absorbed so far, which wasn't much considering it must have taken decades for this lore to develop. But it had all been condensed into a thimbleful of information that seemed more like superstition than fact.

"On the other hand," he thought, "I *have* been there. I *have* seen it. And there *was* something strange about the place."

Cory could hear a dozen voices in his head, all talking at the same time, as if they were calling to him from the great beyond, but he couldn't single out any one particular message. An unidentifiable supremacy was hard at work, urging him to learn more.

He wasn't ready to discredit any of the claims, and the more he recalled his experiences at Tanglewood he convinced himself that the hilltop miles out in the middle of nowhere *was really haunted.* What he thought to be his imagination yesterday – the sounds of a piano, the voices, the gunshots and the breaking glass – today were quite real. *He had heard them.*

And what of the statements Slinky and Jimmy made that "nobody gets out of there alive?" Someone had to have escaped the evil Mack or else there wouldn't have been anyone to carry the tale back to civilization. No one would know he was there.

And is he really evil? Cory couldn't remember ever feeling threatened while he was at Tanglewood, unless he considered the fact that Mack could've been at the throttle of the phantom train when it nearly ran him over.

His uncontrollable urge grew. "The Public Library. I'll go to the

Public Library. If Silver Spring was once a town there's bound to be some information about it somewhere."

Cory gazed around the clutter covering the living room floor. It didn't look much different now than it did two days ago, other than now it was scattered over a much larger area.

It could wait.

And wait it did. Four days went by. Cory's blue and white Bronco became a familiar sight parked outside the front door of the Library. And after four days of searching, he was probably more of an authority on the history of Wellington than anyone living there an entire lifetime. A vast selection of books depicting local history was there at his fingertips; twenty-five years of newspaper archives. But nothing about Tanglewood or Silver Spring Hills. Nothing about people dying or disappearing there. Nothing about Mack. Only verbal contacts with other library patrons confirmed Slinky's and Jimmy's story, but no one seemed to have any more solid information.

Silver Spring Hills had to have a beginning. Tanglewood Lodge and Mack had to have an origin – somewhere – sometime. If that town really did exist, there had to be some recorded history of it. Maybe he was looking in the wrong places. Cory had another idea.

"Is there an Historical Society in Wellington?" he asked.

"Yes, but it's only open Saturdays. What on earth are you trying to find? You've been here all week."

"I'm looking for anything about Silver Spring."

The librarian's smile turned to a questioning frown. "You're not going out there, are you? To hunt for the treasure?"

Cory chuckled. "Well... no, but I am curious about the stories I've heard."

"The Historical Society is over on Johnson."

Not too eager to be of any further assistance, the gray-haired librarian politely went about her business leaving Cory with nothing new except a location on Johnson Street.

Okay. So the librarian did mention the treasure. That could only mean this part of the myth was common knowledge, whether anyone actually believed it was really there or not. But what if it *was* there? And what if there really was an evil Mack? Had he been out to lunch when Cory visited his domain a few days ago? There had to be answers, and now Cory felt even more compelled to find them.

SIX

Daniel Crane, jolting over the rutted roads sitting high on the box seat beside the driver with a shotgun in his lap, was learning the lay of the country.

Not far to the east lay the fair-sized village of Wellington sprawling in the shade of the lofty cottonwoods and shining birch along the banks of the Pike, a muddy little river barely wide and deep enough for the smaller variety of steamers. It was their first stop on the way out, and the last stop on the return. With its many stores, saloons and hotels, Wellington dwarfed Silver Spring in size, but its people seemed so protective of their serenity. Gamblers would come in on the riverboats and by train, but they were never welcome. Often they would crowd into the Wilson Stage, leaving the quiet streets of Wellington behind, and seeking the livelier Silver Spring.

Daniel saw it all. The lumber camps. The limestone quarries. Remote and isolated ranches with sparse cattle herds. And with the establishment of more and more farming settlements, cattle rustling was also becoming common. Stolen cattle from distant prairies were driven into Gopher Hole Valley, where the Lawton boys rebranded and sold them to the local ranchers.

What a dreary, impoverished existence, he thought. Prospecting alone through those empty hills, laboring in a lumber camp or mine or mill, or running a few head of tick-infested cattle. He was always glad to get back to Silver Spring. The bright lights, the pianos tinkling in the saloons and gambling halls, the huge ore wagons rumbling down the street under a cloud of dust, the swarming people – all this commotion and swelling prosperity moved him. He loved the excitement and the pleasure.

On this particular spring evening, another young man rode below him inside the crowded stagecoach, looking out upon the same austere landscape. His name was Alexander Malone. During the past few years, he had done his share of traveling. A talented musician, Alexander had performed with a traveling vaudeville show throughout the East, played accompaniment for singers on a theater circuit in the Midwest, and had even spent a season with a circus. But now he was seeking a quieter life. Alexander Malone was ready to put away his suitcase for good.

He had met another man, Austin Smith, in Minneapolis just a month before. Mr. Smith told him of his mining company and of Silver Spring, and of the grand new hotel there nearing completion; the owner would soon need an entertainer, and Smith possessed the connections to land him the job if he wanted it.

The stage rounded the corner at the end of Main, went down the hill on Connor and in a flurry of dust came to a halt in front of the depot on Railroad Alley. Brook was already there and waiting to take the tired team to a well-deserved water trough and feed box just across the alley at the stables. Daniel carefully got down from his high seat. Malone tumbled out with his luggage. The two men confronted each other briefly.

Malone was a little awed at the imposing figure before him – his steely gray eyes, the six-gun buckled around his waist, and the shotgun across his arm. Daniel Crane, on the other hand, was not impressed.

Malone in his rump-led store suit looked exactly the tenderfoot he was. Daniel saw him as just another common, discouraged city dweller seeking the thrill and adventure awaiting him in this vast, wild territory. Of all the possibilities for his presence, Crane could be certain he wasn't a prospector and he surely didn't have that gambler's look in his eye.

"Is this Silver Spring?" asked Malone.

Daniel gave a condescending glance, nodded, and strode off to the Silver Pick Saloon. There was plenty of time to settle down to a drink at the bar, and maybe a few poker hands before going home to the hearty meal Kate would have waiting for him.

SEVEN

The Wellington County Historical Society occupied the old Opera House on Johnson Street. Not much had been altered to accommodate the museum other than many rows of seating in front of the stage had been removed to make room for the countless displays of artifacts. Even the balcony surrounding the entire arena housed a walkway through time past, but most everything was a portrayal of the City of Wellington from the years of its infancy in pioneer days to the World War II era. Cory soon abandoned the tour and headed for the library occupying the stage.

"There used to be a town called Silver Spring about five or six miles from here," he said approaching the attendant. Cory thought he might save some time by seeking help. "I'm trying to find some information about it. Do you know if there's anything here?"

"I've heard of it," the young girl replied, "but I don't know much about it."

Finally. Someone who didn't cringe at the sound of that name. "There is a book, right over here, that might tell you something. It gives the history of Wellington County back to the Eighteen Hundreds. And right over there is the Newspaper Archive."

"Do you mind if I sit here a while and read through them?"

"Oh no. That's what they're here for. If there's anything else I can help you find, just let me know."

"Thank you..." He looked at her nametag, "...Terri, I will."

Cory made himself comfortable at the reading table and began paging through the book simply entitled "*Wellington County*." The format seemed to have all the cities of the county arranged in alphabetical order. He went to the S's. No Silver Spring. He turned back to the copyright page. 1946. He turned to the page where "Wellington" started. Perhaps, being the nearest city, there would be some mention of the neighboring lost town.

In the entire chapter, the only reference to "Silver Spring" told of "the sixty-some residents who migrated to Wellington when raging fires destroyed nearly every home and business there in 1899." The author gave credit to a man named Theodore Sanford, a former Silver Spring denizen now residing in Wellington, for supplying the information.

Now he was getting somewhere. Silver Spring really did exist –

until 1899. The town really did burn, although there was no mention of how the fires started. And now he had a name – Theodore Sanford. If this man was still alive, and if he was still in Wellington, he might have a real story to tell.

"Terri? Excuse me... I was wondering if you know a man named Theodore Sanford. I found his name in this book. It says he lives here in Wellington."

Terri strained a moment in thought. "Oh! Sure. That must be Ted. He stops in here a lot... brings old stuff in to us all the time."

"Has he ever talked about Silver Spring?" Cory asked.

"Hmmm. No, not that I remember."

"Well, do you know how I can get in touch with him?"

"I think he lives over on the East side of town, but I don't think he has a phone. But like I said, he does stop in here quite often."

Cory paged through the old newspapers the rest of the day. The old gentleman never showed up, but the newspapers – issues of The *Wellington Weekly Star*, as it was called prior to the Second World War – produced a few bits of information that held little meaning to him, except the front-page story of July 27, 1899, unmistakably the description of the event that meant the end of Silver Spring's existence. Rather than photographs, an artist's rendition of burning buildings and people fleeing them covered a quarter of the page, and a bold headline proclaimed: "A TERRIBLE CON-FLAGRATION." In the overheated style of the day, *The Star* told the story:

"The most terrible conflagration which has ever visited the county occurred at Silver Spring last Tuesday afternoon, by which the entire town was lost.

"Words are utterly inadequate to picture the terrible scene – the conflagration, the consternation and the dismay. Business places and homes alike blazed up like a torch in a moment, rendering escape difficult for all.

"The livery stable, railroad depot, and numerous other buildings surrounding the Market Square were immediately wrapped in flames. The picture then presented the roaring conflagration, the terror, the alarm, the uncertainty, the exaggerated rumors of the loss of life, the eager crowds of people – their faces lit up by the flames, all formed a scene to appall the timid and awe the brave.

"It is reported, however, that miraculously only one life was lost during this tragic and devastating event. The resulting casualty was that of the man suspected of being responsible for starting the blaze,

and who allegedly shot and killed Jeremiah Crane, proprietor of Silver Spring's Tanglewood Lodge Hotel. Ironically, he was bludgeoned to death by falling debris. The man was identified a short time later as Zachary McDowell, from Council Bluffs, Iowa. McDowell's daughter and son-in-law arrived in Wellington by train on Friday to claim the body and transported it back to Council Bluffs for burial.

"Terrible as it was, the loss could have been worse. Despite flames and blinding smoke, all residents of Silver Spring fled to safety. The scene presented is, indeed, a sad one. What was once a thriving settlement is now a mass of charred and blackened ruins, strewed with the debris of the great conflagration."

At least now Cory had a baseline. The article named the key players; Silver Spring flourished as a seemingly important contribution to the area. But what events led up to its demise? What happened after? And why had the knowledge of its existence elapsed into the deep, dark recesses of time? Surely, an entire city, though ravaged by disaster, could not be simply expunged from the pages of history and reduced to an inaccurate myth based on the man responsible for its destruction. Or, could it?

EIGHT

On that balmy day late in May of 1891, after eleven long months, Jeremiah Crane flung open the front door to Tanglewood Lodge. Alexander Malone's fingers danced across the piano keyboard sending a flurry of improvised show tunes flooding into the street, announcing the Hotel's official opening. "Fingers'" flair for attracting attention with his music did exactly what it was supposed to do. Jeremiah had planned the timing perfectly: the three o'clock Red Hawk Express was just about to arrive. Every day a parade of travelers marched from the Railroad Depot past his door, turning the corner down Main Street in search of a cold beer, a hot meal, a good time, and a comfortable bed. Today he could offer those people a reason to end their journey at *his* front door - Tanglewood Lodge - he had all those things, and in fine style.

There were other hotels: The Lincoln House, the smaller of the two largest, and The Royal, with its fifteen rooms, grand saloon and gambling hall, until now, had been the most popular places in town, although the beer wasn't always cold and the games not always honest. The dining room menus were most common and the piano players terribly average. The Continental Saloon and Billiard Hall offered but six tiny rooms upstairs - most of which rented long term to miners without families, and although somewhat luxurious and ornate, the North Star was gaining a bad reputation with its dishonest proprietor.

Now there was Tanglewood. Its long, polished mahogany bar, its floors laid with plush carpets, the white linen-covered dining tables, the aroma of fine cuisine, the highly entertaining sounds pouring out of that upright and sometimes keeping rhythm with the clicking ivory roulette ball and clattering dice - all the enticing ingredients that would lure customers off the street and into its parlors. Jeremiah Crane dedicated himself to providing the very best liquors and wines, the tastiest dining room fare, and the warmest hospitality money could buy.

By the time the Red Hawk Express deposited its load of adventure seekers on the depot platform, Tanglewood was only an hour old, but already the saloon had filled with curious, thirsty citizens, the gambling tables nearly all occupied, and even the restaurant was serving up a few late lunches. With the arrival of the afternoon train, the hotel rooms were nearly all booked for the night, and travelers arriving on the stagecoach at seven o'clock would probably take the ones remaining. Jeremiah was quite pleased with the immediate success.

NINE

Professor Percy Barkley walked into the classroom from his adjacent office. He was fashionably five minutes late, and by then the room overflowed with the chatter of the twenty or so students getting acquainted. Gradually the noise diminished to nothing. Everyone was staring at the podium and the gaudy, light green plaid sport coat standing behind it.

"My name is Mr. Barkley." His voice boomed with power and authority. "As a teacher, I'm only as good as my students will allow me to be." While he spoke, he made direct eye contact with every individual in the room. His opening speech was clear and to the point. "My job entails one objective: to teach you to be good, effective, creative writers. I can accomplish that only if you have the desire to learn."

Cory listened intently to every word he said, trying desperately to ignore Barkley's bad taste in clothes. He was here to learn from the renowned Professor who had turned out dozens of successful journalists and authors over the years. Now it was his turn to absorb the wealth of wisdom this man had to offer.

"This course involves a lot of hard work," Barkley went on. "And you'll get out of it only as much as the effort you put into it."

Cory thought back to his first two years at the University, and how then, he had felt little sense of direction wading through the mechanics of all the general courses he was enrolled in there. Only last year did he discover his true calling -- he wanted to be a writer. He had always been good at it, but often ignored his High School teachers' encouragement. But now it was different. Now he had direction. Now Professor Barkley would hone the edge on his talent and lead him to the success he wanted so much.

"We're not going to waste any time getting down to the nitty-gritty. For your first assignment..."

Cory heard a few moans drifting around the room. Apparently not everyone in the class expected the shock of ending their summer vacation so abruptly. Mr. Barkley detected the murmurs too. He peered out among the students over the top of his reading glasses.

"For your first assignment, you will write a short story, twenty-five hundred words, ten pages, about an actual childhood experience."

More groans echoed across the room.

"Choose your subject matter carefully. You'll be coming back to it in later weeks. Typewritten, double-spaced. Due on Friday. And I'll see you here again this Wednesday. Class dismissed."

By the end of the day, Cory had the campus layout submitted to memory. It sprawled over an area about the size of four city blocks, unlike the University where sometimes a half hour walk between classes made for a tightly scheduled day. Here the pace was less demanding, less stressful. He knew he had been quite preoccupied most of the day thinking about his first writing assignment for Mr. Barkley. He had made only one acquaintance the entire day when he paused for lunch in the Student Union cafeteria, and socialized with Buck Paxton over a plate of gummy mashed potatoes and chipped beef swimming in gravy that tasted like one of the main ingredients might have been dish soap.

"God!" Buck said. "The food isn't any better this year."

"How long have you been here?" Cory asked.

"Third year."

"The food always this bad?"

Buck nodded. "But I don't have a car. Too far into town to get lunch every day."

"Aren't there buses?"

"Yeah. But they never seem to fit my schedule."

"I have a car. You can ride with me."

From there the alliance grew. Buck seemed grateful for the friendship and Cory was glad to have met someone who knew his way around.

The assignment didn't seem all that difficult. The hardest part would be selecting the topic. Cory scoured his childhood memories for the right event, but he realized his earlier years lacked anything of much interest. Living in the suburbs all his life rendered little excitement. A daily softball game at the park with the neighborhood kids just about summed up the high points. He fell off his bike once and broke his collarbone. And then there was the family vacation trip to Mt. Rushmore. Not much of a story in any of that.

He gazed around the living room. The place was still in shambles, and now the whole apartment looked more like a battlefield. "If only I hadn't taken that little excursion out in the woods."

Tanglewood! It occurred to him that he *still was a kid*. He still worshiped "Wiley Coyote and Roadrunner," and he still twisted apart *Oreo* cookies to eat the frosting first. No one would ever have to know that this childhood experience happened just two weeks ago. He could disguise the episodes at Tanglewood; change a few details, and make it sound like an adventure from another time, say, when he was ten years old while on a visit to Grandma's.

It was the perfect subject. What better topic than a haunted house could there possibly be? Surely it would be the unique one of the entire class.

The messy apartment could wait. Starting the story couldn't.

The Smith-Corona clicked away, spewing out words far into the night. His Bronco that ran out of gas was now a bicycle that broke a chain. He created the spookiest old "Applegate House" in the shadows of towering pines, deep in a glen he called "Sand Valley." But the piano remained, and without the railroad tracks he had no great climax. They had to stay too. The ghostly sounds once again came to life in his mind and on the page as well. The locomotive rumbled through as if it came crashing right out of the paper.

The story was magnificent. Certainly Mr. Barkley could be nothing but impressed with these ten pages. How could he not like it?

TEN

"Ten percent of the profits... Charlie Daggett will pay me ten percent of everything we get to work for him at his placer mine," Clancy announced at the private supper in the Cranes' living quarters at the back of the Hotel. "And Brook has a two-year-old stallion I'd really like to buy."

"Who's going to do your chores here?" Jeremiah asked.

"I'll only be away on the weekends. Charlie does his farming during the week, and he goes to his mine only on the weekends."

"And what about Church on Sunday?" Millie said. The Crane family faithfully attended Church every Sunday morning.

"I'll take my Bible with me, Millie, and I'll say a prayer before we start working on Sunday morning... I promise."

"If it's what you want to do," Jeremiah said, "I guess we can't stop you. You're fifteen now, and a boy of fifteen ought to be learnin' how to earn a living."

Tanglewood Lodge was entering its fifth successful year. All that time Jeremiah had relied on his young brother to help with the everyday tasks to keep the Hotel running smoothly. Clancy tended the horses and kept their carriage in perfect condition. He trimmed the grass and the hedges, and burned the trash. On market days he knew how to get the best produce for the Hotel kitchen by rising early and arriving at the Market Square before the other shoppers. Clancy had proven himself reliable and trustworthy. He certainly deserved this bit of independence, and Charlie Daggett seemed to be an honest, hard-working man who wouldn't cheat a fifteen-year-old boy of due wages.

Charlie only sat still long enough to eat a meal or to drink a cold beer in the saloon. He was one of those hard-boiled men with artificially serious face, rarely smiling, his actions instant, bold as a cougar and shrewd as the fox. Never tiring, never complaining, he would labor from sunup to sundown, carefully nurturing a crop of potatoes and green beans that found their way to just about every dinner table in Silver Spring.

Part-time prospecting had rendered for Charlie a mediocre placer mine six miles to the north. So profoundly hidden away in an obscure ravine blocked from view by cottonwoods and granite boulders, a natural spring oozed from the hillside creating a trickle of a stream that fed the North Branch Creek, and that no one but Charlie knew existed. It was in that little quarter-mile-long stream where he dug from its sand and gravel bed a few gold nuggets, and soon Charlie had his one-man mining operation in full swing.

But his farm remained top priority. It was a sure thing. The mine could fizzle out at any time, although it continued to produce a handsome income working it just two days a week. With a helper he could increase the production during the summer months before the frigid winter buried the ravine under snow and ice.

So off they went, every Saturday morning at 4:00 o'clock; Charlie, Clancy and an old pack mule Charlie called "Sooner."

"Why do you call him Sooner?" Clancy asked on the first long hike to the mine.

"Because he'd sooner eat and sleep under a shade tree than pull a plow," Charlie explained without cracking a smile.

They'd arrive at the mine by 8:30, go right to work digging and panning, stopping only long enough to eat lunch at mid-day. Every Sunday morning Clancy would read to Charlie from the Good Book, and then offer a little prayer for a successful day and a safe return home. By Sunday evening, they would be trudging back to Silver Spring with at least two hundred dollars worth of gold ore.

During the week, not a single day went by without Clancy's visit to Brook's stable to spend some time with the chestnut stallion he named "Shiner" because of the dark patch around his right eye. He'd ride Shiner bareback around the corral, and often Brook would allow a longer ride out into the countryside. The gruff old man would force a smile as he watched Shiner trotting alongside the railroad tracks with Clancy proudly on his back. Brook knew they made a perfect match.

Late that August, Shiner came to his new home in the stable on Connor Street, and Clancy moved back into his old room in the carriage house.

ELEVEN

The handwriting on the envelope in the mailbox was familiar. It was from his father. Without opening it, Cory knew the envelope contained the money for his apartment rent and his allowance -- something his father had sent religiously every month for the past two years. Sometimes there would be a short letter – bits of news from the home front, and sometimes even a newspaper clipping or two – but often it was only the check made out to the landlord and some extra cash for groceries and gas tucked neatly between the folds of a sheet of yellow legal pad paper. Cory stuffed the letter into his back pocket and led the way up the stairs with Buck Paxton following close behind. It was Friday afternoon. Surviving the first week of school warranted a night on the town starting with a Goliath-sized burger at Abbey's, or maybe a pizza at Papa Leo's. They hadn't decided yet.

"Whoa! What happened here?" Buck said. He was entering Cory's apartment for the first time. "Looks like a tornado hit while you were gone."

"Oh yeah. Sorry about the mess," Cory said, stepping over a cardboard box on his way to the couch. "Just haven't found a place to put everything."

"Cory! That's what cupboards and closets are for."

"Yeah... well... I kind of just unloaded the *U-Haul* and that's as far as I got."

"In a week's time you haven't—"

"Three."

"Three?"

"Three weeks... I've been here three weeks. Are you going to come in and sit down or are you just going to stand there with your teeth in your mouth?"

Buck carefully stepped over the obstacle course and found the other end of the couch.

"What have you been doing all that time?"

"Well... the first day I ran out of gas out in the woods. But I found this really neat place."

"Okay. That's one."

"Then the second day I had to walk back out there with a can of gas... long walk."

"Okay. That's two days."

"And the rest of the time I spent at the library trying to find out about it."

"About what?"

"The place I found out there."

"What place?"

"There's an old building out there... a hotel I guess. Used to be a whole little town, but it was abandoned years ago, and now all that's left is the old hotel."

"Really."

"Yeah. I'd like to go back out there sometime... maybe camp out for a weekend. You like camping?"

"Sure! When do you want to go?"

"How about next weekend?"

"Sounds great. It'll be fun." Buck looked around the room at all the clutter. "But let's get some of this stuff put away...so you can at least walk through here."

Cory remembered the letter from his father and pulled it out of his pocket. "Okay, but I have to see what Dad has to say first."

Buck started plucking books from a box and stacking them on an end table. "Where do you want to put these?"

Cory offered no response. He was concentrating on the letter. Buck opened another box containing dishes and silverware. "I'll find a place for this in the kitchen."

Still no response from Cory.

Another box filled with shirts brought Buck to ask, "Are there hangers in the closet? I'll hang these up for you." He noticed a look on Cory's face as if the letter had caused him to disconnect from reality. "What's wrong, Cory?"

Cory snapped out of a trance-like stare. "Oh! Ah... it's nothing. Yes, there are plenty of hangers in the bedroom closet." He folded the letter, laid the check on the table, and placed the cash in his wallet. "You ready to get something to eat?"

"Not until this stuff is all put away." Buck wasn't going to let Cory get away with postponing the clean-up another day.

All through the large pepperoni pizza Cory had little to offer in the way of conversation. Buck persistently tried to drag him up out of the sudden mood dive, but Cory would just glance at Buck briefly and respond with less-than-enthusiastic answers, then continue to stare distantly into the red-and-white-checkered tablecloth. Even though Papa Leo's was packed with the usual Friday night crowd, Cory had tuned out the buzz of gaiety surrounding him. Buck knew there was something troubling his new friend, but their relationship had not yet reached a point where he thought he had the right to openly question Cory's temperament. He would patiently wait for Cory to come around in his own time.

"Got any plans for tomorrow?" Buck asked.

"Tomorrow? Tomorrow is Saturday."

"Yeah. Saturday usually does come right after Friday night."

Cory acknowledged Buck's attempt to cheer him up. "Yes... as a matter of fact..." He drifted off into another distant stare.

"Well? Are you going to tell me? Or is it a secret?"

"No. It's no secret. I kind of want to go to the Historical Society Museum. Ever been there?"

"I'm a History major. Remember? Of course I've been there."

"Oh, yeah. I forgot."

"Why are you going there?"

"Oh... there's someone I want to talk to...and he might be there tomorrow."

"Who?"

"An old guy who might be able to tell me about..." Cory realized he didn't want to say the name "Silver Spring." Buck might suddenly be looking for a new companion.

"About what?"

"That place I told about. The one I found out in the woods."

"Okay. I can think of worse things to do on a Saturday."

"So...do you want to go?"

"Sure. If you don't mind me tagging along."

"Of course I don't mind. I wouldn't have asked."

"Well, then... do you mind if I crash on your couch tonight?"

"It's kind of lumpy."

"That's okay... so's my bed at the dorm."

TWELVE

Millie wasn't exactly pleased to see John Polk and Gus Barrington, two of Daniel's old cronies from Ohio. Not the most upstanding citizens, they had always seemed to be in some sort of trouble – nothing too serious, but trouble, just the same. On countless occasions they spent a night or two in the Sheriff's guest rooms to sleep off a little too much hooch. And then there was the time that John and Gus – and Daniel – were caught target shooting. The only problem being they were using the neighbor's chickens for targets.

And here they were in Silver Spring. They had a third companion riding with them now. Millie didn't recognize him, but Daniel and Kate seemed to know him. His name was Louie LaPointe and by appearance, Millie had him pegged as the same caliber rogue as John and Gus. She could foresee the same kind of trouble starting all over again – the kind of trouble that always prevented Daniel from success. But he had been away from them now for several years; he had a good-paying job, a happy wife and a nice home. She only hoped that that old gang would not re-unite. Not here. Not now.

They didn't ever stay in town for very long at a time, and there was always certain secrecy with the visits. Even Kate wouldn't talk about them. Daniel would spend the evening at the saloon with them. They'd talk, drink, gamble, and then they'd all go to Daniel's house for the night. Early the next morning, John, Gus and Louie would ride off, and no one would see them again for at least a week. As long as they were staying out of trouble, little attention was being paid to them, but Millie feared their good behavior couldn't last. It wasn't their nature.

THIRTEEN

A warm breeze suggested that summer wasn't giving up just yet. It seemed to be a good day to leave the Bronco parked in the driveway, and walk the mile into downtown. Now that the apartment didn't resemble a war zone, thanks to Buck, Cory couldn't think of a single pressing issue that could possibly steal this wonderful Saturday morning from an itinerary of just goofing off. Buck couldn't think of one, either.

About half way they passed a doughnut shop. "Coffee and doughnut sound good to you?" Cory said.

"Breakfast of champions." Buck couldn't resist the cliché.

They sat at an outdoor table until the doughnuts were gone, and then restlessness set in. They started walking again, sipping from the paper cups. Cory's eyes had taken on that distant stare again.

"I have to get a job." Cory's voice was somber.

"You're not going to quit school, are you?"

"No. Just a part-time job."

"Why?"

"Money. It's called money."

"Yeah...but doesn't your Dad send—"

"The company my Dad works for is on the verge of bankruptcy. He might lose his job."

"Oh. Sorry."

"He said in his letter they might be shut down by the end of this month."

"But he'll find another job." Buck tried to feed encouragement.

"He's almost sixty. It'll be hard."

"Does your Mom work?"

"Just part-time... a checker at the grocery store."

"So... what are you going to do?"

"What do you think? You've lived here longer. What kind of jobs do you think there are here?"

"What do you want to do?"

"I don't know... I'd like to work for the newspaper. I want to be a writer, you know."

"Won't hurt to ask 'em."

"Right. I think I will. Monday. After classes."

At least now Buck understood the reason for Cory's detachment the night before. But he didn't want to see Cory being miserable all day. Perhaps he could divert his thoughts to something more pleasant.

"Sure hope the weather is this nice next weekend."

"Why's that?" Cory asked.

"We're still going camping, aren't we?"

"Oh! Yeah. Sure. We have to get all our stuff ready."

"We can do that tomorrow."

Only a few more steps away from the Museum front door, Cory stopped. "Now if this old guy is here, I might be talking to him for a long time."

"That's okay. I'll just look around."

"I hope this isn't boring for you." Cory seemed to be apologizing in advance.

"If I get that bored I'll go down to the Drug Store... there's a few things I need anyway."

Cory headed straight for Terri as soon as he spotted her. "Hi, Terri," he said. "Nice to see you again."

"Oh! Hi." Her smile was a bit flirting.

"By any chance has Mr. Sanford been here?"

"No... but I did see him this week."

"Do you think he'll be in today?"

"Yes... said he found some old books."

"Would you—"

"I told Ted someone was asking about him."

"Oh... well, could you—"

"He'll be here about two."

"Good! Will you—"

"I'll tell him you're here."

"Okay... thank you... I'll be back at two."

Cory glanced at his watch. It was ten minutes to twelve. Buck was still browsing, and now they had plenty of time for lunch, or the trip to the Drug Store, or whatever Buck wanted to do for the next two hours.

Walking to the Drug Store, buck said, "You know? I've been thinking—"

Cory interrupted. "Didn't hurt yourself, did you?"

"Ha... ha... very funny, asshole."

Something grand was happening to their friendship: they could poke fun at one another now without offending. Cory and Buck were finally paddling the same canoe.

"Maybe I should get a job too," Buck continued. "I have only two classes on Tuesdays and Thursdays."

"Yeah?"

"I could help buy groceries."

"What do you mean?"

"At your place. I'd help buy the groceries."

"Buck... listen. I appreciate the offer. But I don't need charity."

"Charity, hell. I was hoping you'd let me eat a few meals at your place. You know how bad the food is at the campus cafeteria."

"Oh... well that's different." Cory contemplated the proposition. "Can you cook?"

"I can open a can of pork 'n beans just as good as anyone."

"I have a better idea. Why don't you just move in?"

Buck picked up a tube of toothpaste and walked toward the checkout counter. "Dorm room's paid for until the end of the semester... but maybe then."

Cory looked at his watch. It was only twelve-thirty. "Want to grab some lunch at Abbey's?"

Just across the street, Slinky and Jimmy came out of the restaurant as Buck and Cory were going in. The foursome stopped to chat a while as friends usually do. Well into the conversation the subject of camping came up.

"Hey! How about going with us next weekend?" Cory suggested.

Jimmy scratched his chin. "I don't have to work next weekend... sure."

Slinky thought a moment. "I guess I could get away for a couple of days. Where are you planning to go?"

Without realizing the possible reaction, Buck said "Silver Spring."

"On second thought..." Slinky said, "...I don't think I can go."

Jimmy followed suit. "Maybe some other time," he said as he and Slinky sauntered away.

The big clock on the wall at Abbey's Cafe seemed to tick so slowly. Cory looked up at it about every two minutes. He didn't want to miss this opportunity to talk with Theodore Sanford. His anxiety was driving Buck crazy.

"What's so important about talking to this guy?"

"Oh... I just want to hear the story first hand."

"What story?"

"About the town that isn't there anymore...he lived there." Afraid to say any more, Cory just kept peeking at the clock every now and then.

While they ate their cheeseburgers, Buck pulled a slip of paper from his shirt pocket, unfolded it, and began to ponder over its contents.

"What's that?" Cory asked.

"A list of topics... I have to pick one... research project for my

American History class." He handed the paper to Cory.

Cory scanned the list. He was glad he wasn't a History major. "I know the one I'd pick," he said.

"Which one?"

"Number six."

Buck reviewed the list again. "Bank Robberies?"

"Sure. Sounds most interesting to me."

"Sounds hard."

"Hard... but most interesting. No one else will pick that one because it *is* hard. It's a sure bet you can impress your teacher."

"You might be right."

"Hey, look. It's quarter to two. I'm heading back to the Museum. You coming?"

"No... I'll poke around town a while. I'll catch up with you later."

"That's Ted... over there, talking to Joanne," Terri said, pointing toward the front information desk.

"Thank you, Terri."

Theodore Sanford's scant, silvery hair barely covered the sides of his head, and his bent-over body leaned heavily on a cane clutched in his left hand. His face was wrinkled with nearly eight decades of experience, but his eyes sparkled with joy and satisfaction as he watched Joanne page through the old book he had just handed her. Cory waited patiently until it appeared their conversation had ended.

Politely he intervened. "Mr. Sanford?"

The old man slowly turned to answer the address. "That would be me."

"Hi. I'm Cory Brockway." He extended his hand toward the old gentleman.

"You must be the young man that Miss Terri told me about."

"Yes, sir, I must be. And I'm so pleased to meet you."

"Well... what can I do for you, young man?"

"Would you like to sit down somewhere... so we can talk?"

"What do you want to talk about? I haven't got all day, you know, what with the dance lessons, rock climbing and sky diving."

Cory gave a little chuckle. "Well I won't take too much of your time, I promise."

"Joking, son, just joking... I wouldn't jump out of a perfectly good airplane."

Cory knew he was in for a treat. Mr. Sanford definitely had spirit.

"Now, what did you want to talk about?"

Cory leaned toward Mr. Sanford and whispered, "Silver Spring."

The old man's face lost its grin. "Silver Spring. Nobody wants to talk about Silver Spring."

"I do, Mr. Sanford," Cory said.

"Forget the *Mr.* crap. Name's Ted. And let's go sit on a bench outside. Kind of stuffy in here, don't you think?"

"Yes... that would be good."

"There's one just down the block under a big oak tree."

The walk to the park bench was slow and deliberate; the shady seat was a welcomed destination to both. Ted sat with his hands folded and resting on his cane handle.

"You aren't thinking of going out there, are you?" Ted's voice had a little twinge.

"Well, actually... I've already been there."

Ted's squinty eyes widened and stared at Cory in disbelief. "Nobody has been there in years... well, no one I know of."

"I know," Cory said. "Looked pretty... abandoned."

Ted perked up. This was the first time in decades that anyone had taken an interest in his home of so long ago. But he suspected Cory was stretching the truth about actually walking on the grounds where he had spent his youth. "What was it like?"

"All grown down in weeds now... only building left standing is Tanglewood Lodge."

"Tanglewood. No one nowadays even remembers that name." Ted looked Cory square in the eyes. "You really were there, weren't you?"

"Yes, sir... three weeks ago today."

Listening to the descriptive details that no one could possibly know unless they had seen the location, Ted was thoroughly convinced Cory really had visited Silver Spring, what was left of it. And if he was courageous enough to venture so deeply into that forbidden territory, to the very heart of an evil existence, and return unharmed, then he must possess some special power to resist its venomous bonds. He deserved any answers he was seeking.

"What is it you want to know about Silver Spring?"

"Well... everything. That book said you lived there."

"Yes. Born there, in fact."

"Everything. Everything you can remember."

"That could take all afternoon, you know."

"I've got all afternoon."

Ted leaned back and crossed his ankles. He began his story.

"'Long about 1885, some old prospector discovered gold out in those hills. Wasn't much – just a few nuggets – but enough to attract every gold-crazy prospector within a hundred miles. Wasn't long until there was quite a bunch of 'em. Some were finding a little gold and silver now and then, and some weren't. Then a big mining company moved in. Paid everybody quite well to work for them. The miners started building homes and farming the valleys, and soon there was a regular boomtown -- on top of the ridge.

"Then the railroad came, and then the lumberjacks. Why, there were so many people comin' and goin' it's a wonder where there was room for them all.

"Then in 1890 a young man named Jeremiah Crane built Tanglewood Lodge. It was said he was quite wealthy, and the hotel proved it – big, and luxurious for that time. That hotel was the hot spot of the town. Saturday night dance hall Saloon, and the Sunday morning Chapel. And of course, plenty of rooms upstairs for weary travelers.

"As time went on, though, the gold and silver mines played out. The big mining company shut down and the town started to dwindle. That's when it started attracting a lot of crooks too. Tanglewood Lodge became a hideout for cattle rustlers, bank robbers and gunslingers.

"Word got out among the thieves that Jeremiah Crane was a wealthy man. Rumors started about his fortune that was hidden somewhere around Tanglewood. People living in Silver Spring were getting real nervous, and some even started moving away.

"Then, in July of '99, a man named McDowell came to town. He was a mean varmint. I was only ten years old then, but I still remember seeing him get off the train. Big, black, beady eyes, and a big, black, bushy mustache, and a big, black hat. Everybody knew he was trouble as soon as they saw him.

"He stayed around a few days, like he was waiting for someone to show up. But they never did. One day in the middle of the afternoon, he challenged Jeremiah – for the fortune, I guess – threatening to kill if he didn't get it. When Jeremiah refused to cooperate, McDowell gunned him down, right in the Hotel Saloon. A bunch of the men tried to track him down, but they never caught him.

"That was the day that Silver Spring began to die. People started packing up and leaving. They knew that more trouble was on the way.

"They had a funeral for Jeremiah the next day, and as soon as the grave was filled in, the last remaining residents of Silver Spring began leaving their town for the last time. My older brother and I were waiting in the wagon just down the road from the hotel. Our house was the last one on that end of town. Mamma and Papa were just coming out of the house when the real excitement started.

"Don't know why, but McDowell started setting fire to every building in town. He was a madman. Me and my brother watched the whole thing. Our house was burning and we were already on our way out of town, but we saw it all. McDowell almost got to the hotel – Tanglewood – and that's when the ghost of Jeremiah rose up from his grave and attacked McDowell from behind and killed him before he could get to the door."

Cory's face blazed with intrigue. The saga seemed so real, so valid. Right up to the part about Jeremiah's ghost. He wasn't quite sure he believed that, but out of respect for Mr. Sanford, he wouldn't question it.

"Wooooow! And you saw it all right to the very end."

"End? The story doesn't really *end* there."

"There's more?" Cory wasn't at all disappointed.

"Oh, sure there is. You see... Jeremiah Crane and McDowell were the only ones who died *with* Silver Spring, but there were many after that."

"After?" Cory felt his skin tingle – he started associating Ted's words with the myths he'd heard earlier.

Ted continued. "Jeremiah's wife and daughter came to Wellington to live. It seemed they had no money. They lived like paupers, so everyone was certain they had not brought Jeremiah's fortune with them, and no one else ever made a claim to finding it. Some people speculated that Clancy Crane, Jeremiah's son had taken off with it, because he disappeared for quite some time after the fire. But then he finally showed up, and he was as poor as a church mouse too.

"In the meantime, just a couple of weeks after the fire, a gang of foolish treasure hunters went out there, but only two came back alive. They told all of Wellington what they saw and what had happened to the others. The ghosts of Jeremiah and McDowell were still doing battle on that ridge, and they had killed the others. The two survivors said they had heard McDowell yelling out that he would kill *anyone* who tried to take his money.

"The train stopped there only one time after that – just long enough for the Sheriff and his Deputies to retrieve the eight dead men."

"So, what ever happened to Jeremiah's family?"

"His wife passed on quite a few years later, and his daughter married a fellow from California and they moved away."

"And his son?"

"Don't know what happened to Clancy."

"And so that's how the story got started of Silver Spring being haunted?"

"Story? Ain't no story. It's fact."

"Ted? Do *you* believe there are really ghosts out there?"

Ted leaned forward onto his cane. "There's one more thing I can tell you about that place."

"What?"

"In the summer of 1937 my brother, Albert decided that it must be safe to go out there. Said the ghosts would surely be gone after so many years. He wanted to go hunt for the treasure. Wanted me to go with him, but I refused."

"So... did he go?"

"He went, all right. And he never came back. Disappeared out there without a trace."

"No one ever saw him again?"

"Nope."

"No letters? Nothing?"

"Nothing."

"Maybe he found the treasure and just took off."

"No... Albert was the sort of guy that if he had found it, he would have come back braggin' about it."

"Are you sure—"

"He died out there. I know it."

FOURTEEN

Millie had a sixth sense about trouble. On several occasions she had correctly predicted bad endings hours and sometimes days before something happened. Perhaps it was just a mother's protective instinct that was producing the premonitions. Ever since their daughter, Clair, was born, she had found herself paying closer attention to everything going on around her. She would always experience some sort of jittery feeling long before the potential danger struck, and would send Clair off to the safety of her bedroom. It happened the day an argument erupted in the saloon and the two men shot each other dead right on the front verandah of Tanglewood. It happened the evening about suppertime when a couple of crazed, drunken lunatics started shooting up the town. Stray bullets wounded at least six innocent bystanders that night – one inside Tangle-wood's front door.

There had been many times Millie sensed approaching danger, and she was feeling the jitters this morning as she viewed the four men sitting at a table in the dining room eating breakfast. She was trying to ignore her feelings – she had *always* felt uneasy when Daniel and the "Polk Gang," as she had come to call them, were together. So far during the past year while they had been spending a great deal of time in Silver Spring, they hadn't been at the root of any trouble. Polk, Barrington and LaPointe had behaved themselves quite nicely, but still, Millie was having difficulty ignoring her sixth sense on this day.

Early the next morning, the Wilson Stage left the Silver Spring Depot with six passengers and $43,000 in silver bars. It would return that night with the Smith-Hayden bank deposit to cover the miners' payroll. Hundreds of these runs had been successfully made, mainly because of the strict confidence in which they were carried out. Daniel Crane and the driver, Wesley Dawson were the only ones to know the large sums of money were aboard their coach. Passengers always climbed in unsuspecting they were riding with the perfect highwayman's target, but with such guarded secrecy, the Wilson Stage Line had never lost a single dime to thievery.

At Wellington the teams were changed after the grueling, steep hills from Silver Spring. About five miles out, where the road made a sharp bend approaching the wooden bridge across the Pike River, five men watched from a hilltop as the stage slowed to negotiate the curve.

At five o'clock, on the return trip from Red Hawk, Wesley Dawson eased the tired teams onto the bridge and the Concord's wheels rattled across the planks. From their hiding spot under the bridge, five masked and heavily armed men emerged blocking the roadway leading away from the bridge.

"Whoa, boys," one of them cried out. There was nowhere for the stage to go. It stopped. Daniel Crane recognized the threat of instant doom with five large caliber rifles aimed in his direction. He knew his one shotgun was no match for five gunmen, and in his mind he was ready to concede to the highwaymen's wishes without putting the passengers' safety at risk. But Wesley panicked. He dropped the reins and grabbed for another shotgun by his side. Before he could even point the gun in the proper direction, one of the robbers fired two shots, one of them hitting Wesley squarely in the chest. He lurched forward and tumbled to the ground, bouncing first off the back of one of the wheel team. The terrified horses bolted away instinctively around the sharp curve, sending the coach careening from side to side, Daniel barely hanging on, and eight passengers inside hearing a continuing volley of gunfire and fearing the worst. With the reins dragging on the ground amidst the galloping hooves and out of Daniel's reach, he braced himself, aimed his shotgun over the back of the stage, readying himself for a second attack. But the gunmen did not give chase.

A short but sharp incline just outside of Wellington slowed the tiring animals. Daniel leaped to the ground and in heroic fashion gained control of the runaway teams, retrieved the reins and guided the stage safely into Wellington.

The timorous passengers clambered out of the coach, and in the twenty minutes until Sheriff Endicott arrived, the news of the attempted stage hold-up buzzed through the streets, while Daniel Crane still nervously guarded the precious cargo. The story was told how he had bravely defended them from the band of thieves and delivered them safely here. The driver's loss was deeply regretted, but they were greatly indebted to Daniel's courage.

The Wilson Stage arrived in Silver Spring an hour late that night. A large posse had already formed in Wellington and was attempting to pick up the trail of Dawson's killers. The shocking news reached Silver Spring long before Daniel Crane and the replacement driver brought the stage to a stop on Railroad Alley. The town was in an uproar. Its citizens were suddenly realizing the threats of a violent faction looming within their territory.

Tom Hargrove, reporter for the *Striker*, waited patiently for Daniel Crane to conclude his business. He had heard countless rumors and unofficial reports. Now he would get the facts.

"There were five of 'em," Daniel said.

"Did you recognize any of them?" Tom asked.

Daniel hesitated. "No, they wore masks."

"Was Wesley Dawson really killed? Or perhaps, was he just wounded?"

"I'm afraid he's dead. A couple of the Sheriff's men brought the body back to Wellington just as we were leaving."

Daniel made it quite clear he didn't wish to say any more about the bungled hold-up just then. Ignoring the rest of Tom's questions he headed for Tanglewood.

Millie didn't need to ask any questions.

FIFTEEN

Cory sat through the entire hour of Mr. Barkley's class on Monday waiting to hear a critique on his paper. The Professor was being rather cruel with all the others, and almost brutal with some. The suspense made him sweat, and the lack of adequate room ventilation didn't help.

"I gave you this assignment to find out where you're at...and now I know. Most of you need a lot of work. Some I would suggest to take up finger painting."

This guy was downright mean. Nasty. But that was his style, and that was what made him a good teacher. He demanded the most from his students - and those that responded with honest effort might some day join the ranks of his long list of success stories.

The session was coming to a close. Professor Barkley had not even mentioned "Applegate in Sand Valley" by Cory Brockway. Did that mean it was good? Or did it mean his story was so terrible it didn't merit even a bad review? Cory hoped it wasn't the latter.

Barkley dismissed the class. "Mr. Cory Brockway… I want to see you in my office."

Cory stood just in front of the desk. Barkley looked down at the ten pages Cory had turned in to him last Friday, displaying no emotional expression. Cory could see a lot of red ink handwriting on the first page.

"Mr. Brockway? What is this?"

"My story I wrote for the assignment, Sir."

Barkley looked up into Cory's eyes. His expression was heating up, approaching a point of anger. "But it's not the assignment I gave you. I told you to write about an actual experience, not a science fiction fantasy."

"But that's the way it really did happen."

"Nonsense. Ghosts and phantom trains? This reads like something right out of Twilight Zone."

"But I—"

"But nothing! You're getting way ahead of me. Do it over. The subject is good, but this time make it sound like something I can believe."

Cory knew there was no use in disputing the issue. Mr. Barkley had made his point. He would have to rewrite the entire piece. "Yes, Sir. I'll try my best."

"Good. Have it with you on Wednesday."

"Yes Sir."

This was the third afternoon in the last four that Buck chose Cory's kitchen over the campus cafeteria, and more than likely he would end up on Cory's lumpy sofa rather than his lumpy bed at the dorm. But Cory didn't mind. Buck was a good friend, and he enjoyed the companionship. And Buck was a better cook.

"Are you going to apply at the newspaper office today?" Buck was by the stove stirring a pot of something that smelled delicious.

"Gonna have to put that off for a couple days..." Cory sniffed the aroma. "...I have to rewrite my story."

"Was it that bad?"

"No… Barkley thought it sounded like science fiction… 'right out of Twilight Zone' he told me."

"Sounds like a compliment."

"Well it didn't sound like a compliment at the time."

"So what does he want?"

"Something more believable."

"Spaghetti is done… you hungry?"

"I'll get the plates."

"I'm going to the library tonight anyway. I won't bother you."

"The one downtown?"

"Yeah. Research."

"You want to take the Bronco? It's a long walk."

"If you think it's okay."

"Of course I think it's okay. I trust you… now let's eat."

By late Tuesday afternoon, after his lightest scheduled day of the week, Cory had nearly finished the second version of "Applegate." He'd worked on it all afternoon, and although he thought it seemed rather boring and bland without the ghostly piano music and the phantom train, he hoped it would be what Mr. Barkley wanted. In another day or so he'd know.

His eyes fell on the rent check his father had sent. This was a good time to take a break and deliver it downstairs to Mrs. Higgins.

He knocked on the back door where she had told him to always come. She spent most of her time in the kitchen or a den in that part of the house; she would always hear his knock on the back door.

"Hello Cory… so nice to see you."

"Hello Mrs. Higgins. I brought the rent money."

"Well, thank you. Won't you come in?"

"Actually, I probably should get back upstairs."

"Oh, come on in... there's a pot of homemade soup on the stove... and I bet you haven't had supper yet."

"Well, no I haven't, but—"

"Then come on in and have a bowl of soup."

"Well, okay." He *was* getting hungry, and the soup *did* smell rather good.

"You just have a seat by the table in the den."

"Thank you, Mrs. Higgins."

"I don't have many visitors, you know. So many of my friends have passed on, or are in nursing homes."

Cory sat down in the den while Clair Higgins continued to fuss in the kitchen. Admiring all the antique furniture, he noticed a very old picture in a frame propped up on the bureau to his right. He leaned toward it to get a better look. It was of a middle-aged man and woman, a small girl and a boy in his late teens, all standing in a family portrait-style pose on what appeared to be a porch. At first glance, he thought the woman might be Mrs. Higgins, but with closer inspection the woman in the picture looked nothing like her.

"Would you like a glass of milk with your soup?" Mrs. Higgins called from the kitchen.

"Yes, that would be fine." Cory studied the picture some more. At the very top edge were the bottoms of letters – a sign painted on the backdrop wall – looked like G-L-E-W-O-O.

Clair came into the room carrying a tray with the steaming bowl of soup and a tall glass of milk. Cory was still staring into the photograph.

"Is this your family?" he asked.

"Why, yes. It's the only photograph ever taken of us together. I was seven years old."

"Where is this?"

"That picture was taken by a traveling photographer on the front steps of my father's hotel."

"Where's the hotel?"

"Oh, that place isn't even there anymore. It's just a ghost town now."

Cory's head was spinning and his stomach was doing flip-flops. Her father's hotel. Ghost town. G-L-E-W-O-O – part of the name "Tanglewood." Could this possibly be? Was Clair Higgins the daughter of Jeremiah Crane?

"Silver Spring, it was called," Clair said. "Better eat your soup while it's hot."

Cory swallowed the lump in his throat. All this time he had

been searching for an explanation, it had been right here – one flight of stairs from his own apartment. But for some reason he didn't quite understand, he decided it best not to say anything about the story he'd heard from Ted Sanford. *Ghost town* was an understatement, but this wasn't the time to divulge his knowledge about any of that.

He sipped at a spoonful of the hot soup. "What was Silver Spring like, Mrs. Higgins?"

"That was so long ago. I don't remember much about it now."

"Don't you remember *anything* about it?"

"Oh, yes... some. I remember the hotel, and all the people coming and going. And I remember some days after school me and my friends would sit on the hill and wait for the train to come through."

A vision of the big, black locomotive bearing down on him flashed before Cory's eyes. "Engine Number Twenty-Nine," he said without thinking.

"Why, yes... I believe it was. But how did you know that?" Clair seemed a little surprised.

"Oh... ah... just a guess." Cory took another spoonful of the soup.

"I don't recall too much else. There were so many bad people coming to the hotel, I hid most of the time."

"What kind of bad people?"

"Mamma told me they were robbers and cattle thieves, and I was always afraid of them, so I would hide when they came around."

"Did you live there long?"

"Only 'till I was eight years old... 'till the day after my Daddy was killed, and that awful man started all the fires."

Cory laid down the soupspoon. Now the answers were starting to get interesting. "What happened to your father?"

"All I really know is that I heard the two gunshots. Mamma said that awful man killed him, and the next thing I remember was Daddy's funeral. And after the funeral that terrible man started burning the town. That's when we left – Mamma and me."

"What about your brother? What happened to him?"

"Brother? Oh, the boy in the picture. Clancy was my Daddy's brother... my uncle. We didn't see Clancy for a long time after that. We were afraid he'd been killed too."

"But he wasn't."

"No... I guess he was scared too, just like the rest of us. He hid out in the woods for about two months, and then one day he found Mamma and me here in Wellington. He told us about what had happened at Silver Spring after we left."

Clair's voice sounded more sincere with every word. Cory knew he was about to hear a version of the story that might be a little closer to the truth. "So, what did he tell you?"

"Cory? You're the first person I've ever repeated Clancy's story to, but he's dead now too, so I guess it can't hurt."

"Why would telling his story hurt anyone?"

"Well, let me tell you the story, and then you'll know."

"Okay."

"Clancy had been hiding behind some bushes near Daddy's grave. There was hardly anyone else left, so he was afraid to come out when that awful man started burning the town. He watched as every building, one by one went up in flames. When the man came to the only building not burning yet - Daddy's hotel - Clancy ran out from the bushes, grabbed a big chunk of burning wood and whacked the man over the head. Killed him!

"Clancy was so scared then, he ran out into the hills and hid for three weeks. By the time he found us, everyone was saying it was my Daddy's ghost who had killed the man, and we never told anyone differently. Clancy wanted it that way."

"Wow! That's quite a story." Cory wasn't quite satisfied. He knew he could get more with the right questions. "Did you ever go back to Silver Spring?"

"Oh, no. Mamma took a job as a maid at the hotel in town, and when she died several years later, I married Mr. Higgins and we moved to California. We lived there until Higgy retired, and then we came back here."

"Your father was the owner of a hotel. He must have been wealthy."

"My Daddy died a poor man. Spent everything he ever made building that hotel. But he was a proud man too. He'd never admit he had no money. He'd say: "My whole fortune is in that hotel." And the rumors started from that. I guess that's what got him killed."

Cory finished the bowl of soup. Now it was time to go back upstairs and finish his *dull* story for Mr. Barkley.

"Thank you, Mrs. Higgins, for the soup and the story about Silver Spring. They were both wonderful."

Silver Spring's eulogy, as delivered by Mrs. Higgins, was quite similar to the legend told by Ted Sanford, however it did clarify the mystery of what actually brought on the demise of "that awful man," Mr. McDowell. Of course he was *awful*. He killed her father and burned the town; certainly the behavior to justify Clancy's sudden act of violent anger.

It corroborated Ted's version of what happened to the town's people, and why Tanglewood Lodge escaped the arson's torch. It explained why Clair and her mother lived like paupers after the tragedy – there was no fortune.

But it didn't resolve the deaths of eight treasure hunters several weeks later, or the disappearance of Ted's brother some thirty-eight years later. Were the ghosts of Jeremiah Crane and Mr. McDowell still dukin' it out several weeks after the town was destroyed and deserted? Was Mack still trying to protect a fortune that didn't exist, even decades later?

Cory wanted to believe a reasonable explanation did exist. After all, there was a reasonable explanation for the sighting of Jeremiah's ghost: Clancy darting from near the grave, only to attack and kill McDowell and then disappear into the woods led some to believe they had seen Jeremiah's spirit acting in revenge. That seemed reasonable enough. And Clancy disappearing for two months simply out of fear – understandable. In fact, everything about the stories appeared quite logical once all the elements from both were combined.

Cory was feeling mixed emotions. He knew the place was real, the people were real, and the events were real. Ted Sanford and Clair Higgins had provided him awareness, but even now that he knew the legend was spawned from a false beginning, Silver Spring and Tanglewood Lodge *was haunted.* He had been there. He had heard the sounds. He had felt the eerie energy. He had seen the train. How else could he have known it was "Engine Number Twenty-Nine?"

And now, he could hardly wait to go back there again.

SIXTEEN

The increasing vulnerability of stagecoach transport of silver and money persuaded Smith and Hayden Mining Company to discontinue the use of the Wilson Stage Line. The railroad seemed a safer alternative. Daniel Crane was out of a job.

But he had his sights set on the position of Town Marshall. Although the attempted stage robbery account was somewhat exaggerated regarding his heroism, it certainly didn't hurt his chances of being elected. Rumors quickly spread that his bid for the office was more than his interest in a job; everyone suspected he knew who Dawson's killers were, and that he would be determined to bring the rogues to justice. He soon gained the support and encouragement of the citizens on the street, and saving the miners' payroll meant he would have the backing of the most powerful moneymen, Smith and Hayden. It appeared Daniel Crane would soon enjoy success in the upcoming election.

In an attempt to redeem himself in family eyes, he confided in Jeremiah, Millie and Clancy. He needed their respect and support as well. Millie's suspicions had been right on target. Daniel wouldn't ever admit to being a part in the hold-up plan, but that the Polk gang certainly had the capability of such an act. He knew they had been hobnobbing with the Lawton boys over in Gopher Hole Valley; it wasn't beyond the Lawtons to recruit the Polk gang to help pull off the stagecoach heist. Daniel thought it might have been one of the Lawtons who fired the fatal shots.

It wasn't only Daniel Crane and Wesley Dawson who had gotten a good look at the highwaymen. A passenger aboard the stage had gotten a glimpse, too. He was a storekeeper in Wellington with a widespread exposure to the surrounding residents. Not entirely certain of a positive identification, his story spawned rumors that began circulating the territory: the Lawton boys were involved in the attempted stage robbery and Wesley Dawson's murder.

That rumor found its way to the Lawtons who had been making themselves scarce since the hold-up. Now that Daniel Crane was a sure candidate for Marshall – the only living soul who could possibly identify their presence at the scene of the murder – they had a score to settle.

On the Saturday before the election was to be held, Jeremiah and Millie, Daniel and Kate, their neighbor and Councilman Ralph Longhorn and his wife Nancy walked slowly among a crowd exiting an evening stage show at the Opera House. They all buttoned their overcoats against the chill October night air, but in spite of the cool weather, Daniel lingered at the doorway to shake a few hands of well wishers. Millie, experiencing one of her spells of uneasiness wished to return to the Hotel. Kate and Nancy accompanied her to the front door of Tanglewood, and then continued on to their homes some five blocks away.

A few minutes later Daniel turned to his brother. "Would you care to join me for a game of billiards?"

"No, I'd better get back to the Hotel. Clancy is there alone tending to business. Maybe another time." Jeremiah turned and walked toward the Hotel.

The soon-to-be Marshall turned to the Councilman, now joined by Tom Hargrove. "How about you, Ralph? Care for a game before we call it a night? You're welcome to join us too, Tom."

"Sure... why not?" Ralph replied.

"It would be a pleasure," Tom added.

The Continental Tavern and Billiard Hall was just a couple blocks down Main and right around the corner from the Market Square. While they walked, Tom Hargrove asked, "What will be your first order of business as the new Marshall?"

Rather tired of campaigning, Daniel said, "Put your pencil away, Tom. I'd just as soon not think about that any more tonight."

The Continental wasn't crowded. Daniel and Ralph took up cues and began play, while Tom and several other gentlemen watched. Ralph bent over the table to make a shot. Daniel, his back to the alley door and window, stood by chalking his cue when suddenly the window glass behind him shattered. The blast of a six-gun sounded from the alley. Daniel dropped his cue, spun around and collapsed onto the wood floor. A second shot rang out, but the slug lodged harmlessly in the side of the pool table.

The breeze had scarcely blown the gray smoke away when several by-standers raced to the door. When they returned from the empty alley, Daniel was dead.

Jeremiah had barely removed his coat when the messenger dispatched by Tom Hargrove flung open the front door, yelling in terror to the Innkeeper. "Jeremiah! Come quick! The Continental! Daniel's been shot!"

Jeremiah hastily instructed Clancy to remain a while longer, grabbed his coat and ran with the messenger out the front door.

Thinking it was just another drunken barroom brawl, a big crowd already jammed the Continental's entrance. Jeremiah pushed his way through the curious onlookers only to find Ralph Longhorn and Tom Hargrove kneeling beside his dead brother.

SEVENTEEN

On Cory's third attempt, Victor Gladstone finally agreed to talk to him. Friday afternoons weren't any less hectic at the *Wellington Daily Record*, but the small town paper editor would eventually find the time to talk to someone as persistent as Cory had been.

Still wearing yesterday's five o'clock shadow, he sat behind his cluttered desk in the equally cluttered office shielded by a divider screen separating him from his receptionist.

"What can I do for you, Sport?"

"My name is Cory Brockway. I'd like to talk to you about a job with your newspaper."

"Brockway. I worked with a guy named Richard Brockway in upstate New York about ten years ago. Any relations in New York?"

"No, I don't think so. I'm from Southern Illinois."

"Well, Mr. Cory Brockway, what kind of job are you looking for?"

"I'd like to be a reporter."

"Reporter?"

"Yes Sir."

"Any experience? Qualifications?"

"No experience with a newspaper... but I *am* a pretty good writer."

"Any school?"

"I'm at Wellington now. Third year. Journalism major."

"Barkley?"

"Yes Sir."

"I see. Well, Cory, I'll tell it like it is. At a paper like this anyone without experience usually ends up digging through grandma's recipe box or recapping the Friday night results at the bingo parlor. And right now I've got more stringers than I know what to do with."

"Okay... well—"

"But, tell you what. Pick up an app from Elaine. Come back and see me next week – say, Tuesday. I might have something else for you."

"Thank you, Mr. Gladstone. I appreciate your time, and I'll see you on Tuesday."

A light rain started to fall when Cory came out of the Newspaper office. Buck leaned against the front fender of the Bronco, looking up into the gloomy sky. The rain wasn't even enough to settle the dust yet, but enough to dampen a camper's spirit.

"Radio says this is supposed to stop during the night," Buck said.

"What about tomorrow?"

"Partly cloudy… but no rain."

"Still want to go camping tomorrow?"

"Hell, yes. Been waiting for this all week."

Cory was certain now that Buck didn't believe in the ghoulish Silver Spring legend, or he didn't know about it at all. He hadn't voiced any objections to their weekend destination. He hadn't heard the stories either. Cory considered telling him, but it might put an end to a Tanglewood visit. He'd save the stories for around the campfire tomorrow night.

Except for a few faint traces of the tracks Cory had left on his previous visit, the trail to the creek crossing showed no sign that anyone else had been there since. One thing was certain: they wouldn't be competing with anyone for a choice of campsites. The clearing alongside the stream appeared the best spot they had seen so far -- a supply of water, a level area for the tent, and plenty of stones in the creek to make a fire ring.

Mother Nature hadn't delivered the clearing skies by noon the weatherman promised. It was already past two o'clock and still overcast. Occasional sprinkles had threatened the cancellation of the outing all morning, but now they were here without any regrets, no matter how wrong the weatherman had been.

Cory stood at the edge of the stream gazing up toward the hilltop where Tanglewood Lodge was just barely visible. Without any bright sun, it was difficult to see amidst the shadows, but he knew it was there. Recalling the stories he'd heard and read, he tried to imagine the sight in 1899 when the entire top of that ridge was ablaze. He tried to imagine the feeling of devastation the people leaving that day must have felt, looking back from this spot only to see their homes – their entire town – engulfed in flames.

"We can pitch the tent right here," Buck said, kicking away some pebbles and sticks.

Cory broke his concentration of the imagery and agreed. The sooner they had the campsite established, the sooner they could start exploring the hills. He opened the Bronco's tailgate and began lugging the gear.

Buck unrolled the tent bundle. "By the way," he said. "How did your interview at the newspaper turn out?"

Cory tugged at the other end. "Don't know for sure yet. I'm supposed to go back on Tuesday."

"Did it sound promising?"

"He said he might have something for me, but he didn't say exactly what."

Buck drove the stakes into the ground at the corners. "I wasn't going to say anything yet, but..."

Cory hoisted one end of the tent up and put the upright pole in place. "Wasn't going to say anything about what?"

"That I got a job starting next week."

"Where? Doing what?"

"At the Chevy garage... washing cars."

"That's great! What hours?"

"Tuesday and Thursday afternoon and Saturday morning." He put the pole in place at the other end. "Now pull that rope tight while I drive in this stake."

The tent was beginning to take shape. Now it was just a matter of adding a couple of sleeping bags and pillows and their accommodation for the night was ready.

"You get some rocks for the fireplace," Buck told Cory. "I'll go cut some firewood."

Within an hour they had the place looking like they could survive there for at least the weekend; a heap of firewood, a cooler full of food and beer, and a tent to keep them dry. It was time to do some exploring. The clouds were breaking up and patches of sunlight raced across the wooded hillsides. The day was going to turn out okay after all.

Instead of climbing the steep hill directly to Tanglewood, Cory thought there must be an easier route. There had to be some sort of road up to the ridge that the people of Silver Spring would have used. At the far end of the valley, the stream disappeared around a slope that looked less aggressive. They started walking toward it.

A trail did exist, although it vanished in some places under a growth of brush and saplings, and years of heavy rains had entirely washed it away in others. But it was still an easier climb than the steep hillside.

Half way up the grade, they began to see the ruins of houses and sheds that had evidently escaped the fires of 1899, but now were no more than barely identifiable heaps of rubble. Nature was gradually erasing the evidence that man had once blemished this spot of beauty.

Rising up to the top of the ridge, the trail led past more and more of the decaying piles that had once been structures, and then at a point within visual distance of the remaining Tanglewood Lodge, the heaps of debris ended. From there to the Lodge, only rows of rocks outlined the locations where buildings had burned, and now not even the ashes remained – only a few stone fireplaces and the remnants of a brick chimney here and there.

Cory led Buck to the front of the hotel, hoping the piano would start playing. He wanted Buck to hear it.

"So, this is it, eh?" Buck said. He peered up at the barely distinguishable sign painted on the front of the building.

Cory stood silent, listening for the piano. He heard nothing.

Buck stepped up onto the porch. "What's inside? Have you looked inside?"

Cory remained silent. He *wanted* to hear the piano.

Buck stepped toward the window. He heard the board snap and felt his weight pushing through the floor, but by then it was too late. His right leg had penetrated the deck up to his thigh.

"ARE YOU OKAY?" Cory envisioned the possibility of a serious injury.

Buck was making some awkward movements trying to get his leg out of the hole. "Just a broken leg, dislocated shoulder, fractured scull, and a punctured lung... nothing a full body cast won't fix."

Cory chuckled. "No. Really. Are you okay?"

"Well, I didn't feel anything break except that board."

"Good. Now I don't have to shoot you."

Buck looked back at the hole in the porch deck after he jumped to the ground. "Guess somebody doesn't want us snooping."

"Yeah, and they'll probably send you a bill for the damage."

"Can't. They don't know my address."

"Are you sure you're not hurt?" Cory was still concerned.

"I'm just fine. What time is it?"

Cory looked at his watch. "Quarter to five."

Buck rubbed his stomach. "I'm getting hungry. Let's get something to eat. We can look around up here some more later."

Cory agreed, but rather than backtracking the same route to their campsite he suggested following the ridge in the other direction. Not more than a hundred feet from the front of the hotel Buck noticed something off to his left. A flat slab of stone protruded up out of the weeds.

"Cory, look at this."

"What?"

"Looks like a gravestone."

Sheathed in a furry coat of green moss and brown fungus, the three-inch-thick stone sat firmly planted in the earth. Cory looked at the stone, and then toward Tanglewood. He thought about Ted's tale, and then about Mrs. Higgins' account of how Clancy Crane ran from this spot to avenge his brother's murder. He dug out a pocketknife and began slicing and scraping away the moss.

"What are you doing?" Buck asked.

"I want to see the name."

"Why?"

"You're the historian...aren't you just a little curious?"

"No. Doesn't really matter to me who's buried here."

Cory started finding letters of the inscription; he scraped some more until the whole name and dates were clearly visible: JEREMIAH CRANE, 1851 – 1899.

"There," Buck said. "Now that you've seen that, let's go eat. I'm starved."

A crackling fire gave enough light to find the beer cooler, and sent a column of smoke vanishing into the inky black night. Murmurs of the water in the stream sloshing its way along the rocks was accented by an occasional owl's hoot and somewhere off in the distance the lonely cry of a coyote echoed across the hills.

Buck and Cory sat by the fire nursing their cans of *Bud*. Their bellies were full with hot dogs and potato chips, and now they had talked about everything from cars, to school; from their friends back home and stupid things they did in High School, to speculations of their future jobs; from Buck's noisy dorm room, to Cory's more desirable apartment. Nearly out of new subjects to discuss, they sat in silence just listening to the sounds of the night. It was so peaceful here.

Suddenly Buck jerked his head to peer into the darkness behind them. "What was that?" he whispered.

"What was what?" Cory asked.

"I thought I heard... a banjo."

Cory held his breath and listened. Now he heard it too. "Piano," he said. "Saturday night dance hall Saloon," Cory quoted from Ted's story.

"Huh?"

"Oh yeah. I forgot to tell you. This place is haunted."

"Haunted?" Buck listened to the music he couldn't quite distinguish.

"Yeah. Haunted. Like ghosts and stuff."

"Cool." Buck's face lit up with intrigue.

"You're not afraid of ghosts, are you?"

"Hell no. But I never met one, either."

"Neither had I 'till I came here."

"What do you mean?"

"When I was here before... and ran out of gas."

"You *saw* a ghost?"

"Well... not exactly."

"What then?"

"I was standing in front of the old hotel. The piano music was coming from inside."

"So what did you do?"

"Went in. Thought there was somebody there."

"And was there?"

"Nope. Not a soul."

"So, where was the music coming from?"

"Don't know for sure, but there *is* an old piano in there."

"Wow! What'd you do then?"

"Nothing. Walked back to town for some gas. But the next day when I went back? That's when I actually saw something."

"What?"

"I found these old railroad tracks down on the other side of the hill. Bridges washed out on both ends. I was walking along the tracks and the next thing I knew there was a locomotive coming right at me."

"So what happened?"

"Went ass over crock pot jumping out of the way, and when I looked back the train vanished into thin air."

"Cory? You're joshin' me, right?"

"No! I'm not kidding! It really happened!"

"Kind of hard to believe."

"Then tell me... where do you think that music was coming from? You just heard it yourself."

Buck didn't have an answer.

"Remember when I told you Barkley thought my story sounded like something from Twilight Zone?"

"Yes, I remember."

"Well that's the story I wrote."

"No wonder."

"Well, if you'd heard the story Ted Sanford told me... and then what Mrs. Higgins told me after that..."

"Mrs. Higgins? Your landlady?"

"Yes."

"What does she have to do with it?"

"Her father was Jeremiah Crane."

"The grave on the hill."

"Yup."

"So that's why you're so interested in this place."

"It's not her so much as the stories she and Ted told me."

"So what's the story? Can you tell me?"

"Word for word. Got it memorized."

"So let's hear it."

For the next hour, Buck listened just as intently to Cory as Cory had listened to Ted and Mrs. Higgins. He heard both versions just as Cory had. Cory didn't leave out a single detail – from the myths told by Slinky and Jimmy right through to the facts Clair Higgins had provided.

When he was finished, Buck made some conclusions. "So, Mack is McDowell, he wasn't killed by Jeremiah's ghost, and there isn't any treasure."

"Right."

"And who do you suppose killed all those other people?"

"Don't know. Hard to say if *anybody* knows for sure."

The campfire had long since diminished to a heap of embers, and the baying coyote seemed more distant now than it had when they first heard it earlier. Inside the tent Cory laid awake, wondering if Buck had fallen asleep. He kept going over and over the saga he had just recited to Buck, trying to discover some little detail that might offer a clue to the mystery of Silver Spring Hills, and where he could seek any further information. Ted had not mentioned any other names of surviving Silver Spring residents. Nor had Clair Higgins. At this point in time, to Cory it seemed as if he had reached a dead end. Perhaps he had already exhausted all the available sources, and maybe it was foolish to think he would ever find any more.

He thought about Mr. Barkley's current assignment and how he would use the information he did have to create a fictional story around his original ten pages. It was clear to him now why Barkley had refused to accept his first effort: it probably did appear to Barkley that he had skipped over the first step of the process, but from now on, he intended to follow the rules to the letter.

Outside the tent there was a rustling sound, and then a rattling of cans, as if someone had stumbled into their trash bag. Cory sat up, as did Buck. Both their hearts were playing hopscotch inside their chests.

"What's that?" Buck whispered.

The can rattling continued, and twigs snapped under some heavy footsteps.

"I don't know... *something* is out there." Cory pulled back on the tent flap far enough to open it just a crack. Buck scrambled to find the flashlight he had by his pillow.

"Can you see anything?" Buck whispered.

"No. It's too dark."

Buck took his turn at peeking out. He couldn't remember just exactly where the paper garbage sack was in relation to the tent opening. The threshing and rattling went on. Cory thought he could see some movement off in the direction of the fire ring but he couldn't make out the form. Was this Mack searching for a cold beer? Or was he there to kill any trespassers who intruded upon his turf? Was this the end?

Buck threw back the tent flap and switched on the flashlight illuminating the area between the tent and where the fire had been. Past the fire ring and far beyond the reach of the flashlight beam, what appeared to be a dark-clothed human figure darted away into the darkness and disappeared. Nearer to them, two glassy blue eyes stared back toward the tent. Cory gasped and Buck almost dropped the flashlight. It would have been hard to say who was more startled at that moment – Cory and Buck, or the bandit-masked raccoon rummaging the trash bag.

The raccoon scurried off into the brush. Neither Cory nor Buck wanted to admit what they thought they had seen off in the distance.

"Jeez!" Cory said. "Thought I was having a heart attack."

"And I thought I was going to finally see a ghost."

"Now I know I won't get to sleep."

"Why? It was only a raccoon."

One lone scrub oak beside the tent offered little shade from the mid-morning sun. Cory opened his eyes. He could feel his whole body drenched in sweat, the air inside the tent so hot he could hardly breathe. Buck wasn't there. He poked his head through the opening between the door flaps.

Buck had a small fire going and was poking at a few strips of bacon sizzling in a frying pan on a rock in the middle of the fire. The aroma was magnificent.

"Smells good," Cory said. "How long have you been up?"

"Oh, just long enough to do the laundry, wash the car, and mow the lawn."

"Okay, wise guy."

"Hope you're hungry. How do you want your eggs?"

"Over easy."

"Okay… scrambled it is."

Cory finally convinced Buck to join him on another hike. Being lazy for a while had been quite relaxing, but he had come there precisely to get on more intimate terms with a place that whispered to him the decades of mysterious history. To take a walk on Silver Spring's wild side would let him see the passage of time etched plainly on that hilltop. He wanted to feel the energy that would help him capture Tanglewood's chronicle on paper. And now there were only a few hours left until they would have to pack up and head for home.

He picked yet a different route up the steep hillside hoping to spot something they might have missed before. Convinced there was more to be discovered here, Cory kept searching. They wandered for nearly an hour along the ridge, poking and probing but finding nothing more than rocks, trees, and prickly bushes taking dead aim on their bare arms.

"Where are the railroad tracks?" Buck asked.

"Right down there." Cory pointed toward the slope. "It's all grown down in weeds, but it's there."

"I'm going to check it out," Buck said.

"Go ahead. I'm just going to keep looking around up here."

Buck had been off viewing the collapsed trestle for a while when Cory heard the faint sound of the shrill whistle. He looked down toward the railroad grade. Buck was walking the tracks and he appeared to have a puzzled stare on his face. The

whistle sounded again. It was much closer this time. Cory couldn't see the train, but he thought a warning to Buck was in order. "GET OFF THE TRACKS!" he shouted, pointing to the area behind Buck.

Buck looked at Cory, noticing the gesture, then turned to look behind him. He froze for just a second, and then made the similar dive into the weeds Cory had done a few weeks earlier.

"ARE YOU OKAY?" Cory yelled.

Buck scrambled to his feet, peering down the tracks, first to the east and then to the west. "WHAT THE HELL WAS THAT?"

Cory met him half way up the slope. "What number did you see on the front of the locomotive?" Cory asked, speculating what Buck had experienced.

Buck thought a moment. "Twenty-nine."

Now Cory knew he hadn't imagined the vision. "Thought so. Now do you believe me?"

Still suffering from what-the-hell-was-that-syndrome, Buck stared down at the railroad bed. "Did you see that?"

"Not now, but I saw it three weeks ago... guess you have to be on the tracks to see it."

Buck stared into Cory's eyes. "It was there! I swear! It was there!"

"I believe you, Buck. I really do." Cory looked at his watch. "Come on. Let's go up to the hotel."

They stood next to the hotel verandah. Just as before, the breeze rustled the leaves and the birds sang as if this was just another day. Buck kept peering toward the railroad tracks that could not have carried a train in decades. He still couldn't believe what he had just experienced. Then his concentration was interrupted by more noises. It sounded like someone tuning a radio to a weak station. Music. Piano music. He looked at Cory. Cory was grinning.

"What's so funny?" Buck whispered.

"Listen," Cory replied.

"I hear a piano... and people laughing."

"Where's it coming from?" Cory asked.

Buck looked around, concentrating on the sounds. He looked back at Cory, and then at the hotel front door. "In there, I think."

"Now do you believe me?"

Buck just stared in astonishment.

Two gunshots rang out and glass shattered. The voices stopped, but the piano played on.

Buck flinched with the sound of the gunfire. "What was that?"

"Same thing I heard before," Cory said.

Buck stepped up onto the verandah, being careful to avoid the broken boards he fell through yesterday.

"You'll see a busted mirror on the back wall," Cory said.

Buck pulled the door open. The hinges screeched. The piano music stopped. "Cool," was all he said.

EIGHTEEN

The early hours of dawn barely shed enough light for Clancy to see the pages of his tattered little notebook he had purchased for a dime at the General Store and had carried with him everywhere he went. For weeks he had been writing everything he could remember about his life in Silver Spring. Whenever he would think of an event he would stop and jot it into the notebook. He had written so much that his pencil was barely long enough to hold.

Inspired by Millie's journal-writing routine, Clancy developed his daily entry habit as well, and though he knew his language skills were perhaps inferior to those of Millie's, he didn't let that discourage him. He knew others kept journals too: Alexander Malone, the piano player at the Lodge wrote in one often, and Tom Hargrove constantly recorded his observations and activities – a ritual he carried out every morning at his breakfast table at the Lodge.

Struggling with the stubby pencil, notebook resting on his knee, Clancy looked up from where he sat on the verandah steps. He hadn't noticed Tom Hargrove approach, now standing at the foot of the steps. Tom held out a small package tied with string around the brown wrapping paper – the kind of paper the General Store used to bundle customers' purchases.

"This is for you," Tom said. He handed the package to Clancy.

"What's this?" Clancy asked.

"Just a little present from me to you. Go ahead. Open it."

Clancy carefully pulled off the string and unfurled the paper, exposing a thick, leather-bound book. He fanned through the 200 blank pages, staring curiously at Tom.

"I've been watching you write every day and I thought you should have a *real* journal instead of that flimsy little notebook."

Clancy's face beamed with joy. "Thank you, Tom, but it isn't even my birthday."

"It will be someday." Tom reached into his breast pocket, pulled out two new pencils, and with a grin of satisfaction said, "Here, you'll be needing these too."

"Thank you, Tom. I don't know what to say."

"You've said enough already. Just keep writing."

Tom went on his way to gather the daily gossip from town and the mines. This was Market day, and there would be an ample supply of it floating around.

The sun was just beginning to scatter its first sparkles to the morning dew. This was Clancy's favorite time of day, especially on Market days. He could hear the clippity-clop of horseshoes and the rumbling wagon wheels on the cobblestone street. The Market Square was a noisy, busy, and sometimes exciting place. At first glance, it might seem the domain of the giant dray horses – the Percheron, the Belgian, the chestnut and dapple-gray trotters of the merchants, the oxen, the mules and the fat Morgan and Clydesdale mares of the farmers. It was, though, the very heart of the business community. A block off Main Street, the Square was surrounded by feed and grain warehouses, a butcher shop, fruit and vegetable dealers, a blacksmith, and a plow and harness merchant. On market days when farmers brought produce in to trade, the square echoed a constant roar of rumbles, whinnies, shouts and whip cracks from sunup to sundown.

At the far end of the Square, with its backside facing the Railroad Depot stood the Silver Spring Livery Stable. It had always been one of Clancy's favorite spots. But he didn't have time for one of Brook's classic tales today. A delegation of high-ranking officials from Smith & Hayden Mining Company would be arriving that afternoon for their quarterly inspection of the mine operations and two days of board meetings. Tanglewood Lodge was always host to their banquets and overnight stays in Silver Spring, and that meant some extra preparations at the Lodge. It was always worth the effort; the big shots at Smith & Hayden were always big tippers. They appreciated Tanglewood's complimentary coach that shuttled them to and from their headquarters building, and all the extra hospitality Tanglewood extended them during their stays.

A spooky strangeness hung over the Square. It seemed less spirited today for some reason. Unusually quiet and somber faces replaced the normal laughter and gaiety as if it were a funeral rather than Market day. Clancy headed straight for George's wagon. It was always his first stop. George's chicken eggs were always in demand, and even though Clancy knew there would be a crate reserved for Tanglewood, he still made it his top priority. Always cheerful, George usually had the latest and most accurate news of what was going on in the rural areas around Silver Spring.

"Why all the long faces?" Clancy asked.

"Ain't you heard?" George replied.

"Heard about what?"

"The mines."

Clancy had been hearing about the mines all his life. In Silver Spring, that was a common, everyday topic, and there was seldom anything extraordinary about mine gossip.

"We just got the word yesterday," George went on. "They're shuttin' down the mines. S & H is pullin' out."

"But why would they do that?"

"Ain't makin' a profit anymore."

It seemed a little odd to Clancy that this news hadn't yet reached Silver Spring. "But the Board is comin' today. They'll be at Tanglewood tonight."

"It'll be their last. Word is they're comin' to close everything down. And that kinda puts all of us outa business too."

"But George... we'll still be here."

"You and who else? The rabbits? Most everybody in this town works for S & H Mining. If they go, so will all those people. There won't be anybody left."

This all seemed quite outrageous. Just the thought of the miners' absence boggled Clancy's mind. Certainly this had to be just a crazy rumor. But while he made his usual stops around the Market, the entire buzz sounded the same; even the farmers were already talking about pulling up stakes and moving on.

Tanglewood's carriage sat poised and ready at the Depot when the three o'clock Express arrived. By now the entire town had heard the shocking news and everyone was anxious to hear an official announcement. A crowd had gathered at the Depot, but not even the reporter from *The Striker* could coax a comment from any of the seven dignitaries as they stepped off the train, briskly boarded the enclosed carriage and rode off to the Smith & Hayden Mining headquarters at the far end of town. Something was in the air, and it didn't look good.

The doors at S & H Mining remained locked the rest of the day. No one left, and no one entered the secret proceedings. Tom Hargrove, *The Striker's* reporter tried knocking; he even tried peeking and eavesdropping through the windows, but nothing so far was gaining him access to the hottest story Silver Spring would ever hear. The people would be expecting a full account in the next edition of *The Striker* that was due to hit the street the next afternoon. But so far, he had nothing but rumors and wild speculation.

More people swarmed into Tanglewood's Saloon on this Wednesday afternoon than on a Saturday night after payday. Jeremiah knew it was only because of everyone's awareness that the Directors stayed at the Lodge when they were in town. The dining room would fill to capacity with the bigwigs and their guests – or at least, that's the way it usually happened – and tonight a lot of curious citizens, and a few irate ones were hoping to learn the fate of the mines, and perhaps of Silver Spring.

This was a bittersweet day for Jeremiah Crane. Business was better than he'd seen for quite some time, but he couldn't help wondering if there would be any more like it – ever. If the mines closed down, the hundreds of miners and their families would be forced to leave; there certainly weren't other jobs for them here. And without the miners spending their pay on the streets of Silver Spring, the town would surely die a painful, lonely death.

And what would become of Jeremiah Crane? In the eight years he had just barely paid off the thirty-thousand-dollar mortgage on Tanglewood Lodge. He had come here with money in his pocket and a big dream, and on more borrowed money he fulfilled his dream, raised a family, and became a cornerstone of the community. Now that dream – Tanglewood Lodge – a mere building at the end of Main Street in a town with its future in the balance was all he had.

It was well past ten o'clock by the time anyone realized that Clancy had snuck the Directors in through a back entrance and quietly ushered them to the upstairs rooms, unnoticed by the rather noisy, and now slightly tipsy crowd. Only the shrewd and keen-eyed Tom Hargrove had spotted them, and with Clancy's assistance had managed to finally convince the dignitaries to grant him an interview and to divulge the facts. "Otherwise," he told them, "I will be forced to print only rumors in tomorrow's paper, and all of you will be portrayed as nasty, greedy bureaucrats here only to ruin the lives of a thousand honest, hard-working people."

It was so quiet perhaps a spider could have been heard walking across the floor when Hargrove raised his voice above the crowd. He stood halfway down the front staircase overlooking the eager faces that filled the room. Dead silence prevailed with the anticipation of the bad news they really didn't want to hear, but they felt the need to hear it anyway, just to ease the tension. Even "Fingers" stilled the keys of the upright.

"The full story will be on the front page tomorrow," Tom began.

All eyes were on the newsman they trusted.

"I have gotten the official word from the Board of Directors. As of noon tomorrow, all mining operations at Silver Spring run by Smith & Hayden Mining Company will cease."

It was what they had expected – and feared. There didn't seem to be any need for answers to any other questions. Murmurs and mumbles started replacing the silence. Slowly they began filing out the front door, heading for homes somewhere in the darkness beyond the hazy glow of the street lamps.

NINETEEN

Victor Gladstone, elated with the addition of Cory's energetic enthusiasm to his staff, took time out of his busy schedule every day to introduce the newcomer to different operations. For the time being, Cory would be a floater, providing assistance wherever it was needed. After nearly four weeks, he had been exposed to a whole new world contained within the walls of that big, old building. He rapidly learned that newspaper publishing was a fast-paced business demanding concentrated emphasis on time management, schedules, and deadlines. The three or four hours he spent there each day went by rather quickly because of it.

Sometimes there were copy proofs of advertisements to be delivered to and from local businesses. Sometimes there was the monotony of inserting flyers, but often Cory would be delegated to what was becoming his favorite assignment – assisting the production staff, cutting and pasting articles and ads on the page layouts.

And then there were Fridays. For the fourth one running, his efforts were directed to more of a janitorial nature. He didn't care for it, but he was beginning to believe that was Gladstone's test, and he didn't complain. Today, a specific task was added to the usual chores. Three large, newspaper-sized, hardcover books had been delivered to the receptionist's office earlier that day.

"These need to be carried down to the basement," Victor said.

"What are they?" Cory asked.

"Archives. A copy of every issue ever printed here is in books like this. You'll see them down there."

"How far back do they go?"

"Since the paper began... 1875. But it was called the Wellington Weekly Star back then."

As of yet, Cory had not been in the basement, and it appeared that few people had recently ventured into the dimly lit rooms; obviously the catch basin for antiquated desks, chairs, typewriters, lamps and anything that someone didn't have the heart to discard in the trash.

There, among all the unwanted furniture was stack after stack of the huge books. Nearly a century's worth of Wellington history was collected in this room. To the rest of the world, it might only represent trivial local news – news that would have little effect on the nation. But to Cory, it was a bonanza. Within this room, perhaps, were the details missing from the Silver Spring legend, as he knew it so far. Finding those details might be a challenge; there didn't seem to be much organization to the books, but a quick survey indicated the really old ones were definitely in the back of the heap.

Cory gently knocked on Victor's open office door. "Mr. Gladstone?"

"Yes... come in."

"Would it be okay if I come in tomorrow to look through the archives?"

"Looking for something in particular?"

"Yes, sir. Research for a school project."

"I don't see a problem with that."

"Great! I'll be here first thing in the morning."

Cory had until noon to locate the book containing the 1937 editions of the Star. And even if he did find it, there was no guarantee the information would be there. As well kept as this secret was, chances were good that not much of the actual events were ever recorded, but this would be time well spent to find out.

After two hours of rearranging the stacks, one book at a time, he began to find volumes of the right era, and finally, there it was - 1937. He hoisted it up onto the top of another stack and carefully opened the cover. The print was perfectly preserved and clear on the yellowed and brittle pages, but nowhere was there any mention of Albert Sanford's disappearance.

There was still time to dig a little deeper. Unlike the Historical Society's archive, this one had *every* issue of the Weekly Star. But it seemed that after Silver Spring burned, the town had been forgotten quickly, even in 1899. One story did make the news, though, and it was the one Cory had hoped to find. Three weeks following the fire, an article told the account of eight Wellington men mysteriously killed in a gun battle on the site of the destroyed town and two of the original party of ten, Casey Fitzsimmons and Elmer Dickens, had narrowly escaped the flying lead. The report went on to say that Fitzsimmons and Dickens were convinced they had seen the ghosts of Zachary McDowell and Jeremiah Crane shooting it out on the streets of Silver Spring.

"Aha!" Cory thought. "Ted Sanford's saga wasn't so far off." But Clair Higgins had already discounted the ghost theory.

Buck made his not-so-surprising entrance into Cory's apartment after working a longer-than-usual Saturday.

"Here," Buck said. "This letter for you was in the mailbox."

Cory glanced at the familiar handwriting on the envelope. It wasn't necessary to look at the return address; he knew the letter came from his father. He tore it open. The usual rent check, some cash and a lengthy yellow letter were inside. He sat in a chair by the window and began reading the letter while Buck took off his damp shirt and flopped onto the lumpy couch.

A few minutes passed. Buck watched Cory's face display a pageant of expressions ranging from that of surprise to one of indifference. It appeared Cory was re-reading the letter over and over. "What does he say?"

Puzzled, but somewhat relieved, Cory relayed the unexpected news from home. "They've offered my Dad an early retirement... and he's taking it."

"Well, that sure solves the problem of finding a new job," Buck said.

"Not only that," Cory continued. "Mom and Dad are going to Florida for the winter... and they're even thinking of moving there permanently."

"Florida! I've been there. They'll love it."

"Yeah, I suppose they will, but I can't imagine not going *home* for Christmas."

"It's not so bad. I don't go home for Christmas, either. And think of it this way: you *are* home... right here."

TWENTY

Clancy trotted down the front steps off the verandah and paused on the small grassy lawn between the Lodge and the street. He breathed deeply to take in the cool, crisp dawn air. It had rained during the night, enough to make little puddles here and there in the street, and the air exceptionally fresh. He loved early mornings like this. It was nearly the only time he could clear his mind and enjoy the peacefulness. And lately there seemed to be plenty of issues to keep anyone's mind off anything resembling calmness.

Several weeks had gone by since the mining stopped. Every day since, Clancy had watched a steady parade of wagons crawling along the valley, cross Silver Creek, and then disappear over the next ridge. It looked like a never-ending band of gypsies; every wagon loaded with entire households, or at least as much as would fit in the wagons. It was a painful sight seeing hundreds of people leaving their homes behind, packing their dreams in a wagon, and taking up a nomadic road into the vague future.

Clancy thought about the many who had come here with almost nothing, and now they were leaving with not much more. But his heart was going out to those who had found success and happiness in Silver Spring, and now it was being stripped from them. It just didn't seem fair.

The morning was unusually quiet for a Market day. The restless clamor in the Square should already be awakening the town. It wasn't. Rumbling wagon wheels, horseshoes clicking on the cobblestone, whinnies – all the fanfare that announces Market day at the break of dawn – today was hardly noticeable. Only a small fraction of the usual vendors had showed up. Clancy headed straight to George's wagon.

"So… where is everybody?" Clancy asked.

"Moved on, I reckon."

"Where'd they all go?"

"Some said they was goin' to California. Some to Oregon. Others mentioned the Mississippi Valley."

Clancy could detect some distance in George's voice. He suspected George was considering some faraway destination as well. "What about you?"

"Don't rightly know, Clancy, but you 'n the rabbits won't be needing enough eggs to keep me here."

Before he delivered the eggs and other produce to the cool cellar below the kitchen, Clancy paused at a bench in the back yard. He ran to the carriage house to get his journal from the table beside his bed. Drastic changes were taking place in Silver Spring, and Clancy felt compelled to write it all down, just as Tom had encouraged him to do. So many people he knew had already left town, and now it seemed even more were preparing to leave. It saddened him to think he might never see those friends again – writing in his journal helped ease the pain.

Clearly, Silver Spring was in the grips of decline. It had suffered the devastation of losing its lifeblood industry, and now the Clearwater Brewery and the Silver Spring Sawmill were the only places of employment keeping anyone there, and even they were beginning to show evidence of possible failure. The population had shriveled to a handful, and the merchants' only customers were each other and the few loyal citizens who stayed to brew beer and cut lumber, a sad economic scenario, indeed. All over town, the evidence that Silver Spring was destined for ghostdom showed itself; "Closed" signs in the front windows of stores and shops, and hand-lettered messages left for the postman on the front doors of homes that read "Gone to California," "Send my post to Coolidge, Montana," and the classic, "For Sale – Real Cheap."

For the few people who stayed, life went on quietly. The Clearwater Brewery was still putting out about forty barrels of Silver Creek Beer each week that was shipped off to nearby towns, and the Silver Spring Sawmill still produced a few hundred board feet of lumber a day to be loaded onto railroad cars once a week.

A different breed of patrons started showing up at Tanglewood Lodge. Some were quiet and nervous, and some were boisterous. But they all had one characteristic in common; they were hiding from the law.

The news had spread quickly about Silver Spring. Every outlaw in the country knew by now that the town had no lawmen. There wasn't a need anymore. The Hotel there was a comfortable, safe hideaway for a day or two while the trail cooled, and for a few extra bucks the Innkeeper would keep his mouth shut.

Jeremiah was no fool. He saw an opportunity to keep his business alive, and as long as he kept his word, the money would keep coming in. Millie continuously voiced her opposition, frequently reminding him that this lifestyle was not one in which to raise Clair, their eight-year-old daughter.

"Let's sell Tanglewood and move away from here," she would say.

"And who do you think would buy a hotel in a deserted town?" he would ask.

The conversations never seemed to get beyond that point. Millie would once again accept the fact that they were stuck there.

Not all the residents of Silver Spring were as comfortable with this different kind of clientele visiting their town, as was Jeremiah. But no one really dared to challenge the presence, or even pull in the Welcome mat. The outlaws were about the only outsiders bringing money into the town. Whether or not anyone was particularly pleased with the near constant presence, the revenue they brought in seemed to be almost necessary for Silver Spring's survival. They'd rent rooms at the Lodge, drink Silver Creek Beer in the Saloon, buy food and traveling supplies from the General Store, and then they'd be gone, only to make room for the next ones to come through.

The regulars would drift into Tanglewood Saloon like they usually did after every workday. There wasn't a newspaper any more. The pub served as the community gathering place to exchange news, what little news there was these days. An ice-cold beer, some friendly conversation and a talented honky-tonk piano player, "Fingers" Malone, provided just about the only source of entertainment left.

Hans Stengahl, Clearwater's brew master, wasn't usually among the early arrivals, but today nearly the entire crew from the brewery followed him in.

"Jeremiah! Give everybody in the house a mug o' Silver Creek!"

It appeared that a celebration was in order, although no one other than beer makers seemed to know its significance.

Jeremiah began drawing glass after glass of the foamy brew that had become everyone's favorite. But the celebration wasn't over necessarily good news for Silver Spring. Just as this room had been where the official word of the mine shutdown was delivered eight weeks ago, so too would it be where the closing of Clearwater Brewery would be announced. Hans and all his men would soon be making their brew in nearby Wellington.

No one cheered. The brewery closing only put Silver Spring one step closer to extinction.

TWENTY-ONE

Cory had been at the typewriter for a couple of hours. "Applegate In Sand Valley" was coming to life. Now he had heard and read several different viewpoints – all with just a slight variation, but each one providing details to make a great story.

The tale of Silver Spring in itself was quite amazing. Cory couldn't help thinking how incredible it seemed that the facts of this colorful bit of history had been kept hidden for so many years, and that superstitious legend had completely dominated the beliefs of local residents for generations.

He sat in front of the Smith-Corona staring at a blank sheet of paper trying to imagine some logical chain of events that might have occurred just before the fatal shots that killed Jeremiah Crane were fired. He had already created his little town of Sand Valley in his last assignment, and now it was time to sprinkle the scene with action. Just as his village had been fashioned after Silver Spring, so were the citizens of Sand Valley fashioned after those in the stories told by Ted Sanford and Mrs. Higgins. Some of his town's people had come there because they were desperate miners. Some were there because they were dreamers, just like the real settlers of Silver Spring. Sand Valley attracted its share of outlaws, too: gamblers, cattle rustlers, and holdup men who loved their liquor and noise in a crowded saloon on Saturday night.

Footsteps on the stairway broke his concentration. He glanced at his watch; it was almost 9:00 p.m. Buck was returning from the library just as he said he would.

"Remember that list of topics?" Buck said, flying through the front door. "Well, I did pick *Bank Robberies*, and I ran across something I think will interest you." Buck was excited. He plopped a whole armful of books on the table and sorted through them to find a particular one.

Cory had forgotten about the list, but he was impressed that Buck had chosen his recommendation. "What did you find?"

"Here. Read it yourself." A small piece of paper marked the page. He opened the book.

Cory grasped the book, not knowing what to expect. He didn't notice, at first, the reason for Buck's enthusiasm with the material. It appeared to be a piece about a bank in Sioux Falls and its history of hold ups in earlier years.

"So, why should I be interested in this?" Cory asked.

"Read on... and turn the page."

Cory continued to read the chronicle. A black-and-white photograph of two men, apparently from the Wild West days, was at the top of the next page. Quite similar in appearance with bushy, black mustaches and both wearing black hats, their only difference was age. Cory suddenly realized the significance of Buck's find. The text told of a particular bank heist occurring in July of 1899, and the perpetrators being Zachary McDowell and his son, Zachary Junior. Both escaped capture and disappeared. Zachary Jr. was arrested some time later, tried, convicted, and imprisoned. But his father met an untimely death before the authorities caught up with him. Ironically, he was killed in a fire that he started in another small mining town.

It went on to say that the money from that robbery was never recovered, and that Zachary Jr. died in prison in 1927, never revealing to anyone where he had hidden the $3000.

"Now do you see why I thought you'd be interested?"

"Yeah! This is great!"

Now the Silver Spring saga took on a whole new perspective. This gave Ted Sanford's story more depth. He had told of McDowell appearing to be waiting for someone to arrive. That someone must have been Zachary Jr. Perhaps they had planned a rendezvous at Silver Spring, but Junior was late. When he finally did arrive, he couldn't have known his father was dead, and there was no one left in Silver Spring to tell him, so he waited.

Cory's speculation kept building. He had the other stories to help reconstruct the events that followed. "It was *Zachary Jr.* who the looters saw."

"Yeah, they did look alike," Buck agreed. "But who was he fighting?"

Cory thought a few moments. "Of course. Clancy Crane."

"Clancy?"

"Sure. Mrs. Higgins said he hid out in the woods for two months. He could have come back."

"And he *was* mistaken for his father's ghost the day of the fire."

"And the mistaken identity happened again."

"And the looters who got away heard *Junior* yelling he would kill to protect *his* money."

"Buck! Maybe there *is* treasure buried out there."

"That was an awful long time ago, Cory."

"But it *could* be."

They had a speculated explanation for the eight looters getting caught in the crossfire of the fight between Zachary Jr. and Clancy Crane. The evidence was unmistakable, and the possibilities were obvious, but somehow the true story had been lost to imagination and a classic, ghostly legend.

And what about Ted's brother who disappeared while on a treasure hunt in 1937? Zachary Jr. died in prison ten years earlier; he certainly couldn't be credited with that deed.

Where was Clancy Crane by that time? Maybe Mrs. Higgins could supply that answer.

Cory's curiosity was growing and he realized there were other questions that needed answers. Learning the facts and knowing the people behind them was, perhaps, of little value, but it sure was creating some great ideas for his writing project. Now there was an understandable reason for Zachary McDowell to be in Silver Spring, and his mirror-imaged son and a bank robbery certainly added flavor to the mix.

Mr. Barkley's current assignment was to intensify the plot and to give the characters life. "Make them interesting" he'd said. Characters like Cory had just discovered would definitely be interesting. And who could possibly know what this legend would be when it finally flowered? In the haunting unreality, vaguely outlined by mysterious hills threaded by a slow, brown creek unwinding through shaded valleys, shadowy figures and somber faces would take on new identities, and the saga of Silver Spring would be revived with new translation, nearly the way it really happened.

TWENTY-TWO

Jeremiah Crane leaned back in his chair. He had an uneasy feeling for some reason, like there was a sinister cloud waiting over the horizon, and the wind was blowing in his direction.

Like a blood-curdling savage war whoop, the steam whistle of the afternoon train yelped and echoed across the hills; there was no mistaking the Red Hawk Express was about to arrive. As usual the children were gathering on the hillside above the tracks like a flock of pigeons sunning themselves on a silo roof on a cold winter day. No matter how many times they saw the billowing black smoke and the clouds of white steam, and no matter how many times they heard the screaming whistle and the thunderous rumble, it always seemed a spectacular event to them.

Jeremiah strolled out onto the verandah as his daughter, eight-year-old Clair, joined her friends on the hillside. Little Teddy Sanford, Clair's best friend, was there too. His father worked at the Clearwater Brewery, and now they would soon be moving away. Clair would be losing her best friend.

He pulled out his pocket watch. Three o'clock. The Red Hawk Express was right on time.

Long gone were the days when at this time the hotel saloon would fill with the new arrivals – desperate miners, lumbermen, and dreamers. But whoever they were, and for whatever reason they came here, they were the reason Crane's Tanglewood Lodge never knew a slow day or a dull night.

But now, instead of the honest, hard-working people who came to Silver Spring to eke out a living in the mines or cutting timber, it was the gamblers, cattle rustlers, gunslingers, and outlaws of nearly every variety frequently seeking refuge here. They knew they were safe; for a price, they could be scarce from the rest of the world in comfort and style.

When Zachary McDowell's silver-spurred boots lit on the pebbly walkway beside the railroad tracks, few noticed the dark aura surrounding him. No one knew him or where he came from, but there was no question of *why* he was here: he was trouble looking for a place to hide.

He had that look about him; his black, beady eyes could stare a hole through a boilerplate, and nervous hands seemed always ready to draw the intimidating .44 from its leather sheathe on his hip at any given moment. Darkly mysterious, carrying nothing more than a saddlebag over his shoulder, he ambled into the Lodge.

"Need a room… meeting my son. Is he here?"

This was the first time Jeremiah had ever felt intimidated by a guest in his hotel. "Wh-what is your son's name?"

"Zachary McDowell Junior. He looks kinda like me… only thirty years younger."

"I – I don't believe he has been here."

McDowell glanced around the room. "Pecu-liar," he mumbled. "He should've been here days ago." It was as if McDowell didn't believe Crane.

TWENTY-THREE

Cory recalled all the newspaper articles he had seen in the archives. The names haunted him. The events he had read about in those chronicles were more than stirring his curiosity. He began to realize that whether it is for rigorous learning or just lighthearted fun, the past is packed with innumerable attractions. There exists an untapped well of history in every hill, in every river, in every city across the country. Cory knew he had found a niche.

But *this* project was supposed to be fiction. He would have to keep disguising the story somehow, as much as he hated that thought, now that he had become so deeply involved in learning the facts.

"Well, hello Cory!" Mrs. Higgins said. She opened the back door. "Won't you come in?"

"Thank you, Mrs. Higgins. Do you have time to talk a while?"

"Certainly. Come on into the den. What would you like to talk about?"

"Well, I thought you might like to know that... I found your father's grave."

Clair's first reaction was that of alarm, but it slowly melted into a pool of sorrow. "Oh dear. You surely must be mistaken. My father's grave is –"

"Out in Silver Spring... right next to Tangle-wood Lodge... on the hill overlooking Silver Creek."

"Guess I told you he's buried there, didn't I?"

"But I really was there, and I found the gravestone. It was all covered with moss and I scraped it clean. It says 'Jeremiah Crane, 1851 – 1899.'"

"How could you dare go out to Silver Spring? You know what they say about it, don't you?"

"Well –"

"It's haunted, and it's a very dangerous place to go," Clair scolded.

"Yes, I've heard all the ghost stories, and I've heard about Mack, and about people disappearing out there, but I've been there three times now, and Buck and I camped there over night just last weekend, and the ghosts didn't try to harm us."

Clair softened. "What is it like there now?"

"The whole town is gone... except for Tanglewood. Everything else burned down or fell down."

"Is the carriage house still –"

"Gone," Cory said quickly.

"The stables?"

"They're gone too."

Clair just sat quietly, staring off into a reminiscent past. Cory could tell she was having no trouble at all picturing in her mind a place that was still dear to her heart.

"Mrs. Higgins? I found some old newspaper articles at the Historical Society, and I was wondering if you might remember any of the people."

"I don't know... what people?"

"Who was Daniel Crane? A relative of yours?"

"Oh yes. He was my Daddy's brother. They came to Silver Spring together."

"One article says he saved a stage coach from getting robbed."

"That's what the newspapers said, but according to my Mama's journal, it might have been the scared horses that did the saving."

"Your *mother's journal?*"

"Oh, yes. Mama wrote in her journal everything that was goin' on. She saved copies of *The Striker* too."

Cory had seen the name *"Striker"* mentioned in editions of the *Wellington Star*. He knew it was Silver Spring's own newspaper, but since the entire town was destroyed by fire, he didn't think there was much chance of any remaining copies being found. "So, did you ever get a chance to read any of your mother's journal?"

"Heaven's sake, of course. I read from it every now and then."

"You mean... *you still have it?"*

"Sure, I have it right here." Clair pulled open a drawer in the bureau and retrieved a thick, leather-bound book. "It's about the only thing of Mama's I ever kept – this and her collection of newspapers. She loved reading them, and I can't imagine there's anyone else around with copies of The Striker."

"Y-you still have the old newspapers too?"

"Yes, but why are you so interested in all this?"

"Ah... it's a project for school. I'm writing a story about it, but I'm changing all the names."

"Well, plenty of interesting things happened in Silver Spring. I was too young to understand what was goin' on, but Mama told me the stories when I was older, and then she gave me her journal."

"Mrs. Higgins, I know that journal is pretty special to you, but do you think... I mean... could I... well..."

"If you promise not to let anything happen to it, you can take it up to your apartment and read through it. Ain't nothin' personal in it."

Cory couldn't believe the bonanza he had just struck upon. This journal was more valuable than anything discovered so far. Millie Crane had recorded everyday events, views and opinions, and observations from a different eye level than any reporter could achieve. Her statements were bold and she held nothing back. The hand-written journal spelled out the rise and fall of the Crane Empire, from its meek beginnings when they arrived at Silver Spring in 1890, forced to reside *much* too close to the "dead line," their home overlooking that part of town occupied by bums, tramps, gypsies and thieves – a neighborhood all others feared and avoided at all cost. Then she wrote of the joyous day the carriage house was completed and they moved away from that dreadful site. She wrote about Tanglewood Lodge and Alexander Malone's splendid music, the barroom fights and some of the shady characters coming and going.

About the stagecoach robbery she wrote:

"I know I shouldn't say this, but I suspect my brother-in-law was involved with the gang that tried to hold up the Wilson Stage. Daniel knew who they were. That's why he didn't fire a single shot, or even try to stop them in any way. Ever since John Polk, Gus Barrington and Louie LaPointe started coming around, I knew they were up to something. And now I know they tricked Daniel into telling them when the stage was carrying a large sum of money..."

A month later she wrote of Daniel's murder:

"We laid Daniel to rest today after he was shot in cold blood in the Continental last Saturday night. I know who shot him – it was the Lawton boys. Daniel knew it was them and the Polk gang who held up the stage and killed poor Wesley Dawson. They killed Daniel because he knew too much. And now Kate has left to return to Ohio. I will miss them both."

Millie wrote about the mines shutting down and about the people moving away by the hundreds, about Clearwater Brewery relocating to Wellington, and more people moving away.

With but a few pages remaining, Cory read Millie's interpretation of her beloved husband's violent death in 1899 – the misunderstanding and the argument from which she walked away, only to hear a few moments later the deafening, fatal shots echoing through the Hotel.

The entries after that were less frequent – weeks and months apart, and near the end almost a year. The final entry dated March 12, 1917 answered one of Cory's questions as, in a shaky hand Millie sadly wrote of Clancy's death in the Great War. All that remained of Clancy were fond memories and a box of his personal belongings sent home by the military.

Now Cory had a few more pieces to the puzzle. The journal gave him more clearly an understanding of what Silver Spring was really like. Reading that journal was like turning on a 100-watt bulb in a darkened room lit with only a candle. It revealed details he would have never otherwise known: Jeremiah Crane catered to the crooks as well as the townspeople; he had barely repaid a large debt to the bank when the mines closed; his brother was murdered by a band of unsuccessful stagecoach robbers; Clancy, the younger brother – not a son – remained in Silver Spring to defend Tanglewood long after everyone else had fled. Millie's account of Clancy's encounters with Zachary Jr. was sketchy, but complete enough to understand what really happened.

But it left one issue still unsolved: What happened to Albert Sanford? By 1937 when he disappeared, everyone was held at bay by a legend claiming the ghosts of Jeremiah Crane and Zachary McDowell still roamed the hills at Silver Spring. The ghosts seen by the looters just weeks after the 1899 fire were really Zachary Jr. and Clancy. Millie's journal confirmed Cory's speculation about that. But they were both dead long before 1937. Albert Sanford's disappearance remained a mystery.

That didn't stop Cory from adding more installments to his story. He knew if he had to, he could invent something when he reached that point.

He had spent many hours during several nights reading the journal, taking notes as he went along. Sometimes Buck would sit with him pouring over the pages after returning from the library. It almost seemed at times like actually being at Silver Spring – in 1899.

The fourth night Cory happened to think of something Mrs. Higgins had said the evening she gave him the journal. Clair had in her possession copies of *The Striker.* There could be no better source to obtain some solid explanation for Millie's stories that sometimes lacked in adequate background and detail for a complete understanding. As long as Clair had allowed him to borrow the journal, Cory couldn't see any reason she wouldn't let him view the old newspapers as well. The next day he would return the journal and request permission to use the papers a few nights.

When Buck stopped by after work on Thursday evening, the first words he heard as he came through the door were: "Buck! Come look at this. You're not going to believe it." There on the floor in front of the lumpy couch sat a stack of at least a hundred or more neatly folded newspapers. *Old* newspapers. Across the top of the front page of each one the big, bold letters spelled out the name: *THE STRIKER*. Appearing with the name consistently on every issue was a drawing of crossed pickaxe and shovel, and the dates ranged from June 1895 to June 1899. The last date seemed to correspond with Millie's journal where she wrote about all the businesses closing, including the local newspaper.

Containing little news from anywhere beyond the immediate area, *The Striker* reported mostly local gossip and items of interest pertaining to the citizens of Silver Spring, with concentrated focus on the small town's development and the marks of progress. Week by week installments depicted the construction of the new Railroad Depot culminating with a front-page photograph of the newly completed terminal, a steam locomotive - Engine Number 29 - and a host of passengers poised on the boarding platform. Other similar articles showed the progress of new city streets and sidewalks, and the addition of street lamps on Main and Connor Streets.

Just as construction and progress, reports of destruction and setbacks found their way to the front page. Devastating fires consumed homes and business establishments; on two occasions, entire city blocks destroyed, leading to the organization of a volunteer fire department and the construction of a firehouse. That addition seemed just in time to save the Hayden and Smith Smelter building from total destruction when it caught on fire a short time later.

The mines attracted their share of attention - good and bad; new silver veins discovered and increased production, and the occasional cave-in and regrettable loss of life.

Silver Spring, not void of crime encountered numerous incidents, some as minor as a mischievously broken store window on Main Street, or a missing horse and buggy from a local farmer's stable. But the ugly face of violence frequented the streets of Silver Spring as well. Rowdy cowboys, after quenching their thirsts at the many saloons and gambling halls would challenge the just-paid miners on Saturday night resulting in gunfire, and often bloodshed.

A school picnic and the Autumn Miners' Ball; a change in the Railroad schedule and increased stagecoach service to and from Wellington; a new church bell arriving by rail, and the new addition to the municipal building to include a clock tower; elections of the city council members, and the installation of a new minister at the Presbyterian Church; and even text and photographs announcing an anniversary party to be held at Tanglewood Lodge.

Overwhelmed by so much information, Cory desperately continued his search. After several hours, he noticed Buck equally intrigued with the forgotten history of a forgotten place. Buck had found a story about a laborer at the smelter who had allegedly stolen three 70-pound bars of silver to be delivered to the Smith and Hayden Banking House the next day. In the cover of darkness, he buried the silver bars somewhere in the wilderness, but evidently not all in the same place. He had been suspected of the thievery, and was watched. Late one night about a week later, a cunning Deputy Sheriff followed him into the hills and caught him red-handed as the man unearthed one of the bars. A gun battle ensued. The thief was shot and killed; the remaining two bars of silver were never found.

"I guess this would almost qualify as a bank robbery," Buck mused.

"Wow," Cory added. "There's more treasure buried out there than anybody realizes."

"Maybe we should..." Buck hesitated.

"Should what?" Cory asked.

"Oh... it would be like trying to find a pumpkin seed in a pile of sawdust."

"What do you mean?"

"Well, maybe we could get lucky out there."

"Are you serious?"

"Sure. Why not?"

"It's getting too cold to go camping now, but maybe next spring. Right now I want to keep looking for some answers."

"What is it you're looking for?"

"I want to know what happened to Silver Spring... why it became a ghost town."

Cory continued to scrutinize the papers. The search netted many more interesting stories. He located the full account of the attempted Wilson Stagecoach robbery, the murder of its driver, and Daniel Crane's heroic acts to protect passengers and cargo. He saw the article announcing Daniel's bid for the office of Town Marshall in an upcoming election, followed just two weeks later with the report of Daniel's murder in a billiard hall on a Saturday night, shot from an alley window by an unknown gunman who escaped without a trace.

Reporter Tom Hargrove captured Cory's attention with a blow-by-blow account of the events leading to the mine closing and the devastating economic plunges following. Two weeks later, *The Striker* informed readers they were holding the final edition.

A few days later, Cory basked in the glory of having discovered so much information about Silver Spring. In his wildest dreams he never imagined his luck could be so profound.

He was just returning home after a long day of classes followed by three hours at the newspaper office. Autumn had a crisp chill in the air. The days were getting shorter. A blanket of dry, bright yellow leaves covering the driveway crackled as the Bronco tires rolled over them. Mrs. Higgins, clad in a winter coat stood at the open garage door as if she were waiting for Cory to arrive. Cory had never seen the garage door open before. He had never seen the 1952 Oldsmobile sedan Clair had spoken of. The chrome bumper and grille sparkled in the beam of Cory's headlights.

He stopped the motor, got out and walked toward Mrs. Higgins. "Hello, Mrs. Higgins. What are you doing out here in the cold?"

"I've been waiting for you. There's something in the garage I want to give you, but I'll need your help to get it down. It's up too high for me to reach."

Everything in the garage was neatly organized just like the inside of her house. The '52 Olds looked brand new and perfect, other than a little dust.

"Up there on that top shelf... that gray box." Clair pointed to a rectangular wooden box, the name "C. Crane" stenciled in black on the side. "If you could just get it down... I don't think it's too heavy."

Cory's height and strong arms retrieved the box easily. His curiosity, though, was higher than the top shelf.

"I happened to think of it this morning. I know how interested you are in Silver Spring."

Cory's curiosity was climbing somewhere in the rafters now. He set the box on the floor. Mrs. Higgins stooped down, lifted off the lid. Cory just watched. Resting on top of a neatly folded, faded Army dress uniform of World War I vintage lay a brown, leather-covered book. Mrs. Higgins picked it up and caressed it.

"This is for you to keep," she said, and gently handed it to Cory.

"What is it?" Cory asked.

"Just a little present. I'm sure it will be of great interest to you."

Cory opened the cover. On the first page he read the penciled words: "My Journal - Clancy Crane." For a moment he was stunned. "Mrs. Higgins! Are you sure you want to—"

"Of course I'm sure. I want you to have it. It might help you with the story you're writing about Silver Spring."

"But, it's Clancy's journal, a family treasure."

"I have no need for it, but you do. Take it. It's yours. Now, could you please put that box back up on the shelf?"

Cory hoisted the box onto the shelf. He helped Mrs. Higgins close and lock the garage door and escorted her to the back door of the house. "Thank you, Mrs. Higgins. I don't know what else to say."

"You don't have to say any more. Just write a good story." She disappeared into the house.

He had plenty of studying to do that night, but Cory couldn't put down the book written in Clancy Crane's hand. Although the penmanship elementary, spelling not always accurate, and grammar less than perfect, Clancy's words sang with a voice of eloquence that seemed to bring him back to life, and as if he were speaking to Cory in particular. As far as Cory was concerned, Clancy Crane *was* alive. His journal was simply a letter that had been lost in the mail.

TWENTY-FOUR

Several days had gone by. Zachary McDowell still lingered. It was a hot, sticky day, just past three o'clock. The train had come and gone, and now the regular afternoon patrons were beginning to gather in the Saloon for their daily dose of Silver Creek. "Fingers" Malone had the crowd singing, in spite of all the misery looming throughout Silver Spring.

With bushy, drooping mustache, and long, narrow face drawn into an unemotional mask, his appearance and actions added up to fear among everyone who saw him. Just who was he, and why was he hiding in Silver Spring? Obviously a marked man, he stood stiffly at the bar, hands open and dangling loosely at his sides. His cold gray eyes narrowed to slits in his somber face, focusing a mysterious, guarded conversation with Jeremiah.

No one heard the beginning of that conversation between Jeremiah Crane and Zachary McDowell under the mask of the joyous piano and a blanket of laughter. McDowell was convinced that Crane was not being truthful about his missing son. It had been more than two weeks since Zachary and his son split up after they robbed the bank in Sioux Falls and made their successful escape. The plan was to meet again in Silver Spring, and there was no logical reason Junior – who had the money from the bank heist -- hadn't shown up yet.

"Your son has not been here," Crane insisted.

McDowell's temperament was heating. Anger filled his eyes. "I know he's been here… where is he, and where's the money?"

"I haven't seen your son, and I haven't seen your money."

"You're lying! WHERE IS MY MONEY?" McDowell yelled.

A few people in the room took notice now. And Jeremiah took notice of McDowell's twitching right hand poised at the butt of the big gun on his hip. He sensed the danger and foolishly reached beneath the bar where his own firearm lay ready in case of such threats.

The piano played on. Not everyone immed-iately realized what had happened when the two shots from McDowell's pistol shattered the huge mirror behind the bar, and one mortally wounding Jeremiah. It wasn't all that unusual for an occasional fight to break out, but the punctuating gunfire usually occurred outside. Chaos erupted. Taking advantage of the confusion, Zachary McDowell slipped away.

Several months had passed since the rough-and-tumble miners left; since such occurrences were more commonplace; since Silver Spring had witnessed much rowdiness at all involving bloodshed. But now the people here were experiencing a new wave of terror. The uneasiness they had sensed when the mysterious strangers started showing up was manifesting itself as a menacing evil force against which they had no defense. The danger was real, and just one more reason to seek the security and safety of nearby Wellington, where many of their neighbors had already taken up new homes. Of the very few residents left, most of them were planning their final Silver Creek crossing too.

But now a more pressing issue was at hand. Everyone saw Millie Crane weeping over her murdered husband – a man the entire town had learned to admire and respect over the years. His brother's untimely death less than a year ago had occurred without justification, and the killer never apprehended. Jeremiah's murderer, though, would not be so lucky. Few actually witnessed the attack, and although not many knew McDowell by name, nearly everyone knew his face. He would not escape from Silver Spring.

With much of the town already abandoned McDowell could choose a number of places to hide. And with fewer than forty adult men remaining to form an armed search party, he might easily be missed. But the vigilantes were driven by determination. Crane's murderer would not get away. Clancy was to stay at Tanglewood with Millie as the pursuit began, and it was agreed by all to shoot to kill. Such a ruthless scoundrel deserved no mercy.

While the manhunt continued into the night, Millie solemnly made the arrangements with the Reverend Miller for Jeremiah's funeral to be administered the very next day. He would be laid to rest in the open yard in front of the carriage house. Tanglewood Lodge had been his dream and a labor of love for so long. Millie thought it only fitting this should be his final resting place.

Clancy sat writing in his journal in the dim light of an oil lamp at a table in a lonely corner near the piano. Tonight, there was no joyful music as Mr. Malone was among the vigilantes attempting to bring Jeremiah's murderer to justice. Through an open window he could occasionally hear the men talking as they combed the darkened village. Now, more than ever, he realized that not only was Silver Spring changing, but his own life, too, was undergoing dramatic alterations. With his two brothers gone, now he was the man of the family; Tanglewood Lodge was now his responsibility.

Daniel was gone. Kate had moved back to Ohio. And now Jeremiah. Now there was only Millie, Clair and Clancy. Millie knew it was over in Silver Spring for the Cranes. As soon as the funeral ceremony was finished, their stay here would be too. Reverend Miller had already agreed to escort them to Wellington. He had friends there who could help them begin a new life.

Clancy was not at all in harmony with those plans. "I'm not going," he said upon hearing Millie's decision.

"But there's nothing for us here anymore," Millie pleaded.

"I'm not going."

"But what will you do?"

"Someone has to stay to look after Tanglewood. I'm not going to Wellington."

"But everyone is leaving."

"I don't care. I'm not going."

"But Wellington is a nice town. You'll like it there."

"I'm not going. I'm staying here."

"You'll be all alone."

"I'm staying!"

Millie realized nothing she could say would change Clancy's mind about going to Wellington. Not right now, anyway. Perhaps in time he would realize there was no reason to stay, after the town became completely deserted. He would get lonely, and then he would come to Wellington.

Periodically one of the vigilantes reported to Clancy during the night. There were no missing horses; all were accounted for, and all roads and trails leading away from Silver Spring were being closely watched. McDowell was still somewhere within.

TWENTY-FIVE

It was an unusually quiet night at the Public Library. Buck found himself sharing the History wing with only one other student, and by 8:30 she was gone too, as were most of the younger children who had been at the opposite end of the building. He was alone, and no distractions. Buck liked it that way.

He had found a particularly interesting piece of research material on a bottom shelf nearly at the dead end of the last isle. Rather than going to a reading table, he sat right there leaning against the wall with the open book resting on his knees. The library would close at nine and he wanted to make use of every minute he had left. Deeply involved with the material, he heard the librarian shelving some returned books a couple of isles over. Then there were footsteps from farther away but coming closer, and a man's voice said "Miriam? Is that you?" Buck kept reading. He didn't pay much attention to the activity until he heard the librarian say "Hi Honey."

"Honey?" he thought. "This gray-haired old lady had a honey?"

"Hi Miriam," the man said. He seemed to be bypassing any courtship pleasantries and immediately started speaking in a serious tone. "I thought we got rid of all the books here that had anything in them about Silver Spring."

That name really perked Buck's attention. He held his breath and listened.

"There were only a couple, and yes, they are gone," the librarian said.

"Well one of my students' writing project is almost a carbon copy of the history of Silver Spring."

Student? Writing project? Buck had never met Mr. Barkley, much less ever heard him speak, but this must be him talking to the librarian.

"You mean he's copying something from a book?" she said.

"No. It's not that at all."

"What then?"

"Somehow he's learned the facts and he's using them in his story."

"I'm sure a lot of people know the facts."

"Not the details he knows."

"What difference does it make?"

"Miriam? Did you ever read the story about Silver Spring?"

"Most of it."

"Remember the man named McDowell?"

"The man who killed the hotel owner and started the fires."

"Yes. But he was also a bank robber."

"I don't recall reading that, but it doesn't surprise me."

"Well, Cory Brockway has found all that information."

Now Buck knew this had to be Barkley, and the information he was referring to had to be that which Buck had found right here in this library.

"Bad writing?" Miriam asked.

"No. Quite good, actually."

Buck smiled inside. He thought of all the times Cory had expressed his fear of Mr. Barkley not liking his work, and how relieved he would be to hear this report.

"Then why is it so terrible he should write the story?" Miriam said.

"Zachary McDowell was my Grandfather."

"Oh! I see."

"I'm worried about how much Brockway really knows."

"What's to know? That your Grandfather was a bank robber?"

"Miriam, I love you, and I trust you, and I need your support on this."

"Well, sure but –"

"There's something I have to tell you."

"What?"

"Zach Junior, my Uncle, went to prison for that robbery."

Miriam just listened. So did Buck. All this was old hat to him, but it sounded as if this were going somewhere.

Barkley continued. "He died there. But before he died he told my father about hiding the money at Silver Spring."

"Oh dear! And it went up in smoke." Miriam said.

"No. It was after the fire, and he didn't know Grandpa had been killed."

"So your father went to find the money?"

"No, *he* didn't."

"Oh, but *you* did."

"I had just graduated from college. It was 1937 and times were hard. I thought if I could find that money..."

"Did you find it?"

"No. Spent the whole summer digging through the rubble, but while I was there someone else showed up."

"Who?"

"Don't know who he was. It all happened so fast."

"All of what?"

There was a pause and a couple of footsteps, as if Barkley was making sure there was no one else within earshot.

"I was digging along the foundation of a building that had burned, and... well... this man kind of snuck up behind me."

Miriam said nothing while Barkley paused again.

"He startled me, and I swung my shovel and hit him in the head."

"You didn't -"

"Killed him, Miriam. I *killed* that poor man."

Miriam gasped. "And the police didn't believe your claim of self-defense."

"I was so scared... I took the body out into the woods. Buried him. Never told anyone."

"And now you're afraid your student is going to discover the truth."

"After all these years I had nearly wiped out all the horrible memories."

"And now this student... what's his name?"

"Cory Brockway."

"Now Cory Brockway has dredged them all up again."

"Yes."

"Maybe a descendent of the man your Grandfather killed—"

"I've checked. All his family is either dead or moved away. There's no one with the name Crane living anywhere near here."

"I don't know why you're so worried."

"Why shouldn't I be worried?"

"If you've never told anyone about this, and if no one suspected you of it then—"

"No one will suspect now, either."

"Right."

"Yes, maybe you're right."

"Of course I'm right. Now I have to close. You can buy me dinner."

Buck could hear the footsteps on the hardwood floor and the wheels of the librarian's cart rolling up the center isle toward the front desk. Waiting for the perfect opportunity to sneak out without being detected, he peeked around the end of the shelves to see Barkley and the librarian well past the front entrance. He certainly didn't want them to know he had been back in that corner.

It would be at least 9:30 by the time he reached Cory's apartment. Tonight, of all nights, he was on foot. But that was okay. It would give him time to think, and to sort out the conversation he had just overheard.

He snickered at the thought of a college professor making such blunders; Barkley didn't know about the book in which his own

Grandfather and Uncle were portrayed as noted criminals; he didn't know about Mrs. Higgins living in Wellington; and not that it would make much difference, he didn't know about Ted Sanford.

This was some extraordinary and rather shocking information. "How much should I tell Cory?" he said to himself. "Or should I tell him anything at all?" He had only one more block to decide. The Bronco was parked in the driveway. He knew Cory was home. Contemplating the thought of just walking right back to the dorm, he looked up toward the window above the garage. The lights were on and Cory was staring down at him. And he wasn't too fond of walking another mile.

There wasn't much point in knocking. He walked in.

"Hi, Buck. Been at the library?" Cory asked.

The thought of secrecy abandoned Buck. Withholding this information would have been like buying him a birthday present, and then not giving it to him. "Yeah. And you'll never guess what I heard there."

Cory pondered a moment. "Batman and Mary Poppins are going to race dog sleds across New Mexico."

"No."

"Snoopy buried Linus in the back yard."

"No… but you're getting closer."

"Okay. What *did* you hear?"

"For starters, your Mr. Barkley and the librarian are lovers."

"No kidding. Who told you that?"

"Nobody told me… I heard them talking. They didn't know I was back in the corner."

"Did they get mushy?"

"A little… but that's not the best part."

"So what's the best part?"

"They were talking about Silver Spring, and all because of your story."

"Really. But how—"

"Evidently Barkley recognizes your story and you've got him pretty worried."

"About what?"

"I don't know if I should tell you all this."

"Why?"

"Because you'll use it in your story."

"If it's about Silver Spring I want to hear it."

"But if you write this in your story, it could get you killed."

"Buck? You're driving me crazy. What did they say?"

"Promise you'll think about this before you put it in your story."

"Okay. I promise. What did they say?"

Buck sat down at the kitchen table and rested his elbows on the tabletop. Cory did the same, curiosity eating him alive. He fixed his eyes on Buck's, waiting for the words to come out.

"Zachary McDowell was Barkley's Grandfather," Buck began.

Cory's eyes widened and his eyebrows lifted.

"And before Zachary Junior died, he told Barkley's father about the robbery."

"So what?"

"Zach Junior hid the money at Silver Spring."

Cory's lower jaw dropped.

"And didn't Ted say it was 1937 when his brother disappeared?"

Cory nodded.

"Well who *else* do you think was out there at the same time hunting for the bank loot?"

"Barkley's father?"

"No! *Barkley."*

"What are you getting at, Buck?"

"Mr. Barkley killed Ted's brother."

"How do you know that?"

"I heard him tell the librarian the whole story."

Cory took a few seconds for all this to sink in. "And he never got caught?"

"Nope."

"Did he find the money?"

"He said he didn't."

"So it's probably still out there somewhere."

"Guess so."

"And Ted's brother –"

"His bones are buried somewhere out in those hills."

"What do you think we should do?"

"Like I said... think about it before you use it in your story."

Cory did think about it, long and hard. He couldn't just abandon the project after all the intense effort he had put into it. And now the man who would be rating his work – the man who held his ticket to the future – was directly connected to the story he had recreated. Mr. Barkley was a part of it; by his own admission *he was "Mack"*— at least the one that existed in 1937.

Maybe Buck was right. Maybe he should leave out the 1937 incident.

TWENTY-SIX

The long, black dresses that Millie and the other women wore, gathered around the gravesite punctuated that gray, dismal day. Fully understanding the scope of the occasion, eight-year-old Clair clung to her mother's waist. Reverend Miller had to speak loudly to be heard over the wind whistling and roaring through the trees and between the lonely buildings. The only other men present were Clancy and the six bearing Jeremiah's casket on the short, final journey from Tanglewood to the gravesite, and who would fill in the grave at the close of the ceremony. All the others were still hunting the empty town for McDowell. As the Reverend recited the interment service, Clancy could barely focus his attention. He detected the faint sounds of men running and shouting voices somewhere off in the distance.

"...Ashes to ashes, dust to dust..."

The women wept as the Reverend continued. Clancy could still hear the commotion; it sounded as if it were coming from the Market Square.

"...We commit Jeremiah's body to the ground..."

The ruckus at the center of town seemed to get louder. Clancy saw that the other men were noticing it too.

"...Forever and ever. Amen."

The six men began shoveling soil into the grave. Clancy turned to Millie, putting his arms around her in a loving, caring embrace. "You'll be just fine in Wellington," he whispered softly. Then he leaned down to Clair and hugged her. "Take good care of your mother," he whispered to her.

The few belongings Millie would take with her to Wellington, already loaded in the Reverend's wagon and team, waited at the front steps of Tanglewood. Clancy untied the team from the hitching rail, and assisted the Minister, Millie and Clair aboard. "I'll come see you in Wellington... soon," he said.

Millie nodded, and Clair gave a pathetic little wave. The Reverend snapped the reins over the horses' backs and drove off. When they were out of sight, Clancy wandered off beyond Jeremiah's grave to a clump of trees beside the carriage house. He sat on the ground with his knees nearly to his chest, clasped his hands in front of his shins and rested his forehead on his knees.

He could still hear the clamor in the Market Square as if all the search party had gathered there. He could hear voices, but the wind muffled the words they were speaking. Suddenly a loud voice yelled out, "He's in the livery stable." Those were the only legible words, but hearing them didn't stir Clancy. He sat with a heavy heart; nothing seemed to matter to him right then.

A gunshot was heard. Then another. Then several more. Clancy remained still.

Barricaded inside the livery, McDowell saw no escape from the vigilantes gathered outside without creating a diversion. On the stable floor enough dry straw remained to kindle a fire. Once a smoke screen filled the air, he could make his exit through a rear window without being detected. It seemed his only chance of escape.

"FIRE! FIRE!" Clancy heard the screams, but he sat still.

The sight of smoke curling through the cracks in the walls of the abandoned stable, and then the flames licking the air beneath the eaves sent a dozen of the men running toward the fire house. But by the time they could hitch a team to the wagon carrying the water tank and pump, flames had eaten through the roof and were shooting fifty feet into the air, the wind whipping them about in every direction. Fireballs leaped out of the billowing smoke and within minutes the Railroad Depot across the alley succumbed to the fiery beast sending up more smoke and more flames. Like a burning fuse, one by one, the buildings surrounding the Square ignited, out of control. Fanned by the wind the flames lapped against the walls and roofs of Main Street, and soon the buildings there began bursting into flames. There was no stopping it.

Realizing their efforts were in vain, the vigilantes-turned-firemen abandoned the possibility of saving their town from the hellish destruction, and with fear in their eyes and terror in their screams rushed to their homes in hopes of saving what little they could and escaping before this monster consumed everything in its path.

Clancy stood now, watching from the clump of trees as the fire raced along the row of buildings on this side of Main. Clouds of black smoke rolled overhead turning the daylight to near darkness. Ashes and sparks sailed on the wind igniting nearly everything they touched. People everywhere were scrambling for the safety of anywhere but here. Families loaded in wagons and buggies behind skittish teams frantically made their way to the edge of town and toward Silver Creek.

Through the flying ashes and swirling smoke, Clancy saw a man hurriedly walking and occasionally stumbling among the blackened debris strewn in the street. He seemed to be heading for Tanglewood

Lodge. Nearly to the front door, he paused and turned to view the raging furnace behind him. As he turned, Clancy recognized the cowardly bastard who had killed his brother the day before. McDowell turned back toward the Hotel, momentarily rubbing his eyes and brushing the soot from his face. Clancy, now dusted with a goodly amount of soot himself, bounded from out of the trees, picked up a burning piece of timber from the street, held it like a ball bat over his shoulder and made an approach toward the unsuspecting McDowell. The sound of his footsteps covered by the roar of the fire allowed him within four feet before McDowell realized he was there. McDowell started turning toward Clancy just as Clancy swung the blazing club. McDowell went down. He never knew what hit him.

Clancy threw the smoldering timber down beside the lifeless body. Thick, black smoke engulfed him where he stood. It burned his eyes and throat; he could hardly breathe. To his right was the carriage house and just beyond that was the stable housing a single riding horse, Shiner. Through the near blinding smoke he made a dash for the stable, bridled Shiner and charged into the woods behind the Lodge and out of the smoke. Fifteen minutes later he stopped. He had reached another ridge across the valley to the north. From there he could see the dark smoke rising from the burning town a half-mile away, filling the sky like a huge thunderhead. There was no point in going back now, but there didn't seem much point in going any farther, either. He dismounted, tied Shiner's reins to a sapling, sat at the base of a huge oak, leaned back and closed his eyes. Confused. Scared. Angry. Alone – very alone. He didn't understand why he had refused to go to Wellington with Millie and Clair, even now, with visions of every square foot of Silver Spring fueling an inferno. Both of his brothers were dead; any plans for the future he might have entertained floated into the great beyond riding billows of black smoke.

Exhausted from turmoil, Clancy drifted into a restless sleep.

TWENTY-SEVEN

Springtime embraced Wellington. Once again, robins pulled worms from the green lawns, and shorts and T-shirts were becoming the common apparel.

A month had lapsed since Victor Gladstone received a copy of Cory's "Applegate," and the final manuscript left on Mr. Barkley's desk. Cory anxiously awaited the Professor's grade for his efforts on the carefully massaged work of eight months. But more importantly, he desired that favorable nod of approval from Victor Gladstone, confident that these two hundred pages were about to launch him into a writing career.

Sunday afternoons and evenings were usually the time to catch up on all the chores, and if there weren't a heavy weekend study load, the night would find Cory and Buck at Papa Leo's. Tonight, though, the warm weather had coaxed everyone out. Papa Leo's was packed and the waiting line stretched out into the parking lot. Pizza was out of the question. The *Country Cook* was just down the street. That place was busy too, but there were some empty tables. Burgers and fries would have to do tonight. The service was usually quite slow here, and on a busy night it would probably be even slower. But that was okay tonight. It would offer a chance to just talk.

They chatted about their jobs, and possible plans for the summer. Buck intended to work full-time, in order to earn enough for at least a down payment on a car. Cory wanted to keep working at the newspaper, too, but he wasn't sure how he was going to break the news to Mom that he wouldn't be coming home for the summer.

Only a month remained to the end of the school term. But even Spring Fever couldn't squelch the topic of school to creep into the conversation.

"How did your research project turn out?" Cory asked.

"Which one?"

"Bank robberies."

"Professor Harris said in all the years he has had that on the list, no one has ever found the Zachary McDowell robbery."

"So how'd you do?"

"Got an A."

"Way to go, Buck."

"Yeah, and it's kind of neat how that helped you with your story too."

"He still hasn't posted any grades."

"What's taking so long?"

"Twenty stories, each two hundred pages or more. That's what."

"If it's this nice next weekend, do you want to go camping?"

"Sure. Where should we go?"

"Why not *out there* again?"

"Oh, I get it. You want to look for the hidden treasure."

"Well, you never know. We could get lucky."

"Do you really think it's still out there?"

"Who's to say it isn't?"

Cory and Buck were once again feeling the urge to get out into the wild. A springtime camping trip had been on their minds all winter, and now the warm weather had given them a touch of the fever. They could hear their campsite in Silver Spring Hills calling them.

The gray-haired lady in the next booth laid down her fork. Miriam's full attention was directed to the conversation behind the divider. She couldn't see them, but she knew who was talking.

Anticipating the weekend activities, Friday night seemed to take forever to arrive. Cory read off the list of camping items while Buck checked to make sure everything was loaded in the Bronco.

A pickup truck with a canoe loaded in the bed pulled into the driveway. "Hey! Bronco Boy!" Slinky said, slipping out of the driver's seat and Jimmy out of the passenger side, both wearing nothing but swim trunks. "We're gonna canoe down the Pike. Want to come along? I can get another canoe."

The invitation was tempting. "I'd like to, but I have to work in the morning," Buck said with disappointment.

"But we'll be back by midnight," Jimmy replied.

"I've got a better idea," Cory said. "We're going camping tomorrow afternoon… there's a creek that would be great for canoeing. Why don't you go camping with us?"

"Where?"

"Silver Spring."

"No way! You guys are crazy. You're out of your minds."

Cory wanted to convince Slinky and Jimmy that Silver Spring was as safe as their own back yards, but before any further discussion of the matter could be carried out, Slinky was behind the wheel with the motor running. "See ya, Bronco Boy. Have fun with Mack." They drove away.

Saturday noon, Cory was waiting for Buck outside the Chevy garage.

"Gas tank full?" Buck jokingly reminded Cory of his blunder last fall.

"Full."

"Ice in the cooler?"

"Full."

"Money detector?"

"Huh?"

"Never mind. We're ready. Let's go."

The spring rains had erased all their tracks from last fall, and even the deeper tire prints left on the soft creek banks were washed away. Spring floods had deposited woodland debris on their campsite front yard, and had even rearranged the fire ring stones. But it didn't take long to set up camp, and this time the tent was positioned for *morning* shade beside the scrub oak. Cory kept a close eye on the time. He knew he wanted to be on that hilltop before three o'clock.

Surrounded by a new growth of weeds and wildflowers, Tanglewood Lodge looked much the same as they had last seen it. On the forest floor of that ridge overlooking picturesque valleys flanking either side, lay the unmistakable traces of the lost city. Distinctly evident in the shadowy light, were scattered the crumpled bricks of once-majestic chimneys and undaunted hearths, and the chiseled rock foundations of the buildings that bordered the streets. Long ago nature had begun covering up man's signature of the town that once blazed in the glory of mining history.

Cory and Buck stood at a fallen tree trunk. About twenty yards to their right stood the Lodge, and a hundred yards over their left shoulders lay the "dead line." Straight ahead they could see signs of the cobblestone Market Square, and beyond that they gazed out over the valley below the railroad tracks. They hadn't yet ventured in that direction, but Cory wasn't in favor of starting out just yet. He wanted to be right here at Tanglewood at three o'clock. Buck relented and agreed to wait.

"If you were a bank robber," Buck said, "where would you hide it?"

Cory peered around at the possibilities. Obviously, the scene was quite different now than it was just days or weeks following the fires. He tried to imagine the charred, smoldering site in 1899. "I don't think I'd bury it in the ground."

"Where, then?"

"The hotel?"

"Too obvious."

"Maybe that's why nobody ever found it."

"Well then, maybe we should—"

A gunshot echoed across the hills. It wasn't muffled and subdued like the ones they had heard before. This one pierced through the serenity and sounded very *real*. Almost instantly, Buck flinched dramatically. His body stiffened, listed to one side, his right hand grasping Cory's shirttail as he slowly sank to his knees. Cory looked around trying to detect where the sound came from, not paying much attention to Buck's movements, certain they were just playful antics. He could still hear the echo when he glanced down at Buck and suddenly realized Buck was *not* joking. Unable to speak, Buck let out a painful moan. The back of his T-shirt was bright red with blood. His grip on Cory's shirt went limp and he toppled to the ground.

"BUCK! NO!" Instant terror strangled Cory. He dropped to his knees and lifted Buck's head up out of the matted leaves and dirt. He could feel Buck's pain as he brushed away the leaves from his grimaced face.

Another shot rang out and this time Cory heard the bullet zing just inches past his ear and ricochet off a nearby rock. He dove to a prone position beside Buck.

"Get away," Buck strained to whisper the words.

"I can't leave you here," Cory said, frantically searching for an escape plan. Getting Buck to safety was all he could think.

"Get AWAY," Buck struggled to say again.

Cory knew at that moment Buck was right. He had to draw the assailant's attention away from that spot. If he didn't move, he would become the next victim, and he wouldn't be of any help to Buck. "I'll be back… I promise," he whispered in Buck's ear.

Like an antelope he sprang to his feet and ran as hard as his legs could carry him to shelter behind the Lodge. He paused to look back toward Buck who was partially hidden by the log and tall grass. Another shot and a chunk of brick exploded from the wall. Cory ducked around the corner. He knew he had to keep moving. He paused again only long enough to pick out his next destination – one of the rock foundations, fifty feet away. That would be the next source of cover. There wasn't time to think about it. He just started running.

Cory made a dive to safety behind the line of boulders. Another shot split through the air just above his head. At least now he knew he had drawn the attacker away from Buck. A small cluster of trees and bushes stood just beyond the ruins of a fireplace.

"First the fireplace, and then angle off into the trees," he thought, and then ran. Another shot was fired and a spray of dirt flew up from the ground in front of him. Cory was scared like he'd never been scared before.

He ducked behind the trees and crouched. Cautiously he peeked around the tree trunk. Just the glimpse of the brown jacket and a shiny rifle was enough to get him moving again. The gunman was getting much too close.

Cory made a dash for the slope toward the valley he did not know. Heading into unfamiliar territory was risky, but there wasn't time to think about choices. It was his best alternative. Once over the crest of the knoll, he was sure he would be out of the gunman's sight. He slowed his pace and looked back, realizing that was a mistake when he tripped, finding himself in an uncontrollable tumble down the grade. The bruises and scrapes stung a little but they were the least of his concerns now. As he gathered himself up, he noticed his exact location. Right in front of him were the old railroad tracks. He had an idea. Cory looked at his watch. It was just about three o'clock.

Hoping he would be noticed, he waited for the gunman to appear at the top of the slope. As soon as he was certain the gunman saw him, he jumped down the steep embankment across the tracks, and this time he was in complete control of the fall. It wasn't likely he would be followed too quickly down that drop-off, and he wanted that man, whoever he was, on the railroad tracks.

Well out of sight behind a huge oak tree and a thicket of brush, Cory watched the man slowly pace along the tracks, the rifle butt to his shoulder and the barrel poised toward the lower ground where Cory crouched. Through the brush, he could only see the brown jacket and a brown cap, but he still couldn't identify the man wearing them. The brush was too dense.

Cory looked at his watch. Three minutes past three. Of all days for the train to be late.

The faint, shrill whistle seemed like a message from heaven. A phantom train might do no harm to the man, but at least it would create a diversion for Cory to make a getaway. "A speeding locomotive should startle even a lunatic," he thought.

The train whistles screamed again and louder. Cory could just barely see the man's head turning from side to side. The plan was working. Just as had once happened to Cory and to Buck, the man was startled into evasive action, and as he began stepping off the tracks it appeared as though he had hooked his foot on the rail, lost his balance and fell backwards over the embankment, landing not more than fifty feet away from Cory's temporary spot of security. This was *not* part of the plan.

The man did not move. Cory could imagine a fall like that could knock the wind out of almost anyone. This was probably his best opportunity to get away, yet he was afraid to move from his hiding spot. The man still wasn't making the slightest movement. Cory cautiously started to creep out from behind the tree. It meant getting closer to the gunman and it gave him a better view of the man lying in the weeds. He could see the rifle still clenched in the man's hand, but he couldn't see the man's face.

"Buck!" In the next instant Cory had lost his concern for the man who had tried to kill him. He clawed his way back up the railroad embankment. Exhaustion nearly overcame him, but he forced himself into a run back to the spot where Buck lay, now unconscious. Buck had lost a lot of blood, but he was still breathing.

"BUCK!" Wake up! Can you hear me?"

Buck opened his eyes just momentarily, moaned, and plunged into unconsciousness again.

"We've got to get you to the hospital." Cory could plainly see Buck was in no condition to get up, much less walk back to the Bronco down at the campsite. The adrenalin was pumping. There was no time to waste. The only way to save Buck was to carry him down the hill and across the valley.

During the entire distance he never thought once about the pain of his own scrapes and cuts. He didn't think about the punishment he was exerting on his own body. He didn't think about the man he left in the ravine by the railroad tracks. Nothing else mattered now. Buck's life was at stake.

He swung open the Bronco's passenger door, and as gently as time warranted, got Buck into the seat, retrieved one of the sleeping bags from the tent, folded it into a bulky pillow and stuffed it between Buck and the door.

A twist of the ignition key and the Bronco was splashing across the creek. Although he was traveling twice – maybe three times faster than he ever had on this trail, the distance had never seemed so great. Every time he glanced toward Buck and saw his blood-drenched clothes, Wellington and the hospital seemed farther away.

Cory couldn't stop blaming himself for what had happened to Buck. It was his own obsession with the story about Silver Spring that had enticed them into going there. It was he who had convinced Buck to research bank robberies, drawing Buck's interest even deeper into the curious secrets of this dangerous legend.

Once on the highway, it was only another mile into Wellington. Cory's right foot pressed the gas pedal down so hard his knee started to ache. The tires screamed around the last curve on the outskirts of town; getting to the hospital on the other side of town meant getting through the Saturday afternoon traffic. It would be a challenge.

He put the Bronco into a four-wheel slide making the left turn onto Main Street. The next five blocks went by quite quickly at sixty miles per hour. He slowed to a more reasonable speed, held Buck's left shoulder to keep him from tipping out of the bucket seat, turned right onto Johnson Street and once again stood on the gas pedal. A block later, he heard the siren behind him. He looked in the rear view mirror, realizing the policeman, a half block back, couldn't possibly know the circumstances. But maybe when he made the turn toward the hospital, the pursuing cop would understand. Every second counted. Buck was limp and pale, and Cory knew there was no time to explain to anyone. He didn't care how many tickets would result - Buck's life was on the line.

From a half block away from where he would make the turn toward the hospital, Cory saw a new problem developing. Another police car came to a sliding stop, blocking the intersection. The driver's door swung open and the uniformed officer immediately leveled the barrel of a shotgun in Cory's direction.

"This can't be happening," he thought. Only a block from the hospital - one block from saving Buck's life. But he'd had enough lead flying at him for one day, and this guy looked like he meant business. There was no point in ending this with a bigger disaster than it already was. Cory brought the Bronco to a screeching halt with the chase car stopping almost beside him. Now both officers were cautiously stepping toward him with their weapons aimed and ready.

"I HAVE TO GET TO THE HOSPITAL! MY FRIEND HAS BEEN SHOT!"

By then, one of the officers was near enough to see Buck slumped in the passenger seat. He yelled out the order to Cory: "GET OUT OF THE CAR AND KEEP YOUR HANDS WHERE I CAN SEE THEM!"

Cory wasn't about to put up an argument. The sooner the cops realized the urgency of the situation, the sooner Buck would get help. He swung his door open and jumped to the pavement.

With their weapons still trained on Cory, both officers stepped closer to the Bronco.

"PLEASE! LET ME GET HIM TO THE HOSPITAL!"

The officer who had been in pursuit, the younger of the two, went to the open door. Buck's white T-shirt was soaked with blood, and blood was dripping from the fingertips of his hand that dangled limply off the side of the seat, his head tilted back against the window. The officer holstered his revolver, climbed into the driver's seat and laid his fingers on Buck's neck looking for a pulse.

"CALL AN AMBULANCE!" he yelled from inside the Bronco.

"BUT THE HOSPITAL IS RIGHT THERE! I CAN GET HIM THERE FASTER!" Cory's anxiety was now reaching the threshold of hysteria. He'd kept a cool head all this time but now the policemen were delaying

Buck's aid.

"CALL AN AMBULANCE!" the young officer yelled again.

By then, the senior officer had recognized Cory's sincerity and the urgency this incident demanded. To him, Cory was no longer a threat to anyone. He lowered the shotgun and rushed to the Bronco's open door.

"He's right, Tom. Let him go. You ride with him and I'll call to let them know you're coming."

The younger officer seemed to object. "But don't you think we should—"

"TOM? Shut up and make room for him to drive." The older officer was stern with his command. He assisted Cory into the driver's seat.

Cory started the motor and anxiously waited for the squad car to be moved out of the way. The young officer braced himself and held Buck from moving. "What's your name?" he asked.

"Cory Brockway."

"How did this happen?"

"I'd rather drive than talk right now."

"Look here, smart ass, you've broken every rule in the book. You'd *better* start cooperating!"

Cory didn't answer. He was approaching the Emergency Room entrance and he could see four people dressed in white waiting at the door with a gurney. He stopped beside them. They instantly had the passenger door open tending to Buck.

The officer began talking to them. "Apparent gunshot... I checked his pulse and—"

"Shut up, Tom," the attending doctor said. He and two orderlies were already working at getting Buck onto the gurney. He put a stethoscope to Buck's chest for a few seconds, and then began giving instructions to the nurse beside him. "Get a line in. Get the lab down here - type and cross for six. Tell the O.R. we're on the way."

Brief. Simple. Effective. Without wasting a single movement the white team quickly wheeled the gurney toward the door as if they had rehearsed this scene a hundred times.

Cory had circled around the front of the Bronco and started following them through the door when he felt a strong hand take hold of his arm. He hadn't noticed the other police officer arrive.

"Better just to stay out here," he said. "Let them do what they have to do."

"But Buck is my best friend. I -"

"Nothing you can do for him right now. He's in good hands."

The younger officer strutted up to Cory. He sneered. "Okay, Cory Brockway. Are you ready to cooperate now?"

"Tom?" the senior officer said. "Go back and get your car out of the street."

"But I need some information. I have some traffic citations to issue."

"You're not issuing *any* citations. Now go get your car off the street."

"Well, aren't you going to give me a ride?"

"No. It's a block away. WALK."

Not too happy with the order, the rookie

walked away. His superior watched and just shook his head.

"I'm Sergeant Joe Block."

"Cory Brockway."

"Let's go sit down over there, Cory. You can catch your breath."

Thankful that Sergeant Block showed up when he did, Cory saw him as kind and considerate, unlike the young rookie who was ready to lock him up without seeking the facts. Sergeant Block had already earned Cory's respect.

"I suppose you want to know what happened," Cory said. He knew he had a lot of explaining to do.

"Whenever you're ready." Block was eyeing Cory's bloodstained clothes, and noticing the many bruises and cuts on his arms and face. "You've got some nasty cuts."

Cory was so preoccupied with everything else he had forgotten about his own condition. "I'm okay."

"Should have them looked at," Block said.

"Really. I'm okay. Most of this blood is from Buck. Had to carry him."

"Where'd it happen?"

"Out in the woods. We were camping."

"Whose gun? Yours?"

Cory instantly realized that Block had drawn to an assumption that this was an accidental shooting, and that he was the shooter. "Oh... no! We were hiking up in the hills and someone started shooting at us."

Sergeant Block's expression turned to one of curious surprise. Now the situation had suddenly taken on new meaning. "Neither of you were carrying a gun?"

"No sir."

Block reached into his jacket and pulled out a small notebook and pen. "Cory, what's your friend's name?"

"Buck Paxton."

"Buck. That's a nickname?"

"Roger. His real name is Roger."

"You live here?"

"We're students at Wellington College."

"Live in the dorms?"

"No, an apartment on Harrison. Eight fifty-five."

"What time did it happen?"

"Just a few minutes before three."

Joe looked at his watch. "It's 4:45. That's almost two hours ago."

"Well, I had to carry Buck a long way back to my truck. That was after—" Cory realized he had not yet mentioned the man he left lying beside the railroad tracks at Silver Spring.

"After what?" Joe asked.

"The man who shot Buck chased me. Guess he wanted to kill me too."

"Did you see him?"

"Not good enough to see who he was."

"But you got away."

"Well, sort of."

"What do you mean, *sort of,* Cory?"

"He tripped and fell. Looked like he was unconscious... he could still be there."

Joe's eyes widened. His brows lifted. "Where is this place?"

"About five or six miles out in the country... west of town."

"I have to call the County Sheriff on this. Can you take them there?"

"Yes, sir... but it takes a four-wheel-drive to get there."

"County's got four-wheelers."

"Can I find out how Buck is first?"

"Sure. Right inside that door. I'll be there in a couple of minutes."

A nurse met Cory just inside the doorway. "Oh dear. What happened to you?" She took Cory's arm and started guiding him toward a wheelchair, thinking he was there for medical attention.

"No. I'm okay. I just want to know how my friend is – Buck Paxton." Cory wasn't aware of his appearance, other than the blood stains on his shirt.

"You mean the young man just brought in with a bullet wound?"

"Yes. That's him."

"Are you a relative?"

"No... best friend. I brought him in."

"He's in surgery right now. Let's clean up those cuts," she insisted, and coaxed Cory into an examination room.

Minutes later, Cory was whisked off and instructed to climb into the passenger seat of one of the two Dodge Power Wagons waiting in the parking lot. Both had "Wellington County Sheriff's Department" painted on the doors. Sheriff Morgan Bancroft and three Deputies had been filled in on the known details and would handle the incident from here, as the occurrence was outside the jurisdiction of the City Police.

Cory's only role, for now, was to lead them to the scene, and by the way he had been treated by the brown uniformed men, so far, he had the distinct impression the Sheriff still considered him a suspect. But he knew an injured body grasping the rifle that shot Buck would be found in that ravine below the railroad tracks, and that would certainly get him off the hook.

Or would it? Cory thought about all the other strange happenings he had observed at Silver Spring, and considering the reputation it had gained over the years, nearly anything was possible. What if the gunman *wasn't* there? What if the man he saw fall off the embankment had regained consciousness and wandered off after Cory left? What if the man wasn't really a man – but the *ghost of Silver Spring* – just another apparition like the phantom train?

Cory couldn't express any of these thoughts to the Sheriff who was driving the truck. It would just weave more suspicion. Depending on the outcome of this mess, the story would eventually have to surface anyway, but only if it became necessary. And just yet, it wasn't. Although he wasn't one to wish for bad endings, Cory desperately hoped the body would be there.

Two miles into the hills, the dirt road diminished to only the tire tracks Cory's Bronco had left. The Sheriff stopped. He stared through the windshield, seeing the tracks continue into the woods far beyond the end of the road.

"Just where are you taking us?" the Sheriff asked.

"A few more miles... over a couple more ridges."

The Sheriff glared at Cory. He set the emergency brake, got out of the truck and ambled back to the other truck following them. Cory could see the Sheriff and the other Deputies talking, but he couldn't hear them. They kept gesturing and looking toward the hill ahead. He knew they were now suspecting Silver Spring Hills as the destination. Finally, the Sheriff walked up to Cory's window.

"Did you cross a creek to get to your campsite?"

"It's right by the creek."

"And where's the injured man?"

"Just over the next hill from there."

Sheriff Bancroft looked down at the ground, and then up at the horizon. He turned and walked back to the Deputies. They talked some more.

It seemed clear to Cory now that perhaps the creek marked the boundary of the feared and forbidden territory. Did this mean the mission was scrubbed? Were the peace officers abandoning the quest for a criminal? Were they placing restrictions on their duties because they were afraid to enter that area? Somehow, he had to convince them to continue.

Cory jumped out of the truck and walked back to the Sheriff and his men.

The Sheriff eyed him approaching. "Are you absolutely certain we'll find a body?"

"Absolutely." Cory knew he couldn't show any degree of uncertainty.

The Sheriff looked at his Deputies. They looked at him with puzzled stares. One of them shrugged his shoulders, gazing up the hill. No doubt, the Deputies shared reservations.

"All right," Bancroft said. "We're wasting daylight. Saddle up. Let's go."

They crested the next ridge. Feeling deep concern for Buck, Cory asked the Sheriff "Is there any way you can find out about Buck?"

Bancroft keyed the radio microphone. "Forty-four to headquarters."

The radio crackled. "Go ahead, Sheriff," a distant voice said.

"Any word from the hospital yet on the shooting victim?"

"Nothing yet, Sheriff, but I'll keep you posted."

"Ten-four."

The Power Wagons waded across the creek with ease and came to rest beside the tent.

"Where is it from here?" the Sheriff asked.

Cory pointed to the hill straight ahead. "You can drive as far as the bottom of the hill. We'll have to walk from there."

He led them first to the spot where Buck had been hit, and then followed the same path he used to evade the gunman, ending on the railroad bed. He was almost afraid to look down into the ravine.

"I was hiding in the brush… right down there." Cory pointed. "He tripped and fell over this bank."

Cory peeked over the edge. The evening shade prevented the sight of anything at the bottom. Two Deputies started their way down the steep bank. Cory held his breath. Once they had reached the base he could hardly see them moving about in near silence. Cory could only hear the two mumbling. A few minutes later one Deputy spoke loudly but in a solemn voice, "There's nothing down here anywhere."

Daylight was fading to dusk, but Bancroft wanted to get a few of the facts straight. Cory was almost certain the Sheriff didn't believe everything he was hearing, but Cory didn't falter.

It was a long ride back to Wellington. Cory's only concern now was Buck. There had been no word from the hospital and he feared the worst.

After two more hours of interviews and statement writing, Cory was finally released from the Sheriff's Department. Sergeant Joe Block was there waiting.

"My car is right outside. C'mon… I'll give you a ride." Joe suggested a clean change of clothes before returning to the hospital. On the way, he talked to Cory as a friend.

"You know, Cory," he said, "nobody goes out where you guys were camping."

"I know. I've heard all about Mack."

"Then why did you go?"

"I've been writing a story about it."

"For school?"

"Yes, sir."

"Why that?"

"There's some interesting history out there, and –"

Cory suddenly gave second thoughts about revealing any of the information he and Buck had uncovered. Buck was the only other person with whom he had ever discussed this subject, and until now, he'd never told anyone his story was really about Silver Spring, much less that the story was based on fact. The existing legend was part of Wellington's cultural heritage, and the people of Wellington probably weren't ready for their legend to be unraveled and the mysteries solved. Implicating Mr. Barkley in the murder of Albert Sanford – even though it happened thirty years ago – could only stir up another disaster, and one disaster, for right now, was enough.

Cory quickly changed the subject. "Hey, what about Buck's parents?"

"We've been trying to contact them," Joe said. "But we found out they're traveling in Europe somewhere, and we can't reach them."

"Buck *did* say they were going on vacation for a month."

"Did he say where?"

"No. I don't think he knew exactly."

"Has he ever mentioned any other relatives?"

"No… he doesn't talk about family much."

Buck had just come out of surgery and was being placed in an intensive care unit. Joe and Cory watched from the nurses' station as the gurney was wheeled into an elevator.

"Can I go see him?" Cory asked the nurse.

"Not yet. He'll be in recovery for several hours."

"Well, when?"

"When we get him settled in his room and all the monitors are connected."

"How long will that be?"

"I don't know... but I'll have the doctor come talk to you."

"Is he going to be okay?"

"The doctor will be here in a little while. Make yourself comfortable in the lounge."

Sergeant Block put his arm across Cory's shoulders and guided him to a couch in the waiting room. They sat down.

"I know you're worried, Cory, but try to relax."

"I can't."

"I know how you feel, Cory, but it'll be all right... you'll see."

"How long do you think—"

"I don't know, but I can't stay here all night. You going to be okay?"

"Yeah."

"Anything I can do for you?"

"No. But thanks."

"I'll check back with you later." Sergeant Block's long strides carried him down the hallway and out of sight.

"Hi. I'm Dr. Garvey."

"Hi. I'm Cory Brockway. Is Buck going to be okay?"

"The surgery went quite well. Fortunately the bullet didn't penetrate any vital organs or sever any major arteries... but it did do some damage, and he lost a considerable amount of blood."

Cory took a deep breath. This wasn't good news, but it was better than what he had feared.

The Doctor continued. "We have replaced some blood, he's receiving antibiotics, and he'll be on a respirator for a while. Infection is still a great risk. This was a tremendous insult to his body, but the best thing he has going for him is that he is young."

Cory knew he should feel relieved, but there was still a knot the size of a softball in his gut. "But is he going to be okay?"

"We'll know more after twenty-four hours."

"When can I see him?"

"Probably not until tomorrow morning... but even then there is a strong possibility he'll be in a coma for a while."

TWENTY-EIGHT

Nighttime had been *so* dark under overcast and smoky skies. Clancy waited for the first light of dawn to venture any further than his immediate little campsite. Rocky cliffs and drop-offs along this ridge could mean trouble in such total darkness. He knew of wild grapevines, blackberry bushes and apple trees. With a little daylight he'd be able to find them, and with some luck no one else would have picked them clean. Down in the valley there were the abandoned alfalfa and wheat fields. Shiner could have his freedom to eat well there. He had always come running to Clancy's whistle – no reason to worry that he wouldn't do the same now.

On the next ridge where Silver Spring *should be*, there were no lights glowing or rooftop silhouettes meeting the sky. To Clancy it appeared there was nothing left. Perhaps riding Shiner to Wellington was his best option. All he had was the clothes on his back, a pocketknife and a few coins in his pocket, and Shiner. The wild grapes and blackberries wouldn't last forever, and unless some tools could be salvaged from the remains of the town, it might prove difficult to construct any kind of shelter before the colder weather set in.

During the night the wind had calmed and the sky cleared. By the time the sun came peeking through the trees, Clancy and Shiner had foraged breakfast and stood alongside the railroad tracks peering through the smoky haze that hung in the still morning air like fog hovering a swamp. In silence, he gazed around the charred, smoldering ruins. Sadness overwhelmed him. In just a few short hours, Silver Spring, the place he called home, had been reduced to nothing more than heaps of glowing embers, rubble and ashes. The Depot was gone; Market Square was gone; Main Street was gone; even the shacks and shanties beyond the "dead line" were a blackened mass of scattered debris. The fire had swept throughout the entire town consuming everything in its path all the way to Silver Creek. Shiner stepped cautiously among the burned rubble from the toppled buildings. Unbearable heat radiated from everywhere. Whatever structures weren't completely burned, were damaged to the point of collapse. All of Silver Spring lay destroyed. All except one building.

The only structure in all of Silver Spring built completely with brick and stone remained. Expecting to find the hotel completely gutted and no more than an empty brick shell, Clancy, in awe but yet pleased, rode Shiner closer. As he approached the front of the building, he was quickly reminded of the event he'd like to forget: McDowell's body lay on the street just fifty feet from Tanglewood's front door.

A streak of anger jolted through Clancy. He glanced toward Jeremiah's gravesite. The plain stone slab marker protruded from the ground alone. All that remained of the stable and carriage house was foundation stones and one small corner of the stable. Nearly everything Clancy owned had been inside the carriage house. A charred skeleton of their carriage lay buried under more burned rubble. It was, indeed, a forlorn sight. Even Shiner, it seemed, had tears rolling from his eyes.

Everything at Tanglewood, though, seemed to be intact – the outer walls smudged with soot, but otherwise unharmed. The blustery wind and the threat of a storm yesterday morning had caused all the windows to be closed, so not a single spark penetrated. Had McDowell made it to the entrance, the door would have been standing open, and surely the Lodge would not have been spared. Truly remarkable, Tanglewood Lodge stood unscathed with the rest of the town around it fallen in ruins.

The tiny bells attached to the top of the door jingled as Clancy pulled it open. He stepped inside. "HELLO? IS ANYBODY HERE?" he called out. There was no answer. Just silence. Tipped and broken chairs and tables, smashed bottles and mugs, and the shattered mirror behind the bar revealed the evidence of the riotous melee when Jeremiah was gunned down two days earlier. And the eerie silence.

There on the table next to the piano, Clancy saw one of his most prized possessions – the journal Tom Hargrove had given him – the journal into which he had so diligently made his entries – the journal that he feared had been lost. How fortunate it was he had left it there the night before. He clutched it tightly, thinking of all the recorded memories it contained – memories of Silver Spring, its events, and the people he was so fortunate to have known – the people who were a part of his life.

He slowly climbed the staircase to the second floor. The only closed door down the long, narrow hallway led into the room where McDowell had been staying. Clancy turned the doorknob and kicked it open. Nothing was there except the leather saddlebags draped over the back of a chair. He unbuckled the flaps and dumped the contents onto the floor – a change of clothes, a tobacco pouch and five silver dollars. He gathered up the coins, slung the saddlebags over his shoulder, and went down the back stairway.

A few of Jeremiah's clothes still hung in a wardrobe in the Cranes' quarters at the back of the Hotel, and hidden behind them, resting against the corner was the lever-action Winchester rifle and six boxes of cartridges. Clancy placed the ammo in the saddlebag, stuffed in two shirts, a jacket and a pair of trousers, a blanket, his journal and buckled the flap shut.

Millie had left an ample supply of food for him in the cold cellar - a partial barrel of salt pork, two dozen eggs, flour, cornmeal, rings of sausage, a half-bushel of potatoes, and several cans of beans.

"Well that was mighty kind of you, Millie," he thought. "Maybe this won't be so bad after all." Then it occurred to him that by now she would know the condition of Silver Spring. She would no doubt be worried about him. He entertained the thought of riding to Wellington right away to find Millie and Clair, but quickly dismissed the idea.

He remembered the placer mine he and Charlie Daggett had been working before Charlie took ill. All their tools would still be there, and there was still gold to be taken from that creek bank that no one but he and Charlie knew about. He could spend a few days at a time out there, just as they had done before, and then return to Tanglewood when supplies ran out.

Bed sheets worked quite well to fashion a pack to hang over Shiner's back. He took enough food to last three days.

Atop the higher ground behind Tanglewood, the trail passed a point where nearly all of the town could be seen. Clancy paused to look back over the devastated panorama. Suddenly he could hear the pounding of horses' hooves and the rumble of wagons. Forty or fifty men, each toting a shovel or axe jumped from the six wagons and began swarming the smoldering ruins as if they were searching for anything worth taking. Clancy recognized some of the men; they were former residents of Silver Spring. It didn't take long for them to discover McDowell's body, and soon most of the men were gathered in front of Tanglewood. They seemed to be just as astonished with its unharmed presence as Clancy had been. Two of the men in the group entered the front door, and in a couple of minutes returned. Now Clancy could see one of the men had a shiny badge pinned to his chest - it had to be Sheriff Endicott from Wellington.

Clancy just sat on the knoll and watched as each wagon was pulled to the front door, and chairs, tables, beds, potbelly stoves and even rolls of carpet were loaded into them. Then came out the beer and wine barrels from the cellar.

Loaded to capacity, the wagon train rumbled down Connor Street to the East Hill Road, crossed Silver Creek and disappeared over the ridge toward Wellington. Clancy felt fortunate that he had gotten there first, but now his food supply was probably gone. But the good news was that now he didn't have to dispose of McDowell's body.

Three days of panning produced six poppy seed-sized nuggets. Not a fortune, by any means, but at least he wasn't leaving empty-handed. Clancy thought he would turn Shiner loose in the alfalfa field, walk back to Tanglewood, and rest a couple of days before going back to the mine. There was one task he wanted to complete, too, during his stay there. It had been on his mind all the while he was at the placer mine; Jeremiah's name should be chiseled onto the grave marker.

He gathered up a good amount of grapes, blackberries and apples on the way, not knowing if the food stash would still be in the cellar. He kept thinking about the men who had cleaned out the Lodge. Had Millie sent them? Or were they just looters?

Everything was gone from inside Tanglewood – furniture, pots and pans, stoves, carpet, lamps – everything except a few broken tables and chairs, and the piano. Most of the food was gone too. Only the flour, cornmeal, potatoes and eggs remained. Luckily, he had taken some utensils with him to the mine, and they were still in the pack he brought back. And with the fruit he had picked, he wouldn't go hungry.

In the cool of the evening hours before the daylight slipped away, "JEREMIAH CRANE, 1851 - 1899" neatly graced the headstone. When he was finished, Clancy sat in the grass beside the stone and wrote in his journal, "I wish Millie could be here to see it. Somehow, this seems the proper justification for staying. I think of Millie and Clair often now. I hope they are well, and I hope they have found happiness in their new home."

His next stay at the mine lasted four days. The third day produced quite well – one of the eight nuggets the size of a small pea. But the fourth day, nothing. He returned to Tanglewood. And because he was very tired after panning for four days, he decided to ride Shiner all the way back. He could walk the animal down to the fields the next day.

Only six eggs and about that many potatoes left meant that one more trip to the mine would have to be the last before he finally made his way to Wellington.

TWENTY-NINE

Cory awoke to a gentle nudge on his shoulder. He could just barely remember the nurse bringing him the pillow and blanket during the night. Considering the circumstances, he had been sleeping quite soundly. But this wasn't the nurse nudging him now. It was Sheriff Bancroft.

"Kinda thought I'd find you here."

Cory squinted, rubbed his eyes, and sat up. He said nothing. His experience with the Sheriff the night before had been less than pleasant. Bancroft had tried for two hours to find a reason to point a judicial finger at Cory, and it didn't appear he was ready to let up just yet.

"Have you thought of anything you might have left out last night?" the Sheriff asked.

That question seemed a little odd at that very moment. Then a hundred thoughts began racing through Cory's head. "Ahh... no... nothing I can think of."

"Have you had any arguments with anyone lately?"

"N-no! What are you getting at?"

"Is there any reason anyone would have been trying to kill you or Mr. Paxton?"

"I-I don't think so... why?" Cory knew that might not be the whole truth, but until it became absolutely necessary, he wouldn't divulge his knowledge of Barkley's dark past.

Bancroft stared down at the floor a few seconds. "Well, there was someone else out there. We found some tracks through the weeds early this morning but we lost the trail at the edge of the creek."

Cory felt a tingle on the back of his neck and the hair on his arms bristled. The thought had occurred to him at some point during the night that his story could have caused Barkley to fear being exposed as a killer, and Buck had warned him: *"It could get you killed,"* he had said. Mr. Barkley could have possibly been the triggerman back at Silver Spring yesterday.

"By the way," Sheriff Bancroft said. "We gathered up all your camping gear. You can pick it up at my office."

Cory sat on the couch long after the Sheriff had left. A nurse patted him on the shoulder. "Roger is in his room now. He's still asleep, but if you want to peek in on him, it would be okay – but just for a few minutes."

"Okay... that would be great."

The room on the third floor was dimly lit. The bare, pure white walls suggested loneliness. At the center of the room was one bed, the head raised to a slight angle. The sight nearly brought tears to Cory's eyes. Buck's upper torso was mostly covered in white bandage. Green plastic tubes invaded his nose and mouth, and more tubes coming from a rack of hanging bottles filled with clear and colored liquids were taped to his arm. His face was pale and appeared almost lifeless.

Cory gently grasped Buck's free hand. "I'm sorry I got you into all this. It should be me instead of you. Buck, I'm so sorry."

Another voice, almost a whisper, drifted into the room. "Why would you think it should've been you, Cory?"

Cory glanced toward the door, disappointed that he was not being afforded a few private moments with his best friend. But he soon found comfort with this intruder. Sergeant Joe Block without a police uniform stood at the foot of the bed. He was the only person who had made Cory feel more at ease with the situation.

"It's kind of my fault we were out there... at Silver Spring."

"But it's not your fault someone started shooting at you."

"Well, maybe it is."

"What do you mean by that?"

A nurse entered. "I'm sorry, but you'll have to leave now."

Cory leaned close to Buck. "I'll be back soon... I promise."

Out in the corridor Joe Block suggested the first floor Coffee Lounge. "The coffee's okay, and we can talk."

Being a Sunday morning, not many people had yet gathered in the lounge. Cory and Joe took seats at a table by the window.

"I'm really glad you came down, Sergeant Block."

"Call me Joe. I'm not in uniform now."

"Okay."

"Thought I should come to check on you. I know you don't have any family here."

"I do appreciate that."

"Cory, there seems to be more to all this than you're telling."

"Well..." Cory hesitated as he gazed out the window. "There is something I should tell someone, but I'm not sure who."

"Is it about the shooting?"

"No… well, maybe."

"Cory, I'm here as a friend right now. Maybe I can help you with whatever is troubling you."

"What makes you think I'm troubled?"

"You're troubled. I can tell."

"Of course I'm troubled. My best friend is up there fighting for his life. Yeah. I'm troubled."

"But there's more to it, isn't there? What is it?"

"Well, I was going to keep it a secret, but…"

"Keep what a secret?"

"About Barkley… my college professor."

"What about him?"

"Joe? Do you know the real history of Silver Spring?"

"A little."

"Have you ever been there?"

"No, can't say I have."

"Well, I've learned all about that town. And I wrote the whole story as a project in Mr. Barkley's class. Changed all the names and places, but I kept the facts of the story as accurate as I knew them to be."

"And so what does that have to do with what happened yesterday?"

"Well, Barkley was involved in the history out there more than anyone knows."

"How?"

"Well, first of all, it was his grandfather, Zachary McDowell, a bank robber who came to town, killed Jeremiah Crane, the Tanglewood Lodge owner, and then set fire to the rest of the town."

"Okay. I knew the town burned."

"And then McDowell was killed by the Hotel owner's brother, Clancy Crane, and the rest of the Crane family came here to Wellington. A couple weeks later, McDowell's son, Zach Junior, showed up in Silver Spring looking for his father – didn't know he was dead. About the same time, a gang of looters went out there and got caught in the crossfire of a gunfight between Zach Junior and Clancy Crane. Killed eight of them, but the two who escaped came back and told the town it was the ghosts of Crane and McDowell who killed the others. And of course, everyone believed them. And I guess that's where *Mack* got his start."

Joe seemed interested in the story, but maybe just a little skeptical. "Just where did you get all this information?"

"Books at the Public Library and Historical Society, old newspapers, and a couple of people who lived there at the time. They were just kids then, but they remembered enough, and we pieced everything together."

"You mean you talked to real people who lived there?"

"Yes. Ted Sanford and Clair Higgins."

"Clair Higgins! She owns the house where you live."

"Right. And she's also Jeremiah Crane's daughter. I read her mother's journal and a stack of old newspapers from Silver Spring her mother had kept, and she told me right where to find her father's grave."

"And did you find it?"

"Yup. Right where she said it was."

"And who's Ted Sanford?"

"His family lived in Silver Spring right to the last day – the day of the fires. But his brother, Albert, became more of the legend many years after that, in 1937. And that's where Barkley comes in."

"I was wondering when you were getting to that."

"Albert went out there, thinking he was going to find treasure."

Joe seemed to recall this part of the story. "Was he the guy who disappeared?"

"Yes, he was."

"And I suppose you're going to tell me what happened to him."

"As a matter of fact... it was Buck who actually heard all this first hand... at the library. Seems that Barkley was out there at Silver Spring hunting for the money his grandfather and uncle robbed from a bank in 1899. It's hidden out there somewhere, but no one ever knew that until Buck overheard Barkley tell his girlfriend about it."

"Wait a minute. If no one knew, why were there people going out there to hunt for it?"

"The treasure everyone *else* hunted was a mythical fortune thought to have been left behind by Jeremiah Crane, but Mrs. Higgins assured me that her father didn't leave anything there."

"And how do you know the bank robbery story is true?"

"It probably is... Buck found a book at the library that told about a bank robbery in Sioux Falls just before Silver Spring burned. Zach Junior was arrested and convicted, but the money was never recovered."

"What makes you think it's the same one?"

"Because Zach Junior told Barkley's father, and Barkley went looking for it. He told Miriam at the library the whole story, and Buck overheard it."

"So what happened to Albert Sanford?"

"When Albert went treasure hunting, Barkley just happened to be there at the same time searching for the bank loot. Evidently, Albert caught Barkley by surprise. Barkley whacked him with a shovel and killed him. But he buried the body and never told anyone about it."

"Cory, you're not just making all this up, are you?"

"No. Buck will tell you... well, when he wakes up. And Miriam. Ask the Librarian."

"We will. I'm sure we will... and you said you have all this written down?"

"Yes... well... Mr. Barkley has it. But my boss, Victor Gladstone has a copy."

"Gladstone! You work for Gladstone?"

"Yes... since last fall."

"I'd like to read your story."

"I'm sure Victor will give it to you."

Joe sipped his coffee, rubbed his chin. Silent, he stared off into the distance.

THIRTY

After a day of rest, Clancy awoke at sunrise to a rattling noise that sounded as if someone was at the front door. He had bolted the door from the inside, so he was certain whoever was down there would not get in. He arose and ran down the upstairs hallway to the single window looking down on the street. A horse was tied to the hitching rail, but he couldn't see who was on the verandah at the door. He slid the bottom sash upward, and called out, "The Hotel is closed."

Hearing the voice from the upper window, the man backed away from the door and out beside his horse where he might see who was speaking. Startled by the man's appearance, Clancy jerked back from the window. He studied the bushy, black mustache and the cold, dark eyes set deeply into the ruddy, stern face, as if staring into a reflection of a man rose from the dead.

"I am to meet my father here," the man said.

"Who is your father?" Clancy's voice trembled.

"Zachary McDowell... I am Zachary Junior."

"He's not here. No one's here."

"He said he would meet me here... I'll wait."

Clancy had never felt so threatened. He quietly made his way back to his room, grabbed the rifle and returned to the open window. Keeping back from the window out of the man's view, he cocked the lever action, aiming toward the intruder with the tip of the gun barrel just protruding past the windowsill. "Your father isn't here... now go away."

Zachary Jr. heard the click and saw the weapon. Instinct drew the sidearm from his hip with jackrabbit speed and almost instantly released a volley of shots toward the window. Clancy returned the fire with two rounds. He didn't aim for Zachary; he didn't want to kill him – he just wanted to scare him away.

Dancing with nervous fright, Zachary's horse broke loose from the hitching rail and trotted off, Zachary running after him. He took cover behind a pile of burnt rubble and foundation rocks. Again he let fly several more slugs toward the window, and Clancy answered with two more. He wanted Zachary to know he was still able to defend his stand.

All remained quiet for several hours. Every few minutes Clancy peeked through the window. He knew Zachary was still there; his horse once again was secured behind the ruins, and periodically Clancy saw his black hat bobbing. About three o'clock in the afternoon, Zachary scrambled away on foot toward the railroad tracks. It looked as if he were carrying some sort of bundle. From Clancy's vantage point at the window facing Main Street, Zachary soon disappeared from his line of sight. Clancy went to other windows, but he could see nothing.

Half an hour slowly ticked by. Clancy continued going from window to window trying to determine where Zachary had gone. Then, suddenly he knew. Zach had circled around and was coming in the rear entrance. He had not remembered to secure that door. Crunching and snapping glass under heavy footsteps resounded from the lower floor as Zach Jr. made his way around the saloon, and at one point, Clancy thought he must have stumbled into the piano as it made a loud bang and sounded as if twenty keys had all been struck at once.

Clancy sat as silent as moonlight holding his breath, listening, hoping that McDowell would just leave. Then he heard the footsteps on the back stairway. His heart raced. Surely, McDowell would kill him if he had the chance. Clancy slipped off his boots and quickly tiptoed down the hallway to the room where his gear was stashed. With rifle ready, he hid behind the door. The last thing he wanted was more bloodshed, and especially his own.

He could hear the thuds of Zach's boot heels striking the upstairs hallway, coming closer, pausing at each door. Clancy held his breath again as the footsteps stopped at his door. If Zach entered this room, it would mean a face-to-face battle to the death for one of them. Clancy prayed it would not come to that.

The footsteps continued slowly down the hall and then down the stairs and finally ended with the door slamming shut. Clancy sighed with relief. He tiptoed back to the Main Street window just in time to see Zachary returning to his horse.

Then at four o'clock, as if Zachary's temporary absence had been for the purpose of sending a signal, Clancy counted ten men in a group sauntering up Main Street toward the Hotel. Some of the men carried shovels over their shoulders, but they certainly didn't appear to be miners. Some of them carried rifles, but they didn't appear as gunfighters either.

"More looters," Clancy thought as he watched the men coming closer. He didn't recognize any of the men, unsuspecting of the possible danger they were walking into. Out in the open with no place to hide the first shot rang out. One of the ten men crumpled to the ground. Not knowing from where the sniper had fired the shot, the men frantically looked in all directions. More shots, and more of the men fell. Clancy, terrified with the sight, leveled his Winchester toward Zachary McDowell and fired off three shots hoping to stop the massacre, but McDowell kept shooting. Then the men still standing began shooting their weapons, trying desperately to make a retreat.

The battle lasted less than a minute, but when the shooting stopped, eight of the men lay dead in the street. Two had managed to successfully get away unharmed.

A half hour passed. Clancy sat huddled under the open second story window. He had an idea to rid himself of Zachary McDowell.

"McDOWELL!" he yelled out.

There was no answer.

"McDOWELL!" he yelled again.

Still, there was no answer. He peered out the window. McDowell's horse was still there. In a loud voice he continued to speak to the desperado.

"The two men that escaped will be back soon with the Sheriff. I won't shoot if you want to ride away now."

McDowell answered this time. "I will wait here for my father."

"But your father is dead. He died in the fire."

"How do you know he's dead?"

"I was here. I saw the timbers fall on him. The Sheriff took the body to Wellington the next day."

Silence once again befell the demolished town. Clancy hoped his warning and promise not to shoot would entice McDowell to leave. A few minutes later, he heard the hoof beats as Zachary McDowell Jr. galloped his horse down the West Hill Road.

The Sheriff *would* be there soon. Certainly, the two looters who managed to escape would carry the story of what happened back to Wellington. Clancy didn't think he'd been seen by any of them, so if he wasn't present when the Sheriff arrived to investigate the incident, chances were he'd never have to divulge the fact he encouraged the killer to ride away. He realized now that there really was nothing left here to defend. There was no reason to stay at Tanglewood. Life in Silver Spring was over.

He gave a loud whistle. Shiner came trotting down the trail behind the Lodge. With everything he owned in the pack and the saddlebags slung over Shiner's back, together they walked slowly up the trail and down into the alfalfa and wheat fields in the valley. Clancy never looked back.

The sun faded into a fiery haze on the western horizon. Shiner nibbled at the golden heads of wheat. Clancy stretched out on the soft grassy bank of the North Branch Creek patiently waiting for the potato to bake beside a small campfire. He had no desire to return to the mine, nor did he possess a desire to return to Silver Spring. Now he understood what the miners must have felt as they left their homes behind. Now he understood uncertainty.

THIRTY-ONE

"Why don't you go home and get some rest?" the nurse said to Cory. Fully aware that the whole day had passed, and now when the evening shade was beginning to darken the windows, all he could recall from the entire day was his conversation that morning with Joe Block, and the few times he had been allowed to sit in Buck's room a few minutes.

"Yes, maybe I...but you have my name and my landlady's phone number –"

"Yes, Cory, we'll contact you if anything develops."

On his way past Buck's room, he ducked inside. He gently grasped Buck's hand. "Good night, Buck. I'll see you tomorrow," he spoke softly, and left.

Cool and refreshing, the night air soothed. It seemed to ease the tension a little. With windows rolled down, Cory pointed the Bronco toward the small lake that interrupted the city's sprawl. Slowly he drove along the winding road through the park on the lake's banks. A few Sunday picnickers still lingered here and there, watching the full moon rising up over the distant hills. Just beyond the end of the lake, the road met Roosevelt Street leading through downtown and connecting with the Levee Parkway, the street paralleling the river and Wellington's waterfront. Cory drove by the old freight houses and railroad depot, continuing on out of town on the narrow blacktop road flanking the river. Where the road turned abruptly onto a steel and concrete bridge spanning the river, he steered the Bronco into a graveled parking area where canoes and small boats could easily be launched. He shut off the motor, strolled to the river edge and sat on a large sandstone boulder. Gazing toward the bridge and the roadway making its sharp curve around the boat landing, Cory recalled the story of the Wilson Stagecoach hold-up he had read in *The Striker*. Perhaps this was the very location of that occurrence, and where Wesley Dawson had met his unfortunate fate nearly seventy years ago. He wondered if anyone else in all of Wellington realized the significance of this somewhat historic spot. Chances were they didn't.

For more than an hour he sat in the stillness surrounding him. An occasional breeze whisked at his face. Moonlight reflected on the glassy river journeying silently by. Cory thought about all that had happened, and he worried about how it would affect his so-far-successful year at Wellington College. He thought about his family. He thought about his job at the newspaper office. He thought about Mrs. Higgins and Ted Sanford. He thought about Buck Paxton.

The drone of a lawn mower in the yard next door jarred Cory from his sleep. He lay there a few minutes just staring at the bedroom ceiling. He desperately wanted to believe that the last couple of days had just been a bad dream, but reality dictated otherwise. Buck was not there to make breakfast.

Cory quickly showered, dressed and raced down the stairs. He was just about to get into the Bronco when he heard Mrs. Higgins' voice calling to him from the back door. "Cory?"

"Good morning, Mrs. Higgins."

"Is there trouble?" she asked. "I saw the Police car out front Saturday night, and you didn't come home all day yesterday."

"Well, Buck was..." Cory paused. He thought it best not to alarm Mrs. Higgins. "Um... Buck got hurt while we were out camping. He's in the hospital and I'm going there to see him."

"Oh dear. He's such a nice young man. What happened?"

"I'll tell you all about it later, okay? I really must get going."

Cory took the elevator to the third floor. On any other Monday morning at this time, he would be eating a casual breakfast before getting ready to go to his first class – Mr. Barkley's class – at ten o'clock. But today he was walking through the doorway of a hospital room. There was enough time to look in on Buck before making his way to the class he didn't look forward to attending this day. He didn't know what to expect; the day could very well turn into disaster number two.

Not much had changed, although Cory thought Buck's color seemed to be returning to normal. He was only at Buck's side for a couple of minutes when Dr. Garvey came in.

"Good morning, Dr. Garvey," Cory said in almost a whisper.

"Good morning, Cory," the doctor replied in a normal speaking tone. "No need to whisper. It's good for Roger to hear voices around him, especially ones he knows."

"You think he can hear us talking?"

"Sure. He's doing quite well, considering. Vital signs are steadily improving, he's breathing well, his heart is strong, and I'm confident he will recover rather quickly."

"So he's going to be okay?"

Dr. Garvey pulled the sheet away from Buck's torso, took a blunt scissors from his pocket and began cutting away the bandage to inspect the wound.

"Well, his shoulder will be a little sore for a while... I wouldn't recommend mountain climbing for a month or two."

Cory let out a little laugh. It felt good to laugh.

The doctor turned to the nurse who entered the room. "Lois, help me turn him on his side. I want to get a look at the entrance wound."

They eased Buck to his side and the doctor made his examination, after which he seemed pleased with the results. They redressed the wound while Cory sat in a chair in the far corner of the room.

"There's no bleeding," Garvey said to the nurse, "and there isn't any sign of infection... but continue the O-two and antibiotics, and monitor BP every half hour." Then he turned to Cory. "You can stay with him. Talk to him. It might help bring him out of the coma."

As the doctor and his nurse left the room, Cory slid the chair close to the bedside. He stared into the face that normally wore a perpetual smile but now was expressionless. "Buck? You're not going to believe..."

He'd been carrying on the one-sided conversation nearly twenty minutes. The same nurse came into the room. "I'm here to check vitals...and Sergeant Block is out in the corridor. He wants to see you, Cory." Lois began applying the blood pressure cuff to Buck's arm.

Blue uniformed Joe Block greeted Cory with a smile. "How are you today?" he asked.

"I'm fine, thank you."

"And how's Buck?"

"Doc says he's doin' okay...he's got his color back, but he's still not awake."

"Oh. I was hoping he could tell us where his parents were planning to be on their vacation."

"Still haven't found them?"

"No. *TWA* told us they arrived in London last Wednesday, but we don't know where they went from there, and their return flight isn't for three weeks. London police are checking all the hotels."

"What about any other relatives?"

"Nothing, so far, but we're still checking."

"Well, at least I'm here," Cory concluded.

Joe raised his forearm to look at his watch. "I have to be going now, but I'll stop back later...when I get off this afternoon. And by the way, I picked up your manuscript from Victor this morning. I'll read it tonight."

Cory was five minutes late for class. Mr. Barkley turned toward the door as Cory tiptoed in.

"Glad to see you could work us into your busy schedule, Mr. Brockway," Barkley said.

Cory could feel the blade of contempt slicing through the room. A few snickers erupted from classmates.

"Our class will be shortened today," Barkley continued. "I was involved in an auto accident over the weekend and I'm not quite up to par today."

It was then that Cory took notice of Barkley's appearance. Besides his usual bad taste in clothes, Mr. Barkley wore an unsightly bruise on his right cheekbone and temple, his face pale, his actions shaky and slow, and his voice weaker than usual.

Without going into the normal lecture period that everyone in the class expected, Barkley advanced directly to announcing the assignment for the week. "Read Chapter Thirty-seven in the text; then use those techniques to write a five-hundred-word essay on a topic of your choice. I'll see you on Wednesday. Class is dismissed."

Cory had a hard time concentrating even on such a simple instruction. Plagued by the thought of Barkley's appearance, and more so by the shallow explanation for his condition, Cory's suspicions of Barkley's involvement at Silver Spring on Saturday ran deep. Barkley had been the triggerman. The bruise on his head was from the fall off the railroad tracks. Barkley's pristine '64 Rambler Ambassador was in the parking lot with no damage whatsoever. Cory convinced himself that Barkley was guilty.

How could this be? How could a man with the stature of Mr. Barkley allow his dignity to wallow in the depths of violent crime? Cory tried sorting out the details, but it just didn't make sense that Barkley would take such a risk. The story contained nothing about his involvement in the 1937 episode; Cory had left that out completely – at least in the copy Barkley received. The version he had given to Victor Gladstone, on the other hand, was complete with the solution to Albert Sanford's disappearance, but no one else other than Victor had read that one.

Ever since the beginning of the year when he had stepped off with the wrong foot on the very first assignment and Barkley accused him of writing for *Twilight Zone*, Cory made every attempt to stay as straight as a newly-driven fence post. Until now he thought he had succeeded. But now his efforts seemed worthless; not only was his final grade in Barkley's class jeopardized, his life was in danger as well. He couldn't return to class on Wednesday, and maybe never. Fear of a poor grade point average had suddenly manifested into a death threat. He had to talk to Sergeant Block. Joe would know what to do.

By Wednesday afternoon, worried that his absence from work for a couple of days might have placed his job in jeopardy, Cory stepped hesitantly into Victor's office. He hoped Victor would understand.

Victor let out a sigh of relief. "I've been worried about you." He didn't smile, creating more uneasiness in Cory.

"I'm sorry I haven't been at work," Cory said.

Victor leaned back in his chair. "Joe stopped by this morning. He's been keeping me informed."

"Then you know what happened."

"Cory, I'm a newspaper editor. Of course I know what happened. So does the whole town. It's been front page since Sunday."

"Guess I haven't seen the paper lately."

Victor reached to a table behind his desk, retrieved copies of the most recent editions and handed them across the desk to Cory. "The Sheriff's Department, the City Police Department and the hospital have provided all the information. All we could say about your involvement was what they gave us, and that you were unavailable for comment."

"So, do I still have a job here?"

"Of course you do. I understand the situation. Take some time to clear your head. But I do want your side of the story... it's big news, and Wellington is waiting to hear it."

"Did you read my manuscript?"

"Yes, Cory, I did. And quite frankly, I didn't relate it to Silver Spring until Joe told me about it Monday morning."

Cory studied his feet. Afraid to look Victor in the eye, he hesitated and spoke. "So... did you like it?"

"I did, yes."

"Do you think it's gonna get me in trouble?"

"Cory, from what I gather, the Sheriff's Department doesn't want to pursue this – or any other issue that has anything to do with Silver Spring. They're calling it an accident and kind of sweeping it under a rug."

Cory was just about to excuse himself to leave. Victor posed a question. "When can we have an interview?"

Cory contemplated a long moment. "Tomorrow. How about tomorrow?"

"That would be fine," Victor agreed. "And one more thing... how accurate is the story you wrote?"

"Quite... except for the names."

"Can you document the facts?"

"Most of them."

"Good. We'll talk more about that another time."

Mixed emotions swirled in Cory's head as he walked back to the Bronco. He was glad that he probably would face no further confrontations with the Sheriff's Department, but for Buck's sake, it aggravated him to think the incident was considered an accident and that a homicide was being ignored.

Cory stepped into the elevator and pushed the button for the third floor. Now, more than ever, he wanted his best friend back. A feeling of guilt and self-blame weighed heavily on his conscience. He needed to tell Buck how sorry he was to have caused all this trouble and suffering, and that he might ask Buck's forgiveness.

He slid the chair close to Buck's bed and sat down. "I don't know if you can hear me, but I just want you to know that I'm sorry," he said softly. "Can you ever forgive me?"

Cory leaned back in the chair and sat quietly with his eyes shut, silently praying for Buck's return.

Out of the stillness, a weak, raspy voice said, "Cory? It wasn't your fault."

It seemed only seconds later when three nurses and Dr. Garvey surrounded Buck's bed. Lois suggested Cory should make himself comfortable in the visitors' lounge while they performed some rather extensive examinations. There was nothing more that Cory wanted at that moment than to be in the room with Buck now that he was conscious again, but it seemed the medical staff had first dibs.

THIRTY-TWO

A day's ride cross-country found Clancy roaming the streets of Red Hawk. He'd never been there, and though it seemed not much different from Silver Spring other than its larger size, Red Hawk lacked the warm friendliness of his old hometown.

He located a livery barn for Shiner, and then set out to find the assayer's office. His ore was valued at $37.50. He exchanged the ore for currency and checked into the City Hotel after a mouthwatering roast beef dinner. That was the first night he had slept in a bed for nearly three weeks, and he didn't hesitate to spend the extra twenty-five cents for a warm bath.

The days passed. In a weekly edition of the *Red Hawk News* he read the front page lead story telling of the eight men mysteriously gunned down at Silver Spring. The reporter wouldn't commit to any serious beliefs, but the two men, Elmer Dickens and Casey Fitzsimmons who witnessed the shooting swore they had seen the ghosts of Jeremiah Crane and Zachary McDowell, and it was the ghosts who had killed the other eight men in a fierce gun battle. The article went on to say that both Dickens and Fitzsimmons were employed at the Clearwater Brewery when still in Silver Spring, and that they were close friends of Crane. They had taken a stage to Silver Spring for an afternoon visit with Crane the day he was gunned down in his own tavern.

Clancy suspected similar stories appeared in the *Wellington Weekly Star.* It was time to travel the twenty-five miles, find Millie and set the story straight.

THIRTY-THREE

Sergeant Block sat down on the couch next to Cory. Cory's eyes watered and his body trembled.

"What's wrong?" Joe asked.

"Buck's awake."

"That's good news, isn't it?"

"I guess... but I'm scared."

"Why?"

"Barkley."

"Care to explain?"

Cory gazed into Joe's eyes. Holding back the secret he'd been carrying since Monday was beginning to challenge his sanity. Joe Block could be trusted. "It was Barkley who shot Buck," Cory said in almost a whisper.

Deep wrinkles appeared on Joe's forehead. His eyes squinted with a puzzled frown. "What? How do you figure that?"

Cory had nothing to lose now. His college career was in the dump; exposing Barkley in more criminal activity couldn't make things any worse than they already were. "He's got a lump on his head the size of a baseball...from the nosedive he took off the railroad tracks out at Silver Spring. Said he was in a car accident, but I saw his car in the parking lot at school. Not a scratch on it anywhere."

The frown didn't leave Joe's face. "Have you told the Sheriff about this?"

"No. I've been afraid to tell anyone. I wanted to talk to you first."

Joe scanned the floor and then peered down the long corridor toward Buck's room. "I read your book. If Barkley recognized his part in it, he certainly would've had the motive."

"But I left that out of the copy I turned in to him. He never saw it."

"Then how—"

"I don't know."

Joe stood up slowly. "Stay right here. I'm going to talk to the Sheriff. And don't worry. We'll keep this under wraps until there's some solid proof."

To Cory, the knot on Barkley's head was proof enough.

Ten minutes passed while Cory stared across the room through the glass door at Sergeant Block with the pay phone receiver pressed to his ear. Joe talked a little, listened and nodded repeatedly, talked some more and nodded some more, occasionally glancing toward Cory with a blank expression. Cory couldn't hear the conversation and he'd never been any good at reading lips.

Joe finally hung up the phone and strolled back to where Cory sat. Looking around to make sure no one else was listening, he sat down beside Cory again and spoke softly. "Barkley *was* in a car accident… Saturday about noon. They were in Miriam's car." Joe paused and looked down at his shoes. "She was killed instantly."

Cory's chest tightened. Suddenly his hatred for Mr. Barkley evaporated. "Why haven't we heard about it?"

"Hasn't been in the local papers yet because they're still trying to notify next-of-kin."

A feeling of guilt rushed through Cory's head. "Guess I was wrong about Mr. Barkley, huh?"

"Yeah, but Bancroft told me something else, and you're not to breathe a word of this to anyone – not even Buck. He wanted you to know."

"What?"

Joe looked around some more, double-checking their privacy. "Sheriff's Department has a suspect in the shooting. They've got some pretty strong evidence."

"Who? What kind of evidence?" Momentarily Cory sidetracked the bad news about Miriam.

"Can't tell you that. It has to be kept quiet 'till they make an arrest."

"But Victor told me they were calling it an accident and that they weren't going to pursue it any further."

"Like I said, Cory, they have to keep it quiet. You know how newspapers are."

Cory walked the two flights of stairs with Joe to the front hospital entrance.

"I'm being interviewed by a *Daily Record* reporter tomorrow… about the shooting. What should I say?"

"Give 'em the facts. Don't speculate. And *don't* say *anything* about a possible suspect."

"What if I screw up?"

"You won't. You'll do just fine."

They walked out into the parking lot.

"Where's your squad car?" Cory asked. He didn't see it anywhere.

"I was off duty an hour ago. I've got my own car here." He pointed to a gray Buick.

So much had been on his mind Cory didn't realize the late hour. It was past five o'clock.

Cory tilted his head listening to the ambulance siren approaching. He could see the flashing red lights to the west across the small lake. Joe was trying to ignore it. He was off duty. "I'll see you tomorrow," Joe said, got behind the wheel of his Buick and drove away.

Cory darted up the stairs to the third floor. "Is it okay if I go in to see Buck now?" he asked the nurse.

"Sure, Cory." By now, all the nurses knew him by name. "But he probably won't be much for conversation. He was complaining about a lot of pain so we gave him a sedative. He's pretty groggy."

Buck could barely open his eyes. All the tubes had been removed from his nose and mouth, but the intravenous feeding tube was still attached to his arm. He tried to speak when he finally recognized Cory standing at the bedside. A little smile formed, but the words wouldn't come. Eventually he gave in to the painkiller, closed his eyes and began to snore.

Nine o'clock. Visiting hours were over. Cory drove past the lake paying little attention to the couples strolling along its shore. He turned down Roosevelt Street toward the riverfront rather than heading for home. Sleep would not come easy tonight and he wasn't hungry. At this time of night no one would be at the boat landing by the bridge. Cory had a lot on his mind. That quiet spot by the river offered the perfect solitude to think things out.

He sat on the big rock, mesmerized by the lazy water drifting along the bank. Tonight his thoughts weren't about Wesley Dawson or stagecoach hold-ups. Tonight he worried about Buck's welfare. He thought about tomorrow's interview – what he would and would not tell. He imagined his Mom and Dad relaxing on a Gulf coast beach, and wished he were there with them. He agonized over Miriam's death and Mr. Barkley's injuries, and somehow, now he didn't want the 1937 incident to become known. But it was already too late to wish he had listened to Buck's advice not to write that part of the story.

He wondered whom the Sheriff's suspect might be and what evidence was found to lead to a forthcoming arrest. An arrest would lead to a trial and...

A pair of headlights flickered through the bridge railing. The car rounded the curve and was just past the driveway into the gravel lot when Cory heard the brakes come on hard. It stopped, backed to the driveway and turned, aiming straight toward Cory. The lights went out as the now familiar Dodge Coronet rumbled to a stop only ten feet away. The driver got out.

"Hi, Jimmy," Cory blurted before the car door slammed shut.

"Hi, Cory. I kinda figured that was your Bronco. What are you doin' out here?"

"Just sitting and thinking."

"What about... if it's any of my business?"

"Oh, all the crazy stuff that's goin' on."

"How's Buck?"

"He finally woke up today."

"Yeah, I know. I went up to see him this afternoon; they wouldn't let me in. How is he?"

"Lot of pain, I guess. He was so full of drugs tonight I couldn't talk to him either."

"Is he gonna be okay?"

"The Doc says he will."

"That's good news."

They sat on the rock for a few minutes without speaking at all. Reluctant to bring up the subject, Cory couldn't hold it back. "Guess I should've listened to you n' Slinky," he said softly.

"What? About Silver Spring Hills?"

"Yeah. Wish I could turn the clock back to last August and start all over."

"I hate to say it, but I told you so."

"I know. You don't have to say it again."

"Actually, I never really believed all that stuff, but now I'm not so sure."

Cory thought this to be a good time to change the subject. "Did you hear about the librarian, Miriam?"

"The car accident? Yeah, her husband and my Dad were good friends. We heard a couple of days ago."

"Her husband?"

"He died many years ago."

"Oh."

Several more minutes went by in silence. Both were at a loss for subject matter.

"Where's Slinky?" Cory asked.

"Haven't seen him since last Friday night when we went canoeing. I called his place, but his Dad said Slinky fell off a hay wagon Saturday afternoon... he's had a king-sized headache all week."

"That's too bad."

Jimmy patted Cory's shoulder. "I have to open the gas station in the morning. I'd better get goin' for home."

"Okay. The Bronco needs gas. Maybe I'll see you there."

The Dodge roared to life; again, Cory was alone with his thoughts.

He began recalling all the good times he and Buck had shared, and Buck's quirky little remarks. "How do you want your eggs," Buck had asked. "Over easy," Cory had said. "Okay. Scrambled it is," Buck had replied.

Scrambled eggs. It occurred to him that now he was hungry. There were eggs in the fridge at home.

THIRTY-FOUR

In a town nearly three times the size of Silver Spring, Clancy felt intimidation closing in on all sides. He had been in Wellington many times before; there should be no reason to feel uneasy here. Clancy was a refugee of the county's worst calamity just like dozens of other Silver Spring residents who were probably settled into new homes by now and well on their way in rebuilding their lives. Certainly he would be received as a disaster victim just like the others. But it still wasn't Silver Spring. It still wasn't home.

Millie and Clair were absorbed somewhere in this city. Finding them meant finding security to some degree, but the task might not be an easy one - not in a town the size of Wellington. Seemingly endless rows of houses lined the streets that stretched nearly a mile along the riverbank; the main business district sprawled over ten square blocks; grain storage buildings, freight houses, the railroad depot and Wilson Stage Line terminal stood like a string of dominos flanking the river. And people. People milling about everywhere. Clancy didn't know where to begin.

Roosevelt Street, the predominate avenue through the center of town seemed a likely place to start making inquiries. Clancy found the shade of a large cottonwood where Shiner could rest and began walking the streets. Occasionally he would duck into a store that looked like one where Millie might shop to ask the storekeeper if he knew of Millie's whereabouts. No one was familiar with the Widow Crane from Silver Spring.

People on the street proved less helpful. Most of Wellington appeared to shun the likes of the boy claiming to be Jeremiah Crane's brother. To them he was just another stranger, and the citizens of Wellington weren't too fond of strangers.

Late that afternoon Clancy had nearly given up for the day. Stores and shops were closing; the streets cleared as if a bad storm were about to strike. He had to find a livery stable for Shiner and a hotel room for himself. The search for Millie would resume the next morning.

Logically located near the Stagecoach terminal, Clancy found adequate accommodations for Shiner at a livery barn, although the proprietor had the personality of a rattlesnake. "Ain't no hotel rooms left. They're all full up."

"Well, how about here? Could I sleep on a pile of hay next to Shiner?" Clancy asked.

"Nope. Don't allow that."

"Never mind, then. I'll just ride out into the hills and camp."

"Suit yourself," the stableman grunted.

Clancy mounted Shiner and rode away.

His first day in Wellington had been as difficult as trying to drive a fence post into solid rock. Clancy awoke the next morning thinking "No wonder Daniel always liked returning to Silver Spring." He rolled up his blanket and rode Shiner back into town hopeful that breakfast would present less of a challenge.

The waitress at a little café on the edge of town reassured Clancy he had not stumbled into enemy territory. Freckle-faced, red-haired and quite petite, Beverly Chandler flitted from table to table like a butterfly from flower to flower, her tiny voice friendly and warm. Clancy knew she couldn't be a Wellington native.

"We lived in Silver Spring until the mines shut down," she said. "But I didn't want to make that long trip to California with the rest of the family, so I stayed here."

"I'm from Silver Spring, too," Clancy said, thrilled to meet someone from the old home-town. "My brother owned Tanglewood Lodge."

"Oh... I read about his death. What a terrible thing."

"I'm trying to find his wife. She came here just before the fire."

"I don't know her, but I know someone who might."

"Who?"

"There's a reporter for the Weekly Star... he used to be a reporter for the Striker. He might know where she is."

"You mean Tom Hargrove?"

"Yes, I think that's his name."

"Where's the newspaper office?"

"Johnson Street... right across from the Opera House."

"Thank you, Beverly. I'll come back to see you again." Excitement boiled in Clancy's veins. It would be good to see another old friend, and he *really* wanted to find Millie and Clair.

THIRTY-FIVE

Cory fidgeted with the buttons on his shirt and shifted his weight from side to side in the chair. He hadn't expected Victor and Sheriff Bancroft to be present at the interview – just Ray Frazier, *Daily Record's* foremost reporter.

"Don't be nervous, Cory," Victor said. "We're all friends here."

Cory sipped his coffee and set the cup back on the conference room table, trying desperately not to let his tension show. He knew Victor had overstated; countless rumors of Frazier's off-the-record dislike for Bancroft hovered around the newspaper office, but Ray's professional demeanor wouldn't allow that to surface now.

On the table Cory saw both copies of his manuscript. The one he had turned in to Barkley lay in front of Sheriff Bancroft, Victor's folded hands resting on the other.

Victor launched the probe. "Ray thinks we should use your book as the basic lead-in, and you and Buck make for a good human interest story."

Now Cory realized that Sheriff Bancroft was onto the investigation that was formulating thirty years too late and the facts that had been so cleverly concealed since 1937. He let out a sigh. Telling the whole story with the real names would certainly unload some anxiety, although it would destroy his chances of success in Barkley's class. But right now, his conscience told him to do the right thing.

For two and a half hours Cory answered Ray Frazier's questions about Cory's very first visit to Tanglewood, the camping trip last fall, the research, and finally the horrifying experience of a week ago. Frequently Victor tossed in comments and queries, but Bancroft remained silent, just listening.

Cory withheld very little. He even described the eerie sounds of piano music mysteriously emitting from the old hotel, but he chose not to mention the sight of the steam locomotive; that seemed a bit too much. Ray already envisioned a riveting account of Buck's bloodshed as Cory spilled out the details.

"I think we'll want a picture of you and Buck... at the hospital," Ray said.

When the interview seemed to be drawing to a close, Cory, puzzled, wondered why not one question arose regarding the 1937 killing. Sheriff Bancroft had not spoken the entire time, and surely he was inclined to solve a crime, even if it happened thirty years ago.

"Don't you want to know about Albert Sanford's disappearance in 1937?" Cory asked.

"No," Victor replied. An expression of surprise sprang to his face. "That's all speculation, and we can't afford a lawsuit over accusations we can't prove."

"But we know what happened to him. Shouldn't it at least be investigated?" Cory's frustration peeked through.

Bancroft finally joined the conversation. "It's all hearsay. The D.A. can't, and won't prosecute on hearsay evidence."

"But Buck heard Barkley tell Miriam—"

"Miriam is dead. It's real difficult to get a dead person to testify in court."

"But Buck—"

"Hearsay! It's nothing but hearsay."

"But what if Barkley decides to—"

"Don't worry about Barkley," the Sheriff said. He and Victor exchanged concerned stares. The interview was over.

Friday morning's issue of the *Wellington Daily Record* already had the city buzzing by the time Cory dropped his quarter in the vending machine by the front door of the Country Cook. He had plenty of time for breakfast and a visit with Buck before class.

"Scrambled eggs, bacon and toast," he said to the waitress. He was too busy scanning the front page to look up at her.

"Coffee?" the waitress asked.

Cory just nodded, his eyes soaking up the picture of him and Buck taken the day before in Buck's hospital room. Buck had barely been aware of the photographer's presence and Cory knew his own relaxed pose was artificial.

"Hey, I know you. You're the guy who was looking for Ted at the museum."

Cory looked up. Terri, now a waitress at the Country Cook apparently had a good memory for faces.

"Oh! Hi, Terri. I didn't see it was you."

"I saw your picture in the paper this morning. That must have been a terrible experience."

Cory just nodded. He really didn't want to talk about it.

"I'll get your order in right away," Terri said, and walked away.

The article's bulk continued for almost a half-page on page six. Expertly written in the unique Ray Frazier style, it told of Cory's harrowing escape from the unknown gunman, and his heroic efforts in the successful battle for survival, rescuing Buck from the gruesome grasp of death. It told of their curious interest in the "Land of Legend," their ghostly discoveries, a howling coyote and a ravaging raccoon. It contained some non-revealing history of Silver Spring, and not a word about Percy Barkley or Albert Sanford. Quite apparent, Ray Frazier wasn't ready to kill the legend or dismiss Mack from his ghostly duties; there was too much mileage left in a story that had been alive here for nearly seventy years.

Cory flipped the paper back to page one just as Terri delivered breakfast. He folded the paper in half, set it aside and dug into the scrambled eggs. Something he had overlooked on the front page captured his attention. The headline read: "Wellington College Professor Dies." Cory flipped the half-folded paper over, curious to see if the faculty member was someone he knew. His lower jaw dropped with the first words he read: "Professor Percy Barkley, 56, of Wellington College died at 5:30 p.m. Wednesday in the Emergency Room at Wellington Memorial Hospital. His death was the result of head injuries sustained from an auto crash that also claimed the life of Miriam Taft, 59, Head Librarian at Wellington Public Library. Taft was pronounced dead at the scene. The accident occurred approximately 12:10 p.m. Saturday ten miles East of Red Hawk..."

Cory was stunned. Breakfast no longer appealed to him. And now there seemed little need to hurry getting to class.

More coherent now, Buck smiled when Cory entered the room. A pleasant-looking couple stood next to Buck's bed. The middle-aged woman was fussing with Buck's pillow in an attempt to make him more comfortable.

"Hi, Buddy," Buck said. He was trying to ignore the pain.

Cory fought away the tears. He was so happy to see Buck alert and sitting upright. "Hi, Buck."

"Mom, Dad... Cory Brockway, my roommate and best friend."

Mrs. Paxton came around the bed and shocked Cory with a sophisticated hug. Mr. Paxton extended a firm handshake.

"Pleased to meet you," Cory said.

"As I understand it you saved our son's life. We're most grateful," Mr. Paxton said.

Cory blushed. "When did you arrive?" He wanted to skirt around the heroics for now.

"Just a little while ago. We were lucky enough to get a flight out of Madrid a few hours after we heard the news about Roger."

"Do you have a place to stay?"

"We have a reservation at the *Holiday Inn.*"

Mrs. Paxton went back to fussing over her son; Mr. Paxton turned to gaze out the window.

Cory had dreaded this meeting. He knew it would be unavoidable, and he worried that Buck's parents would bear ill feelings toward him. Now it seemed that worry had been needless. One down and umpteen to go.

This was the first Cory had an opportunity to talk with Buck since he regained consciousness on Wednesday, and there was so much to talk about. But now that Buck's Mom and Dad had just arrived he thought he should not interfere with their time together. A steady stream of doctors and nurses shuffled in and out too, so lessened the chance to talk.

"I'll stop back later. You probably want to be with your folks right now."

"You *will* come back later, won't you?" Buck pleaded.

"I promise." Cory turned to Mr. and Mrs. Paxton. "If there's anything I can help you with..."

"Thank you, Cory, I think we'll be fine, but you're entirely welcome to join us for dinner tonight."

THIRTY-SIX

The search would soon be over. Tom Hargrove knew practically everyone in Silver Spring and by now he would know where all the last remaining residents there had settled after being forced to find new homes. Clancy had been reluctant to come to Wellington when Millie first tried to convince him; now his excitement ran high that he would soon reunite with family.

"Tom is at his desk upstairs," Clancy was told. Covered from neck to ankle with ink smudges and looking as though he was experiencing a rather difficult day, the man speaking barely glanced away from his work at the complicated printing machinery.

"Thank you, sir," Clancy said and headed for the stairway. Tom sat at his desk frantically scribbling some notes. Happy to see Clancy again, Tom laid down his pencil and greeted the boy with a smile and a handshake.

"I know you're busy, but I was hoping you could tell me where I might find Millie and Clair."

Tom frowned and shook his head. "I saw her in town one day last week, but I didn't talk to her."

"Have any idea where she might be living?"

Once again Tom shook his head. "Afraid I can't help you."

Disappointment poured from Clancy's eyes. "Guess I'll just have to keep looking... but thanks, anyway." He turned to leave.

"Go over to the lake," Tom said. "A few families from Silver Spring are camped over there. The Andersons or the Sanfords might know."

"Okay. I'll try that. Thanks, Tom."

Clancy knew right where to find the lake. He had driven Tanglewood's carriage past it once when he made a wrong turn on his way to pick up some passengers from the riverboat landing. It wasn't far.

The scene at the lake reminded Clancy of the Crane's arrival at Silver Spring several years earlier. The womenfolk busied themselves cooking over campfires among wagons and tents and hanging laundry on makeshift clotheslines suspended between small trees. Some of the men and boys dangled fish lines in the lake with cane poles, attempting to catch dinner. A few horses and mules grazed near by, and a couple of large, yellow dogs barked as Clancy trotted Shiner toward Tent City. He could hear the children laughing and playing and he smelled the wonderful aromas of sizzling bacon and fresh cornbread.

It seemed ironic that these people were here living like gypsies, yet they appeared happy and content. They weren't poor; no one from Silver Spring was poor.

Clancy spotted Henry Sanford with a fishing pole at the edge of the water. A regular customer at the Tanglewood saloon, Henry knew Clancy well.

"Doggone. If it isn't the young Crane boy." Henry said. "We wondered what happened to you."

"Howdy, Henry."

They shook hands, and Clancy explained that he had gone prospecting, but he didn't mention any knowledge of McDowell's death or that he had witnessed the massacre of the eight men. He had to act surprised when Henry told him the news. The less anyone knew, the better.

"Why are you living here in tents?" Clancy asked.

"Not everyone was lucky to get houses here."

"That's too bad."

"But Mr. Stengahl let us take some time to start building. We all have lots on the East side of town... we start building next week."

"I'm looking for Millie. Have you seen her?"

"Loretta just saw Mrs. Crane in town a few days ago. She and Clair are living with a family over on the west side... right along the river. It's the biggest house over there. Shouldn't be tough to find."

Loretta Sanford held the skirt of her long dress just high enough so she wouldn't trip as she ran toward Clancy, readying himself to jump onto Shiner's back. "Clancy! Wait!"

Clancy stopped and turned toward her.

"Won't you stay and join us for noon dinner? There's plenty," she said.

"Thank you, Ma'am. That's mighty kind. But I want to go find Millie right now."

"She lives with the Jolstens... down by the river."

"Yes, Henry told me."

"Well, good luck, and maybe you can come back for supper."

"Thank you, maybe I will."

Clancy could see the roof of a very large house towering above the trees near the river. He would have continued the ride directly to it, but as he passed by a riverboat tied up at the levee his attention was drawn to a neatly lettered sign propped against the gangplank. It read: "DECK HANDS WANTED – APPLY HERE." A well-dressed man – the Captain, Clancy thought – sat at a small table on the bow. Clancy tied Shiner's reins to a hitching post and took his place behind the only other applicant waiting, a disgustingly dirty, obese young man of about twenty. Clancy quickly repositioned himself away from the fat character. The odor, somewhat like a pigsty, was more than he could take. The round, chubby face with black, greasy hair drooping on either side turned toward Clancy and sneered.

He hadn't thought about this until sixty seconds ago, but that was long enough to realize he did need a job, and the few times he had seen the big boats he was always intrigued by them. But perhaps, this time, he would decline if "Stinky" were hired too.

A very young boy pleaded with the Captain. "Please hire me… I don't want to go to school again."

"How old are you, son?" the Captain asked.

"Thirteen," the boy replied.

"Too young. Now run along." The Captain motioned for the next one in line.

"Ever work on a riverboat?" Even the Captain backed away from the malodorous mass standing in front of the table.

"I know all there is to know about riverboats… my Pappy rode on one once… he told me all about 'em."

"I see," the Captain said.

"So when do I start?"

"I'll let you know." The Captain looked in Clancy's direction. "Next?" he called out and signaled for Clancy to come aboard.

Clancy waited for the rotund, smelly body to clear the end of the gangplank before he made his approach.

The Captain looked him up and down as Clancy stood respectfully at attention in front of the table. "What's your name, son?"

"Clancy Crane, sir."

"How old are you, son?"

"Seventeen, sir."

"Ever work on a riverboat?"

"No, sir. But I'm willing to learn, sir."

The Captain glanced toward the levee only to see no one else waiting in line.

"We head south for the winter, so you won't be home for a long time."

"That's okay, sir. This isn't my home anyway."

"Where's your home, son?"

"Silver Spring. But it burned down. I really don't have a home."

The Captain smiled. "I think you'll do just fine. Pay is ten dollars a week, meals and a bunk."

Clancy grinned and offered his hand. "Thank you, sir."

"Be here tomorrow morning at seven. Sign in with the Mud Clerk on the Texas Deck. He'll show you where to stow your gear."

"Thank you, again, sir. I'll be here."

Clancy strutted down the gangplank as if he had just conquered the entire Confederate Army. He didn't have a clue about what a Mud Clerk did, or where to find the Texas Deck, but he would learn those details tomorrow. Right now he hoped the foul-smelling fat kid was nowhere in sight.

Millie! He had to find Millie right away.

THIRTY-SEVEN

Cory filled the Bronco with gas, chatted with Jimmy a while and then just cruised the back streets. He knew he should probably be using this time to cram for finals next week, but his heart wasn't in studying. The whole weekend would be free for that.

He thought about stopping at the Academy for a cold beer, but somehow that didn't seem appealing either. The Lake Park already overflowed with college students getting a jump on the weekend. Several classmates recognized the Bronco, pointed and waved as Cory drove past. By now, everyone knew Cory Brockway – his picture was on the front page of The Daily Record, and he wasn't ready for celebrity status just yet.

Jammed in door handle to door handle with cars, pickup trucks and boat trailers, his favorite getaway spot at the boat landing appeared out of the question. Walking the streets presented the risk of being confronted by someone who recognized him from the newspaper article. Retreating to his apartment would be dull, so he just kept driving.

It was just past noon when Cory saw the two County Sheriff's Department squad cars heading out of town to the west. Where ever they were going they seemed to be in a hurry to get there. Seeing the Deputies speeding away reminded Cory of his last conversation with Sergeant Block. "A suspect... strong evidence..." he had said. Cory had been so sure of Barkley. But the Professor was ten miles east of Red Hawk when the shooting occurred – it couldn't have been him. And now he's dead.

"Maybe there really is a Mack," Cory thought. He was convinced of some supernatural activity at Silver Spring; he and Buck shared an esoteric knowledge of it. They were, perhaps, the only living souls to ever experience the haunted qualities of Tanglewood. Everyone else just speculated and believed in a myth. But how do you arrest a ghost? Obviously, Sheriff Bancroft was onto something more substantial.

By three o'clock Cory had driven every street in Wellington, been to Red Hawk and back, drank six cans of soda and eaten four bags of potato chips. Certainly by now he had allowed the Paxtons enough time with Buck.

With his back to the corridor leading from the elevator, Sheriff Bancroft, deep in conversation with Mr. and Mrs. Paxton, didn't see Cory sneak into Buck's room. Cory didn't think the Paxtons had noticed him either. They appeared genuinely interested in whatever Bancroft was telling them. Finally, after all this time Cory could talk with Buck.

Surprisingly, Buck was sitting in a chair, his left arm suspended in a blue sling. A cheerful grin beamed from his face when he saw Cory.

"Wow, I didn't expect to see you out of bed," Cory said, sliding another chair close to Buck's side.

"They had me walking around a while after you left this morning." Buck was enthusiastic with his progress. "But I felt kinda silly parading around with nothing on but this gown." He briefly flipped the hospital gown up exposing his totally naked body. Cory giggled.

"So... how are you feeling," Cory asked.

"A little sore, but it's not as bad as yesterday."

"Did you see today's paper yet?"

"Yeah, I saw the picture. Mom read the article to me... my vision is still a little fuzzy."

Cory contemplated a moment whether or not to mention anything about Barkley and Miriam. He didn't want to cause any more stress. But Buck seemed to be handling stress quite well. "Do you know about Mr. Barkley and Miriam?"

"What about 'em?"

"They're..." Cory paused and took a deep breath. "They're both dead," he said quietly.

Buck's smile vanished. "You're kidding, right?"

"No. I'm not kidding. It's in the paper."

"What happened?"

"Car accident... last Saturday. Miriam was killed instantly, and Barkley died Wednesday night."

"Wow. I can't believe it."

"I know. I've been feelin' pretty bad about it."

"So what'll happen with your class?"

"Don't know."

They sat in silence for a minute or so.

"Doc Garvey says I can go home in a few days," Buck said.

"That's great!" Cory smiled again. "I'll be done with finals next week. I can take care of you until you get better."

"Cory, you don't understand. Mom, Dad and I are going back to Spokane... *home*."

"Why? You'll be okay here."

"Mom insisted. Dr. Garvey said it would be okay for me to travel, and they're clearing everything with the Sheriff right now."

"I saw them talking when I came in."

"You staying here for school next year?"

"I'd planned on it. You coming back?"

"Don't know. Depends on how this turns out."

In all the months Cory had known Buck, and for as close friends as they had become, Buck had never portrayed his mother and father as Jet Setters. He had mentioned once that his father was a stockbroker, but he failed to add that Mr. Paxton *owned* the brokerage firm.

"And what does your father do?" Mr. Paxton asked Cory over a lavish steak dinner.

"Oh, he was a foreman at Archer Textiles, but he's retired. Mom and Dad live in Florida now." Cory hoped Mr. Paxton wouldn't dwell on his blue-collar heritage.

"Archer Textiles... they filed Chapter Eleven a few months ago, didn't they?"

Cory realized Mr. Paxton seemed to be well informed in the business world. "Yes, I believe they did, but Dad was out of there by then." He desperately wanted to change the subject. "Buck said he's going back to Spokane with you in a few days."

"Yes. Sheriff Bancroft told us this afternoon it would be months until the trial. Of course, we'll have to come back here for that, but we thought it would be better to have Roger at home now."

Cory's eyes enlarged. Apparently the Paxtons knew something he didn't. "Trial? The Sheriff mentioned a trial?"

"Well, yes. I thought you knew. They arrested the guy who shot Roger."

"I heard they had a suspect, but I didn't know they made an arrest. Who is it? Did he say?"

"He didn't give a name, but he said it'll all be in tomorrow's paper."

"So, when are you leaving for Spokane?"

"We have a flight booked for Tuesday."

This was all happening much too quickly. Buck would be gone in four days. Finals would be over in five. As he climbed the stairs to his apartment, Cory studied the Air Mail envelope postmarked "Sarasota, Florida" and wondered what would develop now that all the plans were so abruptly altered. He wondered who would be on trial for the shooting.

He plopped down on his lumpy couch and gazed around the lonely room. Since Buck moved in at Christmastime, his good housekeeping habits had rubbed off; the entire apartment was neat and clean, everything in its place, much like Mrs. Higgins' house. He couldn't help but chuckle at the thought of Buck's first visit when the place looked like a disaster zone. Meeting Buck's Mom and Dad unleashed the understanding of how he had acquired the tidy traits. They were very pleasant people but it was easy to see they were a bit domineering, and perhaps spending much time with Buck before they jetted back to Spokane might prove difficult.

Cory held the envelope from Florida under the lamplight at the end of the couch. Never before had a letter from his Dad arrived Air Mail. Postmarked just two days ago, his Dad must have responded immediately to the letter Cory sent on Monday telling of the excitement last weekend. He had tried to be as subtle as possible, not to cause any alarm at the Brockway home, but apparently it had; there could be no other reason for the urgency of Air Mail.

He carefully tore open the envelope and shook the contents out onto the coffee table. Instead of the usual rent check payable to Clair Higgins, the check was made out to "Cory Brockway" for $500.00 – over five times the amount of Cory's share of the rent. A pleasant surprise, but a curious one as well.

The letter explained. Dad didn't sound so alarmed – although Cory suspected he was – as he sounded lonesome for his son. They had met many new friends in Sarasota; they were enjoying their new home on Siesta Key with a view of the ocean and a beach within walking distance, a front yard lined with palm trees and magnolias. "Sold our house in Illinois and bought this one," sounded rather permanent. "$500 should be more than enough to get here when you finish your classes," sounded more like an order than an invitation, but an order that seemed pleasingly welcome at the moment. So welcome, in fact, he would start packing tomorrow. There wasn't much to stay here for now that his best friend was leaving town too.

In the darkness of his bedroom, Cory laid thinking about how his life had changed over the last several months. He recalled the consideration he had given a year ago to colleges in Florida, as well as other places, but chose Wellington simply because of the renowned reputation of Percy Barkley. That was no longer a factor, however he was thankful to have been Barkley's student, gaining valuable writing skills in the provoking manner that only Mr. Barkley could deliver.

The job at The Daily Record – priceless experience; Victor Gladstone – an excellent reference on a resume.

Wellington and Silver Spring had widened his horizons. The time here opened his eyes to historic culture, awakened his awareness of its importance and instilled in him a sense of direction.

And how could he place a value on his friendship with Buck Paxton? Never before had a relationship with anyone outside his own family run so deep. The thought of a whole continent soon to be parting them saddened Cory. Perhaps he could convince Buck to come to Florida to finish college – the Paxtons could certainly afford it.

Like a popcorn popper, Cory's head filled with thoughts so rampantly he feared he would never get to sleep at all. He needed an escape.

He imagined a white, sandy beach and palm trees swaying in the ocean breeze, a gentle, breaking surf and serenading sea gulls hovering overhead, sailboats on the horizon against the setting sun and...

Cory opened his eyes to the hum of a lawn mower, a barking dog and a screaming blue jay. Sunshine flooded his bedroom. By the time he had brushed his teeth, dressed and reached the bottom of the stairs, the blue jay had departed for another neighborhood, the dog had given up trying to intimidate the neighbor's cat and the boy next door had tired of cutting grass and was resting under a shade tree.

"Good morning, Mrs. Higgins," Cory said cheerfully to Clair, already out on this beautiful Saturday morning admiring her tulip bed, pulling a weed here and there.

"Good morning, Cory," she replied. "A gorgeous day, isn't it?"

"Yes, it certainly is." Cory was almost afraid to mention to the sweet, old woman that he would be moving out. "School is almost done, and I'll be going home soon."

"Yes, I know. I got a very nice letter from your father yesterday."

"Oh." Once again, Cory thought it seemed like he was always the last one to learn any news. "Buck is getting out of the hospital Tuesday, and –"

"Yes, I know. His folks stopped by yesterday, too."

"Oh. Then I guess you know they'll be getting his things out of the apartment."

"Yes, Monday afternoon, they said. Will you still be here then?"

"Sure. My last exam is on Wednesday, so I'll be around 'till Thursday or Friday."

"Will you be coming back in the fall? Your father didn't say."

"I don't know, Mrs. Higgins. I might go to school in Florida next year."

"Well, be sure to let me know by the first of August if you want the apartment again. I've thoroughly enjoyed having you here."

Cory knew what she really meant: she enjoyed getting her rent checks on time. "Thank you, I will. And I'll tell Buck in case he wants it."

"That would be fine." Mrs. Higgins returned to the weed pulling.

On the way to the hospital, Cory remembered that the identity of Buck's alleged assailant would be announced in this morning's edition of the Record. He nosed the Bronco into the parking lot at the Country Cook where the nearest newspaper vending machine was located by the front door. It was empty.

The next one was at the doughnut shop halfway to downtown. That one was sold out too. Every dispenser he passed was empty. Obviously everyone in Wellington knew who shot Buck except Cory.

He decided to take the back stairs up to the third floor instead of the elevator. There was a newspaper vending machine just inside that entrance.

Empty.

"Lois? You wouldn't by any chance have a copy of today's paper, would you? All the machines are sold out."

Lois reached under the counter at the nurses' station where she was busy jotting some notes on a patient's clipboard. "You're in luck, Cory. I was just about to take this down to Mrs. Hackleberry in 305." She handed the paper across the counter.

Cory unfolded the paper. Big, black headlines jumped out: SHOOTING SUSPECT ARRESTED.

"Thank you, Lois. Here's a quarter for the paper."

"Keep it. For you, no charge." Lois smiled, returning to her notes.

Cory started down the hall toward Buck's room, reading while he walked. His eyes fell on the name in the first line of Ray Frazier's story. Suddenly, he decided to find a seat in the lounge to finish the article. The news was more shocking than he had expected.

In Ray Frazier style, the scene reconstructed. It told of how, according to reports from the Sheriff's Department, the gunman had paddled a canoe up Silver Creek from a road crossing about a mile downstream from Silver Spring, gone on foot to the ruins of the old town where he fired shots from a rifle toward two hikers, critically injuring one. After regaining consciousness following a fall, the gunman fled, leaving footprints on the muddy creek bank that had investigators baffled until the canoe was found the next day. One live round of ammunition found in the canoe matched the spent casings retrieved from the shooting scene, and the rifle and ammunition found still in the suspect's pickup truck.

Ray explained how the canoe owner was easily identified by the registration number on the canoe. That led to the discovery of the loaded weapon in the truck, and eventually an arrest.

Cory stared across the room, shocked with disbelief. He looked back at the first line of the article to make sure he had read the name correctly. For some unexplainable reason he started recalling all the names that had been dropped in conversation, and those he read in the old newspapers. It all started falling in place.

Mr. and Mrs. Paxton were seated next to Buck on chairs facing the window of his room. Buck slowly stood up when Cory entered. His perpetual smile beamed. Cory forced out a return grin.

"Good morning Buck, Mr. and Mrs. Paxton," Cory said with respect. He turned to Buck. "Looks like you're about ready for some scrambled eggs."

"Scrambled eggs?" Mr. Paxton produced a puzzled expression.

"Yeah," Cory explained. "Buck makes the best scrambled eggs... even if you order 'em over easy."

They all laughed a little, although Mr. and Mrs. Paxton didn't really understand why they were laughing.

Cory turned to Buck again. "Did you see the paper?" His smile turned to a frown.

"Yeah," Buck said. "But who is Milton Sinclair?"

Astonished with Buck's response, Cory glanced toward Mr. Paxton, and then looked directly into Buck's eyes again. "Slinky. Milton Sinclair is Slinky."

Buck sat down again. His smile vanished. "Guess I never knew his real name."

Mr. Paxton spoke up. "Both of you know this guy?"

"Yes, we do," Cory said. "We thought he was our friend."

"Some kind of friends you've been hanging out with," Mrs. Paxton said. "Now I know you're not coming back here to school next term."

Neither of the boys wanted to search for a worthy argument against that statement.

Much to Cory's surprise, Mr. and Mrs. Paxton excused themselves. "We'll let you two talk while we take care of some insurance matters at the main office." They strolled out of the room.

"I can't believe it," Buck said. "Why would Slinky...?"

"I think I know why," Cory said.

Buck just stared at Cory, puzzled.

"Slinky was one of the first people I ever met here. He told me about Silver Spring and Mack after I ran out of gas out there."

Buck nodded and listened.

"When I asked him how he knew all about it, he said his Grandfather told him, and when I asked who his Grandfather was he said the name Elmer Dickens."

"So, how does that fit in?"

"Elmer Dickens was at Tanglewood the day Zachary McDowell killed Jeremiah Crane. I read that in one of the old newspapers."

"I still don't get the connection," Buck said.

"Elmer Dickens was also one of the looters who got away the day Clancy Crane and Zach Jr. had the shootout."

Lights flashed and bells rang inside Buck's head. "And when the bank robbery was public knowledge, and everyone knew the money was never recovered, Elmer Dickens was the only one to suspect it had been hidden at Silver Spring."

"Bingo! Dickens told Slinky, and Slinky wanted to find it – not us."

"I still can't believe he'd try to kill us," Buck said.

Cory just shook his head.

A minute of silence went by.

"I got a letter from Dad. Guess I'll be going to Florida next week."

"To visit or to stay?"

"Probably to stay."

"You're not coming back to school next year, either, are you?"

"Not to Wellington. Mr. Barkley was the only reason I came here in the first place."

"So where do you think you'll go?"

"Don't know for sure yet. Probably somewhere in Florida. How 'bout you?"

"Haven't decided." Buck displayed a little grin. "Maybe I'll check out Florida State."

They were exchanging addresses and phone numbers when Mr. and Mrs. Paxton came in. Cory stood. "I've got some studying to do, and a lot of packing," he said. "I'll stop back tomorrow, okay?"

"Okay. I'll see you tomorrow," Buck said.

Mr. and Mrs. Paxton just nodded.

Sheriff Bancroft's patrol car sat at the curb in front of Mrs. Higgins' house. Not particularly thrilled to see him, Cory faked a smile and waved as he turned into the driveway.

They met midway between the two vehicles.

"Cory, I suppose you're leaving town when school is out," the Sheriff began.

"Yes, sir."

"Where's home? Illinois, isn't it?"

"No, sir. Not any more. My folks just bought a house in Sarasota, Florida. I'll be going there next week."

"You coming back to school here next year?"

"No sir. I don't think so."

"Well, I'll need your home address and phone. You can expect to be subpoenaed as a witness for the trial... if there is one."

"Yes, sir. I already figured that."

Cory wrote the information on the Sheriff's clipboard. "Do you still have my manuscript?"

"It's in my car. That's one helluva story – how much is really true?"

"All of it... except for the names."

"You should get it published."

"Thank you, sir, but can I please get that copy back?"

"Don't reckon I'll be needing it any more." Bancroft retrieved the manuscript and handed it over. It was the copy Cory had originally given to Victor Gladstone.

"Have a safe trip to Florida," Bancroft said. "And don't make me come down there lookin' for you." He got in his car and drove away.

Cory sighed with relief. One more obstacle down.

"Boxes," he thought. "I need to find boxes for packing."

THIRTY-EIGHT

There was no mistaking the Jolsten's house. Majestically poised on the riverbank, towering three stories its gleaming white paint glistened in the mid-day sun. A black wrought iron fence encompassed the biggest, greenest lawn Clancy had ever seen. He tied Shiner's reins to the fence near the front gate, swung the gate open just wide enough for him to get through, and started walking toward the mansion. A manservant came rushing out the front entrance and met him mid-way. "If you're looking for Mr. Jolsten, he's not here. He's at his hotel downtown."

"Actually, I'm looking for Millie Crane. I was told she's living here."

"I'm sorry, but you'll have to come back when Mr. Jolsten is here," the servant said.

Great. Another persnickety Wellington snob.

"Well, can you at least tell me if Millie is here?" Clancy had no sooner spoken the words than he heard a tiny voice call out his name.

"Clancy! Clancy! Mommy! Clancy is here!"

He knew that voice well. From the far side of the house he saw little Clair running toward him, and not far behind Millie kept pace. Within seconds Clair jumped into Clancy's arms, hugging him like she always did when he returned from a weekend of mining.

"It's okay, Jonathon," Millie said. "This is Clancy, my husband's brother. It'll be okay."

"Very well, Mrs. Crane," the servant said. He pointed his nose into the air, turned and walked back to the front door.

Millie hugged Clancy. "I'm so glad to see you. I've worried night and day." Millie wiped the tears of joy away with her hankie.

"I thought of you and Clair a lot, too. Are you getting along okay?"

"Oh, we're okay. The Reverend Miller brought us here, and Mr. Jolsten gave me a job as a maid at his hotel."

"And you live here in this fancy house?"

"We just have a small room up on the third floor, but there's a lovely view of the river. And where have you been all this time? We got word that Silver Spring burned to the ground."

"Everything except the Lodge. Tanglewood is the only thing left."

"Is that where you've been?"

"Off and on. I went prospecting most of the time... at Charlie Daggett's old claim."

"Find anything?"

"A little, until..." Clancy paused.

"Until what?"

"Until Zachary McDowell Jr. showed up at the Lodge."

"Oh dear. What happened?"

Clancy looked around in all directions. "Can we go somewhere a little more private?"

They went to some wooden chairs in the shade of a huge cottonwood tree in a far corner of the yard. Clancy began explaining the whole story. He told Millie about the fire and the true account of what really happened to McDowell, and about the Sheriff's posse that cleaned out Tanglewood. He told her about his trips to the mine and how he kept Shiner fed. When he started telling about the day Zach Jr. arrived, Millie already knew this part of the story involved bloodshed. She had heard the stories brought back to Wellington by Elmer Dickens and Casey Fitzsimmons and had read the articles in the Weekly Star. She sent Clair off to play where she wouldn't hear the gruesome details.

When Clancy seemed satisfied that he had not overlooked a single detail he pleaded for Millie's confidence. "Please don't repeat any of this to anybody."

It didn't bother Millie that Clancy wanted to keep this secret, especially the part about him clubbing McDowell. If the people believed Jeremiah's ghost killed the man who set Silver Spring ablaze, then so be it. She was relieved to know the truth.

Millie sighed. "What are you going to do now?"

"On my way here to find you I saw a sign on a riverboat that said 'Deck Hands Wanted.' I applied."

"And?"

"The Captain liked me, and I report to work tomorrow morning at seven o'clock."

"When will you be back?"

"He said we'd go south for the winter... won't be back 'till spring."

"I'll be sad to see you go away, but I'm happy for you."

"Thank you, Millie. I'll bring you a nice present from New Orleans."

The early morning sunshine danced along the river current; the cool autumn breeze fluttered the flags atop the big boat and stirred the black smoke billowing from the tall stacks. The steam whistle pierced the morning air; the paddlewheels began churning the muddy water.

Millie stood on the levee among the noisy crowd waving their good-byes to the last riverboat they would see for months. She could see Clancy dressed in one of Jeremiah's striped shirts standing proudly on the upper deck but she wasn't sure he could hear her "Good-bye." Then their eyes met and Clancy returned the farewell with a gallant wave. Somehow, Millie knew she might never see him again.

THIRTY-NINE

Elbows on knees, chin resting on clenched fists, Cory sat on the bottom step of the stairs to his apartment. He stared out at the empty street, marveled by the serenity that six a.m. offered. In the stillness of the crisp morning air, he could hear the hum of an eighteen-wheeler out on the highway and the buzz of an outboard motor, an early fisherman out for the catch of the day. Someone in the neighborhood sent the aroma of sizzling bacon through an open kitchen window, eventually getting lost in the fragrance from Mrs. Higgins' flowerbed.

It was Thursday. Final exams done, today he would embark on the long journey to Sarasota, and in a few days he would be basking in the sun on Siesta Key Beach and sipping a pina colada. There was a lot to look forward to, but he couldn't get his mind off the past few days. His visions kept flashing back to Monday evening when he stood at the end of the driveway as Buck climbed into the rear seat of the Paxton's rented Lincoln, and then watched it disappear around the corner at the end of the block. By now Buck would be home in Spokane sleeping in a bed that wasn't lumpy.

Cory's focus drew to his Bronco and the eight-foot *U-Haul* trailer that now contained nearly everything he owned. All that remained in the apartment over the garage on Harrison Street were the furnishings Mrs. Higgins provided, including the lumpy couch, his pillow and a patchwork quilt.

His appointment for an oil change at the *Texaco* Station where Jimmy worked was at eight o'clock. After that he would go to Victor Gladstone's office for one last "Good-bye," close his account at the bank, fill out a change of address card at the Post Office, make a final cruise along the river and around the lake, and then be on his way.

"I'm afraid it's going to be a while, Cory," Jimmy's father said. He looked at his wristwatch. "I'm all alone today."

"Where's Jimmy?" Cory asked.

"He's been actin' kind of funny ever since Slinky was arrested. Sheriff's been comin' around askin' a lot of questions. Jimmy got sick of it and just left town."

"Where'd he go?"

"Didn't say. He just packed some clothes, filled his car with gas and took off."

"Oh. Well how long do you think it'll be 'til the Bronco is done?"

"Probably a couple of hours before I'll get to it. Sorry."

"That's okay, I understand. I have some errands to run anyway. I'll just walk downtown. I'll be back in a couple of hours or so."

Cory didn't want to dwell on the subject of Slinky's arrest with Jimmy's Dad any longer than he had to. He was disappointed that Jimmy was gone and that he wouldn't be able to say "good-bye," but he could relate to both counts of the scenario: Jimmy's best friend was in jail, and he knew how irritating Sheriff Bancroft could be.

One of Buck's favorite expressions, "Breakfast of champions," popped into Cory's head as he pulled the door open at the doughnut shop. It seemed like everywhere he went, something reminded him of Buck.

The large coffee nearly lasted to the Daily Record entrance. Now, for the last time he would swing open the door, greet Elaine, and head directly to the break room for a coffee refill.

"Good morning, Elaine."

"Good morning, Cory."

"Is Mr. Gladstone in his office?"

"Yes he is, and I'm sure he'll be glad to see you."

Cory refilled his coffee cup and briefly recited several "farewells" to the people he had worked with for the last nine months. They were sad to see him leave, but happy for him that he would be enjoying his summer vacation on a Florida beach.

Victor Gladstone sat at his usually messy desk with his usual five o'clock shadow, necktie loosened, gripping a coffee cup with one hand and frantically scribbling notes with the other.

"Hello, Cory. Come in, have a seat. I suppose you're getting ready to head south."

"Yes, sir. I'm leaving today. I just wanted to stop in to say good-bye."

"Well, I'm glad you did. I've enjoyed having you on my staff... sorry things worked out the way they did. I was looking forward to having you here full-time this summer."

"Thank you. I've enjoyed working here. Maybe I'll be back some day." Cory knew the "back some day" statement was probably false, but he thought it sounded good. And after all, it wasn't an impossibility.

Victor scribbled a name and phone number on a scratch pad and handed it across the desk. "Here's Harry Claiborne's number. He's a friend of mine in New York. He's a publishing editor. Might help you with your book."

"You really think...?"

"Sure! I'd rewrite it with all the real names, though."

"Okay. Maybe I will."

"Just tell Harry I told you to call him. He owes me a favor or two."

"Thanks, Mr. Gladstone. I really appreciate the vote of confidence."

"And if you ever get back this way, my door is always open."

"Thank you. I'll write you when I get to Sarasota."

He'd used up another hour by the time he made the stops at the Post Office and the Bank. The Bronco, ready and waiting looked better than it had in weeks. Jimmy's father had given it a quick wash, vacuum and he'd even used a spot remover to rid the last remaining blood stains from the carpet. Quite pleased with the extra service he didn't expect, Cory slipped a nice tip for the generous effort.

"When Jimmy gets back, tell him I said good-bye. Maybe I'll see him again."

"Sure... *if* he ever comes back."

Cory would have driven straight to 855 Harrison Street where the rental trailer sat poised to begin the Florida trek, but there was no time schedule to keep; one last look around certainly wouldn't hurt. Rather than turning toward downtown, though, some strange luring sense drew him to the highway leading west out of town. While his hands did the steering, his mind focused on Jimmy and Slinky.

Mixed emotions changed directions in Cory's head more times than a switchback road up the side of a mountain. Was it suspicious or unusual that Jimmy had left town? He wanted to believe that the true reason had been the irritating prods by Sheriff Bancroft and not because of any degree of guilt. To Cory, Jimmy had always seemed a respectable person with high moral standards. He couldn't think of any indications that Jimmy would have had any willful part in an act of violence. Jimmy just wasn't that kind of soul. He went to Church every Sunday; Cory couldn't think of a single time when he'd heard Jimmy use fowl language; of all the Friday nights when he and Buck would meet up with Jimmy and Slinky at the Academy Bar, he never saw Jimmy under the influence. It did seem a little strange that he would keep company with Slinky, a slightly rougher individual. But then Cory remembered them saying they had gone all through school together. Their alliance began long before Slinky developed his brazen adult lifestyle.

Cory was no longer shocked or puzzled by the authorities' suspicion of Milton "Slinky" Sinclair. In addition to the evidence stacking up against him, Slinky had a motive – Cory was quite certain that had probably not surfaced, nor would it surface unless Sheriff Bancroft were to ever view Cory's manuscript rewritten with all the correct names associated with Silver Spring history.

It was hard to believe that Slinky – as adamant as he was about the fear of Silver Spring and the legends connected to it – would not have dropped some hints at one time or another of his interest in a search for the lost treasure. Obviously, Slinky was not afraid to go there, contrary to the indications he had made so many times. Cory recalled the night he and Buck were scared out of their wits by the scavenger raccoon. He had vaguely seen what appeared to be the form of a man lurking in the shadows; that could have been Slinky, as he was one of the only two people who knew they were going camping at Silver Spring on both occasions.

Now Cory gazed toward the ridge where Tanglewood Lodge hid among the growth of forest that time had so carefully placed there for its protection. He tried to imagine the skyline of rooftops that had once been visible, now only a memory to so few. One last time, he had to climb that hill. One last time, he had to see Tanglewood. One last time he had to feel the energy left behind by the dreams and ambitions of those who worked so hard to establish this doomed fortress.

He perched on a foundation rock and surveyed the lonely terrain, feeling no apprehension for the surroundings. He thought of the terror he had experienced here less than two weeks ago, but now his fear seemed so distant. He thought about Slinky sitting in a jail cell, yet anger evaded him. Something about Silver Spring would not allow dissention to prevail.

Cory recognized the cultural divide on which he teetered. How wonderful, he thought, it would be to restore Silver Spring, and to revive the spirit that once drove its founders to wealth and dignity. One look around, though, proved there was no need for artificial adornment, as the trees, hills and sky provided a grandeur no human effort could ever match, and it also revealed an eerie reminder of the harsh lives led by the people who made Silver Spring their home, now the final resting place of a time gone by. And now all of Wellington shared a hackneyed interest in Silver Spring; no one still seemed to possess any desire to visit these hills that had gained such a reputation. Even Slinky's arrest didn't seem to settle their uneasiness born of a legend. Mack still loomed in the shadows and Silver Spring Hills still remained forbidden territory. The people of Wellington County weren't yet ready to accept resolution. The news of Buck's near-fatal experience had simply rejuvenated the original fable with strong reinforcement.

The thought occurred to Cory that Silver Spring was never granted the chance to completely flourish. What would it be today had it not fallen victim, its vulnerability attacked with a single match struck by the cowardly villain, Zachary McDowell? Would it have eventually survived despite an ailing economy? Or would it have perished anyway? No one would ever know.

Cory thought about Clancy's journal. As he stared out across the ridge, Clancy's message brought all of Silver Spring into plain view. Cory could see Main Street lined with stores and shops, the Market Square buzzing with activity, the Livery Stable and the Railroad Station at the end of Connor Street, Smith and Hayden Mining Headquarters at the far end of town, the dreary shacks and huts across the dead line, cobblestones and gas street lamps, the clock tower on City Hall, and Tanglewood Lodge in its splendid radiance. He could hear old Brook, the stable master, telling young Clancy stories, and the clippity-clop of horses' hooves and rumbling ore wagons. He could smell the smoke from the smelter furnace, sawdust from the Silver Creek Mill, and the aroma of fresh bread drifting on the breeze from the bakery's open back door. He could taste the foamy Clearwater brew moistening his lips.

Cory blinked his eyes and in that instant it was all gone. Only the faint remnants of what used to be, barely visible among the natural camouflage, except for one remaining structure, Tanglewood Lodge, spared from decimation.

How fortunate he was to have stumbled onto this paradise so rich with true American culture, and so alive with the spirit of the past. How fortunate he was to have met all the players on this remote little stage of history through the voice of a boy who grew to be a man on this very soil. Although a lifetime separated them, and they never came face-to-face, Cory Brockway could feel the warm closeness of Clancy Crane's friendship.

Tepid south winds sifted through the trees and the sun bathed the verdant hillsides. The fragile colors of spring had given way to a mass of sun-flecked deep green foliage, and melodious birdsongs now replaced by the raucous demands of newly hatched nestlings.

Content now, that he had satisfied his need to see Silver Spring as he wanted to remember it – not as a scene of violence, but as the placid site of serenity – Cory readied himself emotionally to leave it behind.

A man walked slowly and silently toward Cory on a course where Main Street once was. Cory held his breath. He hadn't seen where the man came from, and he didn't recognize him. There didn't seem to be any reason to feel threatened, but Cory's muscles tensed. The closer the man came Cory could see there was no sign of aggression; the stranger's pace was nonchalant, be carried no weapons, and the expression on his aged face seemed pleasant. Cory released his tension and took a deep breath, relieved that danger indications were evaporating.

The crisp white shirt and black bowtie stood out in sharp contrast against the deep green foliage. He tipped his derby hat cordially as he passed by, not speaking a single word. Cory found himself in deep thought about the silent man's rather uncommon hiking apparel as he focused on the white shirt slowly making its way toward the Lodge. He glanced back in the direction where he had first seen the man, and then toward the Lodge only to see the figure disappear behind the closing front door. Moments later he could hear the muffled tinkling of a piano.

Cory knew which window would give him a view of the old upright. Through the dirty glass he could faintly see the white shirt swaying and elbows gyrating in rhythm to the lively tune he couldn't identify. Now it seemed necessary to go inside and talk with this stranger, find out why he was there, and how he could get music out of that old piano that hadn't worked in years.

The front door made its eerie screech that echoed throughout the empty building. There was no one sitting at the piano. There was no music. Just silence.

Cory's mind flipped through Clancy's journal. He had spent so much time with that journal it was not difficult to recall details from it. "Alexander Malone," he whispered.

Another page of the journal now dominated his mind's eye. Cory recalled the story Clancy wrote about the day Zach Junior arrived at Tanglewood. The picture he imagined was so vivid. He could almost see and hear the crunching footsteps; the dark, shadowy villain stepping carelessly across the broken glass scattered about the floor. He could imagine the terror Clancy must have felt hiding in that upstairs room, thinking McDowell would kill him if he had the chance, and the relief delivered by the sound of a slamming door.

Just as some luring force had directed Cory's hands to steer the Bronco toward Silver Spring, that same force now lured him to the old piano. He pried open the top lid and peered inside.

The corners of his mouth curled into a smile. He was staring down at a lumpy, brown canvas bag stenciled with faded black letters that read: Bank of Sioux Falls.

Part 2

The Private Journal of Clancy Crane

My Journal—Clancy Crane

It was Tom the newspaper man who give me this journal early one morning when I was waiting for the market square vendors to get organized so I could buy produce for our kitchen at the lodge. He give me this book and it wasn't even my birthday. He said he seen me writing all the time in that flimsy nikel notebook that Jeremiah purchased for me at the genral store. Tom and me got to be real pals after that. So now that I have this fancy book to do my writing in I will first copy all that I have wrote so far about us coming to Silver Spring and living here and all that I have seen going on. We come here in wagons and horses. It was Daniel and his wife Kate and Jeremiah and his wife Millie and me. Jeremiah and Daniel are my older brothers I was just a kid then. Ma and Pa died of the plaig back in Ohio so I was all alone and Jeremiah and Millie took me in said I was lucky to servive. I was excited about this new place we come to it was full of people scurryen about the streets so crowded you could hardly drive the teams and wagons. Many new stores and houses were being built. Jeremiah said it was the gold and silver mining that made the town so rich and this is where we was going to stay. But Jeremiah didn't want to wade in no cold creek diggin for gold. He knew then that this is where he would build another hotel like Millie and him had in Ohio he just needed a chance to get started. But we had to camp outside of town for a while because there was no place in town for us to stay. Kate was real upset with all this and it was all me and Millie could do to keep her from starting to walk back to Ohio. She cried a lot. I guess she just wasn't as advencherus as the rest of us. Jeremiah and Daniel were going to the saloons in town every night and roaming the streets every day trying to make friends but they wouldn't let Millie and Kate and me go with them said this was a ruff place for women and children. I hated being called children but Daniel kept telling me I had to stay in camp to protect Millie and Kate and that always made me feel important. Finally one day they met a man named Mr. Grumby who was owner of the newspaper office and most of the vacant land left in the town. He *promised Jeremiah and Daniel temperary housing in a couple of little houses he owned until we could find or build something better. But as it turned out there was only one little house at the very edge of town but we all managed to squeeze in and we got by.*

And so begins the journal of Clancy Crane—the very journal that would mysteriously lead certain members of a future generation to great wealth. Although his penmanship elementary, spelling not always accurate, and grammar far less than perfect, his words bear the innocent truths of a youngster, yet the boldness of a seasoned pioneer. As time evolves and Clancy is schooled, his language skills become more refined; that he has been toughened by the environment and his senses are honed to a cutting edge is only testament to his spirited ability to withstand the rigors of the cruel world around him.

Sadly, Clancy would not live to old age: he died in battle during the First World War. But while he lived his short life, he was privileged to witness the rise of a mining camp from its wild and lawless state, to that of a respectable town, to watch it grow and prosper, and to prosper himself, as well. Growing up in a wild and lawless mining camp, however, wasn't always a walk in the park on a sunny afternoon; it was a harsh environment where less-than-honorable men mingled with, and became lord over many of the hard-working souls who had come there to find a better life. Striking trepidation into the hearts of the general population was their primary tool.

By the time Clancy and his brothers arrived at Silver Spring, a few prominent men had managed to control some sort of order over the community; they made the rules that were loosely enforced by their loyal henchmen, and though there was no formal government, the citizenry, wanting some sort of order, needing it to survive, vaguely accepted the leadership in uncertain terms. But it hadn't always been that way.

Silas Patch, an enterprising Easterner, had been the first to establish a place of business here, a mere trading post on the flat top of a hill overlooking a mystifying valley and a stream providing ample water supply. Simply a stroke of fate did several prospectors wander into his camp during the difficult trek to an unknown destination where he planned to settle into business operations, fully intent on monopolizing the region's trade. The chance encounter with gold-crazed men who spoke of wealth within easy grasp right there in those surrounding hills persuaded him to realize his opportunity; he need not travel any farther; he had found his destination. Within weeks, before the winter set in, his structure was secured, and although the winter's winds would soon howl, Silas basked in the glory of his dream, miners coming to him, their sole supplier of provisions and tools.

News traveled quickly of the rich strikes near the settlement known only as Dog Patch, nothing more than a muddy trail across the top of a ridge flanked by only a couple of sturdy log structures. Patch already knew the elements to keep his subjects loyal to him: liquor, drugs, gambling, and women, not necessarily in that order. To provide the additional services, he constructed the second two-story building with surrounding timber to house a saloon, adequate accommodations for the barroom and gambling downstairs, and rooms for the whores upstairs. It was a celebration, indeed, the day the carriage arrived with the prostitutes.

Within a few months the place had attracted more prospectors and more businessmen. Many of the prospectors took up temporary quarters in any kind of shelter—shacks, huts and tents—on the lower slopes below the trading post, while some brave souls camped right at their diggings. With the businessmen came Mr. Grumby and his ambition to promote a metropolitan district. With his knowledge of the prosperous mining strikes in the area and his keen sense of business prudence, he quietly left to file the claim at the land office, returned and proceeded to plat his town—Silver Spring it would eventually be called—on the remainder of the flat, treeless hilltop adjacent to the already established supply camp. At the center he plotted a large square, adequate, he thought, for open-air markets, outlined with various lots for permanent merchant buildings. A block to the east was a wide north-south thoroughfare—Main Street—and another similar, Lincoln Street, to the west, spanned by a dozen cross streets that extended nearly to the edges of the plateau.

Mr. Grumby didn't sit on his haunches waiting for his camp to populate. He was by nature a promoter, and by profession a newspaper man; his print shop on one of the side streets was among the first structures. His press soon produced advertisement posters and letters distributed throughout the eastern states luring potential merchants and service providers to claim their share in the wealth of this new land.

In a few more months, Main Street was lined with stores and shops, and the square's perimeter was soon the site of livery stable, blacksmith, gunsmith, bakery and more.

And with the prosperous mining ventures came Chinamen; they seemed to follow the gold strikes and formed their own communities within, but segregated from the rest of the population. And rightfully so; they wished to stay within their own culture and live among their own people. As much as they had already contributed to building America, they were not readily accepted socially by Americans, nor were they allowed to work in the mines. Their only purpose in the mining camps was to provide services that the miners—mostly single men without families—didn't want to perform, such as laundry, cooking, butchering and baking. Here, they concentrated their efforts on several blocks stretching along the southern reaches of Lincoln Street and west. They were adjacent to the center of town but were removed from it; they knew their boundaries.

They understood the colossal earning potential in the gold mining camps. In its own quiet way, Chinatown, too, was becoming wealthy, taking the miners' gold for the services it performed. Within their society, too, were the bosses, the leaders, the principal chieftains who ran their operations, and who dominated in the power and the wealth. But they didn't build fancy storefronts or fabulous mansions; rarely did one speak English, so the American miners conversed with them only by simple words and sign language to transact business with them, and the Chinaman was never considered among the higher echelon of wealth.

There was another breed of man that filtered in. The gold in the creeks where the prospectors sifted through the mud and sand

and gravel to find it had been washed down from higher places. Larger quantities of precious minerals lay imbedded in the hills where men of greater ambitions sought to discover their fortunes. It took wealthy men to afford the labor-intense operations of sinking shafts into the rock. Knowing where to do that was a matter of studying where the prospectors were successful, buying up all those claims, and then putting those men in their employ to dig into the source—the hills—for the really huge profits.

Those men of money were also men of power, and in a land of lawlessness where any degree of organization of community had occurred before their arrival, conflicts were bound to arise.

It didn't take long for Silas Patch to realize that his little camp was too far removed from the busy center of the new one, now growing not only in size but in popularity, as well. As the prospectors who had resided in shacks on the hillside below his trading post gained financial status, they abandoned their shabby dwellings and moved into better cabins they built near the swelling community. Silas had lost his monopoly; but with the rapidly growing population he knew his prosperity could continue if he joined the ranks within the metropolis. He had already become quite wealthy, and on Main Street his status would surely improve. Mr. Grumby was more than willing to sell him the last remaining lot large enough to accommodate the grand hotel Silas proposed, and another where he would construct his new general store. In a short time, The Striker, Grumby's two-page newspaper, boasted of the new Royal Hotel soon to offer "Comfortable rooms, fine whiskey, and honest games." The Royal would be much larger than the Lincoln House, the Continental, or the North Star. Until now, the Lincoln House had been the largest, and most advantageously located just across the thoroughfare from the leading edge of Chinatown; the face of the Chinamen's district was a busy place with its many laundries, restaurants, butcher shops and bakeries frequented by the entire population. Silas was content, however, with his Main Street prominence, facing away from the stink emitting from the livestock pens and chicken roosts in Chinatown.

To further enhance Patch's investment, a rich silver vein had been discovered close to the camp. Sam Benson, an old prospector who had already done alright for himself made it known that he alone could not work that claim; he did not possess the knowledge or skill to sink a shaft, or the resources for the necessary equipment it would require. Because of his age and deteriorating dexterity he was more interested in selling it to the highest bidder. When word reached the scouts of Hayden and Smith Mining, they quickly surveyed the site, assayed samples of ore taken from the outcropping of rock, and made their offer of purchase. They were experts who knew, without a doubt, that this was no mediocre strike. It would take a large-scale mining operation to extract the ore—an operation that would go on for years. The people of this new settlement were assured of permanence.

That's when the next struggle for power threatened to put the camp at odds. With the Royal Hotel firmly planted and flourishing as the hottest spot in the town, Silas Patch had once again regained his foothold. Not unusual for his saloon and gaming rooms to take in two thousand dollars a night, he was rapidly becoming the richest—and the most powerful—man in camp. Not much happened without the watchful eye of Silas Patch's monitoring. From the windows in the tower he had constructed atop the Royal for the purpose of random audits of activity at his general store, he observed the rest of the town, as well. His observation was recognized and accepted by the population, but only after an incident that won Silas a great deal of respect. From his vantage point high above the bustling thoroughfare he was the only witness to a cowardly crime: a woman on her way to the grocer was dragged into an alley, stabbed and robbed of her purse containing a substantial amount of gold coin. Silas immediately dispatched two of his strong-arms to pursue the assailant, and a bartender to deliver the badly-injured woman to the doctor's office. Thanks to a capable man of medicine, the woman survived; thanks to Silas Patch's henchmen, the woman's attacker did not. Just minutes after the mugging, the scoundrel was cornered; when he tried to escape, he was shot dead. They found the woman's purse concealed inside his shirt and returned it to her, already in the doctor's care. Justice had been served swiftly, and the woman had been spared an agonizing death, alone in that alley.

For those who did not witness, first-hand, the woman's rescue and the rogue's capture, the deed was justly documented in the next issue of The Striker, and it earned for Silas Patch the deserving unofficial title of Guardian Angel to the camp. A killing of that nature seemed justified, and saving the life of that poor, defenseless woman and recovering her stolen money was certainly most honorable.

But sometimes, guardian angels don't play by the rules. When mining magnate William Hayden arrived to view his new holdings and to initiate the first steps of the operation, he appeared as a threat to the free reins people had on the camp. They had come to this strange and magical place saying "I'm going to make a new life." They intended to go off into the hills and streams and get the gold—and live a wonderful life. But then, along comes William Hayden who has all the money in the world, a powerful force that seems to be saying, "I'll eventually own you all." To him, the power, it seems normal, but to everyone else it was maddening and dangerous. To them, he was taking away their freedom.

First impressions didn't sit well with Silas Patch, either. He saw what was coming: Hayden would buy out all the small mining concerns, funnel all the profits into his own wealth and by doing so, regulate the cash flow into the local businesses. The halcyon days of the prospectors' free spirit spending would be over.

Perhaps Sam Benson—who was still waiting for his two hundred-fifty thousand dollar payoff from Hayden—could be persuaded to back out of the deal; perhaps he could be persuaded to accept another offer from local concerns. Perhaps, Silas thought, he could form a group of shareholders to buy Sam Benson's claim... pull it out of William Hayden's grasp. It would be an underhanded trick, but the future of the camp, as Silas Patch interpreted it, hung in the balance; doing nothing meant watching the treasures of the surrounding hills fly away like a flock of migrating birds.

Sam Benson stayed at the North Star Hotel, a sleazy little joint on Lincoln at the far end of Chinatown. Silas wasted no time in sending a messenger there to request a meeting with Benson at the Royal as soon as possible. He'd talk to the old prospector, get him to hold out on Hayden until the other potential investors could be called together for a secret meeting, pool their assets, and then present Benson a better offer.

Silas handpicked several business proprietors that he knew to be among the most financially sound: Oliver Grumby, not because of the newspaper but because of his dealings in real estate; Moses McCarthy, owner of the Silver Pick Saloon; Warren Stover, master of the Lincoln House; John Uldridge, the Continental Saloon & Billiard Hall proprietor; Ralph Longhorn, his competitor in General Merchandise; and Jack Gilmore, hardware store operator. Behind a closed door in the office just below the Guardian Angel tower, Silas presented his proposal to the assembly. For the first time in its short history, the camp's foreboding issues were getting hashed over by leaders, albeit leaders picked by one man. They all agreed with Silas that a man of money and power—an outsider—was invading their territory, and if permitted a stronghold on the richest mining venture in the region, it was likely to progress to an iron grip on the entire camp as well. But this wasn't like building a hotel or a hardware store; not like ordering wagonloads of whiskey or pickaxes and shovels. All those things happened above ground. This was to be a gamble—a big gamble—and unlike the games of chance that some of these men ran, this was a game they didn't know how to fix. None of them were ready, at that moment, to risk large sums of money on a pile of rock on a hillside that had not been explored farther than its surface.

"I think we should all take some time to think about this," Ralph Longhorn suggested. "If it turns out to be a bust, we all lose. But if it's a bust for Hayden, then *we've* lost nothing."

The meeting was adjourned with the only decision made to assemble again in a couple of days. All were present at the second meeting with the exception of Jack Gilmore. A messenger was sent to the hardware store, only to return with the reply that Mr. Gilmore no longer wished to participate in the proceedings. One less man made little difference, as the outcome still resulted in indecision. "Mr. Hayden has more money and power than all of us put together," Ralph Longhorn argued. "If we get in his way, he could retaliate with more force than we are able to endure." His outlook suggesting negativity toward Silas Patch's plan appeared to be swaying some of the members of the group, and Silas suspected that he had invited a traitor into the newly-formed alliance. He confronted Longhorn. "Are you saying that you want to see all the prosperity of this camp siphoned away? That you are willing to just stand idly by and watch all of *our profits* be carried off by some outsider?"

"No, Silas," Ralph Longhorn responded. "What I'm trying to say is that we all—this entire camp—could be faced with violent destruction if we *do* oppose Hayden. We see enough bloodshed here, already, without provoking more! And Silas... you must surely recognize that it *could* come to that."

The others were deeply influenced on both sides; Silas Patch made a strong case to protect the monetary interest of the camp's businessmen; but Ralph Longhorn's interest was to preserve peace, or at least, to not provoke violence. His was a more diplomatic approach that affected the entire settlement, not just the business district.

"We need more time to think this through," Moses McCarthy said. His saloon was supporting his financial status far above his expectations; he wasn't yet convinced that he should risk what he had gained so far on a hole in the ground.

"Gentlemen," Silas said. "Take more time if you need it. But let me remind you that our time might be running short. I can assure you that Hayden is eager to start operations, and I can't guarantee that Benson is going to be patient much longer. I urge you to make your decision soon."

After the meeting broke up, Silas sat in his office alone, contemplating his options. Ralph Longhorn was not going to contribute funds to save Benson's claim from the mining tycoon—he could be sure of that. As for the others, there were no definite commitments either way. He thought he would pay Jack Gilmore a personal visit... perhaps convince him to rejoin the effort with a little one-on-one counseling.

"Jack," he greeted as he entered the hardware store.

"Mr. Patch," Jack Gilmore answered.

"We missed you at the meeting this morning."

Gilmore didn't respond.

"Is there any chance I can reinstate your interest in our effort?"

"Mr. Patch... I understand your concerns; however, I feel it is for naught. You see, Mr. Hayden and I have talked. I have agreed to his use of the hardware store's back room and rear entrance for a temporary banking house... until he can build a suitable structure of his own."

"A bank? He intends to build a bank here?"

"Yes, sir."

"Well that's just great. Then I guess he intends to have control of everybody's money."

"No, Mr. Patch. I think you misunderstand. He intends the bank to be an institution for the good of the town. He has offered me a position as one of its officers."

The information that he obtained in the conversation with Jack Gilmore wasn't the only surprise Silas would encounter that afternoon. A visitor awaited his return to the Royal.

"May we speak in private?" William Hayden asked.

Silas nodded toward the balcony over the barroom. His expression was not smiling; he did not know what to expect, and he certainly didn't trust William Hayden. When they reached Patch's office, Hayden marveled at the steep stairway ascending through the ceiling and into the tower.

Silas just studied his guest for a long moment. Hayden seemed much too refined, much too sophisticated for life in a mining camp, although he must have experienced this type of atmosphere in dozens of other camps just like Dog Patch. Noticing that Hayden remained fascinated by the elevated room above, Silas offered modestly, "It's been called the Guardian Angel tower."

"So I've heard… a commendable act, indeed."

"You know about that?"

"Mr. Patch," Hayden said as he faced his host. "I make it a point to learn as much as I can about the prominent people in the camps where I hold mining operations."

"So you can learn how to control them?"

"No, Mr. Patch." Hayden was a bit irritated by Patch's attack on his integrity. "So that we might work and exist in harmony."

"But you don't hold any mining operations here yet."

"Mr. Patch. Do you know who you are dealing with?"

"Yes, Mr. Hayden. I know who you are."

"Then you might be advised to call off your task force, in the event that you are indeed attempting to prevent me from acquiring Mr. Benson's claim."

"What makes you think *I'm* trying to stop you?"

"Mr. Patch. How naïve do you think I am? First of all, let me tell you that you will not get rid of me so easily as I already have deeds to four other claims here… four men who are very satisfied with the generous amounts I have paid them."

"And those four men would be..."

"Hans Stengahl, Henry Sanford, Elmer Dickens, and Casey Fitzsimmons."

"You see, Mr. Hayden? That's what I don't like about the way you operate. I know all those men. They were fulfilling their dreams."

"No, Mr. Patch, they were merely toiling, wearing themselves out *searching* for their dreams. I, on the other hand, have *given* them their dreams."

"But what about all those other people who came here trying to find their way in the world... trying to make a new life?"

"All those others, scratching out a meager living in the creeks and gullies—"

"Meager to you, perhaps," Silas interrupted. "But to them, the gold dust and nuggets they pan out of the creek mud, to them it's their fortunes. And you're trying to take that away from them."

"All those others," Hayden repeated. "They can continue to sift through the creek bottoms for as long as they want. I have no interest in that. My interests lay in the hills... the source... the mother lode. That's what separates me from them; I have the knowledge and the capability to get to the really big deposits that they can't reach, and if I have the ambition and am willing to take the risks, then, dammit, I deserve to reap the rewards."

"But didn't you just tell me that you bought out claims from four prospectors?"

"I did. But their claims are where my interests are. They were merely attempting... they would have failed because they lack the knowledge and skills and resources to succeed. Don't worry, Mr. Patch. Those four men still have bright futures. Mr. Stengahl and Mr. Sanford are investing their money in a joint effort—a brewery, right here in the camp. Mr. Fitzsimmons and Mr. Dickens have indicated they are interested in being in my employ. As for all those others... when their claims play out—and they will—what will they have then? Nothing more than ragged clothes, bruised bodies and a few hundred dollars in gold dust if they're lucky. What I am creating here is an opportunity for them to work as long as they have the desire, to prosper and to live the new lives they came here to find... to spend their wages in your saloon and your gambling hall, just as they have been doing. And your hotel rooms will be filled to the limit with all the laborers who will come for work and are in need of quarters. Ultimately, Mr. Patch, we can all destroy one another, or we can form some sort of society with some sort of sanction and reason to it that will allow us—under the illusions of sanction—to find a way to live and work and prosper together. Mr. Patch… don't condemn me for doing what I do best, and I promise you… you will not regret it."

Later that evening, a messenger found Sam Benson at the Pickaxe Saloon, a less crowded watering hole on the north edge of camp. The message he delivered was to meet Silas Patch at the Royal; Patch would buy the beefsteak dinner. The soon-to-be wealthy old prospector promptly showed up. In the little dining room at a table spread with platters of food and a bottle of the best Kentucky Bourbon, Silas invited him to sit down. "Go ahead and finish your deal with Hayden," Silas told him. "But if you are mistreated or cheated in any way, you come to me. Hayden is a smooth talking dandy, and there still remains in me a tiny fragment of doubt questioning the trustworthiness of his conduct."

Sam Benson was a man of few words. He nodded his acknowledgement and simply said, "Thank you, Mr. Patch."

My Journal—Clancy Crane

Once we was settled into that tiny little house on South Street the last real street on that side of town things changed for all of us. Jeremiah had bought a piece of property on the other end of town where Main Street ended. I doubt that anybody but the jack rabbits ever set foot on that ground because it was nothing but a tangle of trees and scrub brush. I spose that is why nobody wanted that land but Jeremiah thought it was perfect just up Connor street from the railroad stashun. He spent most of the summer sun up til sun down cutting trees and brush. Daniel helped him for a while but then he got a job riding shotgun on the Wilson stagecoach. I helped him too some days but he wouldn't let me be there all the time said it was too dangerus for a kid. Jeremiah was always lookin out for me making sure I didn't get hurt like keepin me out of harms way when he was cutting the really big trees down or telling me not to go on the other side of South street where we lived. Everybody called our street the dead line because on the hillside below it was where all the winos and tramps and genrally bad people lived in shacks and huts. They called it that because I guess nobody would be caught dead going there. But he would let me go along to get our team of horses from Mr. Brooks livery and drag the logs he cut to the sawmill down in the valley by the creek. Next spring those logs would get sawed into lumber and that lumber would help build our own stable and carrage house and we could live in the carrage house til the hotel was finished.

Some days when I was not helping Jeremiah I would sneak away from the house while Millie and Kate were busy washing or mending clothes and didn't notice that I was gone. Sometimes I walked down by the stamping mill where the silver ore was crushed before it went into the smelter and melted down. What a noisy place that was the 10 stamp mill breaking all the big rocks into little ones. Then sometimes I would walk up into Main street and look in all the store windows and then go down Lincoln street and watch and lissen to the Chineese people with their funny sounding talk. One time there was somebody arguing with a Chinaman about the laundry they left the day before and a fight got started and next thing you know 10 men was rolling around in the muddy street beating each other up til the China boss come and broke up the fight. I could not understand what he said but he sure sounded angry.

Because I was just a kid nobody paid me no mind. I never seen many kids my age in the town lest they was with a grownup I guess they wasn't allowed to run alone and I probly wouldn't be *allowed either if Millie and Kate knew where I had snuck off to. I did make frends with one man in the big market square. His name is George and he always has a whole wagon full of crates of chicken eggs. Where do you get all these eggs I asked him and he told me he has a farm down the valley and he has 200 laying hens. That was enough eggs to keep everybody in town eating eggs for breakfast cept those who had their own chickens. He is a nice man and he always gives me a piece of hard candy.*

With the businessmen a little uneasy knowing the possible consequences of having a power like William Hayden suddenly taking over the mining operations, everyday life remained somewhat tense for them. However, the general population looked upon Hayden's operation as healthy growth and steady work for those who weren't having much luck panning in the creek mud.

Hayden's partner, Austin Smith, came to the camp for abbreviated periodic visits while construction of their various buildings continued. The Smith & Hayden Mining Company office was the first, a dominating two-story frame structure loomed at the south end of Main Street overlooking the valley. Below it on the slope the silver reduction mill and smelter furnaces soon started taking shape. Other than the mining engineers imported from other operations around the country, the mining tycoons were careful to employ only the local labor force and to use locally cut lumber for construction. Paydays were regular and honest; some laborers were building homes; and some were spending their wages in the saloons and gambling halls and brothels. So far, William Hayden hadn't lied to Silas Patch.

Smith & Hayden Mining continued to influence the development of the camp. When the mining operations proved to be quite successful, their bank—which they called the "Silver Spring Bank," to denote the unstoppable flow of silver from their mines—appeared on South Main Street. The population seemed to like the name; certainly it was more appealing than Dog Patch. Without showing any disrespect to its first permanent resident and merchant, Silas Patch, people began referring to their settlement—which by that time had grown to a population of nearly a thousand—as Silver Spring. In a very short time, the name Dog Patch had become extinct.

Now that the town had an official name, a post office was in order; once again, William Hayden and Austin Smith influenced the Postal Service to establish the Silver Spring Post Office, and as not to appear too domineering, they suggested it to be housed in the general store belonging to Silas Patch located just across the thoroughfare from the bank. A contract was awarded to the Wilson Stagecoach Line to haul the mails to and from Silver Spring.

But the most astounding accomplishment came the following year. Because of its remoteness, the town would have remained without the services of a railroad, even if the many prospector mines continued to be active and prosperous. Austin Smith was from Minneapolis and in close acquaintance with the prominent railroad men; with its place firmly established on the map, and with a large mining company like Smith & Hayden ensuring the town's development into a large city, there was good reason to build a spur line from Red Hawk that lay on the main road linking the central continent and the west coast. With the railroad also came the telegraph; Silver Spring was no longer isolated from the rest of the world.

Adding a means of convenient passenger and freight conveyance, Silver Spring continued to mature. More people came to stay and to work; more business places evolved; and more drifters came and went, too. The town, with its twenty-odd saloons and gambling joints was becoming quite well-known among the gunslingers and professional gamblers. Naturally, an environment such as this didn't exist without an occasional confrontation.

Griffin arrived by stagecoach on a hot July late afternoon. He had managed to escape the long arm of lawmen in Kansas—the Earps—after a shootout over a card game that left an innocent cowhand dead; and for a similar incident in the Dakota Territory, Sheriff Seth Bullock had run him out of Deadwood before vigilantes had their way with a lynching. And now he was in Silver Spring after a week on a river steamer that landed him in

Wellington. Seeing that he was already drunk, Wesley Dawson, the Wilson Stage driver, warned him to behave himself on the seven-mile journey to Silver Spring. The warning should have been repeated when he arrived. He found his way into the gambling hall at the Royal after visiting two or three saloons for refreshments he didn't need. He headed for the faro table and immediately recognized the dealer, Dan Flanagan. Hired just a few weeks earlier by Silas Patch, Flanagan came from Denver, an able faro dealer, and a pistol-packing gambler with a reputation. He was good at settling disputes in the hall; Patch valued his presence.

But Griffin had an axe to grind: Flanagan had beaten him in a high stakes game at a Denver casino. Griffin had accused Dan of cheating, and had it not been for a by-stander who hustled Griffin out of that Denver parlor, the confrontation might have ended in bloodshed on a Denver street. Now, in Silver Spring, too much alcohol had given Griffin a little too much courage. Intending to settle an old score, he pulled out a revolver. After an exchange of words he challenged Flanagan, calling him out into the street with the statement that he was going to kill him. Flanagan calmly rose from his seat, and headed for the front door while the entire crowd watched silently in awe.

Out in the thoroughfare, Flanagan warned his adversary: "You don't want to do this, Griffin... you lost fare and square in Denver, and you'll lose here too."

Without heed, Griffin produced his revolver again and fired four shots in rapid succession toward Flanagan, none of which found their mark. In the next instant, before Griffin could get off another shot, Flanagan drew a pistol from inside his waistcoat and fired once. It happened so quickly that onlookers hardly had a notion that Flanagan had even fired the fatal shot that put Griffin down. A few moments of silence went by; unscathed, Flanagan left others to look after the corpse while he returned to the interrupted faro game. Of all the witnesses present, no one suggested that he had done wrong.

Silver Spring was, indeed, still without law. With men like Griffin roaming about, even to Silas Patch it was becoming evident that a constable of some sort was necessary. There was no telling when the next Griffin would appear, or if there would be the good fortune of a Flanagan to defend against him.

Silas sent a messenger to The Striker office. He wanted a private meeting with Grumby. When the newspaperman arrived, Silas presented his proposal: "You know every businessman in this town better than anyone."

"Yes, I suppose that I do," Grumby replied.

"You talk to them regularly."

"I've spoken with every one of them in regards to placing advertisements in The Striker."

"And I've noticed that you've had a great deal of success with that."

"Dispensing advertisement in exchange for monetary gain is what keeps my newspaper in business."

"How successful do you think you could be to get all those businessmen to contribute—monthly, let's say—to a fund for paying the wages of a constable?"

"A constable?" Such a suggestion from Silas Patch came as a surprise.

"Yeah… you know… a marshal, someone to keep the peace. Someone to keep an eye open for trouble like we had with that Griffin fellow the other night."

Grumby thought a long moment. "Well… I don't know… I guess it's possible."

"We could establish an association," Silas suggested. "Each member to contribute a few dollars a month for protection against guys like Griffin."

"Then, I suppose we'd run an advertisement to get applicants for the position."

"That won't be necessary," Silas said. "I already have the man for the job."

"And who would that be?" Grumby asked.

"Dan Flanagan. He's fit, handy with a gun, and he can smell trouble before it comes in the door. He's perfect for the job. He's already proved himself capable, and he already has the stamp of approval from half the people in Silver Spring."

Silas was right on all counts; he knew the man. Tall and sturdy, Dan Flanagan was a man of confidence and quick with a gun. His gambling experience had taught him to be cool-headed; he'd been in enough scrapes himself to know the necessary points of the law, and his mild-mannered composure ensured levelheaded remedy to any situation. He *was* suited for Silver Spring Marshal.

Grumby's eyes lit up; he saw news in the making. A marshal in this town could provide front-page headlines for every Striker issue. There would certainly be confrontations on the streets, investigations, arrests, incarcerations...

"I will convey your proposition to all the business proprietors expeditiously," he told Silas. "I'm certain they will all favor such an institution."

And so the first official business of Silver Spring had been carried out. Grumby had no difficulty in procuring subscriptions to the "association" as everyone was in favor of bringing some sort of law and order to their town, and no one dared voice objection to Dan Flanagan's appointment as Town Marshal, the first official city employee. Most were aware of his reputation as a gambler and a gunfighter, but somehow that seemed to better enhance his qualifications.

My Journal—Clancy Crane

My fifth year of school is coming to a end. I went to school back in Ohio too. I learned to read and write there so I was way ahead of some kids here. I like the school marm in Silver Spring. Her name is Ellie May Tundle but of course we must call her Mrs. Tundle. She also runs the book store in town and her husband Stuart Tundle is a grocer. Millie and Kate buy a lot of food things at Mr. Tundles store right next to Tinys stashunary store which is next to Julians Hardware store on Main street. They have become good frends with Mrs. Tundle too so I can't get away with any mischif at school. But Mrs. Tundle likes me too. She lets be borow books from her book store if I promise not to damage them or get them dirty. Her book store is next to the bakery with the big glass windows in front on Flatrock street just 2 blocks from the schoolhouse so I walk with her sometimes after school when she opens the store and I can look at all the books. Sometimes other people come in and she won't give me a book then so I pay her the dime if I find one I like...

... The carrage house is almost finished and I will be glad when we can move away from the dead line. Mr. Grumby said the house we live in down there is ment for miners. He has about 20 of them all alike small and not fancy. Of course Millie and Kate fixed ours up with rugs on the floor and curtens on the windows and fernicher and other nice things they brought with them from Ohio. Daniel and Kate were going to move into the carrage house with us too but now that Daniel has a good job with the stagecoach line he is building his own house in a nice naborhood not far from our hotel so Kate won't have so far to walk to visit Millie whenever she gets lonely...

... Now we have moved into our carrage house and I have my own rooms upstairs where Daniel and Kate would have lived if they came with us. But they have their own house now too so I can have their space all to myself. Mrs. Tundle and Kate come calling most every morning to visit with Millie after Mr. Tundle goes to open the grocery store. They have biscits and tea and then Mrs. Tundle helps me with my spelling because she knows I am always writing in my journal just like Millie does. So my spelling should get better now.

Just about every day a load of bricks arrives on the train. Jeremiah is building the hotel with bricks instead of wood says it cost more but it will be worth it in the long run. The hotel is huge bigger than any other in town. It will be called

Tanglewood Lodge. Millie thought up that name said it fit on account of the tangled woods that was there before. She is worried about taking care of such a big hotel with so many rooms but Jeremiah keeps on telling her that she will have plenty of help with maids and cooks and porters to do all the work...

... I could tell that Millie was not always feeling well and Kate and Mrs. Tundle was fussing over her all the time. Then one day Mrs. Tundle let it slip out during my spelling lesson that Millie was going to have a baby...

A town like Silver Spring would never have seemed dull, but without the likes of Simon Bordeaux, it *wouldn't* have had the flair of show business. When he stepped off the train, he looked like any other city dandy seeking some frontier adventure in his red satin vest and gloves, black silk top hat, the heavy gold watch chain, and the gold-headed walking stick. A certain sort of sophistication stood him apart from all the others. Not only was Simon Bordeaux a great showman; he was a shrewd businessman as well. But his sensational appearance was soon lost to the crowd clamoring about in search of misplaced luggage and gone astray children.

He was there on a mission of discovery; he had heard of Silver Spring's continued prosperity and his experience told him that a mining town where the only forms of entertainment were gambling halls, billiard parlors and saloons was an opportune location for an opera house. Everybody enjoyed a stage show—even miners—and Silver Spring had plenty of them.

In a town that had already been influenced by metropolitan social standards via the influx of new residents from various big cities, Simon Bordeaux was soon recognized as someone of importance, or at least, someone with high values in social circles; his elegant apparel suggested it; the manner in which he walked down the street suggested it. At every opportunity he would make it be known his purpose for coming to Silver Spring, that he was seeking accommodations for a theater and to bring cultural entertainment to the town.

Leaving his luggage secured with the station clerk to be picked up later, Simon began his walking journey into town from the depot. He stopped at a diner just past the coal yard on Flatrock Street for a beefsteak and potatoes. Abe Slokum, the proprietor and only attendant in the shabby, dismal little restaurant wasn't much for talking, but when asked for directions to the busiest part of town, Abe pointed down the alley toward the Market Square. To Abe, that *was* the busy part of town because most of his patrons came from there. But a livery stable, feed store, harness shop, general store and butcher weren't exactly what Simon Bordeaux had in mind. He saw a good amount of foot traffic was flowing to and from the street leading west from the square, and from the west end of Market Street he viewed the very busy thoroughfare, however, a casual stroll down Lincoln Street with noisy Chinatown looming on his right, he feared that he had been badly misinformed about the town. It was certainly lively, and it may be prosperous, but he had his doubts about its intellectual and cultural development. Simon ducked into the Lincoln House Hotel, seeking some sort of safe haven, as it appeared more civil—an oasis misplaced in this pit of iniquity. The lobby of the Lincoln House, so far, was the nearest comparison with civilization to which he was accustomed, sparingly Victorian in style but lacking in proper housekeeping and posh.

Behind the desk was a tall, thin woman about forty-five with rough-hewn features and bitter expression of disillusionment. Stella Stover had discovered that the hero she married long ago was nothing more than a drunken liability, although Warren Stover masqueraded well as a successful businessman. For six years Mrs. Stover had earned their living by running the hotel, supporting the bad habits of flamboyant Mr. Stover who had long ago lost his good looks and virility. She did a good job of it, but her character did not make her a soft and sympathetic woman.

Simon approached the desk. "Madam," he said. "Would there

be any rooms available in your fine establishment for a gentleman such as myself? I have just arrived via the train."

"We're full up," Mrs. Stover responded dryly. "But you might try the Royal... Patch's place is bigger... he might have a room."

"And where might I find the Royal? It's a hotel, I presume?"

"Yeah, it's a hotel... fancy gamblin' joint... over on Main... across the thoroughfare from the freight barn."

Simon squeezed out a little smile. Perhaps, he thought, he may have underestimated the town a little too hastily. He looked to the front window, wondering about the safest route to his new destination.

Mrs. Stover read the confusion in his eyes. She pointed in the direction from where he had come. "Go up to Market Street, turn right... go across the Square and you come to Main... up one block... can't miss it."

Simon Bordeaux gave a gentlemanly bow. "Thank you, madam. You have been most helpful."

With a new sense of hope, he proceeded to the Lincoln's barroom where he ordered a shot of bourbon, something to calm his nerves for the next leg of his journey. He gently tossed fifty cents on the bar, and then vigorously tossed the bourbon down his throat.

He exited the Lincoln House and wasted no time on the walk back to the Market Square. Unimaginable was the thought of ever lingering on that street. As he crossed the square and approached Main, he began to feel the magical transformation from slum, to the working class, to metropolis. Main Street had the character of a pleasantly bustling city, albeit only a few blocks long. He saw a maze of clattering horse-drawn drays and crowds of people on the sidewalks. The street was lined with a bazaar of shops, cafés, stores, warehouses and saloons. It roared with an air of ranches and mines and sawmills and energetic business. It seemed a wonderful, incredibly busy place. To his right he passed the Continental Hotel with its saloon and billiard hall; just beyond was the Silver Spring Bank, and then the lumber yard. He realized then that he must have misunderstood the madam at the Lincoln House, as there were only small stores and shops across the thoroughfare, no freight barn, and no big, "fancy gamblin' joint" named the Royal Hotel. He crossed the muddy street to return up Main past a large general store, a pleasant-looking little pub, and in the next block, the Silver Ingot Restaurant that he wished he had encountered earlier, another saloon with a pitiful piano player, and then the Freight Warehouse. There it was; he stopped and peered across the thoroughfare at the imposing, large establishment, occupying nearly half the block, natural wood siding, dark green window frames, and matching rail around an upper verandah supported by pillars of the same green. Two seductively-clad, attractive ladies, their faces rouged and their clothes exaggeratedly fashionable, one in blue and one in red, paraded back and forth on the verandah below, enticing potential customers to come inside the Royal. It appeared that not many *needed* much persuasion.

Simon shaded his eyes from the afternoon sun with one hand and gazed up at the unusual tower atop the Royal, and the well-dressed man *in* the tower gazing back at him. The man leaned out the open tower window and called out to Simon: "You appear to be lost. May I be of assistance?"

Simon could barely hear the man's voice over the noise of horse hooves and buggy wheels. "I say, my good man... I have just arrived via the train and I am seeking some lodging. Are you the proprietor of that establishment?"

"Silas Patch, at your service, sir. I will be happy to accommodate you." Silas had a way of spotting wealth when it walked down the street, and in this case, it wasn't difficult to spot. He would *make* room, if necessary.

Once inside, Simon was immediately intercepted by a voluptuous creature in a scanty black dress, with big blond hair and smiling white teeth surrounded by very red lips. "Hi, handsome," she giggled flirtatiously. "Welcome to the Royal. You must be new in town. My name is Bonnie. What kind of game would you like me to escort you to? Poker? Blackjack? Faro?" Or maybe Roulette or Craps?"

Anyone else might stumble over his lower jaw with such contact so abruptly; however, Simon was in show business—he was used to show girls and their flaunty conduct and exposed cleavage. Although Bonnie was an eyeful and a half, he did not stutter or stammer; his composure did not falter. "Actually, my dear Bonnie," he said calmly. "I am here seeking lodging and I would like to see the man I just briefly spoke with... the man in the tower." He pointed upward.

"Oh! You must mean the Guardian Angel, Silas Patch."

"Mr. Patch. Yes. That's him."

"Well, I don't know if he's available right at the moment, but I'll see if I can find him for you—"

"That won't be necessary, Bonnie," Silas's mellow but strong voice said as he appeared from among a throng of people bustling about. He held out his right hand toward Simon. "Silas Patch, owner of the Royal Hotel."

"Simon Bordeaux, Showman, Entrepreneur," he returned with a firm handshake.

Silas turned to the maiden. "That will be all for now, Bonnie," he said with a wink. "I believe Mr. Bordeaux would like to relax in his room after that long, tiring train ride. Perhaps you can bring him a bottle of bourbon to his room later."

Bonnie tilted her head to one side, returned a sensual smile, winked, and kissed the air in Bordeaux's direction before she departed in obedience to her employer.

Simon tipped his derby in a grateful but admonishing reply.

The hotel owner directed his utmost attention to his potential new guest. "I just happen to have one of my best rooms available, Mr. Bordeaux. It's upstairs on the quiet side of the hotel overlooking Flatrock Street. Very comfortable. Would you care to see it before you decide?"

"Thank you, Mr. Patch, but that won't be necessary. I trust your judgment. I will take the room."

"And how long will you be staying with us?"

"For an undetermined length of time, I must say at present. You see, I am here in search of some property to purchase... a building suitable for housing an opera theater... preferably on this main thoroughfare, in the heart of the vibrant activity that I feel in the magnificent atmosphere of this metropolis."

"An opera house! Well, you're *standing* in the heart of the most vibrant activity, Mr. Bordeaux," Silas replied with a bit of humorous sarcasm. "But I'm sorry to say, my place isn't for sale."

Simon received the remark graciously. "Oh, I wouldn't think of disturbing your activity, my friend," he said with a smile. "But tell me; how did you know that I would prefer bourbon?"

"I know a man of good taste, Mr. Bordeaux. It's something you learn in this business, I guess." He guided Simon to the registration desk. "Now, if you would care to sign the guest register, I will be honored to show you to your room, and I will send word to Oliver Grumby—our reliable property agent *and* the editor of the local newspaper—that you might desire his services."

"Yes, indeed," replied Bordeaux. "However, my luggage remains at the rail depot, and I'm afraid daylight might be of the essence, and I should want to retrieve them before darkness—"

"Don't worry about your luggage. I'll send my messenger over there to pick it up. He has a little buggy to haul it in... no sense in you wearing yourself out lugging suitcases all that way."

"Actually," Simon said grimly. "It's a very large trunk and two valises."

"No matter," Silas replied, waving his hand as to dismiss the thought of it being any bother. "Christian will handle it."

"Thank you, Mr. Patch. And *Christian* shall be generously remunerated."

My Journal—Clancy Crane

After we moved away from the dead line I ain't any closer to the livery barn but I don't have to walk by China Town any more to get there. A man named Brook runs the livery. He's a rough sort to look at but he's kind and gentle with the horses. People who don't have their own barn or travelers that stay at the hotels leave their teams or riding ponies with Brook and he takes good care of them. I go there whenever I get the chance to hear one of his stories. Millie don't understand why I spend so much time there now that we have our horses at our own stable by the carriage house. There ain't many boys my age that live close by so I go visit Brook. Sometimes I walk down Connor street to the railroad stashun and then down Railroad Alley past the Wilson Stage Lines office and cut across the wood and coal yard to the barn. And sometimes I walk down Main street where it is really busy most every day. Just a block down Main from where Jeremiah is building his big hotel is Gilmores Hardware store at the corner where Pine street goes to the water tank by the train stashun. Jeremiah gets a lot of things for building the hotel from Gilmore. It's a big square building with Big glass windows on 2 sides facing Pine street and Main street that let it the sun light and everything in there sparkles. Mr. and Mrs. Gilmore live upstairs. Then 4 stores down from Gilmores is Toms Boots and Shoes where I got a new pair of boots last fall just before school started. That store is painted green with white trim around one big window in front. Next to that Tom has his shoe repair shop on the corner. Tom lives in the back rooms of the repair shop. Then I cross Flatrock street and there's the Royal Hotel and saloon. It takes up half the block and there's always a crowd of people there. I guess the guy that owns it was the first to come here he started a general store and sold wisky and tools to the prospectors. Now he has this big hotel with a saloon inside and there's always a lot of fancy women around flirtin with the gentlemen customers. He still has his general store too a couple of blocks down on the other side of the thorofare and that's where the Silver Spring Post office is. His wife must not want anything to do with his business because the only time I ever see her she's out on the upstairs balcony watering her flower boxes. She must stay up there all the time that's where they live. Next to the Royal is Tundles grocery store where Millie and Kate go to buy food. Mr. and Mrs. Tundle live in a nice little house behind the store across the alley. Next to that is Tinys stashunary shop. Tiny is a big fat man I think it is funny that he is called Tiny. Then there is Julians Hardware store painted gray and one big window and on the corner at Market street is the Silver Pick Saloon. Sometimes I see my brother Daniel go in there it is his favorit place to go for a beer and to play cards. Around the corner on Market street is another shoe store and a clothing store and a bakery. That's where the market square starts. On market days the big lot is full of farmers with wagons full of everything from potatos to crabapples. Brooks Livery is just across the square. Of all the store owners I have met I like Brook the best. He lives in a little room in the front of the barn and just inside the big front barn door he keeps a wooden bench and table where he sits and reads and drinks coffee when there's nothing else to do. Brook is a ruff and tuff old guy his face is rinkled and brown from the sun. He tells me stories about when he was in the US cavalry or when he was a wagon master hauling frate on the high plains. He has fought Indians and road agents and run off cattle russlers. I have learned a lot from him. I like old Brook.

Room number fifteen in the back corner of the Royal's upper floor was indeed quiet, away from the boisterous barroom babble and away from the clattery of buggies and wagons on the main thoroughfare. And indeed, it was comfortable, just as Silas had described, appointed with carpet, sofa, soft armchair, and a four-post feather bed. The room was one that Silas reserved for *special* guests.

Simon Bordeaux went to the wash stand, poured some water from the pitcher into the wash basin and then swabbed his face and hands with a wash cloth. His first afternoon in Silver Spring had been quite an arduous experience; the cool water felt refreshing.

A knock came at the door. Upon opening, Simon's eyes fell upon Bonnie in all her radiance holding a brown bottle and two glasses. "This is our best Kentucky Bourbon," she said with a rosy smile. "Compliments of Mr. Patch."

"Well, thank you, my dear Bonnie," Simon replied as he took the bottle and glasses from her. "And be sure to thank Mr. Patch for me, as well."

"Is there anything else you would like?" Bonnie asked suggestively.

"Oh, no… not right now, my dear. I'm very tired from my journey, and I'm waiting for Christian to bring me my luggage from the depot."

"All right, then," she said, turned and strutted down the hall.

At that moment, Simon was thankful that she had not been persistent. He closed the door, set the two glasses on the table, uncorked the bottle and poured himself a drink. The bourbon was smooth as silk as it soothingly slid down his throat. He poured another and stepped over to the window overlooking Flatrock Street. There he recognized his large blue trunk on a low-slung, rickshaw type cart pulled by a sandy-haired young man in a white ruffled shirt. A few minutes later he heard the trunk make a thud as it hit the floor and a knock sounded on his door.

"Mr. Bordeaux?" the young man said as Simon opened the door.

"Yes, you are quite right. And you must be Christian."

"I am," said the young man as he struggled to regain the heavy trunk. "Your other two bags are downstairs; I'll bring them up, too. Where would you like your trunk, sir?"

"At the foot of the bed would be fine."

Christian placed the trunk as directed and quickly disappeared out the door, only to return within a minute with the other two satchels.

"That's quite an ingenious cart you have," Simon said when he entered again.

"Yes, thank you, sir," Christian panted. "I had Gus, the wagon builder make it for me. It saves trips to the depot and makes my job a lot easier."

"Indeed, it must," Simon replied. "But you still must be exhausted, toting that heavy luggage of mine. Would you care for a shot of very fine Kentucky Bourbon?"

"Thank you, sir. Yes, I would like that."

Simon poured him a drink. He eyed the handsome young man with curious pleasure, seeing in Christian the charisma of an actor. "It's sad to see such a fine-looking lad such as you going to waste on menial labor," he said as he handed over the glass.

"What do you mean, sir? I rather enjoy what I do, and Mr. Patch pays me quite well." Christian sipped from the glass.

"I'm sure he does. But have you ever performed on a stage?"

The question hit Christian unaware. "Well... yes, sir... once... a long time ago... in Denver. I played the part of Romeo in Romeo and Juliet."

"The lead! And why did you stop? Was the show not a success?"

"Oh, it was a great success, but after the performance, the producer skipped town with all the proceeds. None of the actors got paid as promised."

"Why, that scoundrel!" Simon raved in a theatrical tone. "I could never do such a thing! How much did he owe you?"

"About fifty dollars, I think."

"That's terrible! And I suppose that one bad experience would prevent you from ever wanting to perform again?"

"I don't know, Mr. Bordeaux," Christian replied. "I would have to give it some thought." He downed the rest of his drink and set the glass on the table.

"As you should. But I am going to build a theater, here in Silver Spring, Christian... and I assure you, that if you should decide to give it a try again, you will not be denied any just compensation." Simon put two silver dollars in Christian's hand as they walked to the door.

"Thank you, Mr. Bordeaux," Christian smiled. "That's more than generous of you."

"You are quite welcome... and feel free to visit me any time, Christian. And do consider giving the theater another chance."

Not long after Christian left smiling, another knock sounded at the door. Simon wondered if he would ever be allowed to relax for the evening. This time, it was a stranger that darkened his doorway.

"Mr. Bordeaux?" the man asked.

"Yes?" Simon was surprised at how many people in this town already knew him by name.

"Sorry to bother you at this hour," the visitor apologized. "My name is Oliver Grumby… editor of The Striker. Silas sent word to me that you are interested in securing some property in Silver Spring."

"Yes, I am," Bordeaux returned. "But I'm not interested in placing any advertisements in your newspaper just yet."

"That's not what I'm here for, Mr. Bordeaux. I am also the agent for available real estate."

"Oh… well that's different. Please. Come in. Mr. Patch did mention you earlier."

They sat down at the small table. Simon poured two glasses of bourbon. "I apologize for the rude reception," said Simon. "I'm rather tired from a long journey, and it has been a rather exhausting afternoon."

"I can fully appreciate that," Grumby replied. "I won't take up much of your time, but I wanted to let you know that I am always eager to be of assistance."

"That is quite apparent, Mr. Grumby. Tell me, what buildings are available that might be suitable for a theater?"

"Hmmm… there *is* a large, vacant store building on Lincoln… next to the North Star Hotel."

"Did you say Lincoln?" The thoroughfare on which the Lincoln House stands?"

"Yes, sir."

"Out of the question. I will pitch a tent out on the prairie before I will place a respectable opera house on that disgusting boulevard."

"But it's a very nice building, Mr. Bordeaux—"

"I don't care if it's Buckingham Palace. I will not locate my theater on the Lincoln thoroughfare."

"You have been there?"

"Yes. I was misdirected there this afternoon, and I felt fortunate to escape with my life."

"I see… well, there is only one other possibility that I can think of at the moment, but it is only a warehouse… not very attractive."

"All the better. Less to remove in the refurbishing process. Where is this warehouse?"

"Across the thoroughfare from this hotel, sir. The proprietor of the freight company is constructing another facility close to the railroad depot, as this location is not suitable anymore for loading and unloading wagons, being right in the busiest part of town."

"The freight warehouse? Across the street?"

"Yes, Mr. Bordeaux."

"Perfect! When can I see the interior?"

"I can arrange for your inspection tour of the premises tomorrow."

When the din of Silver Spring's night life had faded, Simon Bordeaux had long since drifted into a sound, comfortable sleep. He did not have to witness first-hand the stamina of that night life, for he could faintly hear through his open windows that the people of Silver Spring endured long into the night.

The next morning while he, among others, was enjoying his breakfast in the now much quieter Royal saloon, where side pork, biscuits, coffee and canned fruit had replaced whiskey bottles and beer mugs, Simon was joined by Mr. Grumby.

At a nearby table, the sale of a gold claim was taking place: five hundred dollars would secure a few acres of land surrounding a trickle of a stream. Odds were that it would become the humble beginning of a small farm, once the unsuspecting new-comer discovered the claim to be worthless in terms of gold.

"I have arranged it with Mr. Franklin," Grumby informed. "He will suspend his endeavors at the new building site promptly at ten o'clock this morning to meet with us. He is prepared to negotiate."

My Journal—Clancy Crane

My brother's hotel is the biggest in the town. I've heard folks say that it's the best too. And that's just the way he planned it—the best of everything. He didn't do it just to out-do everybody else and all those other places. He did it because he just wanted to provide the very best service to his customers. Now that the hotel is running great guns, I'm busy most of the time doing all sorts of things to help out. Every day at 3 o'clock I have our team hitched to a fine carriage waiting at the train station. That's when the passenger train arrives, and there is always somebody and their baggage to bring to the hotel. Some days if I get there early or if the train is running late I see Christian there too waiting to escort customers to the Royal Hotel downtown. He doesn't have a carriage but he has a little cart that he hauls the luggage on. He's a nice fellow and we've become friends. But his boss Mr. Patch and my brother Jeremiah aren't such good friends. I mean — they wouldn't have a shoot-out in the street or anything like that, but they are competitors in business, so they are not likely to have morning coffee together on a regular schedule.

Jeremiah and me are on our own now running the hotel because Millie has a little one to look after. She named her daughter Clair. She is a beautiful little girl.

Mrs. Tundle comes to call on Millie every morning for tea and biscuits just as always and just as always she gives me my spelling lessons. Last week she gave me a dictionary from her book store so now I shouldn't ever spell any words wrong.

Every day I still go to visit Brook at the Livery. I got my eye on a young stallion in his corral. He says the hoss is an outlaw been running with wild mustangs but he has a brand and has been broke but he won't let anybody ride him. He comes to me though and lets me pet him and I talk to him and I think he is starting to like me. Some day Brook said he might let me try to ride him.

Charlie Daggett is a farmer that I see on market days he sells potatoes and green beans that I always get for the hotel kitchen. Today he asked me if I would be interested in helping him at his placer mine. He will pay me 10 percent of what we take out of the mine. He goes to his claim only on weekends and does his farm work the rest of the week. I hope Jeremiah will allow it so I can earn enough money to buy that stallion from Brook.

When the Crane brothers, Jeremiah and Daniel, had arrived in Silver Spring with their wives, Millie and Kate, and their recently orphaned little brother— for whom Jeremiah had felt obligated to provide care, and had no regrets in doing so—they were among the many who came there looking for new beginnings. Although they didn't have their sights set on prospecting, Silver Spring seemed to call to them—at least it did to Jeremiah—as the land of new opportunity, a place to make a life of grandeur. He had seen, in the past, the flyers announcing great business opportunities in the prospering and growing mining camp, as he and his wife, Millie, owned and operated a small road house in Ohio. In time, he had convinced Millie to make the move, sold the inn, and headed to Silver Spring. By then, Clancy was in his charge, and he convinced his other brother, Daniel, to accompany them, as well, if for no other reason, to separate him from the less-than-honorable friends and ways onto which he had fallen. Kate, Daniel's wife, was less in favor of the journey, fond of the comfortable lifestyle to which she had grown accustomed. But she had finally given in when Daniel sternly informed her that they were going.

It hadn't been an easy start, arriving at a time when the camp had progressed to a lively and thriving town, far from the primitive settlement it had once been. Available commercial property on which to build was quite limited, and available housing was practically nonexistent. Living in their wagons by a creek outside of town, Jeremiah never gave up hope, and in due time, he came into acquaintance with the right people. Mr. Grumby offered him a large plot of land, albeit away from the busy main thoroughfare, undesirable to other prospective businessmen, and then introduced him to banker William Hayden. The simpatico match provided Jeremiah his desired start, although at first the proposal put before him seemed more of a challenge than he had anticipated. William Hayden, also a partner in Smith and Hayden Mining, recognized the need for a grand hotel in Silver Spring, and his bid of financing such a project appealed to Jeremiah. There were, however, stipulations: the proposed lodge had to be the largest and with the finest appointments to meet the needs and comforts of visitors and travelers; it had to provide the best food and drink, and the most amiable atmosphere possible.

The parcel of land would be perfect—away from the noisy district of night life and disruptive conditions for pleasant, restful accommodations, yet readily accessible from the railroad depot, and within a reasonable walking distance to shops and stores.

Jeremiah accepted the conditions of the proposal, and the project was soon under way. Announcements of the new hotel facility in The Striker weekly newspaper stirred the attention of many, and to some, it appeared an objectionable threat as daunting competition in certain areas of endeavor. Silas Patch was among the first to call on Jeremiah when it appeared that the future hotel project had not diminished from its original design. Dressed in his very best suit, he approached Jeremiah in a cordial manner as not to reflect intimidation, but at the same time to imply his prominence in the community.

Jeremiah had already been made aware of Silas Patch—that he practically ran all of Silver Spring, not as an official governmental leader, but as its influential guardian, seeing to it that all standards met his approval and that they did not interfere with his enterprise. As to the morality of the situation, Jeremiah was concerned, but he knew also that the only course was to accept it.

All during the summer months, Silas conducted much of his business from the verandah overhanging Main Street. It was a few degrees cooler there than in his office rooms. He was only occasionally interrupted by the necessity of going downstairs to settle some disorder that he felt too insignificant to bring to the attention of Marshal Flanagan, and he rarely left his domain, except for special occasions such as a visit to the new hotel proprietor.

"Silas Patch, owner of the Royal Hotel," he introduced himself at the building site of the mammoth new structure. By then, the carriage house and stable had been completed and occupied, and the outer brick shell of the lodge was nearing completion; bricklayers were putting the final touches to their work, making way for the carpenters to begin the next stage of construction.

"Yes, Mr. Patch. I am Jeremiah Crane. My brother and I were in your establishment several times when we first arrived."

"Yes, I seem to remember," Patch said. "I see you have done a marvelous job of clearing this unsightly piece of ground that no one wanted."

"Thank you, sir. It was a lot of work, but I think it will be worth it."

"I trust that Mr. Grumby has informed you of the Businessmen's Association."

"He did, Mr. Patch. He informed me that I will be required to pay two dollars a month for police protection, and another two dollars a month for the sanitation men who clean up horse droppings from the streets."

"And you have no objection to that?"

"Certainly not. Why would I object to safe and clean streets?"

"Good. Now, about our mutual interests in business..."

Jeremiah suspected the conversation would come to this, and he was determined to stand his ground, prepared with honest answers to whatever questions might arise, without any alarming offense.

"What about women?" Silas asked.

"If you're talking about prostitutes, Mr. Patch, there will be none here. My wife would never approve of such business."

"Okay... what about gambling? Will you offer any games?"

"Some, but on a much smaller scale than your place, Mr. Patch."

"I see... and what about liquor prices?"

"I will sell drinks at the going rates... same as every place in town, including yours. And I will serve quality food in our dining room at fair and reasonable prices. Mr. Patch, you needn't be concerned with my trying to take your business away from you. I am here to run an honest and respectable hotel as a much needed addition to the town. I see no reason to intrude into your territory, and it would be greatly appreciated that you did not intrude into mine."

A bit stunned by Crane's bold stance, Patch retreated. "Very well, then," he said as if he were still in command of the forum. "I believe we are in harmony and that there should be no conflicting issues between us."

Jeremiah smiled ever so slightly. "None."

"Good day, then... and good luck." Silas Patch returned to his Main Street domain.

Across town, young Clancy was experiencing yet another kind of encounter. A boy doesn't explore a new town the same way an adult does. He absorbs it as he goes along, and makes friends in the process. He doesn't have to be introduced. He meets boys and other people in various ways, and sorts them all out without even thinking about it. That's how it happened that Clancy Crane and Brook came to be such good friends, despite their drastic age difference, like an uncle that Clancy had never known. Because Brook's Livery had been chosen to stable their horses, merely as a common sense business transaction between Brook and the older

Crane brothers, it became Clancy's daily duty to look after the stock, just to be sure they were cared for properly. His routine visits soon became fond moments in Brook's day. The gruff old codger had never married so he didn't have children of his own, and rarely ever gave a second look to any of them. But he took a liking to Clancy. The boy had little fear of strangers; he possessed a sixth sense that steered him away from those who posed possible danger. Likewise, it allowed him to be drawn closer to those who meant him no harm, only friendship, and Brook was one of the latter.

"You told me once that you run off a gang of cattle rustlers," Clancy said to Brook. The boy was leaned over with elbows on the table and chin resting in cupped hands, eyes fixed on the livery man sipping his coffee. "Tell me 'bout it?"

"Well sir," Brook began. He loved telling of his past adventures to the boy, and he knew the boy loved hearing them. "There was this friend of mine... name was Klem. Now Klem was a good hand... but not above holdin' up a stage or two if things looked right. He knew all the boys on the outlaw trail, and he worked for Harry Talon, too.

"Harry Talon ran a ranch down south and he was havin' rustler trouble. Klem went to him one day and suggested that he had some friends who could handle the rustler problem. Harry knew they was outlaws, but they was good cowhands too. They needed a place to lay low for a while, and Harry needed help with his rustler problem, so he took them on.

"Well," Brook went on. "I was one of 'em. We just rode out to that rustler hide out and laid down the law... told 'em that the Talon place was friendly to us and we'd take it most unthoughtful if any more cattle showed up missing.

"Well... them rustlers didn't take so kindly to us tellin' 'em their business. A couple of 'em started for their side arms, but before they even had their palms on the grips they were lookin' down the wrong end of a dozen gun barrels.

"Them rustlers was small potatoes, and they must've decided right then and there that they didn't want to have nothin' to do with the kind of shootin' we would do, so they laid off... and from that day on there was no more rustlin' of Talon's stock."

Clancy's eyes were as big as the top of Brook's coffee mug.

"You mean... you were an *outlaw* then?"

"Mostly," Brook said, "we was rambunctious cow hands who'd got into trouble by some brainless shecoonery. My first holdup was when I was seventeen; a bunch of us figured it would be smart to stop a train and pick up some drinkin' money.

"Well, we done it. We made the conductor give us twenty dollars. We rode off and was willing to leave it at that. Then some wise jasper sticks his head out a car window and lets loose with a pistol. None of us had figured on that, and all of a sudden it wasn't fun anymore. We shot back but I don't think we hit nobody, but I had to ride the outlaw trail for quite some time after that, 'cause I figured that feller'd seen me."

"Wow," Clancy exclaimed. "What kinda gun did you have?"

"Pearl-handled Colt revolvers... a pair of 'em."

"Still got 'em?"

"Nope... lost 'em in a poker game. Guess that's why I don't never go to none of them gamblin' joints. Don't want to lose nothin' else precious."

"What kinda horse did you ride then? I bet he was fast."

"I had a roan... looked just about like that one you been gettin' friendly with out in my corral."

A young boy can easily change his focus onto a different subject, and Clancy was no exception. "Oh, yeah... I gotta go talk to him now." He ran out to the corral board fence and leaned on the top rail, watching the horses. They stirred, shying away, all except one spirited roan stallion with black ears, black mane and tail. The horse had stopped suddenly, ears perked, and was looking right at Clancy.

"Come here boy," Clancy said softly, and the roan came... hesitated... then sidled away.

"It's all right, boy," Clancy whispered, and held out his hand toward the stallion.

The horse's nose extended, sniffing Clancy's fingers. Gradually he came nearer to get his face and neck petted.

Brook watched from a few yards away. He though back to the first time he'd seen Clancy befriend that horse—that outlaw horse that had been running among wild mustangs, brought in with several others, and discovered to have a strange brand that no one could identify, was familiar with saddle and bridle, but was unwilling to let anyone ride him. Brook had always just called him "Outlaw," but Clancy had insisted that he be called "Shiner" because the horse had a dark patch around his left eye.

Strangely enough, the horse that still had a bit of rogue left in him had found trust in the boy.

"You have a way with that hoss," Brook said.

"He's beautiful," Clancy said, and proudly added, "I think he likes me."

Clancy continued petting the animal that was thoroughly enjoying the attention. Brook just stared in total amazement.

Then Clancy turned to the livery man. "Can I ride him now, Brook? You said I could try to ride him sometime. Please?"

"You sure you know how to ride, boy?" Brook questioned.

"Of course, I'm sure. I told you... I had a pony back in Ohio... of course I can ride."

"Don't want you gettin' hurt, ya know."

"I'll be okay... please?"

Brook finally relented. "I'll get a lasso. We hafta try to get him into the barn so we can put a saddle on him." He headed into the barn and soon came back with a rope.

"I'll do it," Clancy said, and took hold of the rope. Brook reluctantly handed it over, quite certain that the boy would have little success.

Clancy climbed over the fence and boldly stood alone. "Come here, boy," he said softly, and the stallion came. Brook watched in awe as Clancy slipped the loop of the rope over the horse's head and down around its neck. With the rope in one hand and the other clutching its mane, Clancy led Shiner from the corral into the stable.

Brook carried a saddle, bridle and bit out from the tack room. "You wanna do it? Or should I?"

The horse looked at Brook, lowered his head and pressed his face into Clancy's arm.

"I think he wants you to do it," Brook said, and gave the saddle to the boy. He was testing Clancy, of course, to make sure the boy had been truthful; if he could handle the saddling, then he probably *could* ride, as he'd said.

When Clancy had finished saddling the horse, Brook stood at the ready to come to the boy's aid, should the stallion resume the mean streak he had demonstrated with others. But to his utter amazement, Shiner didn't so much as hump his back when Clancy swung himself into the saddle, but started prancing as if he was eager to give the boy a ride. At Clancy's command, Shiner stepped out of the barn and into the brightly sunlit corral, trotted gracefully around its perimeter, around the other horses that watched with little interest. Clancy coaxed the horse into a gait, and then into a slow gallop. Brook saw the broad grin on Clancy's face as he glided along on Shiner's back as if they were one.

Brook summoned the blacksmith, Buster Cartwright, from his shop next door to the livery. "Wanted you to see this, Buster," he related.

The smithy gazed into the corral. "Well, I'll be jiggered. Is that...?"

"Yup," Brook replied. "That's Outlaw... and that's the Crane kid. His brother is the one buildin' the big fancy hotel up on Connor Street."

"Well, I never saw the like," said Cartwright. He'd given that horse a set of shoes, but to his knowledge, no one had ever made use of them. He went back to his hearth and anvil shaking his head, mumbling.

When Clancy thought he should give Shiner a rest and walked him back into the stable, a stranger had wandered in—rough-looking, eyes shrewd and black, heavy-shouldered, and a shock of greasy brown hair. He looked at Brook, studied him. Brook was seated again by his table with his coffee cup, trying to ignore the stranger, it seemed to Clancy. The boy just sat on Shiner, watching, knowing that this man could be trouble.

"I know you... I've seen you before," the stranger said to Brook.

Brook merely glanced at him, then picked up an old magazine and began to leaf through it. "Don't want no trouble here," Brook said calmly, as if he recognized the man. "You should just turn around and walk away."

For an instant there was silence. Brook had spoken so casually in an ordinary tone, that for a moment his words failed to register.

"What was that you said?" the man asked belligerently.

Clancy came down from Shiner's back. He didn't know what was about to happen, but he wanted to be ready to help his friend if it came to that.

"You seem to want trouble," Brook responded. He had lowered the magazine to his lap, fidgeting with both hands. "Don't need none of that here. I politely asked you to leave."

Brook was still half reclining on the wooden bench. The rough-looking man bent over, reaching for him. Brook's left hand caught the sleeve on the reaching arm and jerked the man forward and off balance. The magazine, now rolled tight, in a flash thrust upward, catching squarely the attacker's Adam's apple. With a shove, Brook threw the man to the stable floor, where he rolled onto his back, gasping his last breaths.

"Clancy," Brook called out. "Go fetch the marshal... tell him *only* that this stranger met a most unfortunate accident in the stable."

"Are you okay, Brook?" the boy asked, shocked and afraid to come any closer.

"I'm fine," Brook said with a little anger in his voice. "Now, go get the marshal, and *don't* tell him what you saw."

Clancy fully understood what Brook meant. "Can I ride Shiner?"

"Yes! Now go!"

Clancy mounted Shiner and rode across the square. While he was away, Brook dragged the body to the doorway. A small crowd was gathered when Clancy returned, escorting Marshall Flanagan and Doc Lowery aboard the Doc's one-horse buggy.

"Does anybody know this man?" the marshal asked as he approached the body. There were no responses other than murmurs from the gawkers.

The doctor examined the body. "His Adam's apple is crushed," he said after a few minutes.

"He must've tripped and fallen head-first on that stall railing," Brook explained.

"Is that right, Doc?" Flanagan asked. "Is that what *you* think happened?"

The doctor stared at Flanagan with a perplexed scowl. "I don't know *how* it happened, Dan. How could I? All I can tell you is that his injury is consistent with that explanation... yes."

"Do you know this man, Brook?" asked the marshal.

"Never saw him before," Brook replied. "Just a cowpoke drifter lookin' t' get him a pony, I 'spect."

A couple of bystanders helped Flanagan load the body into the back of Doc's buggy. "We can deliver him to the undertaker," Doc said grimly.

"Well, that's that," Flanagan said as he watched the gathered crowd disperse. He put a hand on Brook's shoulder. "Just an unfortunate accident," he said with a wink. Then he and Doc Lowery boarded the buggy and drove off.

Brook suspected that Marshal Flanagan *might* have recognized the man, but didn't let on. After all, Dan Flanagan had once ridden the outlaw trail, as well.

"You knew that man, didn't you?" Clancy said to Brook after everyone else was out of earshot. It wasn't really a question; it was more a statement.

"His name was Riley... an outlaw... worked for a while on the Talon ranch I told you about... but Talon run him off when he tried to kill me."

"Why did he try to kill you?"

"'Cause I caught him tryin' to rape one of Talon's servant girls... kicked his butt into next week. Guess he was gonna get his revenge."

The next issue of The Striker simply stated that an unidentified stranger had accidentally met his death in Brook's Livery Stable. Since no one in the town claimed to know the man, interment officiated by the Reverend Miller was quietly carried out in an unmarked grave on the hill.

My Journal—Clancy Crane

I earned over $200 working for Charlie Daggett at his mine. Toward the last, just before Charlie took ill and couldn't do any more, we had found very little there, so I guess he was right when he said it wouldn't last forever. Not many prospectors are out in the hills and streams any more—they've all pinched out their claims and some have moved on, some work in the silver mines, some have taken up farming or some other business. I'm just glad that the silver mines are still prospering and keeping Silver Spring alive as ever. Tanglewood remains the best hotel in town, although the Royal is still the busiest gambling joint and Mr. Patch is probably the richest man in town by now, except for William Hayden who owns the silver mines.

The day I had finally earned the first $25 from Charlie was one of the happiest days of my life since we came here. It seemed like it had taken forever, although I know it was only a couple of weeks. Shiner was finally mine! I'm sure Brook would have sold him for much more to someone else, if anyone else would have wanted him. But nobody did, or at least that's what he told me. He even sold me a saddle that he said he didn't need, but I'm sure he bought another to replace it at three times the amount he charged me. At any rate, I'm thankful to Brook, and even though Shiner is in our stable at Tanglewood now, I still go to visit Brook quite often. He's still one of my best friends.

Another good friend has been Tom Hargrove, the newspaper reporter who now works for Mr. Grumby at The Striker. It seems as though Tom does most of the newspaper work these days as Mr. Grumby is quite busy brokering land and property deals. Not everybody that comes to Silver Spring stays, and a lot of property changes hands, and that's what keeps Mr. Grumby so busy. One thing for sure, Tanglewood isn't likely to change hands anytime soon. Rooms are nearly always full, the dining room has a waiting list nearly every night, and the gambling hall and barroom overflow, especially on Friday and Saturday nights when the miners get paid.

I moved back into the carriage house after I got Shiner. Millie thought it was foolish of me to want to leave the luxury of our apartment at the rear of Tanglewood. Shiner was my excuse, but I think Jeremiah understood the real reason, that I needed my own space. Now I have the freedom to come and go when I want without disturbing anybody else.

I get up quite early in the morning, before anyone. I like the early morning hours. The air is clear and crisp, and it is quiet. It's that time after the gamblers have either won or lost it all, after the whores have quit, and even the dogs have given up barking at every night sound. And it's that time before the miners tramp off to work, before the sawmill starts echoing its daily trills, and before the streets are churning the everyday racket of hooves and wagon wheels. It's that time of day when the whole world seems at peace.

Sometimes, then, I go for walks in the shadows of what still remains of the night, that darkest part of the night just before first light. Seldom is anyone stirring at that hour, or else they are stirring just like me, out of sight in the shadows.

Just a couple of mornings ago I saw Oliver sneaking about. I kept out of sight in the deepest shadow so I know he didn't see me, but he seemed to be headed somewhere with a heavy bag slung over his shoulder. He lives upstairs in a room over the Continental Billiard Parlor, and he definitely wasn't headed there. In fact, he was headed directly away from it past the Opera House. I watched him until he was out of sight from my hiding spot before I continued my exploration of my shadowy kingdom. It couldn't have been much more than five minutes later when I encountered Oliver again, but this time he was returning from wherever he had been, back to the Continental. I watched again as he disappeared into the rear entrance.

This morning, though, I sit here on the Tanglewood verandah instead of venturing out into the shadows of early morn. In a short while, I will hear the farmers' wagons coming in from the valleys and hills. They will line up in the Market Square and arrange their displays of produce, live fowl, and other goods of their own manufacture or hunt that they will offer for sale to the public. It is market day, and I will be the first there to get the pick of choicest vegetables, the freshest eggs, butter and cheeses for Tanglewood's kitchen. Jeremiah trusts me to do this well, and I never disappoint him or the fussy cooks who demand nothing but the best.

This morning while I write my observations of the past few days, I see Oliver again, darting from shadow to shadow, as if avoiding to be seen or heard. As he rounds the corner onto Connor Street I notice that he is once again carrying that burlap bag over his shoulder—it contains a heavy object. I am well concealed behind the verandah railing. He doesn't see me. Then I hear the sounds of the first wagon approaching on the road from Silver Creek Crossing. Oliver hears it too and he ducks down Washington Street, out of my sight. A minute later, the wagon passes by. It is George, the egg man. He doesn't see me either, but at sun-up, down in the Market Square, he will give me a piece of hard candy and then he'll point out the crate containing his freshest eggs.

Some days when there was little to do at Tanglewood after his daily chores were done, Clancy was free to do whatever he wanted. Jeremiah Crane was no slave driver, and he certainly didn't want Clancy to appear as his indentured servant. So the boy ventured out, seeking the world, exploring new territory, sharing the experiences with his school chums when they were able.

Joey Lowery and Eddy Swenson were the only boys in Silver Spring close to his own age that Clancy knew. There were others but they didn't attend school, and there were some farm boys and girls who were in town only when school was in session. They lived too far away and were too engaged in farm work all summer to be practical playmates.

Joey Lowery was the son of Doc Lowery who owned and operated the Drug Store on Main Street just catty-corner from the Royal Hotel. Doc's medical office was in the back room of the store, and the family lived in a modest Victorian on South Johnson Street about three blocks north from the "dead line."

Clancy saddled Shiner and rode down Main Street. He tied the stallion to the hitching rail in front of Doc Lowery's Drug Store and went inside. Doc greeted him with a smile, and then he suddenly frowned and said: "You aren't here to report another *accident* at the livery barn, are you?"

"No," Clancy replied, trying to dismiss the memory of the incident at Brook's that he would just as soon forget, but had been reminded of it by the Doc. "Just dropped by to see if Joey was here... if he was doin' anything special today. Thought maybe we could go for a ride."

"Joey's should be at the house," Doc said. "If his ma doesn't need him for chores, then I guess he could join you. But tell him I need him to go to the depot... there's an important package to be picked up."

"Okay... I'll tell him," Clancy said. He saw that there was someone waiting for the Doc at his back office, so he left.

Shiner seemed to be quite eager for a ride in the country, to break away from the noisy streets, to savor the wilderness, and so was Clancy. Even if Joey couldn't go, he was going alone. Instead of taking the back streets to Joey's house, he rode right down Main through the congestion of drays and surreys and people walking. He would stop at Patch's General Store to get some beef jerky, in case the ride turned out to be an extended one. He usually bought such items at Longhorn's on the Market Square, but the downtown was quite crowded that day, and Longhorn's would be crowded too. Patch's store was right on his way.

Clancy browsed a short while; Patch's store was about as big and well-stocked as Longhorn's. He chose three large strips of jerky from a glass jar and the clerk wrapped them in brown paper. Clancy handed the clerk twenty-five cents, stuffed the package inside his shirt, returned to Shiner and proceeded to Joey's house.

Joey had a big black dog he called Bear, a mix of Labrador and German Shepherd. Bear could be rather intimidating to strangers, and there was no mistaking that the corner lot at Johnson and Maple was *his* domain. But Joey had introduced Clancy to Bear as a friend, so Clancy was always welcomed by the protective sentry with a lick of a hand and the offer of a handshake.

Bear met Clancy and Shiner at the hitching post in front of the Lowery house, panting and excited to greet the visitors. He sniffed at Shiner's nose, and then sat on his haunches eagerly waiting for Clancy's handshake. His tail wagged briskly kicking up a cloud of dust behind him.

"Hello, Bear," Clancy said as he accepted the customary handshake from the dog. "Where's Joey?"

Bear barked and ran toward the house, as if to summon his master.

Joey came out the front door. "Hey, Clancy," he said, happy to see his friend.

"Hey, Joey. Wanna go for a ride?"

"Where to?"

"I don't care... anywhere... out in the hills somewhere."

"Sure... I'll go tell Ma I'm goin' and then I'll meet you round back at the barn... I'll get Pokey saddled and ready."

"Oh! I almost forgot," Clancy said. "Doc said he wanted you to go to the depot first to pick up a package for him... sounded important."

Joey waved in acknowledgment, disappeared into the house.

Clancy played with Bear a few minutes and then led Shiner up the pathway to the Lowery's stable. Nearly all the houses in this neighborhood had their own carriage houses and barns. Doc maintained his own buggy necessary for house calls, and his stable had stalls for two horses: the mare that so diligently attended the buggy every day in the lot behind the Drug Store, and Pokey, a painted pony that Joey loved nearly as much as Clancy loved Shiner.

"So... what direction should we go?" Joey asked when he had his mount saddled.

"To the railroad depot... to pick up that package for Doc," Clancy responded. "I don't want him mad at me for you slackin.' Then we can decide."

They rode down Maple Street to Main, and then Joey took the lead around the lumber yard and out Wilson Street to Lincoln. It wasn't the way Clancy would have gone, but he followed. At Lincoln they walked the horses through the congestion and noise of Chinatown, past the Lincoln House, past the back side of the busy Market Square, to Railroad Alley where they trotted along the board fence of Brook's Livery corral.

Shiner seemed to know where he was, and Clancy didn't know whether his sudden excited prance was to show off to his former corral mates, or his eagerness to get away from there.

Then they passed through the coal yard and by Wilson's Stage Line office and finally arrived at the depot. In the station the agent greeted them both by name and gave Joey a small express package marked "Drugs." They lingered a while, listening to the clack-clack of the telegraph instruments and then went into the freight room and weighed themselves just because the scales were there. They went out onto the station platform and peered west. Across the tracks was a ravine, and beyond that Silver Spring had not expanded, as if the tracks were a boundary line. There wasn't a house in sight, only more hills and just to the south, the valley of Silver Creek and piles of logs waiting to be sawed into lumber at the sawmill that was just barely out of sight around the slope.

Joey pointed. "You can't see from here, but about ten or fifteen miles off there are bluffs along the river, and there's a couple of old Indian caves."

"Is that where we should go today?" Clancy asked.

"Na," Joey replied. "Let's go see what Eddy's doing. Maybe we can ride out to Webb's Lake. Do you swim?"

"Not very good," Clancy said.

They walked down the tracks to the big red tank on stilts where locomotives stopped for water. A towering cottonwood, watered by the drip from the tank, shaded a small pump house that throbbed as its steam engine drove the pump. A big red-faced man in overalls who was in charge of the pumping station sat on a bench outside in the shade, watched them as they caught the icy cold drip in their open mouths. They exchanged greetings with him when they strolled past on their way back to the horses.

They delivered the package to the Drug Store.

"Let's take the back way to Eddy's," Joey suggested. "It's a nice ride."

Clancy agreed. They rode up Main to Connor, then over to the new freight warehouse and turned up the North road that arced around, behind and above Tanglewood Lodge, on the hill where the lonely graveyard was partially hidden by the forest. From there a trail wound down past the back of the cemetery, through the woods and came out on the road that led to Silver Creek Crossing, where the stagecoach took the easier route to Wellington. At that point, they were only a few blocks from Joey's house, but the detour had taken them more than a mile. A little farther down that road, another trail went up the hillside to a house so new the boards were still yellow. Eddy Swenson's father had just finished building that house last fall. He worked for Smith and Hayden Mining Company, driving one of the ore wagons between the mines and the smelter.

Eddy was tall and slender, almost to the point of looking frail. His head of ragged blond hair, fair skin and his bright blue eyes gave evidence of his Scandinavian heritage, and he even spoke with a slight Norske accent. But everyone in Silver Spring came from somewhere else, so accents didn't mean much. Eddy was quite a character, often speaking in verse as general, gladiator, great explorer, or safari hunter, perhaps to make up for his slight build, to cover up his lack of physical greatness.

He, too, had a dog, a mutt of so many different breeds, it was difficult to determine the dominant blood line of the yellow critter he called Duke.

Clancy thought maybe he should get a dog, too, but then common sense made him realize that a dog might not be the best thing to have around the hotel.

They found Eddy beside the house, stooped down, weeding a

hardy garden patch, fenced to keep out the rabbits. Duke lay beside him, raised his head to inspect the visitors. "Aren't you done with that yet?" Joey called out to him.

Eddy straightened up with a haughty, superior expression. "Watch thy manners, Pilgrim. Let not thy tongue play viper." Then he grinned a silly grin and squinted his bright blue eyes nearly shut. "What you been doing?"

"Errands... and inspecting the camp. We thought of riding over to Webb's Lake. Wanna go along?"

"Ah! I shall join the expedition." Eddy pointed theatrically with a stiff right arm toward the east and shaded his eyes from the bright sun with his left. "We shall blaze a trail through the wilderness... we shall ascend the highest summit... we shall conquer the unknown. Pause there, fellow comrades, while I make ready my trusty steed." He darted for the barn as Clancy and Joey exchanged smiles.

"While you do that," Joey called out, "I'm going back to town to get Bear. He'd like a good outing, too." Then he turned to Clancy. "I'm only ten minutes there and back. It'll take him longer than that to saddle his *trusty steed."*

"Okay," replied Clancy. "I'll wait here."

By the time Joey returned with Bear loping along beside him, Eddy had brought out the tired old mare that was kept primarily as a buggy horse for transporting the family to church on Sunday and a trip to the General Store now and then. Molly occasionally served the purpose, though, for a light rider like Eddy as well. She couldn't run fast or far, but she was still sure-footed on the trail.

When Mrs. Swenson heard the plans of a trail ride, she insisted on making some sandwiches for the boys to take along. They were placed in a flour sack and tied to Eddy's saddle horn.

Three boys on horses and two dogs trotted off into the hills. It was only mid-morning and the night's coolness still hung in the air, especially in the hollows. They followed no road and as they slipped down into the shaded Silver Creek valley it was like easing into a cool stream. But the hilltops were already warming up and they knew that by noon it would be a blazing hot day. The clear blue sky was bigger than the ocean and the fragrance of yellow loosestrife was in the air.

On the high ground the meadow larks sang. By then they had

stuffed themselves with beetles and grasshoppers, and now they perched, their bright yellow chests with ink black Vs, their heads pointed up, and they seemed to be putting their very hearts into song.

About three miles into their slow, lazy journey, the dogs kicked up the first jack rabbit and went yelping after it, not in the spirit of catching a rabbit; they just wanted the world to know they were chasing one. The rabbit sprinted ahead as Bear and Duke used more breath barking than running, but they kept at it. Nearly fifteen minutes later, they came back to rejoin the boys, panting and thoroughly pleased with themselves. They had been outdistanced in the first five minutes, but the very act of chasing a rabbit was self-gratifying, as if a major accomplishment.

Another half mile, in a ravine about two hundred yards up from the rocky creek, they came onto an abandoned shack. Its bare boards were weathered to a silver-gray, only a few shreds of tar paper left on its low-pitched roof, not even a sliver of glass in its two windows, and its battered door hung half open on one rusted hinge. The yard around it was littered with rusted tin cans, broken dishes, and small shards of broken brown glass bottles that sparkled in the sunlight. They poked around in the discarded junk, looking for clues about the long ago vanished occupant, but found nothing of any value.

"Old prospector's shanty," Joey said. The previous summer he had found the rusted remains of a Smith & Wesson revolver at a similar site, but here, only a rusted pocket knife with half its bone handle missing and a broken blade. They pushed past the sagging door to look inside. Only the remnants of a mattress lay in one corner, robbed of its stuffing by mice, and a faded calendar dated 1879 still tacked on one wall.

Outside, the dogs had scared out another cottontail and were giving only a token chase. The boys returned to the horses and went on, knowing Bear and Duke would catch up when they tired of the futile pursuit.

Five miles from their starting point, where the high bluffs and rugged slopes had diminished to rolling hills carpeted with buffalo grass, Joey and his painted pony led the others; at the top of a rise, they overlooked a wide valley. Webb's Lake lay before them, about five acres in size. This was a catch basin for spring melt and summer downpours, and now its surface shimmered in the hot sun, but by summer's end, it would be nothing more than a bed of dry, caked mud. Its banks were pocked with the hoof prints of cattle, for it was the watering hole for the livestock that grazed the whole area.

They walked the horses to the edge so they could drink, dismounted and sat on a high, dry bank. The sun was hot on their heads and the buffalo grass soft to their bottoms. Across the little lake, two herons waded among the reeds, and a few mallards paddled about. The horses whinnied in delight of the cool treat; the herons froze momentarily, watching them, and then went about their business of hunting frogs.

"I'm hungry," Eddy said, and he retrieved the sack of sandwiches from Molly's saddle horn, and Clancy got his canteen from Shiner. They sat on the bank eating the cheese sandwiches, and then Clancy shared his beef jerky with the others when the dogs finally arrived, poking cold noses to necks and nearly knocking the boys down in rejoice of the rendezvous. Then they went splashing into the water, lapping noisily with their tongues as if they hadn't drunk in a week.

The herons, frightened by the ruckus, took flight in a low, wide circle around the lake.

"Hark!" Eddy announced. "The great majestic beasts take wing into the wide expanse of the universe, seeking new horizons."

The horses had wandered higher on the bank and were nibbling at the tall grass, when Bear and Duke, sopping wet and dripping mud galloped back to the boys, got as close as they could, and shook water and mud in all directions. Clancy and Joey saw it coming, flopped down on their bellies and covered their faces. Eddy, though, was less alert to the imminent disaster, still watching the flight of the herons. He called the dogs every name he could think of as he wiped the dirty water from his face. Joey and Clancy laughed; they collected the horses, mounted Shiner and Pokey, and led Molly to Eddy. "Come on," Joey said. "Let's start back for home."

My Journal—Clancy Crane

Tanglewood is always a busy place. But that's what Jeremiah wanted and that's what he got. When he first talked about his plans to Millie and me—how Mr. Hayden had insisted the hotel had to "meet certain standards" in order for him to loan the money to build it—I was quite certain that all I would ever do for the rest of my life was sweep floors, empty slop buckets, and wash dishes. But life hasn't been that way for me at all. Oh, I keep busy, all right, but there are maids to do all the cleaning and cooks and cook's helpers to handle all the kitchen work. Sometimes when it's really busy, I help clear off dirty dishes in the dining room and set the tables for more people to eat. The dining room is behind the big main front hall. It's a fair-sized room with low ceilings and lit by four hanging oil lamps with crystal glass shades. Along one wall is a large table with ten chairs. The rest of the room is filled with ten smaller tables and four chairs each. That's 50 place settings. That's a lot of dishes.

The main front hall is where the barroom is, and the gambling tables and the piano and dance floor. We have the best piano player around. His name is Alexander Malone, but we call him "Fingers" because he can tickle the ivories better than anybody in the whole town. He starts playing most every day at 3 o'clock. That's when the passenger train arrives and his music draws a lot of people in. He has told me about the days when he played for vaudeville acts in New York, and sometimes he roamed all over the East to accompany famous singers, and he even traveled with a circus for a couple of seasons. But then he wanted to settle down somewhere, said he was tired of tramping all over the country. He came here, struck up a deal with Jeremiah and he's been here ever since.

Jeremiah spends most of his time there in the main hall taking care of business. He has a little office room behind the bar, and he spends a good share of his time tending bar so he's always close to his office. Sometimes he wants me to help him there, refilling whiskey and brandy bottles from the kegs down in the cool cellar and lugging them up to the bar, or washing and polishing drink glasses when he doesn't have enough time.

But most of the time, I have other things to do, such as taking care of the stable, feeding the horses, maintaining the carriage, and such. If I don't have enough room in the stable for a guest's team or mount, I see to it that the animals are boarded at Brook's Livery. Most days I hitch our horses to the carriage and drive to the train depot to pick up guests and their luggage. Tanglewood Lodge is the only hotel in town that does that, and maybe that's *why we're so busy all the time. And on market days, Jeremiah trusts me to buy all the fresh produce for the cooks. They give me their list the night before. Then I get up really early in the morning and go to the market square so they don't have to be gone during the busy breakfast time.*

Yesterday morning before dawn I walked down Washington Street on my way to see if there was a light at Tom's house. Sometimes he's up early too. That's when I saw Oliver again, toting his burlap bag past the Flower shop heading out Flatrock. When I got to the corner he was in front of the Butcher shop at the next corner. By the time I got there, Oliver was already past the Lamp Store. It was too dark to see him after that.

Simon Bordeaux had created a fabulous, ornately appointed theater from that nondescript barn of a warehouse. Over the course of a few years the Crystal Palace Opera House had become more luxurious than anyone would have ever imagined, and Simon knew that it was certainly destined for greatness, as it was his best creation yet. Even the finest opera houses of the east had little better to offer.

The Crystal Palace had become a very popular place with regular presentations of every type: operas, Shakespeare and Dickens plays, musical concerts, variety shows—entertainment to please and stimulate nearly everyone. On the day of a performance, all through the afternoon the excitement mounted in the hotels, saloons and stores of Silver Spring. It could hardly be said that there were in the prospective audience many real lovers of opera or classical music. The more experienced ones familiar with the opera went with expectations of seeing great performers; but most people went because it was a "show" and because it offered a kind of romance in a place where that particular kind of romance was scarce. There were many who had never seen anything more elaborate in the way of a "show" other than the performances put on by the men who sold Swamproot and other cure-all snake oil remedies, or the itinerant preachers with their one-night tent revival meetings down by the creek.

But now there would be a week-long break in the Crystal Palace schedule to accommodate a circus. Simon had engaged the event and arranged for the use of the large open field on the south end of town between Birch Street and the row of miners' houses on South Street. That area had been left undeveloped because every spring it became a marsh with snow melt and early rains. But by mid-summer it dried up, and the grassland was grazed by city cows and horses, so it wasn't really considered wasteland. And it would be perfect for a circus.

The Cole Circus arrived via its special train on Wednesday morning just as the dawn was breaking. The engine rolled to a stop and sighed with a loud hiss of steam. Men hopped down and immediately began the task of unloading and moving to the lot. Horses were led from the cars and wagons were pulled off the flats and onto Railroad Alley. The men worked smoothly, quickly, efficiently, as if they had done this a thousand times, and more than likely they had.

Soon there was a steady stream of people and horses and wagons loaded with canvas and poles toward the lot where the advance men, the day before, had measured and put stakes to mark the location of every tent and wagon. Burly hammer gangs went to work rolling out and anchoring the massive sheets of canvas that would become the tent city. Elephants pulled the center poles into place and dragged the canvas up until the Big Top was an immense brown shell. People with nothing better to do watched in total awe as the tent city rose up from that empty pasture, transforming the weed-covered lot into a carnival of lights, music, games, and displays of ferocious beasts from foreign lands.

There was to be a parade of all the wagons carrying exotic animals and the performers as sort of a preview to instill the interest and curiosity of the town's people. And elephants! No one in Silver Spring—except for Alexander Malone—had ever seen real live elephants! The Striker had run several previous announcements and printed hand bills that were tacked up all over town. A new experience for Silver Spring, the circus promised excitement and thrills for all. By ten o'clock Wednesday morning, the parade route was lined solid with spectators anxious to get their first glimpse of something so spectacular.

Joey Lowery and Eddy Swenson had come to Tanglewood and were directed out to the stable where they found Clancy; Clancy took a break from his usual chores—as almost everyone in Silver Spring had—and with his friends they ran to Doc Lowery's Drug Store. They were just in time to claim a space on the corner where the parade would turn from Flatrock onto Main; they had a front row view, and they weren't going to miss a thing. From across the street, perched on the Royal Hotel's upper balcony, Christian waved and called out to Clancy. He was among several of Silas Patch's guests, there for a bird's eye viewing.

At eleven o'clock, after all the equipment was unloaded from the rail cars and lined up along Railroad Alley, the procession began its way up Flatrock, heralded by the echo of a brass band blaring out a lively fanfare and the clop of horse's hooves.

First came riders, impressively uniformed men shouting greetings and announcing: "The elephants are coming!" Then came the ringmaster in his flamboyant, long-tailed, red Prince Albert coat, silk top hat, shiny gloves and boutonniere, driving matched horses that danced along, merely toying with the high-wheeled buggy. Banner and flag bearers and buglers, all mounted on spirited white horses came next, flags flying and trumpets glistening in the sun. Then a string of ten horses two abreast with red, white and blue plumes over their heads pulled the gigantic bandwagon, the driver astride the last horse. The bandwagon was a rainbow of color, ornately carved and with sunburst wheels, and on it were twenty or more uniformed musicians playing at a volume the whole town could hear.

There were bright and gaudy wagons pulled by teams of high-stepping Clydesdales. Mysterious, majestic creatures lay in the wagon-sized cages, peering out at the crowd, visible just enough to cause curious cheers. Some wagons carried groups of circus performers clad in flashy outfits, waving and smiling, encouraging everyone to witness the forthcoming extravaganza. Clowns walked along, displaying silly antics, some nearly hidden in huge clusters of balloons.

And finally came the elephants—four of them—trunk to tail, with ornate blankets draped over their backs and fringed crowns on their heads, drawing the most enthusiastic cheers, for their oddity was nothing but awesome.

Bringing up the rear was the calliope, singing out a joyous invitation to follow the parade and visit the circus soon to start.

The procession found its way down Main and at Birch Street it turned as directed and populated the tented space. This and the next three days were going to be incredibly spectacular!

Among those who followed along with easy strides to where the tents were erected, nearly ready for the opening evening performances were Clancy Crane, Joey Lowery, and Eddy Swenson. They could hear the noise and music from several blocks away; there seemed to be merriment everywhere, and the day was charged with a different kind of excitement that Silver Spring had ever known.

Near the entrance they came upon the first calliope they had ever seen or heard—the one that had been part of the parade. They lingered a while listening to the music they would forever associate with the circus, until they saw a man with a waxed mustache mount a small platform. He wore a derby hat; white cuffs protruded from the sleeves of his dazzling blue jacket. He held a gold-headed cane which he twirled and pointed.

"La-deez and gen-tul-men!" He began his spiel in a clear, crisp voice that penetrated the grounds. "If you will give me your attention for just a moment... welcome to our collection of the most outstanding attractions ever assembled in one place, brought to your fair city by that master showman, Mister William Washington Cole." He pointed with his cane to a big canvas square hanging behind him that pictured Dora, the fat lady, considerably larger than life size. Surrounding the fat lady were paintings of a strong man, a fire eater, an armless man writing with a pen grasped between his toes, a bearded woman, and a goat with two heads. Entwined among them all was a green and blue serpent with red eyes and breathing flames.

"Let me assure you, la-deez and gen-tul-men, that every attraction is exactly as represented... many exhibits await you, and you have ample time to see them all before the first spectacular show in the Big Top begins."

Clancy, Joey, and Eddy strolled up and down the midway, their eyes and ears absorbing this vast, extraordinary picture. Surrounding the entire area now were carriages and wagons and saddled horses that had delivered loads of curious adults and excited children; the hum of the crowd blended with the music and the attraction barkers to form a great, confused symphony of noise. In the air were the odors of fresh sawdust, lemonade, fried onions, tobacco smoke and licorice, plus the smell of wild animals and horse manure. They watched young bucks try their skill and strength at the games and people lining up to view the various displays of oddity.

It was nearly three o'clock. "I have to get back," Clancy told the others. "The train will arrive soon and I have to get the team hitched to the carriage." There would likely be several trips to and from the depot that day to accommodate the many people arriving to attend the circus. But he would return that evening for the trapeze and tight rope acts in the Big Top.

My Journal—Clancy Crane

Jeremiah gives me plenty of time off to do the things I want to do, says he doesn't want folks to think I'm his slave. Oh, he pays me to work at Tanglewood a dollar a day. That's not as much as most folks make here in Silver Spring. This town and everybody in it is quite wealthy, some more than others. But Jeremiah keeps reminding me that I am still just a kid, and someday when I finish school I'll have a business of my own and I will make more money then. The good thing for me now is that I have time to explore and meet other people.

Yesterday I saw my good friend Tom the newspaper man and he invited me to see the newspaper office and presses and all that goes on in the printing shop. The Striker is the only building on that side of Johnson Street between Flatrock and Oak. It's a long low building with a porch roof across the whole front and a big window on each side of the front door to let in plenty of light. On the wall above the porch roof is a painted sign that says Striker News & Printing. It's one of the few places around town where there are trees.

I could see a rack of type cases through the window, and when we went in I sniffed the odors of a print shop—paper, ink, lye, benzene, and the oily smell of the printing presses. The whole inside was one big low ceiling room. Opposite the door was a big roll top desk with a clutter of letters, paper, and scribbled notes. In the middle of the room was what Tom called the composing stone. It was a thick slab of marble polished like a mirror about three feet wide and six feet long set like a table top on a cabinet of drawers. On it were metal frames that the type was locked into and put on the press. In the far corner sat two printing presses, one big and one small. In the other corner was a big paper cutter and an open paper cabinet. Across the other end was a long wooden table with various tools and supplies. That was Tom's printing shop. And that's where I was the first to see the hand bills he had just printed for Simon Bordeaux to advertise the circus that was coming to town. He paid me $2 to help him tack them up all around town. It was great fun to watch in our wake the crowds of people that gathered around to read the signs after we left each one tacked to a store wall or on a fence board. By the end of the day we had put up about a hundred of them, and I could hardly wait to see lions and tigers and elephants.

Having traveled to and performed in Europe, Asia, and Australia, the Cole Circus was a rather prestigious organization, quite self-sufficient, and extremely professional in its manner of operation. By noon, the camp was assembled and the Big Top and two dozen other smaller tents were erected with absolute precision. Although numerous other preparations continued on through the night by a diligent crew, most of the performers and animals were comfortably bedded down after the show in their temporary canvas quarters as routinely as a family in a permanent house.

The Cole Circus drew large crowds of people together wherever it went; naturally, in its shadow traveled any number of sneak thieves and pick-pockets capable of fleecing the crowd of its valuables and disappearing before anyone was aware of what had happened.

"I've lost my pocketbook" was the cry heard frequently among the crowd, and then it became apparent that it was being heard *much too frequently* to be a common occurrence. It was brought to Marshal Flanagan's attention before the end of the next day; he quickly enlisted a half-dozen deputies to patrol the circus grounds, and he mingled with the crowd, too, keeping a watchful eye. Their efforts reduced the "lost pocketbook" problem, but it left the streets of Silver Spring wide open for larger endeavors.

As Clancy Crane and Joey Lowery walked down Main Street Saturday morning, on their way to meet Eddy Swenson, and then take in the last lion tamer act at the Big Top, they came across a man—a stranger—standing in front of Patch's General Store. There were a lot of strangers in town during the circus, but what was so unusual about this stranger was that he stood there just staring across the street. Clancy and Joey looked, curious as to what had captured the man's attention to such an intense degree. They saw nothing; just the bank and a few pedestrians. But the stranger's stare didn't seem to be focused on anyone walking. To the boys, his behavior seemed rather odd, but they were keener to the circus tents and the adventure in store for them there.

They could hear the circus band playing vigorously in the Big Top as they entered the grounds, and when the boys got in line to buy their tickets, Clancy noticed a familiar head of sandy-colored hair a little ways in front of him.

"Christian?" he called out.

The head turned to look. Christian gave a big smile, and then relinquished his spot in line to join his friend.

Like Clancy, Christian had not lived in Silver Spring all his life, so he, too, learned as he went along. Working for Silas Patch had given him an edge; he had become callous to the all too frequent bloodshed, the bawdy activity of the whores, the drunken behavior in the bars and gambling halls, conditioned to handle almost anything that came along. Although Christian was not above having a little sip of liquor now and then, Silas knew he probably wasn't capable of pointing a gun or drawing a blade, and he never expected Christian to be the remedy for some raucous act requiring forceful discipline.

Christian loved music, and he loved watching performers on stage—any kind of performers. He had not missed a single show since the opening of the Crystal Palace Theater; the sights and the sounds and the smells of the circus offered a different variety, but it was a show, just the same, and he was thoroughly enjoying it.

They marveled at the dancing elephants and the acrobats riding the sleek white horses galloping around the ring; they laughed at the comical clowns; they cheered with delight for the jugglers; and like everyone else in the audience, Joey and Eddy were at the edge of their seats holding their breath as the lion and tiger tamer coaxed his wild beasts to sit obediently in a row and wave to the crowd. Clancy, though, was quite certain the lions and tigers were probably as tame as house cats and were merely trained to act ferocious; it was still an impressive sight.

All during these grand finale performances, Christian was clearly attuned to the lively music and its perfect timing with the acts in the ring. Clancy noticed. He leaned toward Christian. "Have you ever heard our piano player, Fingers Malone?"

"I've heard about him," Christian replied. "But I've never heard him play."

"You should come to Tanglewood sometime. You'll like Fingers."

"Yeah," Joey chimed in. "He's a great piano player. He's so good… I've heard that Simon Bordeaux has been trying to steal him away from Tanglewood… wants him to work at the opera house."

"Think he'll do it?" Christian asked.

"I don't think so," Clancy replied. "Fingers likes where he is."

"Well, your Mr. Malone isn't the only one Simon has been trying to steal."

"Really? Who else?"

"Me."

Clancy threw Christian a startled look.

"He found out that I've performed on stage before, and he's been after me ever since I brought his luggage to his room from the depot."

Just then a clown act brought the circus to its official conclusion. Everyone stood and cheered wildly as the Ringmaster announced a final farewell and all the performers gathered in the ring to wave their farewells. The cheering continued while the spectators filed out of the Big Top, and by then most of the midway attractions had been dismantled. Workmen were busy loading all the gear into wagons, and everyone knew it was over. Clancy was saddened to think it had ended, but what a joy the last few days had been. Now all that was left was the departure parade back to the railroad depot.

"Let's walk along with the bandwagon in the parade," Christian suggested with a great deal of enthusiasm.

"Let's not," Eddy responded.

"Why? Don't you like music?"

"Of course, I possess a fondness for fine arts… but we must forge on, ahead of the column, to a place near its final destination, so that we might embrace and enjoy the entire procession."

"What he means," Joey added with a big smile, "Is that we want to see the whole parade."

"Okay," Clancy said. "I'll walk with Christian. We'll meet you at the corner by the drug store when we get there."

It seemed an agreeable arrangement, so Joey and Eddy followed the crowd up the street while Clancy and Christian waited for the musicians to get situated on the wagon.

The bandwagon drawn by six prancing Percheron horses was nearly at the head of the procession. Excitement filled the street as throngs of people lined up on the sidewalks to get one last look at the most spectacular show ever to perform in Silver Spring. It would soon be over, and soon the town would be back to its usual self, and everyone wanted their money's worth.

As the circus parade started up Main Street, Christian and Clancy kept pace with the bandwagon among many others who were enjoying the lively tunes. When they approached Patch's General Store, Clancy noticed three men crossing the street toward the bank. One of them was the unusual fellow he had seen that morning standing and staring so oddly. Clancy watched the men as they lingered a short time in front of the bank, and then two went inside and one stepped out of sight into the alley beside the building.

The passing parade had drawn the interest of one of the bank cashiers to the front door, leaving Jack Gilmore alone behind the counter. William Hayden was in his private office in the back behind a closed door. A lull in depositors entering the bank during the parade allowed Jack to talk to a stranger who had just come in wanting assistance at the teller's counter. He engaged in conversation with the smartly dressed gentleman wishing to exchange a one-hundred-dollar note for some smaller denominations. Since there seemed to be some question as to the doubtful appearance of his note, the conversation went on at length, demanding Jack's full attention in protecting the bank's best interest, the stranger being quite insistent that the note was legitimate.

With his back to his own desk and the rest of the cashier's area, Jack didn't notice when the second man who had entered with the stranger crouched down on hands and knees. He crawled around the far end of the counter and to the desk where Jack had been preparing stacks of greenbacks for deposit into the safe. Sweeping the desk clean of four thousand dollars in cash, he wrapped the money in a red handkerchief, proceeded to the back door and disappeared out into the alley. When the stranger arguing with Jack saw that his partner had escaped safely, he gave up trying to defend the validity of his note and left, disappearing into the crowd on the street.

When the parade reached the corner where it made its turn toward the railroad depot, Clancy and Christian joined Joey and Eddy on the sidewalk. They were watching wagons with the lions and tigers pass when Clancy saw the three men again, this time appearing to be in quite a hurry. Something seemed rather strange about their movement as they darted down an alley away from the rest of the crowd.

My Journal—Clancy Crane

Of all the things I have seen in Silver Spring, the week that the Circus came to town has been most exciting. I got my first ever look at lions and tigers and elephants. The beat of the circus never stopped — there seemed to always be something happening on that lot. All afternoon and into the night barkers sang out luring people into the side shows and games. Every afternoon and night the Big Top thundered music and excitement with the fantastic shows — the wild animals, the clowns, the acrobats on fast and beautiful horses, the tightrope walkers and the flying trapeze acts —even a man shot from a cannon!

I had never imagined all those spectacular things! And when there weren't any shows, after the crowds had left, all night long there were workers doing all sorts of chores, picking up trash, tightening tent ropes, caring for the animals, and I even saw one fellow painting a wagon at 4 o'clock in the morning. That was just before I saw Oliver toting his burlap sack through the churchyard on Johnson Street and up to Flatrock. I stayed in the shadows so he didn't see me.

A really good thing happened for me during the circus. Christian and I have become much better friends. The time we spent together watching the shows and wandering around the circus grounds looking at all the wild creatures and all the strange people, and tagging along with the band wagon in the parade, I have learned what a kind and wonderful person Christian is. He works for Silas Patch at the Royal Hotel doing the same kind of things I do every day so I suppose we have plenty in common that way. His hotel, though, is more of a saloon and gambling hall, and of course the whores, so there aren't as many rooms for travelers like Tanglewood. Our restaurant serves ten times more meals, but the Royal serves ten times more liquor. So instead of going to the Market Square as often as I do to pick up eggs and fresh vegetables, Christian goes to the cellar to fill whiskey bottles. But I know that Christian wants to be an actor, to perform on stage in front of big audiences. He's a good singer too. He told me that once in a while he sings songs in the variety shows at the Royal, but their piano player isn't very good, and someday he wants to perform at the Crystal Palace. Simon Bordeaux wants him to join the theater group, and he probably will someday, but I think part of Christian likes the job at the Royal, likes the rough crowd, likes the excitement. I have invited him to come to Tanglewood some night to hear our piano player Fingers Malone and maybe sing a song or two. I hope he will come. I really like Christian. He is a good friend.

The excitement of the week didn't end with the Circus. Three men robbed the Silver Spring Bank while everyone was busy watching the Circus Parade. Poor Mr. Gilmore. He felt so bad that he had not realized what was happening when that stranger kept him busy while his partner sneaked behind the counter and took all that money. And it was a lucky thing that I saw those three men cross the street by the bank and then again later when they were in a hurry to get away. I told Marshal Flanagan about it, and then he knew just who he was looking for.

There was no one else in the bank, so Jack Gilmore came from behind the teller's counter and stepped over to the front window to view a portion of the circus parade. Jeffery Winslow, the other cashier was just entering through the front door and acknowledged Jack's presence at the window. By that time, most of the procession had passed, so both men returned to their posts. Jack was suddenly reminded of his previous task and was a bit confused when he saw his desk cleared of the bundled bills he had prepared for deposit in the safe. Thinking that he may have placed the money in the cashier's drawer and forgotten, he asked Jeffery to check the drawer. The four thousand dollars was not there. It wasn't anywhere. Jack was certain that he had not opened the safe.

Mr. Hayden's office door was still closed; he had shown no interest in the circus parade. Jack knocked and entered. "Mr. Hayden," he said in distress.

"What is it, Gilmore?" the bank president said.

"I think we've been robbed!"

William Hayden and his two officers discussed the circumstances briefly and came to a rapid conclusion that it seemed almost impossible for anyone to steal that much money and walk out of the bank unnoticed when there had been cashiers present the whole time.

"Winslow," Hayden said in a demanding tone. "Go find Marshal Flanagan... right away!"

"Yes, sir. I'll look for him."

The last of the parade had passed, but there were still a lot of people lingering on Main Street. Jeffery wove his way through the crowd, every now and then asking someone he recognized if they had seen the marshal. With little success in his inquiries he continued the search. Finally, he spotted Flanagan at the corner of Main and Flatrock Streets talking to young Clancy Crane. "The last I saw them," he heard the boy say, "they were in a big hurry, and they ducked down the alley behind Tom's Boot Repair Shop."

Flanagan gazed in the direction where Clancy was pointing.

"Marshal!" Jeffery interrupted. Then he discreetly leaned in close to Flanagan and stated quietly as to not cause alarm to other people nearby, "The bank has been robbed!"

"When?" Flanagan asked.

"Just a little while ago... during the parade."

"How many were there? Did they hold you up at gunpoint?"

"No... no guns... and we didn't even see them."

The marshal turned to Clancy once again. "Where did you say you first saw those men?"

"Crossing the street by the bank... just as the parade started. Me and Christian were walking with the bandwagon."

Flanagan thought for a long moment. From the description of the men that Clancy had given him, he had a good idea who they were. "Sly" Black and "Red" Morrison were a couple of sophisticated and slippery thieves who usually worked together; about the third man he was unsure.

"Chances are they'll hide out and then try to get on the afternoon train," Marshal Flanagan said. "I'll alert my deputies to start a thorough search. Meantime, Jeffery, go back to the bank. I'll be there in a little while."

After Jeffery Winslow had taken his leave, Dan Flanagan asked Clancy to show him where he had last seen the three men. They pushed their way through the crowd down Flatrock Street to the alley behind Tom's Boot Repair.

"They went up this way," Clancy said. "And they were in a big hurry."

"All three men came this way?"

"Yes, sir."

The marshal gazed around in all directions. "There's a lot of places they could have gone from here. And with so many people in town, it'll be easy for them to move around without being noticed."

"I'll get Christian," Clancy said. "We'll look for 'em too. We both saw them, so we'll know 'em when we see 'em."

"If you spot them," Marshal Flanagan warned, "Just come and find me... don't do anything foolish."

Dan Flanagan hurried off to find his deputies. He sincerely hoped that the large gathering of people on the streets would clear out now that the circus was over and was loading onto their train. Tracking down and catching up with these bank robbers could easily result in gunfire, and fewer people around meant less possibilities of innocent casualties. Dan knew two of the men from his time in Denver; Black and Morrison were big time gamblers, and they were accomplished thieves, as well. Always dressed as if they were headed to a formal ball, they didn't look the part of bank robbers, and maybe that was why they could be so successful. But Dan wasn't sure about the third man; he didn't sound familiar by Clancy Crane's description, and that bothered him—he didn't know what to expect. If Black had recruited a trigger-happy accomplice, there could be trouble.

After Flanagan had relayed the information to his deputies, he went to the bank to confirm Winslow's story, and perhaps get some more helpful clues.

"The man I talked to," explained Jack Gilmore, "Was tall, slender, narrow face and a thin, black mustache, dressed in a fine black suit and bowler."

"Sounds like Sly Black, alright," the marshal responded.

"But I never had him out of my sight," said Gilmore. "He didn't take the money from that table."

"Was anyone else with him?" asked Flanagan.

"Come to think of it... yes, there was another man who came in with him, not so tall and wearing a brown suit, I believe, but when I started talking to the man with the hundred-dollar note, I don't remember seeing that other fellow after that."

"Did you see them leave?"

"Now that you mention it, only the one I had been talking to."

Marshal Flanagan looked over the interior of the bank; noticing the position of the rear door, and considering where Jack had been standing while talking to the stranger, it seemed entirely likely that the second man could have gotten to the table with the stacks of money and then exited through that door without Jack seeing. The mysterious third man was probably standing guard outside that door during the robbery, ensuring that no one saw the exit. He couldn't have come in that way, as the door was fashioned with a spring lock that was impossible to open from the outside, even with a key.

"I know the men who robbed you," the marshal said. "My special deputies are searching the town for them right now."

"You think they're still here?" Hayden asked.

"My guess is that they'll either try to board the afternoon train, or they'll show up at one of the gambling halls tonight… probably the Royal."

"What makes you so sure?"

"It's their style… I've seen them operate before, and I've sat at the same poker table with them. If they don't try to leave town, they'll hit the Royal tonight… bigger stakes and more crowded, where they won't be noticed."

Although they might have covered more ground separately, Clancy and Christian chose to roam the streets and alleys together for the next hour, hopeful of catching a glimpse of the bank robbers. It seemed unlikely to them that fugitives who had just made off with four thousand dollars from a bank would still be within the town. But Marshal Flanagan knew these men, and he was certain their mode of transportation out of town would be the train.

Now and then they saw some of the deputies patrolling the back alleys, and now there seemed to be a growing number of citizens joining the watch. With so many strangers in town because of the circus, Clancy wondered if any of the searchers knew who they were looking for.

After a walk through Chinatown, a place where Clancy would rather not walk alone, Christian looked at his watch. "I have to go back to the Royal," he said as they crossed the Market Square. "There are some of our guests leaving on the three o'clock train, and I have to take their baggage to the depot."

Clancy looked at his watch. "Yeah, and I have to get the team hitched to the carriage. I'll see you at the station."

When the three o'clock train whistle sounded from the hills, Tanglewood guests were stepping off Clancy's carriage and making their way to the platform. Christian was there, too, his buggy fully loaded with baggage, the owners of which were quickly claiming. A large crowd had gathered around the depot to watch the circus train depart just minutes before the passenger express arrived, more people than Clancy had ever seen there. And among the crowd, he noticed the deputies and Marshal Flanagan carefully scrutinizing everyone on the loading platform. Even Sheriff Endicott from Wellington wondered about, on the lookout for suspicious characters.

As usual, the sign on Clancy's carriage—*Tanglewood Lodge*—drew the attention of prospective guests. But there were only two gentlemen.

"We'll wait a little while," Clancy told them. "There might be someone else."

The sign on Christian's baggage cart—*Royal Hotel*—however, had not drawn any attention by the time the train was pulling away from the station. "Looks like it's gonna be a quiet night for me," he said to Clancy.

"Then why don't you come to Tanglewood tonight?" Clancy asked. "Hear Fingers... and maybe you can sing a song with him."

They were both directing their attention toward the loading platform where the entire police force, including the County Sheriff, were gathered and discussing their dismal failure, so far, in capturing the bank robbers. They had closely watched the activities around the circus train as well as monitoring every passenger that boarded the express. Black and Morrison had not left by rail; Flanagan was still certain that they were still at large somewhere in Silver Spring. "We'll watch the gambling joints tonight," he told his men. "They think no one knows of their identity as the bank robbers because they got out clean, without anyone seeing them. They'll be brave enough to visit the Royal tonight."

Clancy delivered his two passengers to the front door at Tanglewood, and then drove back to the carriage house where he unharnessed the team and led the horses to the corral. He anticipated the visit by his friend that evening; Fingers Malone would surely enjoy it, too, as only on rare occasions did he perform with any other musicians.

My Journal—Clancy Crane

Marshal Flanagan still had not found the bank robbers when people started coming to the hotel for supper. Since the Circus left, the whole town got quieter and even Tanglewood wasn't real busy. All my chores were done and I had already eaten my supper when Christian came through the front door. I was so happy to see him there. He seemed quite surprised when he came in though. I guess he'd never been here before, and Tanglewood was a little classier place than the Royal Hotel where he worked. He stared quite a while at the crystal chandeliers and then the carpeted floor. Our saloon and gambling hall isn't as big as the Royal, but there were a lot of people there drinking and gambling just the same as always. Alexander "Fingers" Malone must've been taking a break just then so there was no music playing. But it wasn't long after I introduced Christian to my brother Jeremiah when the piano came to life again. Earlier I had told Fingers about Christian maybe coming and that maybe he would want to sing a song or two. Fingers thought it was a good idea, and when I asked Jeremiah if it was okay, he liked the idea too.

The next of many surprises came then as Simon Bordeaux stepped up next to us at the bar. Mr.

Bordeaux was seen quite often in our dining room and bar and gambling parlor, but this time was different. He seemed quite pleased to see Christian, and was curious about him being here. "Spying on the competition?" he asked with a little laugh. "No. My good friend Clancy invited me to come and sing a song with Mr. Malone."

That really pleased Mr. Bordeaux and he insisted on allowing him to introduce Christian to the audience when he was ready. Of course, there were many more surprises to come!

The saloons of Silver Spring, just as the saloons of any Nineteenth Century settlement, existed and thrived because they filled the basic human needs. They were places of comfort, a refuge, even a place of refinement where one could rub elbows with a fellow human being. It was where they spoke cow talk, mining talk, and timber talk. The saloons were places to expel the loneliness of a month on the range or two months at some remote diggings.

The saloon was all things to all men; besides a drinking place, it was an eatery, a hotel, a bath and comfort station, gambling den, dance hall, barber shop, social club, political center, news exchange, and theater. For the wrangler, the lumberjack, the miner, it was the portal back to society; for the drifter, it was a temporary home; for the professional gambler, it was his workplace.

Marshal Dan Flanagan was a man who thoroughly understood the saloons' many functions. Before his position as a lawman, he had lived his life depending upon them, not only for the comforts and entertainment they offered, but also for his livelihood. He had been a member of a gambling fraternity that turned to the saloons as friendly ports in a storm, where the barkeepers were watchdogs over the safety of their faithful patrons who weren't afraid to spend money on whiskey, women and games. He was familiar with the characteristics and habits of scores of gamblers, rowdies, and outlaws, for he, himself, had been one of them. But now it was his job to protect the citizens of Silver Spring against the evil deeds of such desperados like Sly Black and Red Morrison.

Flanagan stationed his deputies at strategic locations in and around the Royal Hotel's saloon and gambling hall. With his badge neatly concealed behind the lapel of his coat, Dan took his position as dealer at the Blackjack table, Sly Black's game of choice. He was quite certain that Black would show up, ready to wager large amounts from the bank heist loot, and his partner, Red Morrison would spend his night at the Roulette Wheel. All the exits were well-guarded inconspicuously; neither of them would suspect; neither of them would get out.

At the Tanglewood piano sat the dark-haired man in white shirt with black sleeve garters, a vest but no coat, and gray serge pants. His big hands and long fingers danced over the keyboard, producing a dance tune that had the whole room swaying. He bobbed up and down on the piano stool, threw his head back and laughed, seeing the enjoyment he was creating. Finally, he ended the tune with lots of runs and flourishes, and then three loud chords. He drew a deep breath as the applause and cheers washed over him, and then he saw Simon Bordeaux approaching. He'd known the showman for quite some time, and although they were on friendly terms, Alexander sincerely hoped this was not another of Simon's attempts to lure him away from Tanglewood.

"Ah, my good friend, Mr. Malone," said Simon, clapping the piano player's back. "I must commend you on your usual extraordinary performance."

"Thank you. And... how are you this evening, Mr. Bordeaux?"

"Wonderful!" replied Simon. "I come to you with a request..."

Clancy watched the two from the bar, knowing that Simon was briefing Fingers about the surprise appearance of some new talent. Then Christian appeared at their side.

"What song would you like to sing?" asked Malone.

"I know a lot of songs," replied Christian. "Can you play the accompaniment for—"

"Young man!" Malone exclaimed. "I can play any published song you can name."

"All right, then... how about... *Listen to the Mocking Bird?"*

Malone put his hands to the keyboard and played the first few bars of the melody. Christian smiled and nodded.

"Ladies and gentlemen!" Simon announced in a showy style, and everyone in the room gave him their attention. Local residents of Silver Spring were familiar with Simon's stage presence as most of them were theater goers. "It gives me great pleasure to introduce to you a special guest as your entertainment." He gestured toward the boy next to the piano and Fingers Malone began playing an arpeggio. Simon went on. "May I present to you... Christian Parker!"

Some of the people in the crowd recognized Christian and had heard him perform at the Royal variety shows. However, their low expectations were pleasantly surprised as he began singing with a pianist who actually knew the melody. His virtuous tenor voice brought many smiles as it painted the air with the beautiful song:

I'm dreaming now of Hally, sweet Hally, sweet Hally;
I'm dreaming now of Hally,
For the thought of her is one that never dies;
She's sleeping in the valley, the valley, the valley,
She's sleeping in the valley,
And the mocking bird is singing where she lies.

As Christian sang on, Clancy gazed about the hall, noticing the delightful expressions persuaded by this charming new voice. When Christian had finished the song, applause filled the hotel with cheers begging for more. The singer leaned toward the pianist and whispered, "How 'bout *The Sidewalks of New York?"* Fingers nodded, and immediately went into the introduction for the tune. Without delay, Christian sang the ballad as if he were on a Broadway stage:

Down in front of Casey's old brown wooden stoop
On a summer's evening we formed a merry group
Boys and girls together would sing and waltz
While Tony played the organ on the sidewalks of New York .

Clancy noticed more than just the smiles on the faces in the audience gathered around the musicians. Beyond the piano, at the Blackjack table, sat a tall, well-dressed man who seemed more interested in the poker game than in the music. At the Roulette table was his partner intensely studying the numbers.

"Jeremiah," he said to his brother. "See that man at the Blackjack table? The one in the fancy black suit?"

Jeremiah glanced in that direction. "Yes. He's one of our guests... checked in this afternoon just after the train arrived." He reached for the guest register book. "Here it is... his name is Sylvester Putnam."

"No," Clancy whispered. "That's not his real name."

Jeremiah threw Clancy a curious stare.

"That's one of the men who robbed the bank this morning... Marshal Flanagan says his name is Sly Black... and his partner is the fellow at the Roulette table, Red Morrison." Clancy gave his brother a quick explanation about how he knew this information. "Keep Christian singing songs," Clancy said. "I'll go find the Marshal."

Being as inconspicuous as possible, Clancy slipped out the back door and set out on a sprint toward the Royal Hotel. He knew the marshal and his deputies planned to watch the most popular gambling casino in town, anticipating Black's appearance there. But apparently, Black had outsmarted the lawmen one more time.

Nearly out of breath, Clancy scurried into the Royal.

"Hello, handsome!" a sensuous voice said to him as he entered. "I'm Bonnie... what's your hurry?"

Clancy's eyes widened at the sight of the bare-shouldered, bare-legged beauty greeting him, although he didn't hear her words clearly over all the crowd noise and the frightfully bad piano music muttering from deep within the hall.

"I... I..." he stammered, and then he darted past Bonnie. He looked up and down the long bar occupied by miners and ranchers and lumberjacks, but he saw nothing of the marshal. Somewhat intimidated in strange surroundings, Clancy cautiously approached a gap between two men at the bar, hoping to get the attention of the bartender.

In the tradition of saloons of the day, the barkeeper wore a white shirt, sleeve bands and calico cuffs. On one side of his red vest was a horseshoe diamond pin above the pocket holding a gold watch, the massive gold chain draping across his belly. On the other side of the vest were a geranium and a sprig of fern wrapped in silver paper. He sported a well-waxed handlebar mustache, hair parted in the middle, well oiled with *Lucky Tiger*. His highly respected occupation held the same social status as the lawyer, newspaper editor, or banker. He was a gentleman and a patient listener to endless problems, an impartial umpire of wagers and disputes.

"What can I do for you, young man?" he said when he noticed Clancy with elbows sprawled on the bar, propping him up taller than he really was.

"Is Marshal Flanagan in here?" Clancy whispered, a worried expression on his face.

"He is," the bartender replied, gazing out into the gambling parlor. "But he's rather busy… and he shouldn't be disturbed."

"But this is important," Clancy cried. "I really need to see him!"

"Dan is dealing Blackjack… I'll give him the message when he's free."

"But this can't wait!" Clancy could tell that the bartender wasn't going to cooperate in a timely fashion; he *had* to talk to Marshal Flanagan right away. He turned toward the gambling parlor and dashed away, scrambling through the noisy crowd of men, call girls, cigar smoke and the smell of stale beer.

After pushing his way past two Faro banks, the Roulette wheel, and a Craps table, he spotted the marshal behind a Blackjack table, no less than six men across from him engaged in a serious game. Clancy sidled up to him, knowing that he was overstepping his bounds. "Marshal!" he said in a loud whisper.

At first, Flanagan wanted to ignore the intruder; he had eleven showing in front of him, but then, with a quick glance he realized who had summoned his attention. He turned to the gamblers. "Excuse me, gentlemen, for just a moment." He turned back to Clancy. "What brings you here with such urgency?" he asked the boy.

Clancy leaned in to whisper in Flanagan's ear. "The men who robbed the bank… they're at Tanglewood."

"Are you sure?"

"Possitive."

"What are they doing?"

"Gambling. Blackjack and Roulette. Jeremiah said they checked into the hotel just after the train arrived."

Dan Flanagan ran a few quick calculations through his head. With a couple of deputies, he could easily apprehend the crooks in a surprise ambush, right at the Blackjack table. "Wait by the front door," he told Clancy. "...while I finish up here." Then he turned to the gamblers again. "Withdraw your chips, gentlemen. All bets are off. There is an urgent matter that I must attend to. Another dealer will be here shortly."

When he rejoined Clancy waiting at the door, the marshal had two deputies with him, Casey O'Rourke and Jack Coonan. Together, the four marched up Main Street toward Tanglewood.

"How many exits at the hotel?" Flanagan asked Clancy.

"Just two... front and back."

"Good. Casey, you'll cover the back door, and Jack, you'll stay at the front. I'll go in and pay Sly and Red a surprise visit."

"What d'ya want me to do?" Clancy said.

"Just stay out of the way."

Christian was just getting into another song when Dan Flanagan threaded through the crowd.

After the ball is over,
After the break of morn,
After the dancers' leaving;
After the stars are gone...

While the music kept spirits lifted, Dan kept a watchful eye on Red Morrison at the Roulette wheel as he casually walked over to the Blackjack table. He whispered something in the dealer's ear, and when the dealer rose from his seat, Dan sat down. He smiled across the table at the tall man in the fancy black suit. "Hello, Sly," he said cordially.

Sly Black gave a look of astonishment, and then returned the smile. "Well, if it isn't Dan Flanagan! What brings you here?" The two of them had been gambling rivals for a long time, but Dan Flanagan was the last person Sly Black expected to see here.

"Oh, I just came to town to do a little gamblin' a while back, and I liked the town so much I decided to stay."

"So now you're a dealer here?"

"Among other things."

"What other things?" Black quizzed.

"Oh... like making sure some people don't get out of line." Still smiling, Dan looked Black in the eyes.

Sly Black gave a nervous little twitch.

Dan picked up the deck of cards and began shuffling, as if he were preparing to start a game. "Actually," he said. "I was waiting for you to show up at the Royal... thought you'd like the bigger stakes. But we can settle our business right here instead."

"And what business would that be?"

"Well, Sly... there seems to be a little matter of a bank that got robbed here this morning..."

The other men on either side of Sly suspected some kind of trouble; they pocketed their poker chips and quickly left the table.

"Well," Sly said. "I don't know anything about that. I just arrived on the afternoon train."

Flanagan set the deck of cards on the table and casually pulled back the lapels of his coat, exposing the sparkling badge. "On the contrary," he said. "I have several eye witnesses that saw you there this morning...you and Red Morrison—"

"That's ridiculous!" Black said eyeing the badge, almost in shock.

"Is it?" the marshal said sharply. "While the circus parade was going on, you and Red went into the Silver Spring Bank. You kept the teller busy while Red slipped behind the counter, grabbed a stack of cash, and then he slipped out the back door. Then you managed to stay hid until the three o'clock express arrived, and I happen to know you *didn't* get off that train."

Christian was just finishing his song:
Many a heart is aching,
If you could read them all;
Many the hopes that have vanished
After the ball.

Both Marshal Flanagan and Sly Black stood up; Flanagan thought it appeared that the confrontation was about to end without any further trouble, and he was prepared to take the two men into custody. But the surprises and excitement weren't over; as the audience applauded Christian, Flanagan glanced to the front door, thinking he would get his deputy's attention.

That was the opening for Black. In one swift movement, while the marshal's head was turned away, he withdrew a pistol from inside his jacket, stepped over to the piano and grabbed Christian from behind in a strangle hold. Shouts and screams erupted from the astonished crowd. Christian struggled a bit, but when he realized there was a gun involved, he froze. Then Red Morrison appeared brandishing a revolver, and he, too, collared an innocent by-stander from the audience. Together, with their captives as shields, they started for the front door, a wide berth being cleared by the frightened saloon patrons. No one else was armed except the marshal, and he knew better than to draw gunfire in a crowded room.

Jeremiah shoved Clancy behind the bar, out of harm's way, and then reached for the Winchester he kept under the bar. When Red Morrison caught a glimpse of the rifle, he unleashed a deafening shot from his revolver in the bartender's direction. The bullet hit nothing but the wall, but it served its purpose in discouraging any further interference of the escape.

At the front door, Deputy Jack Coonan recognized what was happening. Although his six-gun was ready for action, there was too much danger of hitting Christian, or Jimmy Cooper, the other hostage that Morrison held. He could do nothing but let them pass.

Black and Morrison backed away from the hotel, down Main Street, Christian and Cooper stumbling along, vulnerable, held in their merciless death grips. Lights were glowing in the hardware store—Jack Gilmore's Hardware Store —where the clerk was finishing with the day's end chores, sweeping the floor and straightening the merchandise in their displays. Sly Black and Christian crashed through the front door, nearly ripping it from its hinges, Red Morrison and Jimmy Cooper following close behind. The clerk was so startled with the intrusion that he just stood silently, staring at the guns in the hands of the crooks.

"WHERE DO YOU KEEP THE GUNS?" Black yelled at the clerk.

"I... I... I don't have a gun!" responded the clerk, so scared he couldn't think. He held his hands out, open palms toward Black to prove he was unarmed.

"NO, NO!" yelled Black. "I mean where are the guns in the store? All hardware stores sell guns!"

The terrified clerk slowly pointed a shaky finger toward the far wall.

Morrison released Cooper, pushed him to stand next to the store clerk, and then hustled to close and lock the front door, all the while keeping his revolver pointed at the hostages. Releasing Christian with a shove that sent him sprawling on the floor, Black went to the gun display and pulled down a Winchester. Then he retrieved a box of ammunition from an adjacent shelf, loaded the rifle, and repeated the process with a second gun. In the next five minutes, he broke the stocks from all the remaining rifles on the wall, smashing the mechanisms, rendering the weapons inoperable, to prevent any possible retaliation.

Christian remained on the floor, watching, fearful of moving.

Out the side door, next to the store was an empty lot where stood several carriages and saddle horses tied to hitching rails. It was a convenient place where many people left their rigs or mounts while shopping in town, or in this case, enjoying the entertainment on a Saturday night. In that lot was Black's and Morrison's means of a getaway. Neither of them were expert riders, but the circumstances were pressing them to it.

Black tossed one of the loaded rifles to Morrison. "Now," he commanded. "The three of you will continue to be our protection until we get to those horses out there." He pointed to the side door and then motioned for them to go to the exit. Herding the three hostages around them, Black and Morrison cautiously maneuvered out into the lot. Twenty-five or thirty feet of open space separated them from the horses.

The lot and the street were deserted, or so it seemed. Just for a moment the robbers might have congratulated themselves on a hasty plan well made and executed. But then Morrison saw the glint of a gun in the shadows behind the Tin Shop across the street. He raised his rifle and snapped off a shot toward the shadowy figure that hit nothing but the corner of the building. Then catastrophe for the bandits struck: all three hostages saw their opportunity to run for cover, as the gunmen were quite occupied with scanning the barely lit street for more opposition. The hardware clerk made a dash back to the side door and dove behind the counter by the time Black could get off a couple of shots at him. Jimmy Cooper ran around the front corner of the hardware store toward Main Street, and Christian fled past the horses and hid in the shadows behind a carriage house next to the alley. Morrison opened fire on the fleeing hostages, but they didn't stop running and were all out of sight and out of range before he could do them any harm. In that short time the outlaws found themselves alone and unprotected.

Clancy could not bear to think of what might happen to his friend. He saw the terror in Christian's eyes, and he saw the evil glares emitting from Sly Black and Red Morrison as they drug their captives out into the street. He had seen those looks before that so many times had resulted in bloodshed.

"They're heading into the hardware store!" he heard someone say by the front door. Marshal Flanagan was busy organizing a plan of attack with his two deputies and several other men, and it seemed to Clancy that valuable time was being wasted. He darted past his brother and headed for the back door. He reached the carriage house in seconds, retrieved his Winchester Model 73 rifle, quickly loaded fifteen shells into the magazine, and then headed for the stable. There he rapidly slipped a halter over Shiner's head and swung himself onto the bare back of the animal.

"Okay, boy," he said to his horse. "We have to help Christian."

He galloped Shiner around the back of the hotel, then westward down Connor Street. He could sneak down the alley behind the Tin Shop and get to the rear of the hardware store. But just as he approached the halfway point to Pine Street, he saw the muzzle flash at the side of Gilmore's Hardware, heard the blast, and the bullet strike the wall with a splintering thud. It was too dark to see any detail, but he could see the movement in the lot where the horses were tied. Clancy knew he was too much out in the open, so he turned Shiner to the right between buildings; he could circle around and approach from the other side.

As Shiner galloped through the dark alleyways, Clancy heard more shots—at least a half-dozen. They echoed among the structures, sounding like a small-scale war, but he thought they sounded as if they were all coming from the hardware store lot. Apparently, Marshal Flanagan had arrived with his posse.

But as he came near the carriage house behind Gilmore's, all that appeared to be happening was the two bandits fumbling with rifles as they were making their way toward some rather nervous horses. No gun battle. No marshal. No posse. Yet.

"Clancy! Is that you?" he heard a frightened voice say, no more than a loud whisper.

The voice startled Shiner. He whinnied and reared up. Instinct was telling him he had entered a danger zone. Without a saddle, Clancy had all he could do to stay on Shiner's back and not drop the rifle.

"Easy, boy! Easy," he tried calming the steed. When Shiner settled, Clancy looked around in the shadows. Whoever was there had called him by name, so he assumed it was not a threat. Then Christian appeared out of the darkness.

Clancy reached down with his free hand and helped Christian swing up onto Shiner's back behind him. By then, Black and Morrison had managed to mount a couple of horses, but were having great difficulty in gaining their control.

Shiner eased ahead just enough for Clancy to have a clear shot at the crooks. He dropped the reigns as Shiner stood perfectly still, raised his gun and took careful aim. The report from his Winchester caused Shiner to sidestep, but Clancy saw one of the outlaws suddenly flinch, his rifle flying away as he grabbed his right arm with his left hand. Morrison was hit, and now Black was searching the dimness for the aggressor, his horse more nervous than ever.

Clancy levered in another round, once again took careful aim, and fired. This shot missed its target, and Black spotted the muzzle flash. He pointed his weapon toward the alley and fired off three rapid shots, but because the horse he rode was dancing from fright, none of the bullets were aimed with any degree of accuracy.

Shiner was getting a little anxious, now, too, and Christian tightly clutched Clancy around his torso, but Clancy managed to aim and fire again, and this time Black fell from his horse.

A few more shots were fired as Black, only wounded, had pulled out his revolver and emptied it into the dark night. Morrison was on the ground again, too, but neither of them in any condition to put up any more fight as Marshal Flanagan and his deputies rushed onto the lot and made their arrest.

My Journal—Clancy Crane

They found $2200 in cash in Sly Black's and Red Morrison's coat pockets, and the next day when Marshal Flanagan searched their room at Tanglewood he found another $2000. So the bank got their $4000 back, and the other $200 went to Gilmore's Hardware Store for all the guns that they busted up. Tom Hargrove wrote in the Striker that it was busting up all those guns that got them caught—if they hadn't taken the time to do that they might have rode away before some mysterious gunman in the alley stopped them. That's right, I never told nobody it was me who fired the shots that knocked Black and Morrison off the horses. Me and Christian rode away on Shiner before anybody saw us. We circled around back to Tanglewood, put Shiner in his stall, and were in my rooms in the carriage house before anybody came looking for me. Christian was still in shock from the whole thing, or so that's what he led everybody to believe. He said he ran all the way to my place from the hardware store and he didn't see anybody in the alley.

Sheriff Endicott from Wellington took Black and Morrison away and word is that they'll spend a long time behind bars at Leavenworth. Black confessed that the third man was one from the circus they paid a hundred dollars to be a lookout *at the back door of the bank. He made his getaway on the circus train.*

After Doc Lowery fixed up the bullet wounds I gave to Black and Morrison he came to my rooms to check on Christian. He had Christian take off his clothes and that's when I saw the awful bruises Black gave him. But nothing was broken, and Doc said he should just stay right where he was for the night and get some good rest. That was fine with us because that's what we had planned anyhow. That night Christian told me he was grateful for rescuing him from the bank robbers, but he was even more grateful that I had invited him to Tanglewood to sing with Mr Malone. It had made him feel so good to hear an audience applaud his performance. He is sure now that show business is where he belongs. I think Simon Bordeaux will soon get his wish and Silas Patch will be looking for a new messenger boy.

After the bank robbery incident, Christian Parker spent a great deal of his free time at Tanglewood; his friendship with Clancy Crane had strengthened, and Fingers Malone was always willing to accompany a song or two. There seemed little doubt that he was losing interest in carting baggage back and forth between the railroad depot and Royal Hotel, even though Silas Patch took good care of him and paid him quite well. But his heart was in the theater, and the day had finally come when he was ready to make a commitment to his passion. Simon Bordeaux had been pleading with him for quite some time to play the leading role in his planned stage production of *Oliver Twist*; now was his chance to overcome his fear of being cheated like had happened in Denver.

Simon seemed more honorable than that producer who ran out on the entire troupe after a successful run of shows without paying any of the actors. Simon had built and operated the Crystal Palace successfully, and there wasn't any reason he would run out on that.

Christian's small stature and boyish looks made him perfect for the part of Oliver Twist, and Simon was thrilled to hear that he finally had the actor for the role. "We can begin rehearsals right away—"

"Not so fast, Simon," Christian responded. "I'm still working for Mr. Patch. I can't—I won't just walk out on him."

"When do you plan to tell him?"

"Soon... I'll talk to him soon."

But finding the opportunity to discuss the matter with Silas Patch wasn't so easy. Every time Christian approached his employer, some matter of urgency arose: baggage to transport; important messages to deliver to the telegraph office; needed supplies to be picked up at the General Store; always something. Finally Christian thought he would call on Mr. Patch at his upstairs office at the end of the day. He knocked on the door, but when it opened, he was surprised to see Mrs. Patch greet him.

"Well, hello Christian," she said in her usually pleasant way. "Won't you come in?" She escorted him through the office and into the Patch's private living quarters where he was sure Silas would be relaxing after a busy day. "Please... sit and make yourself comfortable. I'll bring in the tea." She seemed delighted to have a guest.

Christian had been there many times before so it was not difficult to feel at ease; he was one of the few people in Silver Spring who didn't feel intimidated by the wealthiest, most powerful man in the town. However, Mr. Patch was nowhere in sight. He graciously accepted the cup of tea, stirred in a spoonful of sugar, and politely sipped, patiently waiting, assuming that the woman knew he was there to see her husband.

Most of the time, Mrs. Patch kept to herself in these rooms furnished to suit her needs on the second floor of the Royal. She was a small, slight woman, her auburn hair turning gray and a prematurely aged face that had once been very pretty.

The rooms were comfortable and cozy with well-worn

furniture and white lace curtains on the windows. Outside the windows were big flower boxes where she grew pansies and geraniums and all sorts of sweet-scented flowers that she loved. Their fragrance, warmed by the afternoon sun drifted in through the open windows creating a soft, pleasant atmosphere, unlike that of much of the rough town that lay beyond the balcony railing.

"I suppose you're here to see Silas," she said. She spoke quietly and with dignity, but she had some inward spirit that made her seem somewhat distant from Mr. Patch. This lifestyle of a saloon and gambling parlor operator was quite different from what she had expected at the outset of their frontier experience—that of a general store proprietor. Now her contempt had grown as Mr. Patch had become richer, more successful, and more powerful.

But she loved her sewing machine. She pedaled away hours on end assembling new nightgowns and dresses, and then decorated them with cross-stitching and lace collars and cuffs. Andorra Patch didn't socialize downstairs, nor did she have many visitors—only on occasion Mrs. Longhorn, Ellie May Tundle, or the Reverend Miller would stop by for tea, and she liked to look her best at those times, and whenever she ventured out on one of her endless shopping expeditions to purchase household gadgets or sewing supplies. Apparently, the one satisfaction she found in her union with Silas Patch and his rise to great wealth was to spend as much money as she liked on the things she could never afford before. Silas was generous with her; she could have spent thousands on perfumes, jewels and other extravagances, but all those luxuries meant nothing to her. She had no appetite for power and wealth like her husband. In her own simple way, she was a wise and happy woman.

"Will Mr. Patch be here soon?" Christian asked.

"Is your business with him urgent? You seem troubled about something."

Christian wiped the sweat from his brow with the back of his hand. "Yes, ma'am," he replied. "I do need to talk to him as soon as possible."

"Well, if it's something about your employment here, you can certainly tell me. Silas won't be back for a couple of days."

"Yes, ma'am, it does concern my work at the Royal..."

"Are you unhappy here, Christian?"

"Oh, no, ma'am. You and Mr. Patch have been very kind."

"Then it must be that you're getting tired of the saloon life."

"Well, it's not exactly that, either."

"Is it an increase in salary? Are we not paying you enough?"

"Yes... the pay is quite adequate... you have been very generous."

"Then tell me, Christian... what is troubling you?"

"Well, you see, Mrs. Patch, I have the opportunity to go back into acting... performing in the theater. Simon Bordeaux has made me a very handsome offer."

"The theater!" Mrs. Patch exclaimed. "Is that what you really want to do?"

"Yes, ma'am."

"How wonderful!"

"Do you think Mr. Patch is gonna be angry with me?"

"Well, he might not take the news well... you've been such reliable help to him and he thinks quite highly of you. But don't you worry about that. I'll take care of him. You just go ahead and do what you must... and Mr. Patch and I will be in the front row at the Crystal for your first performance."

My Journal—Clancy Crane

New people arrive at Silver Spring every day. Some don't stay long—only a day or two. Some stay a week or more if they're lucky enough to get a room at one of the hotels or boarding houses. A lot of them are looking for work in the mines. They come from other mining camps where the mines had played out. So some of them stay. Smith and Hayden Mining built a few more of the little frame houses for the miners down along the dead line. They aren't much—two small rooms each—but they are a roof overhead and glass in the windows that keep the rain out. There's a well and a hand pump for each 4 or 5 houses, shared clothes lines, a privy for each, and a low barn that holds about a dozen horses. But not many of the miners who live in those houses have horses, so the barn is nearly empty most of the time. The yards around them are bare without trees or shrubs, and the buffalo grass is worn thin by footpaths to the wells and privies.

There are some people who can afford to build a house of their own. They're the ones who plan to stay a long time and they start new businesses in town or buy out the ones that are already there.

Of course, there's always a steady stream of professional gamblers coming and going. They are the real aristocrats. I can usually spot them as soon as they step off the train or out of the stagecoach. They're always dressed in fine fashion, shiny boots and top hats of various styles, and at least one—sometimes two six guns bulging under their coat. Some are soft-spoken and some are boisterous, but they all consider themselves gentlemen. They come from everywhere, but mostly from New Orleans and Mississippi steamboats, San Francisco, and Chicago. I've even seen a couple of older gentlemen who were ex-Johnny-rebs, one claiming to be a major and one a colonel in the Confederate army. But no matter where they come from or what they used to be, they're all willing to spend money—lots of it. I always get big tips for a carriage ride from the depot and toting their luggage upstairs to their rooms so I like it when they come to stay at Tanglewood.

There's one gambler, though, who isn't like the rest. Oh, he's a gentleman all right, and then some. But he is so much younger than most all of the professional gamblers who come to town. He and Christian instantly became good friends when they met one afternoon at the Royal. And because Christian visits Tanglewood almost every night and sometimes he even stays overnight with me in the carriage house, I have now become the young gambler's good friend too. His name is Clay Edwards and just the other night he and Christian were my overnight guests at the carriage house so we had all night to talk. They brought a bottle of porter and a bottle of champagne and we drank Velvets, a half and half concoction of the two that is very popular in all the fancy hotel bars. That night I learned how Clay got to be a professional gambler at such a young age.

Clay told his story to Clancy and Christian as they sipped their drinks. Through the open windows of the carriage house they could hear the tinkling of Fingers Malone's piano and the late night merriment from Tanglewood's saloon. Clay kept cocking his head toward the music. "When I was growing up in Woodville," he said. "I never imagined what my life would be."

Clay Edwards was only sixteen when he left his home at Woodville, Mississippi, walked the thirty-five miles to Natchez, where, after a few days he hopped on a tramp steamboat to New Orleans. His good fortune there a week later to meet a riverboat captain landed him a job as a cabin boy aboard the Mississippi River steamer, and within a short time he was filling in as bartender. That, naturally, exposed him to the high society of professional gamblers, and although he had seen their kind many times before in Natchez, this closer proximity to them began to spur Clay's interest in their lifestyle. He took advantage of every opportunity to watch their poker games, and at the bar, to talk to the ones who were willing to teach him the fine points of the games.

Then he started sitting in on small stakes games during his free time, mostly with the non-professionals, people just traveling on the river and passing the time at a game table. Clay liked to think that it was skill more than luck that brought him a sizeable supplement to his income, and he learned quickly not to feel guilty about taking hundreds of dollars a night from the rich.

Then one night on the river, his life was altered for all time. When several others had folded and walked away, it was only Clay and one wealthy, arrogant Louisiana cotton planter left at the table. The man seemed a little irritated—with himself, mostly—for losing over a thousand dollars to this *boy*. He was confident, however, that his luck would soon change, and he was quite determined to recover his losses. But Clay's skill—and maybe some luck—outplayed the wealthy plantation man, hand after hand.

About two a.m. just upriver from Baton Rouge, with a substantial crowd of spectators standing by, the man thought he finally had the winning hand that would, once and for all, put this kid in his place. He wagered all he had left; Clay matched the bet and raised another $500. Out of cash, the plantation owner refused to back down, convinced that his opponent was bluffing. He placed his gold-handled walking stick across the table, atop the $5000 pot. Recognizing that the game was soon over, that the man was broke, Clay accepted the cane as the final bet.

As if every heart in the room stopped beating, and every breath held in, the entire riverboat saloon fell into complete silence, nervous onlookers fearing for the boy's defeat, but hoping otherwise. He had played honorably, and he had not only won a handsome amount of money so far, but he had also won the respect and admiration of his peers.

With an egotistical sneer, the man turned over his cards, a full house—jacks and eights.

"Well," said Clay, still displaying a rigid poker face. "That's a pretty good hand."

Sighs of disappointment were heard around the room, the speculations that the boy was finally admitting defeat. Hearts were heavy.

The man was just about to rake the pot to his side of the table when Clay politely took hold of the cane's gold head, preventing its removal. One by one he turned over the four kings with his free hand.

What had been a deathly silent room full of anxious observers suddenly erupted in astonished shouts, an alarmed upheaval of disbelief, but at the same time, a joyful approval of the boy's success.

Trying desperately to disguise his emotions, the plantation owner got up from the table and left the saloon. Clay caught up with him at the door and held out the exquisite walking stick. "You may have this back. I don't need it." he said, as he urged the man to accept his offer.

With just a fragment of a smile, the man tipped his hat in

gentleman's style. "Y'all won it fair and square... and I have others." He turned and walked away to his stateroom.

Clay's winnings that night were just over $25,000. It was the turning point in his young career; he decided then and there that gambling must be his destiny. When the boat returned to New Orleans, the captain had little expectation of ever seeing Clay again as his cabin boy or bartender. Collecting his final pay, he bid his farewell, and as the newest member of this elite society, he set out to purchase fine clothes and to outfit himself with all the appropriate accessories.

Always dressed in fine black suit, ruffled shirt, brocaded vest, and small, stylish bow tie, Clay spent a good deal of his time traveling the river and increasing his bankroll in the steamboat saloons or in the gambling parlors at the many ports of call along the Mississippi River, winning more than he lost. By then he had gained the typical characteristics of a professional gambler: an affinity for easy living and an absolute aversion to physical work. But he had become a killer, too. He had to be. All professional gamblers knew that they must win to eat. To back down from an opponent that accuses him of cheating—whether he did or not—would ruin his reputation and integrity; it would ruin his belief in himself, his confidence. Sometimes it meant bloodshed, and more than once Clay had been faced with such a situation. By the code of the time, a man accused of cheating, or being challenged to a fight, had a perfect right to bring about the prompt demise of his assailant. In line with the requirements of his surroundings, a sleek Smith & Wesson .45 was tucked neatly in a side holster under his coat, and a double-barreled Remington .41 derringer concealed in a sleeve pocket, and he had become quite proficient in their use.

Although the Lower Mississippi River had provided the perfect backdrop for the birth of his new career, the surroundings were getting dangerous. It was time to move on, and the western gold mining towns, where money was plentiful and the saloons were overflowing with amateurs, sounded like the best option. Deadwood, Leadville, Creede, Central City, and Denver all netted Clay moderate profits, but also a few challenges, so now, here he was in Silver Spring, tired of the need to make hasty relocations via a stagecoach into new and unfamiliar territory. He hoped it would be different here.

"I don't know how long my luck will hold out," Clay said.

"But it's your skill that keeps you winning, ain't it?" Clancy asked.

"It's not the cards I'm talking about."

"What do you mean, then?"

"That I might not be fast enough on the draw for the next confrontation... that some tinhorn hot head loser gets off a lucky shot."

Clancy and Christian seemed a bit disturbed with that explanation. "If you're worried about that," Christian said, "Why don't you just quite gambling?"

"It's not that easy to just stop."

"Well it's not that easy for me to think that tomorrow night at this time, me and Clancy could be sitting here alone, faced with figuring out what to put on your tombstone."

My Journal—Clancy Crane

Joey and Eddy came by yesterday morning. It wasn't market day, and they hoped I could get the day off and go for a ride. They wanted to explore the Indian caves. I hadn't taken a whole day off since the circus, so Jeremiah was willing to let me go. Joey's black dog Bear and Eddy's yellow dog Duke were with them, eager to wander the hills and valleys. Somehow they must have known this was going to be an adventure. Shiner seemed anxious for a ride in the wilderness too when he saw Pokey and Molly all saddled and ready for a journey. We hadn't been out for a long ride in a while.

We all had a canteen of cold water, and Eddy's mom had packed some sandwiches, like she always did for us when we went exploring. But when we passed by Longhorn's General Store on the square we decided to stop for some beef jerky and maybe a few pieces of hard candy. It would be a long ride.

Ralph Longhorn is a tall strong man, full of energy and always full of good business ideas. His store was just a little dry goods shop when me and my brothers arrived in Silver Spring, and he has built it into one of the best stocked general stores in the territory. Just like Jeremiah, he had borrowed from the bank to stock up and meet the needs of a booming camp, and now Longhorn's is usually the busiest store in town.

The windows to the right of the front door display women's wear—everything from silk stockings to hats and ready-made dresses and shoes. The windows on the left have men's clothing, work clothes mostly, shirts, overalls, jackets, but some fine suits too. Inside there are books showing pictures of more dress suits to order for $15 or $18 or $20. The middle of the store is filled with all sorts of house wares, yard goods, and notions. And the whole back of the store is the groceries, shelved to the ceiling. Coffee is in 100-pound bags and is ground in the big mill while you watch and sniff. Cheese comes in 2-foot wheels and is wedged out with the big cheese knife right there on the counter. There's a big glass case for candy sold by the pound, and another glass case for cigars and chewing tobacco. Canned fruit and vegetables line the shelves, and dried prunes and apricots are in wooden boxes. There's a barrel of soda crackers, and off to the side are stacks of bagged dry beans, sugar and flour. Way in the back is the huge ice box for meat and butter. Ice is brought in just about every day from the ice house down by the mill pond. There's usually a side of beef in Longhorn's ice box for the folks who want a fresh steak in the middle of summer. But there's always cured meats, salt pork, bacon, smoked hams, dried beef, smoked sausage, *and beef jerky.*

You can get almost anything you want at Ralph Longhorn's General Store except hardware and hard liquor, but we were there for the beef jerky and hard candy. Eddy stayed with the horses and dogs while Joey and I went in.

Three boys, three horses, and two dogs crossed the railroad tracks and headed out the west road down into the valley below Silver Spring, past the ice house, the lumber and grist mills. The graded wagon road, busy with ore wagons, dwindled to just a dirt path a couple of miles past the mills where it made a sharp turn toward one of the S and H mines. Beyond that, they saw no more ore wagons, and it wasn't likely there would be any farm wagons on the trail on a non-market day.

The morning was cool and bright, alive with meadow larks and sluggish grasshoppers, and sweet with the fragrance of wildflowers. The small army of peaceful invaders whooped and hollered, asserting their presence. They weren't there to kill anything, but they had to let the world know they were there. Even Bear and Duke weren't in the mood to catch rabbits, but merely joined the fun with a bark now and then just to let the rabbits know dogs were in the neighborhood.

There were more abandoned shacks along this trail, and more were visible in the hills, signs of a once-thriving prospector community. Here, Silver Creek had once been bustling with anxious prospectors, and some had been quite successful —for as long as it lasted. Now, many of them worked in the deep mines where Smith and Hayden Mining Company was able to reach the gold and silver that the prospectors couldn't reach on their own. Joey and Bear had already investigated most of the old shanties on previous outings, so there didn't seem much point now. But Duke apparently thought there was reason to scratch and sniff at a few.

The boys rode on down the valley and soon the bluffs along the Pike River came into sight. To Clancy they appeared to be on the opposite side of the river. "How do we get across the river to the bluffs?" he asked Joey.

"You'll see," Joey replied. He'd been there before and was quite unconcerned.

Unlike the trail they had taken to Webb's Lake, over hilly, rough terrain, this one coursed along the valley floor. Now, several miles from town, Silver Creek was wide and shallow and crystal clear, and on either bank laid green pastures with cows grazing lazily in the late morning sun.

"So this is where our milk comes from!" Clancy exclaimed.

"Most of it," said Joey. "Lots of farmers down this way. They used to be prospectors. But the claims down this far never produced much, so they just started farming."

A little ways farther the trail led over a slight rise, and beyond Clancy could see the big horseshoe bend in the river. They didn't have to cross the river to reach the bluffs, just merely wade the horses across Silver Creek.

After the horses had a long, cool drink from midstream and the dogs had lain in the refreshing water for a few minutes, they were all ready to move on. Duke and Bear loped along the riverbank in search of a good spot for a swim. The Pike was much too shallow for steamboats this far upstream, but the two dogs managed to find a deep hole and plunged in. Seeing the grand pleasure they were enjoying, Eddy stopped Molly near the bank and dismounted. "Let's go for a swim too," he said to the others.

Joey was off Pokey in an instant. "C'mon, Clancy!" he said as he stripped off his clothes. "Don't you wanna go for a swim?"

"I'm not a very good swimmer... remember?" Clancy replied.

"That's okay," Eddy said. "The water's not too deep here... you'll be fine."

The sun was getting rather hot, and Clancy thought a dip in the cool river might feel pretty good. Joey and Eddy were already in the water playing with the dogs, so he disrobed, draped his shirt and jeans across Shiner's saddle like Joey and Eddy had done. All three horses were nibbling at the long, succulent green grass. Clancy charged for the riverbank and splashed in amidst his exploring companions.

They were all having so much fun, the boys throwing sticks for the dogs to fetch, that they didn't notice the development up on the bank that meant trouble. It could have been a snake, or maybe the nearby presence of a mountain lion, but whatever the reason, the horses were spooked and trotted off.

When the boys finally came out of the water, Eddy was the first to notice the missing horses. "Did anybody see where Molly and Pokey and Shiner went?"

"OH NO!" Joey cried out. "Where are the horses?"

"SHINER!" Clancy called

Panic stricken, all three boys stood on the riverbank, naked, scanning the surrounding area. Not only were the horses gone, but their clothes, too! Only their boots lay on the ground where they had kicked them off.

Then Joey had an idea. "Bear!" he called out to his dog. Bear came from the water and Duke followed. They shook themselves dry when they couldn't get any closer, but the boys were wet anyway, and they really didn't care.

"Bear... go find Pokey," Joey told the dog with arousing enthusiasm. Bear danced around, ears perked, eyes wide and bright, excited and curious

with the challenge.

"Go find Pokey and Molly and Shiner!" Joey commanded again. "Bring them back here to us."

Bear bounced up, nearly standing on his hind legs to make himself taller to see farther, looking this way and that. And then, as if he had made a decision, he launched into a run, leaping in long strides through the tall grass. Duke went chasing after him.

"Think he'll find 'em?" Clancy asked.

"Yeah, he'll find 'em," Joey replied. "He and Pokey are buddies. They spend a lot of time together. And he'll bring 'em back here... you'll see."

"Think we should go looking too?"

"D'ya really want to go trampin' around in the woods with no clothes on?"

"Not really."

"Well, then, let's just stay right here and wait for Bear to bring back the horses."

Quite embarrassed by their precarious situation, Clancy, Eddy and Joey stood by the water, hoping that no one would come by. They were well off the wagon trail that the farmers used to travel into Silver Spring, although there was always the chance that a farmer might come looking after his cows, or to go fishing. But they had no choice. All they could do was wait and hope for Bear's success.

To pass the time they waded in the shallow water near the bank, and Joey pointed out some dark spots on the bluffs high above the river about a quarter-mile upstream. "Those are the Indian caves," he said. "That's where we're going."

"Yeah," Eddy replied with a little uncertainty. "If we ever get our horses and clothes back."

Just then they heard a dog bark. A few seconds later Duke raced to the riverbank, panting and excited. He stood on the bank above the boys and barked twice.

Eddy scurried out of the water and climbed the bank, petting and hugging his big, yellow dog. "Clancy, Joey," he called back to the other two. "Come up here! You gotta see this."

Clancy and Joey came splashing out of the water and climbed the bank next to Eddy. Joey couldn't help but laugh. There, loping toward them was Bear, Molly trotting alongside, her reins tightly clenched in Bear's teeth. Pokey and Shiner followed closely behind.

"See?" Joey bragged. "I told you he'd find 'em and bring 'em back."

"But why is he leading Molly?" Clancy asked. "I thought he was Pokey's buddy."

"Molly was prob'ly less interested in coming back and she needed a little persuasion."

Clancy gave a whistle and Shiner went into a gallop, halting abruptly at Clancy's side. When Bear arrived with Molly and Pokey, the boys, although joyous and grateful that their horses had returned, realized then that their clothes were no longer where they had left them on the saddles.

"Great!" Eddy yelled. "What do we do now?"

"They must have fallen off when the horses started running," Joey speculated.

"If Bear found the horses, d'ya think he can find our clothes, too?"

"No," Joey replied. "But now *we* can go look for them." He slipped on his socks and boots and swung into Pokey's saddle. "C'mon," he said. "They can't be far away."

Clancy and Eddy put on their boots, mounted Molly and Shiner and followed after Joey. Modesty was no longer an issue.

They hadn't ridden more than a few hundred feet when they found their garments scattered in the tall grass.

"Jeez!" Joey said. "They were right here! We could've found 'em before."

Fully dressed again, they stood by their horses and laughed about what had just happened. What had seemed at first an innocent and harmless bit of fun, and what had turned into a temporary disaster, now was simply a humorous memory that they would laugh about for years to come.

"Gentlemen! Comrades!" Eddy began his short oration. "Merely a brief interruption in the day's agenda. We must now rally the troops, gain our bearings, and continue our journey to the unknown—"

"Eddy!" Joey said. "Get on your horse and let's ride."

They followed around the horseshoe bend of the river, and there rose the bluffs, beginning first as a gentle slope but soon rose sharply to a plateau several hundred feet above the valley floor. The steep slope was covered with grass, jack pine, scrub oak, and brush almost to the top. A trail climbed the slope in hairpins and some sweeping curves. From the bottom, it appeared almost impossible for man or horse to traverse such a steep hill, but Joey and Eddy had done it before on Pokey and Molly. Joey led the way.

Shiner seemed almost at home, treading over the steep trail with only the slightest challenge. Sure-footed Molly was slower and more cautious, and fell behind the others, so Joey and Clancy stopped now and then to let Eddy catch up.

At the very top of the bluff was a bare cliff, the edge of a sandstone layer that capped the whole upland. Big chunks of rock had been broken loose by rain and frost and had rolled or slid part way down the slope. They passed several of the large boulders, some as big as an ore wagon. The rocks had been there a long time, as the grass and brush were well-rooted all around them. As they neared the top there was more rubble, tumbled from the bare cliff, which was at least twenty feet high.

A number of hollows dotted the face of the cliff, some large and some barely big enough for a man to crawl into. When they reached the top, there was a wide, flat ledge in front of the cliff where the horses could stand comfortably.

"My hunger is overwhelming me!" Eddy declared. "Would anyone care to join me in the fine feast my dear mother has prepared?"

"Yeah," Joey replied. "I'll have a sandwich."

They had all worked up an appetite; as they sat there on some rocks enjoying the fresh bread, cheese, and smoked ham, Eddy commented, "From up here it looks big as the ocean."

"Have you ever seen the ocean?" Joey asked.

"Not yet... but I will. I'm going to sail around the world on a schooner... yo-ho-ho."

"I thought you were gonna be a trapper in Alaska."

"I am. And I'm gonna hunt lions in the African jungles, too. To be an author and write books, you've got to have a lot of experiences."

"You're gonna be an author?" Clancy asked.

"Yep!" Eddy said. "A lot more fun than being a doctor... hangin' 'round sick people all the time. How long d'ya have to go to college to be a doctor, Joey?"

"Six years, I think," Joey replied.

"Well, an author doesn't have to go to college. He just goes out on adventures... and then writes about 'em."

"And you're gonna be a doctor?" Clancy asked Joey.

Joey didn't answer. He reached over and caught Clancy's wrist, felt for and found his pulse, and then stared at the ground for a long minute, as intent as a cat watching a mouse hole. Then he dropped the hand and said, "You're alive! What are you going to do? When you get older?"

"I don't know for sure," Clancy replied. He pondered for a moment. "I might like to be a newspaperman and printer... like Tom. I like to write down all the things that happen; like our trip today... I'll put down in my journal about our adventure, and if anything exciting happened in town while we were gone, I'll find out about it and put that my journal, too."

"You mean... you're gonna write about us losing our clothes and horses and depending on a dog to find them?" Eddy exclaimed.

"Maybe. Yeah. Sure."

"But that's embarrassing! Why would you do that?"

"Don't worry, Eddy. It's just my journal. Nobody else will ever read it."

They had each eaten two sandwiches and were starting their third—all that was left. The horses had found a patch of rather dry-looking grass, but they seemed to be enjoying it. Both dogs were lying quietly in the shade of the scrub oaks when Eddy broke off little pieces of his bread and tossed it to them, arousing their interest in something to eat. They started snapping and growling at each other, competing for each little morsel until it escalated into a full-blown fight.

"Now see what you did?" Joey scolded Eddy.

"I'm conducting an experiment," Eddy said. "We're trapped on a mountaintop and the wolves are closing in. I want to see how long I can keep the wolves from eating us."

"Some experiment! I'll throw *you* to the wolves," Joey said. He grabbed what remained of Eddy's sandwich, broke it in half, and then yelled, "DUKE! BEAR!" and then tossed each half to them when he had their attention.

"Traitor!" Eddy shouted. "I shall have your life for that!" He watched Duke gulp down his half of the sandwich. "Okay, Duke, my fierce warrior... you kill him and I'll bury him in one of the caves."

Duke licked his chops, panted, yawned, and then returned to his spot in the shade next to Bear, quite disinterested in Eddy's command.

Joey went to his pony and retrieved a small, short-handled spade, one like the miners used in tight spaces. "C'mon," he said to Clancy. "Let's go dig out one of the caves... see what we find."

Just twenty yards from where they had been sitting was the opening to a shallow cavern, recessing only about thirty feet into the sandstone cliff, but only tall enough to stand stooped over. With the shovel, Joey began to dig into the loose, sandy soil of the floor. As he dug, Clancy and Eddy crouched down and maneuvered to the back of the cave to investigate its farthest reaches, making certain there weren't any more passageways hidden from sight. "Do you think this might be an old gold mine?" Clancy asked.

"Not likely," replied Joey. "Not in this sandstone. Gold and silver is usually found in hard rock. But Indians used to live in places like this." He kept digging, and then Clancy noticed some red flecks in the soil he was tossing towards the cave door.

"Stop! I see something!" Clancy said. He sifted through the

loosened dirt with his fingers and found four small glass beads, common to Indian moccasins and headgear. With each shovelful of dirt, they found more, some red, some blue. Then Joey's shovel struck something more solid with a crunching sound. The others peered into the foot-deep trench, curious of what might be there. Joey continued to carefully dig away the soil, first unearthing a yellowed bone about a foot long with a knob at each end. While he examined the bone, Eddy took over at digging, determined to find the rest of the skeleton. A few minutes later he shrieked. "Look at this! It's a skull!"

Clancy and Joey quickly shifted their attention to the hole where Eddy was scooping the sandy soil away with his bare hands. It was certainly a human skull, grinning teeth, empty eye sockets and all. When it was completely uncovered, cause of death to its owner was evident: a jagged, oval-shaped hole about three inches long near the top suggested that this man had died as the result of a sharp blow, perhaps with a tomahawk.

They took turns digging, but no more bones were found. "It's no use," said Joey. "Wolves—or maybe coyotes—were here... carried the rest of it away, all but this humerus, but that was a long time ago."

"This what?"

"Humerus... the upper bone of the arm."

"How did it get buried like this?" Eddy asked.

"Hard to say," Joey answered. "Maybe the murderer covered it up, or maybe the wind and rain did it over the years." There was sadness in his voice. Somehow, it seemed that he felt sorry for disturbing this ancient man's final resting place. Slowly he began to cover the skull with soil again, placing the other bone that he was certain to be the man's upper arm next to the skull, all that remained of a past life. Clancy and Eddy helped push soil back into the trench. When they were finished, it was mid-afternoon and the sun was just passing its hottest point. They mounted their horses and headed for home.

My Journal—Clancy Crane

Now that Christian has been a member of Simon Bordeaux's theater troupe for a while, in a couple of weeks he was supposed to have his first big performance as Oliver in a play called Oliver Twist. But that might not happen. Another actor, Freddy Marrow, has quit and skedaddled, and so Simon is upset about his play not going on as scheduled, and I feel sorry for Christian because he has worked so hard at learning his part.

Meanwhile, Clay Edwards, the young gambler, continues to be the biggest toad in the puddle. So far, he hasn't had to shoot anybody over a card game in Silver Spring, and a lot of people are actually starting to like him. Christian is still trying to convince him to quit gambling before there's bloodshed.

The hot afternoon had drawn a large crowd into the Royal Hotel's saloon and gambling parlors. Miners just finishing their shift were ready to gulp some cold beer and take a chance at increasing their earnings for the day; and there were those who would have been there anyway.

Clay Edwards was taking a break from a series of small stake poker games in which he had netted only a paltry sum. He was hoping for some heavy betters to show up, but the three o'clock train had come and gone two hours ago, and now all he could rely on were the miners.

As he enjoyed a cold drink at the bar, he noticed a man near the front door, dressed all in black except for the white collar, his black hat held in hand. The man looked lost, or perhaps embarrassed to be there, gazing about until his eyes met Clay's, and for some reason he saw in Clay a person he could talk to. He casually walked to the bar, sat on a stool beside the young gambler and offered his right hand. "I'm the Reverend Conrad," he said. "And you are Clay Edwards."

Clay accepted the handshake, puzzled by the preacher's knowledge of his name. "Pleased to meet you, Reverend," he replied. "But... how do you know my name?"

"Oh, we met once before, just briefly... in Denver. And then when you experienced that altercation that I'm assuming caused you to leave town rather abruptly, I prayed for your soul. And I'm glad to see that my prayers must've been effective. You look quite well."

"Yes... er... well,.. yes... I'm quite well," Clay stuttered. "I'd prefer to leave all that behind me," he said with a grim expression. "Things are different here. I've made some friends now, and I really don't want any more trouble. And you, Reverend? What brings you to Silver Spring? Certainly you didn't come all the way here just to make sure I am well."

"No, actually... I came here to build a church, but on the way, road agents relieved me and my traveling companions of all our valuables, including all the money I had, so now I'm here penniless."

"Oh, Reverend, I'm so sorry to hear that. You're lucky they didn't kill you while they were at it."

"Yes, we were fortunate that our lives were spared... and now I must start all over."

"But there's already a church here in Silver Spring," Clay said.

"But not a Methodist church," Reverend Conrad replied. "In a town with this many people, there is room for another church."

Clay had been raised a Methodist among a population that was largely Southern Baptist. Here he knew there were a few Methodists... among Catholics and Presbyterians, and although he had long ago drifted away from the church, he felt compassion for the preacher. "I'll help you!" he said with a sudden surge of enthusiasm. His generous heart led him on. He climbed up, standing above the crowded barroom on his stool, and sounding a shrill whistle he gained the attention of a few. "Hey!" he shouted. "Countrymen! Lend me your ears!"

More people in the crowd turned their heads and soon the room fell quiet as the youngster spoke. "My friend, the Reverend Conrad, here, has recently traveled here from afar to build a church in this fine community, however, he has fallen on bad luck. Road agents! They robbed him clean, and now the Reverend has nothing... not even enough to buy supper!" Clay took off his bowler hat and extended it toward the crowd. "Open your hearts and your pocketbooks and kindly show the Reverend what a great place Silver Spring is..." He pulled a twenty-dollar bill from his pocket and dropped it into the hat, first making sure that everyone near saw it. Mumbles and murmurs quickly erupted into festive shouts and cheers, and hands came toward the hat, dropping in bills and coins. Men from across the room jostled their way through the mob to drop in their contributions. When it appeared the donations were complete and all had gone back to their previous activities, Clay and the preacher found an empty table, and with a few curious onlookers, Clay dumped the proceeds from his hat onto the table and began counting.

"Hell, there's only a hundred and eighty dollars here!" he frowned. "That won't build no church!" He looked sincerely into the preacher's eyes. "Trust me, Reverend," he said, picked up a hundred dollars and headed to the faro table. He winked at the dealer; the dealer acknowledged with a discrete smile. Clay placed his bet on the eight and the king. The second card the dealer drew from the box was a king. "The king is the winner!" he announced. "Five hundred dollars!"

Clay continued to play with smaller, more conservative wagers, and within a short period of time he had converted the preacher's donations into nine hundred dollars. He tipped his hat to the dealer and graciously withdrew.

Upon presenting the money to Reverend Conrad, Clay said, "Do you have a place to sleep?"

"Not yet."

"Well," Clay said. "The boarding house on Flatrock Street will have a room for you. Just tell Mrs. Crabtree that I sent you."

"Thank you... and God bless you, my son." The preacher stuffed the money into his coat pocket, and then vigorously shook Clay's hand. "I will see you again, soon, I hope."

Clay just smiled and nodded as the Reverend turned for the door.

"That was mighty generous of you," a voice said from behind Clay. He turned to see Christian Parker and Simon Bordeaux staring at him with appreciative grins.

"Well, hullo, my covey! What's the row?"

"I'm very hungry and tired," Christian answered."

"You want grub, and you shall have it," Clay recited. "I'm at low-water-mark myself..."

Simon watched and listened to the brief banter between the two. His eyes widened and he was nearly breathless. "What was that you just—"

"Christian said he's hungry and I said that I am hungry, too. Why?"

Simon recognized the lines from *Oliver Twist*. He gazed questioningly to Christian.

Christian finally grasped Simon's confusion. He laid his hand on Simon's shoulder. "Clay's been helping me memorize my lines," he explained.

Simon looked Clay up and down. "And what a charming young lad. Have you ever acted?" he asked the gambler.

"Oh, I put on an act every time I sit down at a poker table," Clay responded.

"No, I mean have you ever performed on stage?"

"I was an elf in a school Christmas play... long time ago, of course."

"Christian!" Simon exclaimed. "He'd be perfect for the part of the Artful Dodger!"

Christian slowly cultivated a beaming grin. "You are absolutely right." He stared at Clay. "And he practically knows all the lines already."

Clay was a bit confused with the conversation.

"What are you talking about?" he asked.

"Freddy Marrow, the actor who I had cast for the part of Artful Dodger in *Oliver Twist* is gone," Simon explained.

"What happened to him?"

"He received a telegram a couple of days ago, and he went to Deadwood to rejoin John Langrishe's theater company there."

"How about it?" Christian pleaded. "You already know the Dodger's lines... well... most of 'em, and I can help you with the rest. How about it? Will you do it? For a friend?"

Clay's eyes wandered around the saloon and gaming parlor as if he were searching for the right answer. Making such a commitment would mean making a drastic alteration in his lifestyle, and he wasn't sure that he was ready for that just yet. But Christian was the best friend he'd had since his childhood days in Mississippi, and he knew how much the performance of this play meant to Christian. His wandering gaze eventually returned to his friend. "Do you think..." he hesitated. "Do you really think... that I can do it?"

"Yes!" Christian replied quickly without the slightest hint of doubt. "You said yourself that you can do anything you put your mind to. Yes, you can do it!"

Reluctantly, Clay nodded. "Okay," he said in almost a whisper. "I'll give it a try."

"Marvelous!" Simon beamed. "Let's have supper and celebrate!"

"Okay," Christian said. "But let's go to Tanglewood. The food is better there."

My Journal—Clancy Crane

Today is market day, so I was awake extra early before anybody else started moving—except Oliver. While I was in the shadows, where I usually stay at that time of morning, Oliver passed right by me not more than ten feet away toting his heavy gunnysack and he never noticed me there. I stood perfectly still until he was a long way down Flatrock Street. Finally I have gotten a closer look at that bag he always has over his shoulder. Some nights I see him in the saloon at Tanglewood. He always sits and drinks alone. In fact, I've never seen him talk to anybody. Next time I see him there, I will have a chat with him, because he must be very lonely.

Oliver Pratt was a loner; he was a schemer and a thief, although most people only knew him as a quiet, solitary, and odd fellow who never seemed to fall in line with any social standards. The nearest he ever came to being social was to enter one of the drinking establishments now and then for a cold beer, but never did he go to the same saloon on consecutive days, always alternating his visits so no one would ever try to get too friendly. And no one ever did.

A tiny one room apartment on the second floor above the Continental Saloon and Billiard Parlor is where Oliver made his home. His seven neighbors in the other rooms—mostly miners—rarely saw him, nor did any of them know him other than by sight. Only two or three times a week he ate a hot supper at one of the diners, and the rest of the time he had cold meals in his room. Oliver Pratt was nearly an urban hermit.

He had worked at the smelter since its creation. His job was to pour the molten gold and silver into the ingot molds, and when they cooled and solidified, he removed the seventy-pound ingots from the molds and prepared them for delivery to the banking house. Since he had been there so long, he was put in charge of the late-night hours, working alone most of the time in the finishing room. Because it was so noisy, the stamping mill didn't operate during the nighttime, so by two or three a.m. the last of the valuable liquid trickled down from the furnace.

In due time, Oliver found his isolation an advantage, and he soon succumbed to the temptation of easily making his own wealth. He discovered that nearly every night he was afforded the opportunity to sneak one of the ingots out an unguarded passage opposite the mounds of ore tailings and dispose of it by easily burying it in the loose soil amidst the shadows of nearby brush. Then it was a simple matter to retrieve it later when he was done working, still under the cover of darkness. One ingot at a time would not be missed. He had found the perfect hiding place, an abandoned mine shaft east of town. The mine had been closed long ago after a cave-in when three miners were buried and lost. Because of the high risk factor, their bodies were never recovered. No one went near that mine shaft. Oliver knew that if he hid a few bars of silver and gold there, it would be a place of safe-keeping. He suspected, too, that the region's mining wouldn't last forever, and when the mines finally played out, like they eventually did at every other mining boom town, the majority of the population—if not its entirety—would move away, leaving Silver Spring a ghost town. With no one left, then, to even question his activity, he could retrieve his fortune with little or no opposition. His scheme, he thought, was near perfect, and it was merely a matter of time until he could cash in on his efforts. Oliver just needed to be cautious and patient. As one of the few residents of Silver Spring who had the foresight of the town's probable future—dismal as it might be—he had his own prosperous future planned, as well. When the mining ended and the social and economic structure collapsed, he would be a wealthy man.

But Oliver became too overconfident with his plan. As clever as he might be, his complacency betrayed him. So far, he was certain that no one had followed him to the abandoned mineshaft, and his seclusion working alone in the finishing room late at night had surely kept his actions there unnoticed. But just by chance, another workman, Elmer Dickens, caught a glimpse of Oliver as he slipped out into the darkness with one of the shiny bars on three occasions. At first, Elmer didn't realize what Oliver was actually doing, but the second and third times he happened to be at a vantage point where he was hidden from Oliver's sight, it became evident that Oliver Pratt was stealing the silver ingots and hiding them in the adjacent woods. On the third night, Oliver thought he saw someone watching him when he returned from the brush. Perhaps he would not retrieve the bar that morning; he'd wait a few days.

"That's a mighty serious accusation," Marshal Flanagan said when Dickens told him of what he had witnessed. "Are you quite sure?"

"Positive," Dickens replied. "I seen him do it three times... three different nights."

"Who else have you told about this?"

"Nobody else."

"Good. Then keep it quiet. Understand?"

Elmer nodded.

Flanagan decided that this matter should be turned over to the county sheriff; he promptly rode into Wellington to report the incident in person to Sheriff Endicott. After a long discussion about how to capture Pratt red-handed, and then bring him to justice, Deputies Johnny Brown and Brice Tatum were assigned to the task. They rode back to Silver Spring with Marshal Flanagan.

For the next three nights, Brown and Tatum remained out of sight in the shadows, waiting for Pratt to emerge from the finishing room with a bar of silver. They planned to wait until he reached the spot where he had concealed the others that Elmer Dickens claimed he saw Pratt carry out. It was the only way they would have the absolute proof they needed. But it was three long nights with no results.

Suspicious of the possibility that he had been seen a few nights earlier, Oliver Pratt went about his usual work, making no attempts at any unauthorized removal of silver or gold from the finishing room. All the while, he planned his next move, which would be to recover the one bar still buried in the nearby woods. He knew he had to do it soon, before someone else discovered it there; he would do it on his next night off, Sunday.

Oliver waited patiently in his room over the billiard hall Sunday night. He had slept quite soundly until eleven-thirty, but by midnight he was wide awake. The minutes and hours ticked by slowly until three a.m. That's when it had always been safe to retrieve the ingots from the temporary hiding spot in the woods and deliver them to their final destination in the abandoned mineshaft. He could return to his comfortable bed by four o'clock before anyone else was awake.

As a precautionary measure, his Colt revolver was tucked under his belt when he descended the back stairs of the Continental carrying the burlap bag rolled up in a small bundle. When he was absolutely sure that he was alone in the darkness, Oliver left the doorway, passed through the alley and crossed the lumberyard to Wilson Street, then over to Lincoln Street and down past the North Star Hotel, the route that he always used bringing the silver bars back from the woods. He held little concern for any Chinamen who might be stirring at that hour, as none of them could speak English, nor would they pay him any attention. Just a short distance from the end of the row of miners' little houses, he darted across South Street—the "dead line"—and followed the pathway down the slope among the tramps' unpainted shacks and ragged tents. Oliver had lived in this neighborhood when he first arrived at Silver Spring, so he knew the way quite well. The remains of a few cooking fires burned and smoldered, filling the air with the pungent smell of burnt garbage, but he hoped none of the vagrant residents would be awake; he didn't worry about them seeing him wandering around at that time of morning, but he didn't want to be delayed by any unnecessary chit-chat from the bums that knew him.

Beyond, Oliver slipped into the strip of woods and brush that was the barrier between the hobo camp and the smelter shed, cautiously and quietly stepping as if he were a stalking savage. When he neared the spot where the silver ingot was buried, he stopped to listen and gaze around to make certain that he was alone. All he heard, though, were the normal nighttime noises from within the smelter.

Scuffing away the loose dirt with his boot, he uncovered the shiny bar of silver. Even in the nighttime shadows its luster gleamed wealth—Oliver's wealth. Slivers of moonlight filtered through the tree branches and made the bar sparkle like dewdrops on the morning grass. He stooped over to brush away the fragments of dirt and sand, and as he slid the bar to the bottom of the burlap sack and hoisted it over his shoulder, he thought about his stunning success in pulling off the biggest heist in Silver Spring's history; a smile came to his face that no one would ever see.

Just as he started back through the woods a voice called from the darkness, startling Oliver to a standstill. "Hold it right there, Oliver Pratt!" the voice said.

But Oliver didn't recognize the voice. It was Deputy Brown. He and his partner, Deputy Tatum had been watching the Continental, waiting for Pratt to make his move. Their stealth pursuit had resulted in the triumphant capture of the ingot thief. "We've got you dead to rights," Brown called out, and not suspecting the need for weapons, the two deputies rushed toward Oliver.

Oliver was still unaware of the identity of his assailants; he drew out his Colt pistol and fired three hasty shots blindly into the dark woods, hitting nothing but trees. In the next instant he saw the muzzle flashes from two guns, and a moment later his body sprawled on the ground, his left hand still clutching the bag that contained his fortune. But now it was all over.

Although they had recovered one of the missing ingots, Deputies Brown and Tatum were too late to find out where the others were hidden. They had silenced Oliver Pratt forever. When daylight came, the entire area where Oliver had unearthed the silver bar was thoroughly searched, but no more ingots were found. According to Elmer Dickens, there should have been three. The two others were evidently too well hidden to be found.

No more investigation seemed necessary. There was the strong probability that Dickens could have been mistaken about *three* ingots. Smith and Hayden Mining Company was satisfied with the return of one, knowing the sole thief had been killed, and was willing to let the matter rest. They would, however, improve the security measures from then on with a few armed guards around the finishing room.

My Journal—Clancy Crane

It was a very special day when the play Oliver Twist was to open that night at the Crystal Palace. Christian was excited, and Clay was a little nervous. Although he knew his part well and the whole cast had put in many extra hours of rehearsals to ensure he was ready, Clay couldn't help but be a little jittery. I had my reserved seat in the front row right next to Mr. And Mrs. Patch. Millie's seat was next to me, but Jeremiah had to stay at Tanglewood and take care of business. He would see another performance another night. The whole town was excited about the play, and almost everybody said they wanted to see it. It was the first real play at the Crystal Palace in a couple of months, since a travelling theater company performed Uncle Tom's Cabin 5 nights in a row. There had only been minstrel shows and variety shows since, with trained dog acts, singers, dancers, acrobats, and a few comedy skits. So everybody in Silver Spring was anxious to see Oliver Twist.

In respect for Christian and Clay on that special day, I decided that I should have some new clothes to wear to the opera house, especially when I had a front row seat where there were the bright lights. I had always sat way in the back at other shows where it didn't matter. So I went to the Men's

Clothing Emporium on Market Street right next to the bakery on Market Square. The frames around the big front windows are carved with fancy scrolls and ribbons and flowers, and they are painted with red, yellow and blue. The window glass is almost covered with signs advertising bargains on socks, shirts, jeans, suits and shoes. Like many other store buildings, the ornate front is backed by an ordinary unpainted two-story wooden structure. The store occupies the ground floor, and the proprietors, Henry Chesterton and his wife Martha live upstairs. They are good people. Henry and Martha were the ones responsible for putting an end to dumping garbage and even chamber pots in the thoroughfare, and they organized the street cleaning service to remove horse droppings.

Henry met me at the front door after he saw me admiring the pale blue ruffled shirt in the front window. It was one like Clay wears, and Christian too, except Christian usually wears white. Henry marched me back to a fitting room where he gave me one of the blue shirts to try on. It was a good fit, but the sleeves were too long. "Not to fear" said Henry. He slipped a pair of sleeve garters over my wrists and placed them just above my elbows so they pulled the cuffs to just the right position. "There" he told me. "That's the fashion now you know." Then he spun me around to have a look in the big looking glass. While I was admiring the most beautiful shirt I had every wore, Henry left a few moments and returned with a dark blue brocade vest that he slipped onto my shoulders, and then applied a small dark blue bow tie at my throat. "There" he said again. "Now you look ready for the theater tonight." "How did you know I want this for the theater?" I asked him. "Because a dozen other fellows have been here before you, all wanting new garments to wear for opening night."

Christian and Clay should feel honored I thought.

When the curtain went up for the opening of the play, *Oliver Twist*, the Crystal Palace Opera House seats were filled to capacity. The same full house would be repeated for another twenty-six performances. Never before had audiences at this theater been so captivated as with these talented actors and actresses, a group that Simon Bordeaux had carefully selected for the roles.

With perfect make-up and proper clothing, it wasn't difficult for the audience to imagine Christian as the orphan boy in the lead role. Although Christian wasn't as diminutive as the undernourished nine-year-old character that Charles Dickens intended, his rather small stature, compared to the rest of the cast, fit quite well, and his practiced soprano voice was quite convincing. By the time the orphan runs away from all the people who have mistreated him, Christian, as Oliver Twist, had captured the hearts of the entire audience. But then, the real surprise to that first unsuspecting crowd of viewers was when he encounters Jack Dawkins—the "Artful Dodger"—played by the young and debonair gambler, Clay Edwards. The people of Silver Spring had learned to admire the young man on the street, but now, on stage, they simply adored him as the prime integer in a gang of juvenile pickpockets.

Simon Bordeaux, Christian, Clay, and the entire theater company enjoyed a long and prosperous run of *Oliver Twist*. But it was after the ninth performance on a chilly November night when a terrifying incident marred the good fortune. It was the night that Clancy's brothers, Jeremiah and Daniel, and their wives attended the play at the Crystal Palace. After the final curtain, several members of the audience paused outside in front of the theater to converse. Among them was Daniel Crane, who then was a candidate for Town Marshal, Ralph Longhorn, and Tom Hargrove, the newspaperman. Jeremiah Crane excused himself to get back to Tanglewood where young Clancy was tending to business so his brother could attend the play.

"How about a game of billiards before we call it a night?" Daniel suggested to the others.

Ralph Longhorn and Tom Hargrove accompanied Daniel to the Continental Billiard Hall, just a couple of blocks down Main Street.

The Continental wasn't crowded. Daniel and Ralph took up cues and began play, while Tom and several other gentlemen watched. Ralph bent over the table to make a shot. Daniel, his back to the alley door and window, stood by chalking his cue when suddenly the window glass behind him shattered. The blast of a six-gun sounded from the alley. Daniel dropped his cue, spun around and collapsed onto the wood floor. A second shot rang out, but the slug lodged harmlessly in the side of the pool table.

The breeze had scarcely blown the gray smoke from the pistol away when several by-standers raced to the door. When they returned from the empty alley, Daniel was dead.

Jeremiah had barely removed his coat when the messenger dispatched by Tom Hargrove flung open the Hotel front door, yelling in terror to the Innkeeper. "Jeremiah! Come quick! The Continental! Daniel's been shot!"

Jeremiah hastily instructed Clancy to remain a while longer, grabbed his coat from its hook and ran with the messenger out the front door.

Thinking it was just another drunken barroom brawl, a big crowd already jammed the Continental's entrance. Jeremiah pushed his way through the curious onlookers only to find Ralph Longhorn and Tom Hargrove kneeling beside his dead brother.

My Journal—Clancy Crane

Joey and Eddy and I had attended and passed all the usual classes at school, but Mrs. Tundle told us that she had prepared some lessons of "higher learning" for us, and insisted that we should come back to school this fall. We all like Mrs. Tundle. She knows how to make school fun and interesting, so we all agreed. She had devised a way to separate the one large school room in half by having carpenters build a temporary wall right down the middle. All the younger elementary children are on one side, and about 10 of us older students have our "Higher Learning" Room all to ourselves. Mrs. Tundle gives us lessons in History, Geography, English Language, and Mathematics. On the other side of the wall she calls it Arithmetic but on our side of the wall it's called Mathematics.

I always get my work around the hotel done early, before the morning classes, and we are out of school in time for me to meet the 3 o'clock train with the carriage. But on Saturdays Jeremiah allows me to do whatever I want to do. Sometimes me and Eddy and Joey ride to Wellington or sometimes all the way to Red Hawk. I always invite Christian and Clay to join us. Sometimes they come, but most of the time they are too tired from their Friday night shows, or they are busy getting ready for a Saturday night performance. They are still some of my best friends, just like Joey and Eddy, and they come to visit me often during the week, but show business takes up most of their time on the weekends.

Friday afternoon when we left the schoolhouse, Eddy was lagging behind Joey and me. We had been discussing our Saturday plans when Eddy finally caught up to us. "What's the secret mission, boys?" he said in a whisper. "Do we need a password? What shall it be? Do we storm the castle at dawn, or go out and steal chickens at midnight?" "The password" said Joey "is jack rabbit. We're going hunting tomorrow. Are you coming along?" Eddy said "I shall lead the expedition, forging the trail through the wilderness, stalking the mighty and ferocious beasts—" "We'll be at your place at 8 o'clock in the morning" Joey interrupted. "We'll leave our horses in your corral and walk from there."

After I took three traveling salesmen and their cases of wares to the depot and then brought back a carriage full of new hotel guests, I put the carriage away and turned the horses into the corral behind the stables. I had to get ready for the hunt. I got out my favorite rabbit gun, a double-barrel 16 gauge shotgun that Jeremiah gave me for Christmas when I was 11. That gun has put a lot of meat on our table. I know how far it will reach, the pattern it *throws, and what it can and cannot do. I wouldn't swap it for any other gun in the world.*

The next morning was raw and cold, overcast, and a damp wind blew from the north. Clancy bundled himself in his warm mackinaw coat, quite certain that he would be glad for it later. When he trotted Shiner up to the Lowery's little barn, he found Joey equally protected against the chilly wind in a heavy sheepskin jacket, complete with a turned-up wooly collar. Bear barked his greeting and sniffed at Shiner's nose. Joey slipped his sleek 12-gauge double-barrel into its scabbard and swung into Pokey's saddle. "Hope you're dressed warm enough," he said to Clancy. "It'll be cold out in the hills."

They both rode off toward Eddy Swenson's house, Bear running out ahead. He knew this was a hunting trip, and he was eagerly ready to chase rabbits with Duke.

Eddy was waiting on the back stoop in his mackinaw, his trusty old 10-gauge resting across his lap. It was the gun that Joey affectionately called "the cannon"—an old, long, heavy, single-barreled shotgun that delivered quite a kick. If Eddy shot quickly without bracing himself first, the recoil from the 10-gauge would spin him around and sometimes knock him down. "Why don't we take the horses?" he asked.

"Because," Joey replied. "You and me are not getting enough exercise. Look at Clancy... he's so healthy he stinks! So he needs to get aired out, and he can carry home the game."

Duke and Bear were off and running ahead, as usual, as the trio headed north of town. They took to the ridge above the railroad tracks instead of following any road; rabbits would be more plentiful there. But after the first mile, they had not spotted a single rabbit. The cold wind had them laying low. Then, about a hundred yards ahead, the dogs scared a cottontail out of hiding and went howling after it to the east, glad for a chance to run, perhaps, and get warmed up. Too far away to get a good shot, the boys continued on with hopes that the rabbit would circle around past them, like jacks would sometimes do. But this one didn't.

The dogs finally returned about a half-hour later. By then the boys had covered another half-mile and were just entering a draw where a couple of twisted old cottonwoods shaded a heap of rotting wood rubble that had once been a cabin of sorts. Little remained to identify anything in particular, but Joey knew this to be an ancient trading post. They stopped and scuffed the sod with their boot heels, turning up nothing more than a green bottle neck, a few rusty nails, and a piece of broken pottery. The cold wind sighed heavily through the bare cottonwood branches, and the dogs kicked up another rabbit while the boys weren't paying attention.

There was an echoing whistle; the mid-morning freight train came rumbling along the tracks fifty yards to the west. Eddy climbed to the top of the rubble heap and waved his arms frantically, shouting "Help! Help! We're being held hostage by a band of cannibals!" The engineer waved back and then the whistle shrieked again in playful short blasts, and the wind whipped a stream of gray smoke over and around the boys with its half-warm, sooty odor.

When the train was gone, the dogs came panting back from their chase and Eddy jumped down from the ruins, flopping his arms to warm up. "I'm freezing to death," he said. "Let's get going."

They turned eastward and by noon, at their slow pace, they reached an outbuilding of a ranch near Webb's Lake. Joey and Clancy had shot only one rabbit each, but Eddy had not even taken aim the entire morning. Duke and Bear chased a rabbit into a hole under the shed and put up quite a fuss, but the boys headed to the lee side of the building to get warmed up out of the wind. After a few minutes, Clancy and Joey were warm enough, but Eddy's teeth were chattering. Clancy thought he was play acting again, until Joey felt of his forehead. "Come on. We're going home," Joey said seriously. It's too cold out here for people to enjoy, and we're not having too much fun."

For once, Eddy didn't have an oratorical reply. He followed along, his jaw set and shoulders hunched against the cold. He was dragging his feet by the time they reached the top of the ridge above the lake. Clancy offered to carry his shotgun for him, but he refused at first with an angry tone. Then, after he reconsidered he said, "Very well, valet, take the cannon."

It was a long, slow walk back to Silver Spring. Eddy had fallen silent, hands deep in his mackinaw pockets and his head down. Occasionally they stopped, Joey and Clancy standing on the windward side of Eddy to give him some shelter. After a few minutes of rest, Eddy started to shiver again, so they resumed walking.

A half-mile from town, the wind carried with it pellets of sleet that stung like birdshot. Within minutes, the grass became slippery with the stuff, and all three were sliding and stumbling. Eddy slipped and fell to his knees; Joey helped him up and tried to assist him by taking his arm as they walked, but Eddy shook his head and pushed him away.

When they reached the top of the knoll behind Tanglewood, Joey said, "We're gonna take you to the drug store to see my dad."

"No," Eddy responded. He turned onto the trail past the cemetery. "I'm going home."

Clancy was still carrying the cannon, but Eddy seemed to have forgotten. Joey argued that they should head to Main Street, but it was no use. Eddy just kept walking down the trail toward his house. The others caught up and walked all the way with him to the Swenson's back yard. Eddy took his gun, shouldered it, and was about to start for the house when a coughing spasm nearly took him to his knees. He stood there for several minutes, Joey and Clancy practically holding him up. Finally, he regained his balance, straightened up and said, "Thank you, gentlemen. I shall be seeing you anon." By then his face was pasty white. He turned to climb the steps, stumbled and nearly fell, caught himself, crossed the porch, and then entered the house without looking back.

"Eddy's really sick," Clancy said as he and Joey saddled the horses.

"Yeah," replied Joey. "Lucky we started back when we did."

"Sure wish he'd gone to see Doc Lowery."

"Me too," Joey said. "I'll get my dad to come see him right away."

My Journal—Clancy Crane

Everybody at school wondered where Eddy was the next Monday. Unlike Joey and me, they weren't nearly as concerned when we told them he was very sick. Then in private, Joey told me that Eddy had an awful heavy cold and that he was running a fever. "What does that mean?" I asked. "It means he's really sick." I asked if his father had seen him yet. "Yes, he's been to their house twice."

Tuesday there was no change. Joey said "My father says he's about the same."

But Wednesday morning Joey had worse news. Eddy had pneumonia and he told me that in a hushed voice. The sickness is so deadly that everybody hesitates to talk about it. Those who recover from pneumonia are considered lucky to be alive.

I was so stunned by the news that I don't think I heard a single word in any classes. I was in a daze all day. After the last class I met Joey outside and told him "We have to go see Eddy." "No" Joey said. "I asked my father and he said we'd better stay away. Eddy's got an awful high fever and he's out of his head." "Well there's got to be something we can do" I said. "Come down to the drug store and we'll see what Dad says."

Doc Lowery wasn't there, but he came in just a few minutes later, looking tired and worn out. He had been called out at midnight to a farm ten miles away to deliver a baby, which was stillborn. He had just returned when he was summoned to another country home where a man had what turned out to be a ruptured appendix. Doc Lowery performed the emergency operation on a kitchen table and hoped for the best. Before he returned to the store, he had stopped at the Swenson's house to check on Eddy. He saw Joey and Clancy waiting by the front windows and invited them to his back office.

When he had put down his bag and taken off his overcoat, he sat down heavily in the swivel chair at his roll top desk. He removed his glasses and began polishing them with a handkerchief. Turning toward the two boys he said, "I'm afraid I have some bad news about Eddy. His lungs are weak and his heart can't take the strain much longer. He may not pull through the night."

Clancy felt like he had just been kicked in the gut by a horse. He reached for a chair and fell onto it. Joey just stood there staring at his father.

Dr. Lowery put his handkerchief in a pocket and put his glasses on again. He sighed. "Eddy has double pneumonia and a bad heart too. He has no reserve left in him. His chances for recovery are getting quite slim." He paused a long moment and then turned to Clancy. "I already told Joey this, and now I'm going to tell you, Clancy… that hunting trip you three took last Saturday didn't have anything to do with this. Eddy had the pneumonia before he ever left the house. If he'd stayed home in bed, he'd still be just as sick by now. Just remember that… both of you… it's not your fault."

"Can we go see him?" Clancy asked.

"No. There's no reason for you to be exposed, and Eddy's high fever has him delirious. He wouldn't even know you."

"Isn't there anything we can do?"

Doc Lowery just shook his head. "You're both pretty healthy and strong. Just see that you stay that way. No, there's nothing you can do for Eddy now." He turned to his desk.

Joey and Clancy left the office and stood silently by the big front window for several minutes. Finally, Clancy said, "See you at school tomorrow," and headed for Tanglewood. He told Millie and Jeremiah what Doc Lowery had said.

"That's just so sad," said Millie. "Some folks live longer than they need to, and others don't have the chance to get started. I suppose it's God's will, but it is so sad."

Eddy died that night.

My Journal—Clancy Crane

Winter in Silver Spring is neither bleak nor pleasant. It is just plain winter, with snow and cold and sometimes bitter wind. When a blizzard sweeps across the hills it seems to have come all the way from the Arctic Circle. But there aren't so many of them—most winter storms are just snowfall without the high wind and bitter cold. And then there are the times when Chinooks, relatively warm winds blow in from the west and give us periods of melt and pleasant temperatures that remind us that there will eventually be an end to winter.

The people in town shovel the snow from the sidewalks, and dig paths to stables, wells, and privies. A track is kept open down the main streets for the drays from the depot, the coal wagons, and the delivery wagons from the food stores for those who are unable to get to the store themselves. The country roads are mostly blocked, so the farmers come to town in horse-drawn sleighs instead of wagons, and some walk on snowshoes. Even the stagecoach from Silver Spring to Wellington is a sleigh during the worst winter months. Travel beyond the local vicinity is mostly by rail, but during the winter the train is usually late, and if there has been a bad storm with a lot of snow, the passenger and freight trains don't make it to Silver

Spring for several days.

Joey and I keep going to school every day. We enjoy our "higher learning" classes with Mrs. Tundle, and because we are the oldest boys at the school, we are expected to keep wood and coal in the heating stove, and to make sure there is a fresh bucket of drinking water drawn from the neighbor's well every morning. School is a good way to spend our time during the cold winter, but we're very much looking forward to spring.

Spring did come right on schedule, and as the warm early summer dressed the surrounding hills in a veil of green, there seemed to be change in the air, but no one could lay claim with any degree of certainty exactly what that change was.

Silver Spring had lost its lawman; Dan Flanagan had moved on, and the only interested candidate to replace him had been murdered by the bandits he intended to put behind bars. Daniel Crane, the brother of Jeremiah and Clancy, the man who rode shotgun on the Wilson Stage to Wellington and Red Hawk, and the only man to witness the murder of the stagecoach driver many months earlier, was viciously gunned down by the cowards who didn't want him to become the law. So the boomtown lay in a state of lawlessness once again, and Silas Patch was finding great difficulty in correcting that situation. No one was eager to fill the position.

The Crystal Palace Opera House had had its finest season ever, Christian Parker and Clay Edwards contributing largely to the reason for packed audiences all through the fall and winter. When the curtain fell on the final performance, the two new young actors had become quite well-known, and theater fans had traveled great distances to view the play, *Oliver Twist.*

For Clancy Crane, spring was a time to renew his bond with the world. In the past six months, he had lost a best friend, and he had lost a brother; he had mourned for both all winter. Even though Eddy wasn't his *only* best friend and he had always been closer to his brother, Jeremiah than to Daniel, their deaths had left him feeling empty and alone, wondering why some people were not allowed to live their lives. But as spring blossomed into summer and Silver Spring was returning to its usual lively ways, Clancy started to realize that no matter what happened, the world and all its wonders went on. Mrs. Patch's flower pots on the balcony overlooking Main Street flourished with color; a new string of horses frolicked in Brook's Livery corral; the smell of sawdust and fresh-cut hay and baking bread filled the air; miners and sawyers and ranchers filled the saloons and gambling halls; and every afternoon could be heard the echoing whistle of the approaching three o'clock passenger express, depositing its load of salesmen and fun seekers and family visitors.

And for Clancy, summer meant the early morning visits to Market Square as the farmers started bringing in their produce, tanned hides, fur pelts, smoked meats, and of course, George was always there with his chicken eggs.

Everything seemed so usual and natural, and yet, there was that mysterious veil of change, seemingly preparing to choke the town. Smith & Hayden Mining had not sunk any new mineshafts for quite some time, and it seemed that the silver and gold production had diminished some, but the thought of the mining coming to an end at Silver Spring was such a preposterous and frightening topic that no one talked about it in public... ever.

But eventually, the rumor mill produced more than could be kept quiet; unfortunately, it wasn't just rumors. As Clancy entered Market Square early Wednesday morning with his one-horse buggy, he noticed a strangely solemn atmosphere among the vendors; the usual cheerfulness and high-spirited chatter between the market people was absent, and no one seemed to be smiling. He had a busy day ahead, as the Mining Board of Directors were due to arrive on the three o'clock express for their quarterly inspection of mining operations and two days of business meetings; they slept and dined at Tanglewood, so there was plenty to do at the hotel in preparation. Clancy headed straight for George's wagon, always his first stop. George's chicken eggs were in high demand, and Clancy made it his top priority. George always seemed to know the latest and most accurate news of what was going on around Silver Spring.

"Why all the long faces?" Clancy asked.

"Ain't you heard?" George replied.

"Heard about what?"

"The mines."

In Silver Spring, that was a common, everyday topic, and there was seldom anything extraordinary about mine gossip.

"We just got the word yesterday," George went on. "They're shuttin' down the mines. S & H is pullin' out."

"But why would they do that?"

"Ain't makin' a profit anymore."

It seemed a little odd to Clancy that this news—if it was true—hadn't yet saturated Silver Spring. "But the Board is comin' today. They'll be at Tanglewood tonight."

"It'll be their last. Word is they're comin' to close everything down. And that kinda puts all of us outa business too."

"But George... we'll still be here."

"You and who else? The rabbits? Most everybody in this town works for S & H Mining. If they go, so will all those people. There won't be anybody left."

This all seemed quite outrageous. Just the thought of the miners' absence boggled Clancy's mind. Certainly this had to be just a crazy rumor. But while he made his usual stops around the Market, the entire buzz sounded the same; even the farmers were already talking about pulling up stakes and moving on.

Tanglewood's carriage sat poised and ready at the Depot when the three o'clock Express arrived. By now the entire town had heard the shocking news and everyone was anxious to hear an official announcement. A crowd had gathered at the Depot, but not even the reporter from The Striker could coax a comment from any of the seven dignitaries as they stepped off the train, briskly boarded the enclosed carriage and rode off to the Smith & Hayden Mining headquarters at the far end of town. Something was in the air, and it didn't look good.

The doors at S & H Mining remained locked the rest of the day. No one left, and no one entered the secret proceedings. Tom Hargrove, The Striker's reporter tried knocking; he even tried peeking and eavesdropping through the windows, but nothing so far was gaining him access to the hottest story Silver Spring would ever hear. The people would be expecting a full account in the next edition of The Striker that was due to hit the street the next afternoon. But so far, he had nothing but rumors and wild speculation.

More people swarmed into Tanglewood's Saloon on this Wednesday afternoon than on a Saturday night after payday. Jeremiah knew it was only because of everyone's awareness that the Directors stayed at the Lodge when they were in town. The dining room would fill to capacity with the bigwigs and their guests - or at least, that's the way it usually happened - and tonight a lot of curious citizens, and a few irate ones were hoping to learn the fate of the mines, and perhaps of Silver Spring.

This was a bittersweet day for Jeremiah Crane. Business was better than he'd seen for quite some time, but he couldn't help wondering if there would be any more like it - ever. If the mines closed down, the hundreds of miners and their families would be forced to leave; there certainly weren't other jobs for them here. And without the miners spending their pay on the streets of Silver Spring, the town would surely die a painful, lonely death.

And what would become of Jeremiah Crane? In the eight years he had just barely paid off the thirty-thousand-dollar mortgage on Tanglewood Lodge. He had come here with money in his pocket and a big dream, and on more borrowed money he fulfilled his dream, raised a family, and became a cornerstone of the community. Now that dream - Tanglewood Lodge - a mere building at the end of Main Street in a town with its future in the balance was all he had.

It was well past ten o'clock by the time anyone realized that Clancy had snuck the Directors in through a back entrance and quietly ushered them to the upstairs rooms, unnoticed by the rather noisy, and now slightly tipsy crowd. Only the shrewd and keen-eyed Tom Hargrove had spotted them, and with Clancy's assistance had managed to finally convince the dignitaries to grant him an interview and to divulge the facts. "Otherwise," he told them, "I will be forced to print only rumors in tomorrow's paper, and all of you will be portrayed as nasty, greedy bureaucrats here only to ruin the lives of a thousand honest, hard-working people."

It was so quiet perhaps a spider could have been heard walking across the floor when Hargrove raised his voice above the crowd. He stood halfway down the front staircase overlooking the eager faces that filled the room. Dead silence prevailed with the anticipation of the bad news they really didn't want to hear, but they felt the need to hear it anyway, just to ease the tension. Even "Fingers" stilled the keys of the upright.

"The full story will be on the front page tomorrow," Tom began.

All eyes were on the newsman they had trusted for several years.

"I have gotten the official word from the Board of Directors. As of noon tomorrow, all mining operations at Silver Spring run by Smith & Hayden Mining Company will cease."

It was what they had expected – and feared. There didn't seem to be any need for answers to any other questions. Murmurs and mumbles started replacing the silence. Slowly they began filing out the front door, heading for homes somewhere in the darkness beyond the hazy glow of the street lamps.

My Journal—Clancy Crane

It has been several weeks since the mining stopped. Every day I watch a parade of wagons loaded with entire households and families crawling slowly out of town. Many of them don't even know their destination. They're like a band of gypsies following the wind. At first I thought it would only be the miners leaving, but now many of the stores in town have closed and the proprietors are in the departing parade. Most of the saloons and gambling joints and restaurants have shut their doors too. Even Silas Patch has closed the Royal Hotel. He and Mrs. Patch left town yesterday. Of course, Mr. Patch is leaving a very wealthy man.

All of Chinatown practically vanished overnight. Everything is gone, even their shacks. Only thing left is footprints in the mud.

Gus the wagon builder sold every wagon he had, and the only horse Brook had left was the one he rode away. He came to say good-bye to me and Shiner, said he and Buster the blacksmith and Gus were going to set up shop together in San Francisco. I wished them all the best of luck.

All the machinery and equipment has been removed from the stamping mill and smelter and hauled away. It seems awfully strange—that place that was always so noisy and busy is now forever silent, only an empty shell left of the monster that had made Silver Spring what it was. A long time ago I can remember hearing people say that this could happen someday, but now that it has, it's almost unbelievable. Watching all the sad faces on the people who are leaving town, I now understand why nobody ever wanted to talk about the possibility of the mines playing out. So many of the men who worked the mines came here with almost nothing, and many of them are now leaving with not much more. While they were here they lived well, enjoying all the comforts and good living that Silver Spring had to offer. They spent their money as fast as they earned it in the saloons, the gambling halls, the brothels. They will surely find another boomtown somewhere and do it all over again, just as Silver Spring was not their first.

But I feel sad for all the people who came here to make a better life, and found success and happiness, built homes and raised families. Now their good fortune has been stripped from them, and they are forced to leave behind their good life in Silver Spring, hoping for a bright future in another place.

A few days ago I rode Shiner out to see the Swensons. Eddy was one of my best friends, and I will always miss him. I had not seen his mother or father since Eddy's funeral and I wanted to see how they were getting along. I was saddened to find their house empty. Later I learned that Mr. Swenson had hauled one of the first loads of machinery out of the stamping mill, and his family had followed with the household in another wagon. I will visit Eddy's grave later today.

Another week has passed, and the most difficult of all good-byes came yesterday. With most of the population gone now, Doc Lowery felt the need to go where he is needed more. The decision to leave Silver Spring came abruptly, and its news to me was rather shocking. His son Joey is truly a dear friend, and I shall sincerely miss all the good times we have shared. Although our parting saddens me, I am also happy for Joey Lowery. He is so smart and capable of great things. I know that he will become a fine doctor someday, just like his father.

At least I still have my good friends Christian Parker and Clay Edwards for companions. Now that the Crystal Palace Opera House has a very limited audience and shows have all but ceased, Christian and Clay have more time for social life, although there aren't too many others to have a social life with. So they spend a lot of time at Tanglewood with me, and sometimes at night, just for fun and the tips people drop in a hat, they put on little shows with Fingers Malone providing the music. Because Tanglewood isn't so very busy anymore, I have time to get away during the day, and Christian and Clay and I roam the deserted streets. We walk all the way down to Silver Creek, past the sawmill and ice house, and we always stop in at the Silver Creek Brewery where Hans Stengahl always offers us a free glass of his brew. Those are the only places left where people still have jobs, but rumor is that Hans will soon move his brewery to Wellington, and the sawmill will only operate until all the logs drying beside the mill pond have been cut into lumber. That stack is getting mighty small.

Then we wander through the deserted silver smelter sheds and occasionally we find tiny bits of silver no bigger than birdshot. Those buildings look as if a good wind would knock them right down.

And then we usually end our journey at the Railroad Depot where the 3 o'clock express still stops every day. But there's seldom more than two or three passengers arriving, and they're usually Silver Spring residents who are returning from a shopping trip in Red Hawk or Wellington to buy the things that aren't available here anymore. Or sometimes there are shady-looking characters that are neither businessman nor job seeker. They always seem to know where to go, though, to Tanglewood Lodge. I have figured out that they are outlaws looking for a temporary place to hide.

Every day Christian expects Simon Bordeaux to arrive. Simon has been away for the past two weeks. He told Christian before he left that he intended to find a new location for a theater. When he did, he would return to pack up all his belongings, and any members of the theater troupe were welcome to follow him to the new location. He especially wanted Christian and Clay to accompany him. I keep telling Christian that Simon is not coming back, and deep down inside, I hope that he doesn't. If Christian and Clay leave, I will have lost all my close friends.

After three weeks of Simon's absence, Christian is beginning to believe that he isn't coming back, and Clay has been showing hints of falling back into a life of gambling and crime. Both are now living at Tanglewood following the absolute closing of the Crystal Palace. The last traveling minstrel show performed only one night before an audience of only twenty-two people.

But Christian and Clay made so much money this last winter as the stars of *Oliver Twist*, they can afford to live at Tanglewood. Besides, neither of them knows how to cook, and our hotel answers all their needs.

Silver Spring no longer has a newspaper—Tom Hargrove, who took over its operation from Mr. Grumby two years ago, finally admitted that it was a losing proposition. First of all, with the mines closed, stores out of business, and the greater population gone, there was no local news to report anymore, and even if there was, there weren't enough people left to read it to make it worthwhile printing. All the other saloons and gambling halls are closed, and with no opera house, entertainment in Silver Spring is non-existent—except for Tanglewood. It's the only place in town to get a cold beer or a shot of brandy, it's the only place to order a restaurant cooked meal, and Fingers Malone is the only source of musical entertainment. The folks who are left gather there to swap bits of news and gossip. Reverend Miller has even found it advantageous to conduct his Sunday morning services there, because it's where everybody gathers for Sunday breakfast. Christian and Clay still amuse the patrons once in a while with their silly skits and sometimes a few songs, but I can tell that they are getting discouraged. I hate to see them in such a sorry state.

The 3 o'clock Express whistle aroused the usual interest yesterday. Christian and Clay and I were just completing our daily patrol of checking the size of the remaining log pile, and we'd had our sampling of Silver Creek Beer at the brewery. Only Clay was anxious to see who might step off the train... perhaps a gambler of sorts, who he could engage in a poker game later that night. As we rounded the corner of the depot and strolled toward the platform, we saw a few passengers had already disembarked. A gentleman in long-tailed coat and top hat stood with his back to us. Clay approached with the intention of making acquaintance, and then an invitation to the poker table. But when the man turned around, to our greatest astonishment, it was Simon Bordeaux!

In an instant my heart sank, for I knew that my only close friends, Christian and Clay, would soon be gone, off somewhere to pursue their already successful acting careers. But then I thought for a moment about how depressed Christian had been for the past few days, and I saw how happy he was now with Simon's return. I couldn't allow my selfish desires to stand in his way.

"Where have you been? California?" Christian asked Simon.

"No" replied Simon. "I've been east."

"New York? Philadelphia?" asked Clay.

"No, no," said Simon. "I've been to a charming spot in Wisconsin. A beautiful lake and hills and breathtaking rock cliffs and pine forest... and tourist hotels and theaters... and the Ringling Brothers Circus!"

I remembered traveling through Wisconsin on our way from Ohio, and marveling at the natural beauty there. I recalled passing lakes and climbing over hills, and crossing the Mississippi River on a ferryboat at a place called La Crosse. If that's where they were destined, they were surely going to a charming place.

"When do we go?" Christian asked with excitement in his voice.

"Soon" said Simon. "As soon as we can get everything packed."

Clay noticed that I was only trying to smile. Indeed I was happy for them, but it was painful to think of their leaving. He put his arm across my shoulders. "Simon !" he said. "How 'bout we take Clancy with us?" Then he turned to me. "Why don't you come with us, Clancy? There's nothing here for you anymore."

The request came as quite a surprise to me. Granted, there was little left in Silver Spring, but I wasn't ready to make such resolution as to leaving the place I called home, and abandoning my only brother, my only family, just didn't seem right to me.

"You are more than welcome to join us" said Simon.

"Yes ! Please do come with us !" said Christian.

"I don't know" I said. "I'll have to think it over."

A few days have passed since Simon arrived back in Silver Spring and Clay asked if I would go with them to Wisconsin. They have been busy packing their belongings and all the theater gear in big crates—wardrobe costumes, props, small furniture, lights, and even the huge dark blue stage curtain. I helped them when I didn't have chores to do at the hotel. All during the packing, they asked me if I had made my decision, whether to stay in Silver Spring or go to Wisconsin. It has been a very difficult choice. When I brought up the subject to Jeremiah and Millie last night at the supper table, Millie said that she wished they had the choice to make. Millie has been trying to convince Jeremiah to move away ever since the mines closed and the town started its downward spiral. But Jeremiah is steadfast in his commitment to Tanglewood, and he has faith that Silver Spring can and will once again flourish. It will just take time for the people to find a reason to come back. As a brother, he told me that I had to follow my heart, and to choose the path that seemed right to me.

Finally, the time came to haul all the crates from the Crystal Palace to the railroad station. Jeremiah agreed to let me do the task with our horse and wagon. I made four trips. We heard the whistle of the Express just as we unloaded the last crate onto the platform. Christian took my arm and dragged me aside.

"I don't see any baggage of yours" he said.

"No" I replied. "As much as I hate to part company with you and Clay, I have decided to stay. Silver Spring is my home. Jeremiah is my only kin. Brothers should stick together."

"We'll miss you" Clay said looking over Christian's shoulder.

I shook their hands and hugged them both and wished them well with tears in our eyes, and then Simon called to them.

"Come, gentlemen. Let us be on our way to Wisconsin!"

They boarded the train and I guessed that I would never see them again. But I was where I wanted to be, and I guess that my spirit will be in Silver Spring forever.

Clancy Crane's journal doesn't end here, but the story of his final, event-filled days in Silver Spring has been told before. Future episodes, perhaps, will bear evidence that his spirit indeed lives on in the place he loved.

Part 3

Piano Man

ONE

"We could use a good piano man."

Clay looked at Christian with utmost seriousness. "And where do y'all think we'll find one here?"

"We could go into the city and find one."

The thought of venturing out to Baraboo was secretly intriguing to both, but rather than jumping up in jubilation to begin their journey, they sat quietly at their table and sipped the dark ale. Simon had been gone all day—again—and the boys were eager to get back to work. Work to them, of course, was performing on a stage, and soon there would be plenty of people to enjoy their performances. All winter they had practiced their skits and songs that had been successful back in Silver Spring at Tanglewood after the theater closed, and they had even tried them out on small groups here in the *Cliff House*. But if they were to perform before larger audiences at the *Chateau*, they needed a piano player to appear more professional. So far, their efforts to find one had rendered nothing.

"Did I hear you say you need a piano player?"

Christian and Clay spun around to face the voice that had just spoken to them.

"I couldn't help but overhear..."

The boys at the table stared at the tall, dark-haired fellow standing there. None of them spoke for a while, just trying to size each other up.

"Do you play the piano?" Christian finally asked. It didn't seem likely; the fellow didn't look the type.

"No," the lad replied. "But I have a friend..."

Clay kicked the chair next to him out away from the table. "Have a seat," he said.

As the fellow sat, pulling the chair closer, Clay half stood and offered his right hand. "My name is Clay Edwards… and this is Christian Parker."

"My name is Roscoe Connor. Pleased to meet you both." He shook their hands and then eyed Clay. "I saw you playin' cards last night at the hotel. You sure 'nough cleaned everybody out."

Christian leaned in. "Best not sit down with this guy at the poker table. He doesn't lose."

"What he means to say," Clay corrected, "is that I *usually* win more than I lose."

"Yes, I saw evidence of that last night," said Roscoe.

"So, who's your piano-playin' friend?" Christian asked, looking around. "Where is he?"

"Oh, he's not here. His name's Marty Mason. He's in Baraboo."

"Where can we find him?"

"That's hard to say."

"Well… could you take us to him?"

Roscoe stared at Christian for a moment with reluctance in his eyes. "I'm here for a week of fishing. After that?"

"I'll pay your train fare if you'll go with us tomorrow."

"I don't know…"

"Aw, c'mon, Roscoe," Clay pleaded. "How long can it take? A couple hours there and back?"

"I'll have to think about it."

"The first train to Baraboo is at eight o'clock in the morning," Christian said. "We could be back here by ten."

"And you'll hardly miss any fishing time at all," Clay added.

"Well, I suppose…"

"Great!" Christian said. "We'll meet you at the depot at seven-forty-five."

Clay Edwards had been eagerly waiting for spring since the very first November snowfall. His peculiar little drawl that stamped him as Southern born made it quite clear he was never conditioned for Wisconsin winters. Content to stay by a warm fire, he'd managed to find a few poker games to keep him occupied during the cold months. Many a visitor from the big cities went back home with lighter pockets after an evening or two at the game table across from Clay. Here, though, the stakes weren't always as high as in the gold and silver boomtowns of the West, but Clay didn't really care; it was simply a good way to pass the time, and to keep spending money in his pocket.

Christian Parker, though, was accustomed to winter; he'd grown up in Denver. Winter was just a normal part of the year to him; he had skated on the frozen lake and had enjoyed the horse-drawn sleigh rides, although he, too, vigorously welcomed the springtime.

Nearly nine months had passed since they left Montana and arrived at Devil's Lake Village. They had endured the bitter Wisconsin winter, but now the ice was gone from the lake; warm spring air gave promise to the forthcoming summer. Nothing seemed grander than the verdant luster creeping onto the forested hills, for the dreary chill of winter and its blustery wind, the messenger of frosty and snow-filled days had erased the memory of crimson and gold and fiery orange that had painted those glorious October hills. Devil's Lake stretched and yawned as it awoke from its long, icy sleep, welcoming the warmth of the April sun and clamor of ducks and geese upon its placid waters. Soon it would host bathers and rowers and anglers, as the lake and its hotels and campsites had become a most popular resort destination to people from far and near. The *Chicago and Northwestern* railway trains would deposit vacationers from the big cities like Chicago, Milwaukee, and St. Paul by the hundreds and thousands all summer long, and Devil's Lake Village would be a very busy place.

Simon Bordeaux, the man responsible for them being there at Devil's Lake, had envisioned something grand. In the recent past, his endeavors in the theater business had all been relatively short-lived, moving from one mining camp to another, satisfying the entertainment needs and desires for communities that were destined to ghostdom when the mines played out. But nearby Baraboo was different; it was a show town, home of the Ringling Brothers Circus. One thing was certain: unlike the boomtowns in the West, Baraboo was a well-established city that would be there for a long time. It held a population quite ample to support a theater for the performing arts, and it would only be a matter of time until Simon had one established.

When Simon, Christian, and Clay boarded the train in Silver

Spring, Montana nine months ago, they were parting with good friends; they were leaving behind a magnificent opera house. But they were also saying goodbye to a town that was destined for destruction. The mines had played out and the majority of the population had moved on, abandoning homes and deserting businesses. Within a few short months, a madman gunned down the proprietor of the only operating hotel left, and then set fire to the rest of the town, leaving nothing but ashes and charred memories.

That winter, Christian received a telegram from his good friend Clancy Crane who, by then, was working aboard a riverboat on the Lower Mississippi River. They exchanged many letters after that, in which Clancy told of the devastating events that had destroyed Silver Spring and his harrowing experiences of survival. After the smoke cleared, warding off looters and outlaws in order to protect his dead brother's hotel, the only remaining building—Tanglewood Lodge—had not been easy, and finally, it seemed best to just leave. *"There was nothing to stay for,"* Clancy wrote. *"Somehow, I knew nobody was ever coming back. I bid farewell to my sister-in-law and my niece in Wellington, and hopped on a south bound steamer working as a deck hand. Three weeks later our boat was in St. Louis, and two weeks after that we arrived at New Orleans. We will stay on the Lower Mississippi all winter."* Of all the friends they had left behind, they missed Clancy most. His brother's hotel had been home for them after the opera house closed, so they had spent much time together. But their combined efforts and coaxing couldn't get Clancy to accompany them to Wisconsin.

Young as they were—Christian barely nineteen, and Clay, twenty, although his boyish looks made him seem much younger—they were seasoned stage performers. Christian's angelic singing voice melted half the ladies' hearts, and Clay's delightful Southern acting charm liquefied the other half. There could be little doubt why Simon Bordeaux, the troupe manager and producer, had lured them to Wisconsin with him; audiences loved these two adorable personalities, and rarely failed to fill the house when they performed. But those audiences had been in the wild Western mining camps; this was Wisconsin, where audiences had already been exposed to sophisticated stage arts for quite some time. Simon, though, was still optimistic that his two star performers could capture hearts in the Midwest just as well as in the Western theater. He was counting on it.

And there could be little doubt that they were getting restless, eager to be performing again.

As the train slowly pulled away from the Devil's Lake station the next morning and rolled along the edge of the lake, Roscoe Connor gazed out over the water, yearning to be there with a fishing pole in his hands. His father, a merchant in Baraboo, had finally relented, and given him a week to spend at the lake before the busy tourist season began, when the place would be overrun by big city dwellers. And now he was giving up precious time he had been longing for all winter, to find his friend Marty Mason, just because Marty could play the piano.

"Don't look so sad," Clay said. He stretched his arm behind Roscoe's neck and playfully patted his shoulder. "You'll be back out there fishing in no time."

"That is," Roscoe replied. "If we can find Marty right away."

"Why should he be so hard to find?"

"Mason could be anywhere. Until the Ringling Brothers come back for the season..."

"Ringling Brothers? They're the circus people?"

"Yeah... one of the most popular circuses in the country. Marty worked for them all last summer, and he says he's gonna work for them again this year, too."

"What does he do in the circus?"

"He's a musician. He traveled with them last summer."

"Hallelujah! Did y'all hear that, Christian? Our new piano player traveled with the circus! Just like Fingers Malone."

"He's not *our* piano player yet," Christian returned. "And if he already has a job with the circus, we might be wasting our time." He turned to Roscoe. "Why didn't you tell us that before we started on a wild goose chase?"

"You didn't ask," Roscoe replied. "Why do you need a piano player anyway?"

"We're performers of a theater troupe. We came here from Montana, but we came *without* a piano player."

"Montana!" Roscoe said.

"Yes," Christian explained. "We had a very successful theater in a mining town, but when the mine was finished, so were we. All the people of the town moved on..." Then, with a bit of melancholy in his voice he added, "And our opera house, the grand Crystal Palace died."

"So Simon went scoutin' for a new place," Clay added. "And we ended up here."

"Who's Simon?" Roscoe asked.

"Simon Bordeaux is our director. He owned the Crystal Palace... and he kinda runs the whole show. But he couldn't talk Fingers into coming with us."

"Who's Fingers?"

"He was the piano player at the hotel where we lived," Christian said. "When our theater closed, Clay and I kept performing at the hotel now and then, and Fingers provided the music."

"So, what happened to your theater musicians?" Roscoe asked.

"Most of them joined up with other troupes, but Simon thinks some of them... and some of the actors, too... will rejoin us here. He's been sending a lot of telegrams and letters."

By then, the train was rumbling along at speed through the countryside. Baraboo was not far; in ten minutes they would arrive at the station, and their search for the pianist would begin.

TWO

"I reckon we can start lookin' at his house," Roscoe suggested when they had disembarked the train.

It did seem a logical place to begin, however, Marty was not there, nor did his mother have a clue where he had spent the night. "I thought," she said, "That some of the circus people had returned, and he was with them."

But the circus people had not returned yet; their summer quarters were empty and quiet.

"So where to now?" asked Clay.

"We'll just have to walk around town... try to spot him somewhere."

"So *you* can spot him," Christian said. "Clay and I don't know who we're looking for."

"He's about my size," Roscoe explained. "Maybe a little taller."

"Well... that narrows it right down. What color is his hair?"

"Like sand. But it's cut short, and his cap covers most of it."

"What color is his cap?"

"Like sand."

"Now we're getting somewhere."

"Marty's got freckles," Roscoe offered.

"Okay! Okay!" said Clay. "We'll just follow y'all."

They toured the town, all except one street that Roscoe explained he had to avoid. "My father's store is on that street, and if he sees me here in town, he'll make me come back to work. I'm *supposed* to be out at the lake fishin', y' know."

The whistles of the next train to the lake had been heard long ago, still with no sign of the piano player. But a few of Roscoe's acquaintances had seen Marty that morning; he couldn't be far away.

By noon they had nearly given up all hope of finding Marty when Roscoe stopped in his tracks to take another look down an alley. "There he is," he said, pointing to a group of rough-looking characters. "Marty's the one in the yellow shirt."

Clay and Christian were glad to have finally ended the hunt; but the gathering in the alley didn't look like a friendly one. The yellow-shirted fellow was certainly outnumbered by five slovenly-attired ruffians; it appeared as if Marty Mason was about to become the recipient of some brutal treatment.

"HEY! MASON!" Roscoe called out.

That drew the attention of the gang from Marty just long enough for him to slip away, around the corner from his attackers. By the time they realized he was gone, Clay, Christian and Roscoe had taken advantage of their confused state to make an exit as well. They dashed down the street and ducked into the next alley. On a dead run, Christian and Clay followed Roscoe; he knew his way around the town, and they sincerely hoped he would lead them to an effective escape.

After two more blocks they stopped and listened at the corner, trying to detect any approach by the gang. They heard running footsteps, but it was only one pair of feet. Clay boldly stepped out to look. A bright yellow shirt was coming right at him at full speed. He reached out to grab the runner, spun him around and pulled him into the alley.

The fellow in the yellow shirt was taken by such alarm that he was winding up for a good fist fight before he realized that his friend, Roscoe was there.

"Go ahead!" he said to Clay. "Take your best shot!" Both his fists were clenched, drawn back, ready to strike. But then, as he eyed Clay dressed in a fancy black three-piece suit and bowler, standing before him with no intensions of engaging in battle, he relaxed a little, but still poised for defense if it became necessary.

"Take it easy, Mason," Roscoe said.

Marty Mason reluctantly turned to the familiar voice. "Connor! What are you doing here?" he asked his friend, still ready for a skirmish.

"Relax, Mason. They're friends."

Marty stared at Clay, and then at Christian. "How do I know I can trust 'em?"

"You'll just have to take my word," Roscoe replied as he gripped Marty's forearm.

They could hear the angry growls and shouts of Marty's

enemies about a block away. There was little time to discuss the merits of friendship; escape for Marty from these thugs was top priority.

"I have a plan," Clay informed the others. He hastily inspected Marty and Roscoe, comparing their size. "You two… trade shirts and caps."

The two friends stared at Clay, puzzled. "What—"

"Don't argue," Clay insisted. "Just DO IT! QUICKLY!"

Marty and Roscoe seemed to realize that Clay might have a good plan in mind. They swiftly followed the instructions, exchanging the clothing. The malicious voices were coming nearer.

"Now," Clay said. "Marty? Do y'all have any objections to taking a little train ride with us?"

Marty peered up the alley where the gang would appear any second, and then back at Clay. "Train ride?"

"No time for questions," Clay said. "It's that or we can leave y'all here to face those *friends* of yours on your own."

"Okay…" Marty answered. "I'll go with you."

"Christian," Clay said. "Take Marty down this alley and then go to the train station. Roscoe and I will stay here long enough to draw their attention with this yellow shirt. It should give y'all enough time to reach the station… they won't know where you went."

"And what about you?" Marty asked.

"Don't worry about us. I'll think of something. Now, GO! We'll catch up with y'all at the station."

Christian and Marty, now clad in Roscoe's faded blue shirt and dark blue cap, rushed down the alley and around the corner. Clay instructed Roscoe to turn his back to the other end of the alley where the gang was just entering.

"THERE HE IS!" the gang leader yelled. "LET'S GET HIM!"

Clay sensed Roscoe's fright as they listened to the hurried footsteps coming toward them. "Don't be afraid," he told Roscoe. "Simply turn around nice and easy when I give you a nod."

Clay counted five of them, all toting clubs of some sort; there was definitely murder in their eyes as they marched closer. The leader was a big fellow, at least six feet tall and rather stocky, built like a steamer trunk with legs and arms, clothes ragged, dirty and stained with sweat. The rest varied in size, but none were dressed any better than their chief, and all were determined to do harm to the fellow in the yellow shirt. They were about ten feet from Roscoe when Clay nodded. "Nice and easy," he reminded Roscoe in a low tone.

Roscoe slowly turned to face the assailants. "Hello, Jasper," he said. He tried to look unconcerned, but he knew he wasn't being very convincing. Even on this cool day, nervous sweat trickled down his back. Clay stepped beside him.

Upon seeing Roscoe's face, the gang leader stopped abruptly, holding his arms out to halt the others behind him. A jumble of shock, confusion, and disappointment washed over him as he stared at the target that had mysteriously changed. "Okay..." he said. "So... where's that rat?"

"To which rat would y'all be referring?" Clay said quite calmly.

Jasper still seemed baffled, and snarls kept coming from his followers. "Mason," the brute growled. "The one we followed here."

"Well," Clay replied. "There's no one else here... as y'all can plainly see."

Trying to make sense of the strange situation, Jasper looked Roscoe up and down, and then turned his focus on Clay, studying the fine clothes. Clay Edwards, in the prime of his life, just a little beyond twenty, not so tall but erect, continued to dress in the typical costume of the river gamblers—a dark, long-tailed coat, white shirt and black string tie, brocade vest, dark trousers, narrow at the bottom, and high-heeled boots polished like a mirror. He stood with supreme self-confidence without showing a hint of arrogance.

Jasper slapped the club he was holding into the palm of his free hand. Encountering a total stranger—especially one with the striking looks of Clay Edwards—was not what he had expected to find in that alley; he was stalling, trying to figure his next move, quite sure he had been hoodwinked but didn't know how. "Well, I think you must've helped him get away."

"Just why do y'all want to catch up with this *rat?*" Clay asked. He was buying time as well.

"That's none of your business," Jasper snapped, and then it was quite clear that Jasper and his gang intended to make short work of the two standing between them and their intended victim.

Roscoe was familiar with the ruffians; they were the most feared bullies among the population of Baraboo. Those who *did* attend school—Jasper among them—passed their classes only because the teachers were afraid to fail them. As far as Roscoe was concerned, he had always stayed clear of them, and right now he would sooner be running away at full speed than to be standing there facing these thugs. At this point, his confidence was melting like ice cream under a July sun; neither he nor Clay were big enough to take on all five in an alley fight, particularly when the opposition was armed with clubs... and no doubt, some with knives. He wondered how Clay could stand there so calm in the face of imminent danger. Clay's good plan had turned sour, and now they were about to pay for their bravery.

As Jasper and a couple of his buddies stepped forward, muscles flexed for combat, Clay's right hand gave a sudden jerk. In the next instant, the aggressors were staring at the business end of his double-barreled .41 caliber Remington derringer that was always tucked in a pocket inside his coat sleeve, ready for any unexpected need of defense. Jasper and the other two abruptly stopped their advance, eyes as big as fried eggs in a pan fixed on the weapon. Even though it was small in size, its large caliber barrels appeared rather intimidating.

"Y-you c-can't h-hit the b-broad side of a b-barn with that little pea-shooter," Jasper stuttered nervously.

"On the contrary," Clay said. "At this range I *don't* miss."

"B-but you only have two shots," Jasper said. "And there's five of us."

"Maybe," replied Clay. "But the first one will find *you*, Jasper, and then your friend beside you." He held out his left hand, palm up, revealing two more cartridges. "And I can reload before the two of you hit the ground. Believe me... I've had plenty of practice."

The two roughnecks beside Jasper swiftly and meekly retreated to their comrades behind them.

Roscoe stared at the gun with surprise, too, and then his eyes raced back and forth from Jasper to Clay. Although he had suddenly regained a little confidence, his instincts governed a couple cautious steps in retreat. Jasper, although stunned by the sight of the firepower, wasn't backing down.

Clay remained steadfast with his stiff right arm outstretched, the derringer pointed at Jasper's chest. "Now," he said calmly. "Maybe you boys should reconsider your desire for rat hunting today. I'm sure y'all could find something more constructive to do." His poker face never flinched or displayed any sign of emotion. His unblinking eyes were welded to Jasper's.

There was a chance, Jasper thought, that this Southern silver-tongued dandy was bluffing. But there was also the chance that he wasn't. He didn't look like a killer, but he acted much too calm for any man in his position. "Y-you won't pull that trigger," Jasper taunted nervously, stepping closer.

Clay pulled back the hammer and it sounded its distinct, unmistakable click that echoed between the buildings. "Take one more step in this direction, Mr. Jasper, and your pals will be carryin' y'all out of this alley."

"Y-you're bluffing."

"I've shot men before under much less threatening circumstances," Clay said in his soft, calm Southern drawl. "Y'all are comin' at me with a deadly weapon. I don't take kindly to getting beat over the head with a lead pipe."

Jasper's four disciple dogs were backing away. "Come on, Jasper," one pleaded with him.

"This ain't worth gettin' shot," another called out.

"I don't think he's bluffing, Jasper!" another cried.

"Let's get outa here 'fore this lunatic shoots us all," the fourth one urged.

Their voices were shallow and scared. Jasper listened to their petitions, and without admitting his own fear, he took a step back and dropped the pipe to his side. He now had his excuse to retreat: "Okay, you donkey spit," he snarled. "I guess the boys aren't wantin' t' fight today… so I guess I'll stick with them." He took several steps backward to rejoin the gang, and then they all started back stepping rapidly out of the alley. Half-way, they turned to walk forward, but still glancing over their shoulders to see Clay still standing in the same position with outstretched arm and derringer pointing their way.

Clay remained in that posture until the last one disappeared around the corner. He took a deep breath, dropped his arm, relaxed, and turned to where Roscoe stood six feet behind him. A little shaken by the incident and still quite tense, Roscoe stared in disbelief. No one had ever stood up to Jasper Blackburn and his bunch without receiving at least a black eye, multiple bruises and a knot on the head, if not worse.

Clay deposited the Remington back in its sleeve pocket, completely out of sight. "We have to get to the train station," he said. "What's the shortest way?"

Roscoe pointed his thumb over his shoulder, the opposite end of the alley from where Jasper left. It wasn't necessarily the *shortest* route to the depot, but he didn't want another confrontation. Clay gripped his arm, spun him around and started walking briskly toward the street. "Lead the way to the station," he told Roscoe.

THREE

Christian held four tickets to Devil's Lake. He breathed a little easier when he spotted Clay and Roscoe entering the crowded, busy station house. Marty Mason had hunkered down in a chair back in a corner, trying to stay out of sight. Neither of them was aware of Clay and Roscoe's narrow escape, nor of the gang's close proximity to the station. Clay had seen them, and he was quite certain that Jasper had followed them, perhaps seeking revenge.

"We have to get on that train... NOW!" Clay informed the others. He pushed Christian and Roscoe toward the platform door, and then grabbed Marty's arm and hoisted him up from the chair, practically dragging him to the boarding platform.

Roscoe spoke up: "But this train—"

"No time to be choosy," Clay interrupted calmly and continued to urge the others to a coach door. Once in the coach, Clay instructed the others to sit in seats away from the windows. Christian knew Clay's background well enough to know that he was a master at hasty get-away, and he also knew that Clay must have good reason for this one.

They heard the "All aboard" call by the conductor, and a few seconds later the shrill cry of the whistle. The train jolted forward, rumbling slowly away from the station. Clay saw Jasper and his gang through the windows, but it didn't appear they had any clue that the foursome was on the train. They seemed to still be searching among the people on the platform.

A few minutes later the conductor came by asking for tickets. Christian handed them over to be punched.

"How far are you boys going?" the conductor asked curiously.

"To Devil's Lake."

The conductor laughed. "You're on the wrong train "We're

headed to North Freedom and Rock Springs."

"Where's North Freedom?"

"The opposite direction from the lake."

Roscoe joined the conversation. "I tried to tell you back at the station."

"Well," Clay said. "We'll just have to buy more tickets to North Freedom."

"Tell you what," the conductor said. "I'll just let you boys get off at North Freedom. Next train back to the lake will be along in about two hours."

The station at North Freedom wasn't so crowded. A few other passengers had gotten off there, but most of them were already gone. The foursome stood on the platform watching the westbound train disappear around the bend.

"What are we gonna do here for two hours?" Christian asked no one in particular.

"One thing you *could* do," Marty said, "Is to explain what I'm doing here with a couple of people I don't know. You practically kidnapped me, y' know."

"I'd call it more like savin' your ass from getting beaten to a pulp!" said Clay. After a dramatic pause he added: "A little appreciation?"

Marty thought for a moment; he hadn't said much the whole time since the miraculous rescue by these strangers. Christian had introduced himself at the Baraboo station, but Marty had responded only by speaking his name—no more. He realized that he had probably been somewhat rude and ungrateful for not thanking his saviors. "Thanks," he said in a meek tone, and then offered his right hand to Clay. "I don't know who you are, but I *am* grateful for what you did."

"I'm Clay Edwards, and I'm sure you already know Christian. Y'all prob'ly had a chance to get acquainted back at the last station."

"By name only," said Marty. He nodded to Christian. "I guess I wasn't too talkative back there."

Roscoe had remained silent, too, since the incident in the alley; Clay's behavior had extended far beyond what he expected, and so smoothly executed, there could be little doubt that experience in such matters had to exist. "Why do you carry a pistol?" he asked

Clay in a tone that offered his suspicion of an outlaw.

"It's a derringer," Clay corrected. "Simply a means of protection associated with my former occupation."

"What are you talking about?" Marty broke in. "What pistol?"

"He pulled a gun—from where I don't know," Roscoe said. "That's how he got Jasper to back off."

Now Marty's curiosity rose to a new plateau; he had wondered why two finely dressed strangers had snatched him away from a hazardous state of affairs, potentially placing themselves in danger as well. They had no reason to jeopardize their own safety to help someone they did not know. "What kinda outlaws are you mixed up with, Roscoe?"

"Relax," Christian intervened. "We're not outlaws! It's true... Clay carries a derringer because he used to be a professional gambler."

"Gambler?" Marty sputtered.

"Yeah, that's probably so," said Roscoe. "I saw him playin' poker at the Cliff House... and he doesn't lose."

"Looks pretty young to be a professional gambler," Marty said.

"I started playin' poker when I was sixteen," Clay explained. "On a Mississippi riverboat where I worked. Thought I was just lucky at first, but then, one night I cleaned out a rich plantation owner of twenty-five thousand dollars. Decided right then and there that gambling was the best work for me."

"But you said... *used to be a gambler.*"

"I left the Mississippi—I'd had a few *bad experiences*—headed to the gold field boomtowns... that's when I eventually met Christian... after a few more hasty moves from one town to another."

"Bad experiences? Hasty moves?"

"It's unwritten law that when a man is accused of cheating... or he's challenged to a fight, he has the perfect right to promptly bring about his challenger's demise. But once that happens—and particularly if the man on the floor is a local—it's not a good idea to linger in that town too much longer."

Roscoe's and Marty's eyes widened like two little kids hearing a ghost story. "You mean... you... you..."

"Answered a few challenges?" Clay completed the question. "Yes... I did... but only when I was confronted with a deadly situation. Y'all must understand one thing: if a gambler backs down from a threat like that, one of two things happens... your self-confidence is destroyed and your reputation is ruined... or... you're dead."

"So," Roscoe said. "That's why you didn't back down from Jasper."

Clay nodded.

"Would you have shot him?"

Clay hesitated; he calculated the odds of these two fellows grasping the concept. "Yes," he said softly. "He was a deadly threat to both of us. If he'd taken another step toward us and started swingin' that pipe... yes... I would have pulled the trigger."

"You would have killed Jasper?" Marty exclaimed.

"He was gonna bash our heads in with a lead pipe," Clay replied. "It wasn't even us he was after in the first place. And I'm quite sure he wouldn't have hesitated to finish us off. What would y'all do?"

"I... I don't know," Marty said modestly. "I wasn't there."

"Sure seems like a lot of trouble to get a piano player," Christian laughed.

That seemed to lighten the serious nature of the conversation. He was tired of Jasper as the focal point; he was gone; Clay was the victor; it was time to get on with the business they came for.

Marty looked at Christian as if he had two heads. Then he glared at Roscoe. "What's he talkin' about, Roscoe?"

"They said they need a piano player."

Marty scowled at Christian and Clay again. "You mean... you rescued me from Jasper's gang because you need a piano player?"

"Well... yeah..." Christian replied. "But we weren't counting on Jasper when we came looking for you."

"How did you know where to find me?"

"We didn't... that's where Roscoe comes in."

"I've been at the lake fishing," Roscoe explained. "I met them at the Chateau last night. I told them about you."

"What gives you the right to stick your nose into my business?" Marty gave his friend a shove, and then lunged toward him.

Much smaller than either of them, Clay stepped between them before Marty could do any more damage. "Take it easy, Marty!" he said, holding the aggressor back. "Y'all should consider yourself lucky that he did... or maybe you'd be layin' back there in that alley right now."

Marty knew he was acting irrationally; his temper—that he usually kept in check—was flaring only because he was experiencing an extremely bad day. He abruptly surrendered to Clay's intervention; a fist fight with Roscoe wouldn't solve anything.

"Listen," Christian said trying to calm him down. "We heard you're a pretty darn good pianist. It was us who wrangled Roscoe into coming to Baraboo to look for you, so don't blame him."

"So why do you need a pianist?" Marty said in a calmer tone.

"Well, you see, it's like this," Christian said putting a hand on Marty's shoulder and steering him off to the side, away from Roscoe. "We're part of a theater troupe..."

While Christian and Marty wandered off, Christian explaining how they came to Wisconsin without the rest of the actors and musicians, Roscoe and Clay found a bench in the shade of the depot.

"Are you really a professional gambler?" Roscoe asked.

"Was," Clay responded. "I made a good living at it. Guess y'all could call it that."

"But now you're an entertainer. Why did you quit gambling?"

"Poker was gettin' mighty risky out there in the gold fields... too many hotheads with itchy trigger fingers... if y'all know what I mean."

Roscoe nodded. "And the hotheads were probably the usual losers at cards?"

"Y'all got it figured just about right... and 'cause I kinda take a liking to stay breathing a while longer, I decided to change my line o' work."

"But you're so quick with that gun—"

"The derringer y'all saw was only my backup. When we get back to the hotel, I'll show you the *equalizer*... my Smith n' Wesson forty-five."

"You carry a forty-five?"

"Not so much anymore... just the Remington derringer. It gives me a sense of safety."

"Will you teach me?" Roscoe said.

"What? To shoot?"

"No... cards. Poker."

Two hours seemed to flash by once good conversation took over. Other people started gathering on the boarding platform and then the faint sound of a whistle echoed. The eastbound was only ten minutes behind schedule, but the engineer and the conductor were determined to make up the lost time, somehow. Belching smoke and steam like the big iron monster it was, the engine rolled past the loading platform a little faster than usual. A frantic conductor nearly lost his cap as he stepped off the still moving cars. When the train finally came to an abrupt halt, he was already urging those waiting to get ready for boarding. Only a few passengers disembarked, and then the dozen people besides Clay, Christian, Roscoe and Marty were hurriedly shuffled aboard. The routine fifteen-minute stop was reduced to ten.

It was impossible to shorten the stop at Baraboo with so many travelers getting off and on the train. Clay was confident that Jasper and his dogs would be nowhere in sight of the station, but he scanned the area through the car windows anyway. Roscoe leaned toward the window, his eyes searching the crowd. "Any sign of 'em?" he whispered.

"No," Clay replied. "I'm sure they've given up by now."

Marty and Christian were too busy talking about music and entertainment to demonstrate concern. Brief accounts of Marty's circus life the previous summer intrigued Christian, although Christian didn't think it was a life for him. "When we travel on the train," Marty enlightened, "performers and musicians have their own cars... men and women in separate cars, of course. Each person has their compartment... kinda like bunk beds. That's where you keep your personal belongings and where you sleep. Not much room, but you get used to it."

"We had our own theater," Christian said. "So we never traveled. But there were a lot of vaudeville acts that traveled to us. When we weren't performing, we were running the opera house."

"All aboard!" the conductor called out. The whistle sounded. The train jerked ahead and started rolling away from the station. They were finally on their way back to the lake.

FOUR

Although he hadn't done any fishing that day, Roscoe couldn't help but feel good about the outcome; he'd made some new friends, and his old friend, Marty Mason, had been saved from a terrible fate. And miraculously, he'd managed to navigate the search for Marty without his father discovering him back in town. Now that it was nearly suppertime, he remembered that he hadn't eaten since breakfast. But as the foursome walked to the *Cliff House* from the Devil's Lake depot, he wasn't the only one who was hungry. It had been a long, tiring day for them all.

At the supper table in the hotel dining hall, the conversation between Christian and Marty continued non-stop; Roscoe and Clay listened mostly:

"The circus came to Silver Spring," Christian said. "It was great... all the animals and clowns... and the horses! There was this one young girl who performed acrobatic stunts on a white galloping stallion! And the trapeze artists..." He went on like an excited little kid telling about the circus.

"Last summer," Marty said, "We had a band of pickpockets following us around... happens a lot with circuses. Police never did catch any of 'em."

That reminded Christian of another story: "Bank robbers hit the Silver Spring Bank during the closing parade. Me and my good friend Clancy saw the men go into the bank while we walked along with the band wagon. But we didn't think anything of it at the time... until the Town Marshal came looking. We'd seen those same men running away down an alley. When we told the Marshal about it, he knew who they were from our description."

"Did they catch 'em?" Roscoe asked.

"Well," Christian resumed. "That turned into a night I'll never forget. I got taken hostage by the bank robbers later at the hotel where I was singing."

"You were kidnapped?"

"Yeah... when the Marshal confronted one of them playing

poker there, he grabbed me and held a gun to my head, dragging me out the door."

Clay had heard this story before so he managed to stay calm, but Marty and Roscoe were on the edge. Their eyes widened and they leaned in to hear every word Christian told about him and another bystander being used as shields to protect the outlaws in their retreat out of the hotel. "They drug us at gunpoint into the hardware store just down the street. But we broke away from them when they tried to steal a couple of horses there, and our good friend, Clancy, rescued me on his horse in the back alley… and he actually shot the crooks off the horses they were going to steal."

"Wow!" Marty exclaimed. "Did he kill 'em?"

"No, he just wounded them so they couldn't ride away, and then the marshal and his deputies captured them."

Roscoe and Marty were thrilled to be in the company of these new friends who had experienced firsthand the excitement of the gold and silver mining western frontier. They had read newspaper accounts of wild west episodes—bank and train robberies involving the likes of Jesse James, Butch Cassidy, and many other notorious outlaws, Indian uprisings, buffalo and cattle stampedes—all the things that kept the west a glorious and exciting place in the eyes of those who hadn't yet experienced it for themselves. Marty and Roscoe had never rubbed elbows with anyone who actually had.

Clay had been waiting for the right opportunity to question Marty about his run-in with Jasper's gang. "Why," he asked, "was Jasper so intent on making you a bloody mess?"

"Oh, that," replied Marty. He gave a sheepish little grin and his freckled cheeks turned a bit red. "I just suggested that he could get a job as a clown in the Ringling Circus."

"And for that y'all just about became a pile of chop suey?"

Marty nodded. "Yeah. I was just trying to be helpful, but I guess it doesn't take much to get Jasper all riled up."

When they had finished their pork chops, potatoes and gravy, they realized they were the last ones left in the dining hall. Because the hotel wasn't full yet at this time of year, there had been a small supper crowd, and everyone else had already left. "Hey, Marty," Christian said. "How 'bout giving me a little sample of your piano playing?"

"Where are we gonna find a piano?" Marty asked.

"Oh... we have a piano. It's in the extra room Simon rented to store all our theater gear."

"You brought a piano with you to the hotel?"

"Well... yeah... we couldn't just leave it behind."

The extra room was in the back of the hotel, between Simon's room and the one occupied by him and Clay. Christian kept a key. He opened the door and they all went in, although there wasn't much empty space among all the trunks and wooden crates.

"What *is* all this stuff?" Roscoe asked.

"Costumes and props, mostly," Christian replied. "Some of it is Simon's personal belongings, and those long rolls of canvas are stage backdrops... with scenery painted on them."

The bed had been pushed into one corner to make more room, and beside it stood the upright piano, a thin layer of dust covering its otherwise polished mahogany finish. Christian shoved a couple of trunks aside to give access to the keyboard, and then gestured to Marty as if he were giving a sacrifice to a God.

Marty's freckled face beamed as he lifted the keyboard cover and pulled back the stool. Then his fingers danced across the ivory and a few bars of a lively circus march filled the room, followed by the familiar *Man on the Flying Trapeze*.

Christian smiled and looked at Clay. "It's a little different than Fingers' style, but we can work on it." Then he tapped Marty on the shoulder. "Do you know *Sunny Side of the Street?"*

Marty stopped playing abruptly, bobbed his head a few times as he thought, and then stumbled a little on the melody with his right hand, but within a short time the full harmonious sound had Christian singing the lyrics.

Clay didn't need to hear any more; he was convinced that Marty was an accomplished musician. He turned to Roscoe. "Y'all wanna go next door and play some cards?"

FIVE

It had been nearly midnight when Roscoe and Marty went off to Roscoe's room. Marty was adjusting to a vaudeville piano style, and Roscoe had learned the value of a poker face, and that a full house was a pretty good hand. But they both had a ways to go yet.

The next morning, Clay and Christian looked for their new friends at breakfast. Roscoe, however, was an early riser; he had already wandered out to the lake with his fishing gear, trying to make up for lost time, and he already had two very nice bass on his stringer. Marty, though, came sauntering into the dining hall, sleepy-eyed, just as the other two were well into platefuls of scrambled eggs, fried potatoes, and bacon. He stood silently by their table, as if waiting for an invitation to sit down.

"Good morning, Marty," Christian greeted. "Won't you join us?"

"Mornin'" Marty responded, pulled out a chair and sat down.

"Are y'all havin' breakfast?" Clay asked.

"I... I... don't have any money with me," Marty said. "I left town yesterday in a bit of a hurry..."

"Yeah, we know." Clay waved to a passing waitress. "Would y'all please bring my friend a breakfast plate? I'll pay for it."

"Thank you," Marty said sheepishly after the waitress had left. "You really didn't have to do that."

"Sure I did. Y'all are hungry. Can't stand to see a friend go hungry."

"Why are you being so kind to me?" Marty asked. "You saved my skin back in that alley; you treated me to supper last night; and now breakfast..."

Clay saw that satisfying twinkle in Christian's eyes; he knew how much Christian wanted to be performing again, and he knew how he appreciated a *good* piano player for his accompaniment. Apparently he was enthused by Marty's ability. "Well, let's just put it this way, Marty," he said with a gleam in his eye. "We kinda like you, and now that I've risked my reputation… almost havin' to shoot someone because of y'all… I guess I just wanna protect my investment." He grinned.

"Um, that's what I wanted to talk to you about this morning," Marty said. But then the waitress interrupted him as she set a steaming hot plate of food in front of him. He eyed it with appreciation. "Thank you," he said to the waitress as she turned to leave, and then, as if embarrassed to make his request, he stared at the center of the table as he continued. "I… I was kinda wondering if I could hang out here with you for a few days… until Jasper cools off… I mean… I'll pay you back for the room and the food and all… I have money back at my Ma's house… but if I go back there now I know Jasper will be watchin' for me… and you must've seen what kind of guy he is."

Clay frowned. "Are y'all saying that you want me to be your bodyguard?"

"No… no… not at all… well, maybe… but Jasper's not smart enough to come out here looking for me."

Christian washed down his last bite of potatoes with a gulp of cold milk. "But we were hoping that you'd stay on with us anyway… join our troupe. You're the best piano player we've seen since we left Silver Spring."

Marty's expression turned solemn. "But I've got a job with the Ringling Circus."

Christian's face drooped as if every last bit of good in the world had drained away. This had been his only hope in several months to have a talented musician join them, and now that hope was melting.

Marty noticed his dismay. "All right… I'll play for you until the circus people get back."

"When's that?"

"First of May."

"Well, that's less than a month… but it's a start," Christian said. His good spirit partially returned. "You might change your mind after you get a taste of vaudeville. I think it might be a little better lifestyle than the circus… from what you told me yesterday. And you're gonna like Simon."

At three o'clock that afternoon the *Chicago & North Western* delivered about forty vacationers at the Devil's Lake depot. Among them was Simon Bordeaux returning from one of his frequent scouting trips, and accompanying him were Claudia and Vivian Moon, who had been actresses in the troupe back in Silver Spring. By chance, Simon had run across the Moon sisters in Chicago; they were headed to New York, as their thrill of the West had worn thin. But Simon convinced them to give Wisconsin a try. "Christian and Clay are there with me," he had told them. He knew they were rather fond of the two young actors. "All right," they finally gave in. "What could it hurt? We'll give it a whirl." And so then, Simon's theater troupe was about to be partially reunited; and if some of the others who had responded to his telegrams and letters could find their way to Devil's Lake Village, he would soon have nearly a full complement of actors and musicians.

As Simon approached his hotel room door he heard the piano in the storage room. He was quite sure that Christian had the only other key, and Christian couldn't play the piano—not like that! And then he heard Christian's singing voice, so he had to be in there with someone who could. Simon tried the door; it was unlocked. Standing in the doorway, he watched and listened to the duo with their backs to him, unaware that he was there. *After the Ball* sounded as good now as it ever had at the Crystal Palace in Silver Spring. Obviously, Christian had found a piano player.

"You two must've been rehearsing a long time," Simon said as he clapped his hands in appreciation of what he had just heard.

Christian and Marty spun around, startled by Simon's voice. Christian stepped briskly to the door to greet Simon. "Hi, Simon! Welcome back. Did you have a good trip?"

"Yes, actually, I did... and you'll never guess who I found in Chicago."

"Who?"

"Claudia and Vivian... they're checking into a room right now."

"Claudia and Vivian are here?"

Simon nodded and then glanced toward the piano player. "And who's this you've been rehearsing with?"

"Oh! Yes! This is Marty Mason," Christian said as he led Simon to the piano. "Marty? This is Simon Bordeaux."

"Pleased to meet you, Mr. Bordeaux," the freckle-faced lad said as he shook Simon's hand.

"Marty played with the Ringling Circus last season," Christian explained. "And we've only been tryin' out a few songs for the last couple of hours. Clay and I just met him yesterday."

"Where is that rascal, Clay?" Simon asked.

"Oh, I think he's out fishing with Roscoe."

"Who's Roscoe?"

"Marty's friend. We actually met him first, and he told us about Marty."

Simon examined Marty's less-than-fashionable attire as if he were choosing a puppy from a litter. "Well, I suppose we can groom him a bit."

"Marty's here as the result of a hasty maneuver," Christian said. "So he didn't have time to get dressed up."

"And where do you call home?" Simon asked.

"Baraboo," Marty replied.

"You were a windjammer with the Ringlings."

"Yes sir."

"A *forty-miler*, no doubt."

"No, sir," Marty said proudly. "I was *with it*... stayed the whole season."

"What's a *forty-miler?"* asked Christian.

Marty explained: "That's what the other performers call you if they think you're not gonna make it. But I was *with it*... didn't quit."

Christian eyed Simon curiously. "How do you know all this lingo?"

"I've been in show business nearly all my life... talked to a lot of circus people."

SIX

Warmer weather was beginning to attract more people to the lake; the lodges were filling with vacationers at a steady pace, and the private cottages showed signs of awakening. With every train arrival, Simon anxiously awaited the appearance of his troupe members. One by one, they started showing up—Henry Holland, the drummer; Victor Abbot, an actor; Clyde Cameron, the violinist, comedian and actor; Charlotte Van Horn, a singer, dancer, and actress—and there would be others. Christian and Clay saw Simon's confidence building and they knew they would soon be back on the stage.

Even though Marty didn't know any of the returning troupe, he could sense Christian's energy and enthusiasm—the kind of energy he had felt performing at circus shows. But this seemed different, somehow; in the circus, he was just one little digit among a multitude, blending his presence and talent with so many others that he was barely noticed. Here, though, Christian and Clay were stars among a much smaller group—a group in which every member shone as a significant player, contributing their individual character that everyone noticed. *Perhaps this was the very element that Christian meant,* Marty thought, *when he tried to convince me that I'd be happier here... or... sleeping in a hotel bed every night instead of a crowded, rumbling rail car amidst the putrid odor of sweat and stinky feet of fifty other men, and bathing in a hotel bathtub instead of an occasional bucket bath.*

In all honesty, Marty did enjoy traveling with the circus, even though the traveling accommodations weren't the most pleasant. His space on the train car had been a four-foot-by-six-foot compartment with its "crumb box"—a small storage space for his personal belongings. The compartment served as his bunk, that, occasionally he had to share with another *First of May*—a newcomer—or *Forty-miler*. The sharing usually didn't last long, as most of the newcomers didn't last. They were quickly labeled a *Forty-miler* when it became evident they couldn't cope with the lifestyle of the circus, and then they would soon be gone, leaving Marty the full expanse of his tiny dwelling again.

But now there was a new option looming before him: Christian seemed to appreciate his musical talent, and if the singer could convince Simon, the master of the organization, to let Marty join the troupe, he could say good-bye to the tiny sleeping compartment on the train car. *Is that what I want?* he thought. *Do I want to say good-bye to all the friends I made there? Do I want to leave that exciting life of the circus and the thrill of seeing new places?* It would be a tough decision, perhaps.

Marty had a couple of weeks to make up his mind. He'd have to be certain that he was compatible with this new "family" and that they would readily accept him. He wasn't at all concerned about the pay; Christian and Clay appeared to be financially well-endowed, and Simon Bordeaux seemed to have not a care in the world; he could afford to travel to far-away cities, stay in luxury hotels, and wear the finest clothes. No, Marty wasn't concerned about the potential earnings.

There was, however, one other concern that merited consideration. Now that his home base would be Baraboo again, it could not be ignored. As long as he had been traveling with the circus, away most of the time, and when he wasn't away, Marty had been shrouded by the circus people, able to remain out of reach by his nemesis... Jasper Blackburn. They had been arch-rivals for as long as Marty could remember, and just a few days ago, Marty had renewed the rivalry by attempting to resolve it—by suggesting to Jasper the possibility of a job with the circus. His intentions had been sincere, but Jasper Adler had misinterpreted the offer of being a circus clown as an insult. Marty's scheme to try befriending his enemy had kicked back like a stubborn mule and had almost gotten him killed.

Thanks to his good friend, Roscoe, he was saved from that horrible doom, although Clay Edwards had played the key role, and because of that, Clay gave him a feeling of security. The ex-gambler wasn't afraid of Jasper, or at least he knew how to summon up the courage to defend against the bully. And now that Jasper knew about Clay, maybe there wouldn't be any more trouble.

Clay spent a lot of time with Roscoe during his week at the lake. Other than his friendship with Marty Mason, Roscoe seemed more a loner, although he also seemed to know nearly everyone who lived in Baraboo. Familiarity with so many people stemmed from working in his father's store; he'd never had any trouble making acquaintances, but seldom did he wish to spend longer periods of time than a casual, passing conversation with any of them. But Clay was different, just like Marty had been different. Marty was always the courageous one, always ready and eager for some new adventure, and Roscoe was usually quiet and more recluse. But their personalities fit together like bacon and eggs. Marty had tried to convince Roscoe to join the circus a year ago, and it might have happened, but Roscoe's father put a stop to it. They had been close friends since their early school days, and Roscoe might have preferred accompanying Marty on the circus trail, however, being the obedient son, he remained loyal to the family business. Staying in his father's good graces seemed the right thing to do at the time.

Now there was Clay. In some respects, he was much like Marty—genuinely friendly, but in that warm, southern biscuits and gravy sort of friendly that was difficult not to like. Clay was bold; he, too, had ventured out on his own from a small Mississippi town that folks in other parts of the country had never heard of. At only sixteen, he had left his home and family in Mississippi, making his life the way he chose. There was no reason to doubt that he had actually gained his apparent wealth by gambling; he was exceptionally good at poker, and his swiftness with a gun was unmatched by anyone Roscoe knew. That didn't make him an outlaw, as first impressions had led Roscoe and Marty to believe in the alley in Baraboo, but it still did cause some curious thoughts.

SEVEN

It was a gray day. The fish weren't biting. Roscoe had only one more day at the lake after this one. He gazed up at the overcast sky, wondering if Clay would once again join him, as he had the previous three days. His new friend had been good companionship whiling away the time waiting for the big ones to take their bait.

All along the rocky shoreline, other anglers were having no more luck than he was; perhaps it would be a good day to do something else. So what if he missed a few more hours of fishing? He thought of hiking into the bluffs overlooking the lake, to view the breathtaking panorama. That had always been one of his favorite pastimes when there was nothing better to do. And maybe he could go to the hotel first, and ask Clay to join him on the hike.

Dozens of vacationers had just arrived at the Cliff House via the train; it was a madhouse, people pushing and crowding, tripping over each other's baggage trying to get to the registration desk. Roscoe skirted around the small mob of impatient guests and headed to the back of the hotel where he thought he would find the others, perhaps rehearsing some musical numbers. He found Christian alone in the extra room with the piano. "Where is everybody?" he asked.

Christian looked up from the sheet music he had been practicing. "Marty and Simon are having a private discussion."

"Private?"

"Yeah… I think Simon is making Marty an offer."

"Offer?"

"Yeah… to join our troupe."

"Oh. Think he will?"

"Don't know," Christian said. "Hope so. He's a good pianist. Thanks for introducing us."

"Sure," Roscoe replied. "So, where's Clay?"

Christian peered past Roscoe toward the open door. "I thought he was with you. He left here a half-hour ago to look for you at the lake."

"I... I must've missed him. The fishing's no good today so I came back, and I was on the opposite side of the lake today."

"He said he would walk the shoreline down to the Kirkland Hotel. If he didn't find you along the way, he'd ride the boat back here."

Roscoe looked at his pocket watch. It was already past two o'clolck. He remembered seeing the *Capitola* at the dock, the crew building steam. "I think the boat is leaving here soon, so I guess I'll get on it."

"You'll be sure to find him, then."

Roscoe hurried down to the dock. Dark gray smoke boiled from the smokestack of the *Capitola,* the small steam powered excursion boat that gave vacationers a leisurely cruise around the lake, and often delivered travelers to the *Cliff House* from the train depot. On Saturday afternoons during the summer, it ferried passengers from the South Shore hotels to the North Shore *Chateau* shows and dances. A trim little vessel, the *Capitola* could comfortably carry about fifteen or twenty passengers; Roscoe counted only a half-dozen or so on the dock waiting to board.

"Will you be stopping at the Kirkland dock?" he asked the boat captain as he approached.

The boatman nodded. "Will you be getting off there?"

"No... well, maybe, but a friend might be waiting there to get on."

"Okay," the captain said. "Have a seat and enjoy the ride."

The side paddlewheels started churning the water and the sturdy little steamer puffed away from the dock, navigating along the East side of the lake about fifty yards out from the shore. This was a new experience for Roscoe; the many times he had visited Devil's Lake, he had never taken the *Capitola* cruise. It sure beat rowing a skiff, as he sometimes did when he came here to fish. Now it was just a matter of sitting back, relaxing, and keeping an eye on the shoreline hopeful to spot Clay. In the meantime, he had time to think about what decision Marty would make about leaving the circus to join a band of strangers he hardly knew.

Back at the hotel, that very decision was being discussed. Simon had auditioned Marty Mason, and he had heard him play accompaniment for a few of Christian's songs; so far, he liked what he heard, although Marty needed a little grooming—both in physical appearance and his musical style. He had to gain some elegance in his dress, and he had to lose the circus flair at the keyboard. In time it would all come around.

When Simon invited him to a private conversation, Marty didn't know exactly what to expect; it would either be rejection or persuasion to become part of this show. If it was rejection, he still had his job with the Ringling Circus, and if it was persuasion, he wasn't ready to make a commitment just yet. He liked Christian and Clay, and Simon seemed to be a likeable sort, too. But he had only met briefly the rest of the group and he hadn't gotten to know them very well.

"I'm sure by now," Simon began, "that Christian has informed you all about our theater troupe."

"Well, he's told me some, yes."

"And has he said anything about you joining us?"

"Yes... yes, he has mentioned it."

"Good," Simon said. "Then this won't be a complete surprise to you. Have you given some thought to the idea?"

"A little... but I haven't made any decisions yet. Are you saying that you want me to stay?"

"Yes, I want you to stay with us. I think you belong with us."

"But I really don't know any of the others. What if they don't like me?"

"You know Christian and Clay, and they seem to like you."

"Well... yeah... but the others..."

"Did you know everyone in the circus before you joined them?"

"No... but—"

"I wouldn't worry about the others. They all adore Christian and Clay, and they'll like you, as well."

"How can you be so sure?"

"I know my people," Simon declared. "And I recognize your talent as a musician, and so do they."

"I'll have to think about it," Marty said. He was being cautious.

"What are you so unsure of, Marty?" Simon asked.

"That I won't fit in... I won't be good enough."

"I already know that you're good enough, Marty. All you need is a little polish."

"But if I feel bullied or abused in any way, I'm gone."

"I will... we *all* will... do our best to keep you from feeling that way," said Simon. "But if you choose to stay, you will have to abide by my rules. We're a company. We have procedures and laws, much like you experienced traveling with the circus. We all pull together as a team, and everyone works his share, and everyone is treated equally."

"I don't expect any favoritism," Marty said.

"And you won't get any. However, I will expect perfection from you. The pianist plays a very important roll, and I think you understand that."

Marty smiled. For the first time since Christian had praised his performance, he felt a sense of pride heating up inside.

"So, will you stay with us?" Simon asked again.

"Let me sleep on it."

At the other end of the lake, the little steamer, *Capitola*, was nearing the South Shore dock. Roscoe spotted Clay walking along the bank. He stood up on the boat deck, waved his arms over his head and called out: "CLAY!"

Clay heard the call and looked toward the boat. When he noticed Roscoe, he returned the wave. "I'LL MEET YOU AT THE DOCK."

The grayness of the day didn't seem quite so dreary as the two friends met. "Not out fishin' today?" Clay asked.

"They weren't biting, so I thought I'd see if you were interested in a hike up to the bluffs." Roscoe's voice had an overtone of cordiality.

Clay balanced his companion's proposal for an indecisive moment, focused his gaze to the tops of the hills surrounding the lake. "Up there?"

"Yeah," Roscoe replied. "The view is fantastic."

"Should we see if Marty and Christian want to join us?"

"Just came from the hotel," Roscoe said. "They're kinda busy right now."

"Well, then... lead the way."

EIGHT

The climb to the top of the rocky bluff was quite demanding, but Clay finally admitted that it was worth the effort. He had grumbled a bit during the long, strenuous climb, but when the amazing vista lay before him with the lake far below, he changed his tune. Even on this dismal, gray day, the view was breathtaking, just as Roscoe had said it would be.

They sat on some high boulders gazing at the scenery, neither one speaking. Because the weather was less than favorable for hikers, they were alone.

Roscoe finally broke the silence. "So, what was that town in Montana really like?"

"Silver Spring?" Clay replied. "It was no sleepy little town... a wild and uncurried timber wolf, and it howled every night."

"Howled?"

"The streets were lined with more saloons and gambling halls than y'all can imagine, and they were full every night... miners and cattlemen and lumbermen, drinking and gambling their money away, and they *weren't* a quiet bunch. Payrolls were large, and there were plenty of gamblers, gunmen, and thieves gathered for the pickings."

"You gambled in those places, too?"

"Not all of 'em... just a couple. Occasionally at Tanglewood Lodge, but mostly at the Royal Hotel. They were classier joints, higher stakes, and not so many rowdies."

"Rowdies? Like Jasper?"

"Roscoe, my friend... Jasper is a toddler compared to the rowdies I'm talkin' about. In Silver Spring, just about everybody carried a gun, and they drank whiskey like y'all drink water. It would be an odd day to walk down the street and not see at least one fist-fight, and maybe some gunplay."

"Didn't the police try to keep a lid on all that?" Roscoe asked.

"Police? We only had one Town Marshal... Flanagan... and he

did what he could. But keepin' a lid on *all* the drunken disputes was somewhere between a bad idea and impossible."

"Sounds like a real nasty place."

"Actually," Clay smiled. "Silver Spring was next to paradise."

"How can you call a place like that paradise?"

"Because... for the most part, all the people there—besides the rowdies—were kind and friendly; Silver Spring was nestled in the mountain foothills, and it was a lot like here, except instead of a lake, we had a small river, an' just like here, a prettier place would be hard to find. Everybody there had plenty of money and lived comfortably. Life was good there."

"If you ever go back there," Roscoe said. "Could I go with you?"

"Don't reckon anybody will ever go back to Silver Spring, Roscoe. We got letters over the winter from Clancy, our last friend there; he told us that the whole town was destroyed by fire after we left. Ain't nobody there anymore."

"The entire town is gone?"

"Yup... according to Clancy."

"Wow... hard to imagine a whole town disappearing."

"I guess me and Christian got out of there just in time."

"So, how did you and Christian meet?"

"Christian worked for Silas Patch, the proprietor of the Royal Hotel. He'd escort travelers from the railroad depot to the hotel and carry their baggage on a cart. Just about everybody arriving at Silver Spring ended up at either the Royal or Tanglewood, depending on which messenger got to them first—Christian, from the Royal, or Clancy, from Tanglewood. Anyhow, that's where I first met Christian. He took me to the Royal to get a room, and after that we happened to bump into each other a few times around the saloon and gambling hall. One evening, he invited me to join him at his table for supper, and we became good friends."

"D'ya think he'll get Mason to quit the circus?"

"I'd say the chances are good."

The corners of Roscoe's mouth curled into a little smile; he hadn't liked it when his best friend ran off with the circus, leaving him to spend most of the last summer alone.

"It'll be gettin' dark early... with this cloud cover," Clay said looking up into the grayness. "Maybe we ought to start back."

Roscoe led the way down the steep trail back to the lake. It was dusk; the warm air of the early spring afternoon was being crowded by an exhilarating evening chill. In the half-light the golden beach sand acquired the smooth texture of a thick carpet, spreading out to the thin woods, and down to the shimmering lake with the stolid little steamer perched beside the long, narrow, jutting dock. Beyond, the landscape sloped gently up, dissected by the railroad tracks, and to the gray square shape of the hotel, and then the wooded hills rose abruptly forming the high horizon against the darkening gray sky.

"See y'all at supper tonight?" Clay asked as they were about to part.

"Yeah," replied Roscoe. "It'll be my last one with you… I have to go back home tomorrow afternoon."

Unbeknownst to Clay, supper that evening was to be a gala affair; Simon had invited all the returned cast members to join him in the dining hall, and he insisted that Marty Mason be there, too, even though he wasn't officially a part of the troupe yet. "It will give you a chance to get to know them better," he told the pianist. "You have to start somewhere."

Marty hesitantly accepted the invitation; he didn't know the reason for his reluctance, but he was determined to figure it out during a solo walk along the lakeshore. As he stepped onto the gravel path that led over the railroad tracks, he felt strong and durable with the sound of his boots on the hard surface. But he sensed once again that he was helplessly sliding back into the foggy social bottomland where beginners dwell. Not that he was an outcast; all the time he had been with the circus, he had never been treated adversely by the other windjammers, nor had it ever been suggested that he gather his belongings and determine the next appropriate jumping-off spot to exit the train. Such victims *were* genuine outcasts. But that was not Marty. He had actually gained a couple of rungs on the social ladder among the circus people, and he had succeeded in becoming accepted and even respected by the entire band.

He stepped cautiously along the trail, only a few feet from the water's edge, suddenly realizing the trees were mere silhouettes and the dusky chill added to the already dreary conditions would soon devour everything in darkness. The lake surface magnified and reflected what little light was left; Marty stopped and stared at it. "Am I doing the right thing? Leaving the circus and joining this bunch I don't really know?" he asked, as if he expected a reply from some unseen spirit. Taking a deep breath of the cool, refreshing air and then sighing, he remembered once again that he had merely inhabited that nether world of the unregarded where no one bothered him or bothered about him. In the circus band he had just been one small integer of the body, rarely recognized as anything significant. Being a part of Simon Bordeaux's theater troupe, however, he could advance to the status of a star performer. The thought of it was intoxicating. Visions swirled in his head: he, Marty Mason, dressed in a fine tuxedo, bowing in the footlights before an appreciative crowd after a brilliant performance. What more could he possibly want?

Standing there staring into the water, motionless, he suddenly felt a shiver in his bones as he gradually slipped back into reality. He wasn't certain how long he had been standing there in that daze, but now darkness had swallowed everything. The lights from the Chateau gave him direction, and then the warm, friendly glow from the hotel reminded him that he was expected in the dining room. Exercising willpower, he walked, holding himself back from running; he didn't want to appear out of breath when he arrived at the supper table.

NINE

Adorned with appointments characteristic of such inns—polished walnut woodwork, the tan and green wallpaper depicting Colonial scenes, and a friendly fireplace—the dining room purred with the many quiet conversations by an increasing number of guests. At the far end of the room, Marty saw his supper partners huddled at a large corner table. He strode past other tables, bright with white linens and silver, aware of the murmuring groups here and there, but his focus was on the far corner table. He was surprised to see Roscoe there, sitting next to Clay; Roscoe appeared to feel out of place, and rightly so, among all the actors and musicians. But Marty was glad Roscoe was there; it perhaps seemed as though he had been ignoring his best friend the entire week, spending most of the time with Christian.

It was Roscoe who first noticed Marty's approach. He nudged Clay and nodded toward Marty. Clay, in turn, patted Simon's shoulder.

Simon looked up, eyeing Marty dressed in the clothes he had borrowed from Roscoe. "For Heaven's sake," he whispered to Christian. "I thought you were going to get him a jacket from our wardrobe."

"I did," Christian responded. "But he disappeared before I could get it to him."

"Well, take him back and dress him properly for dining."

Christian rose from his chair and met Marty before he reached the table. "Come with me," he said as he turned Marty around and started walking him out. "We're going to get you into some different clothes."

"Why do I need different clothes?" Marty whispered.

"Didn't you see everyone else at the table? Even Roscoe has a coat and tie."

"Why is Roscoe there?"

"Clay invited him. And where were you? We were beginning to wonder if you were gonna show up."

"I was out walking... thinking some things out. You and Mr. Bordeaux are asking me to make a big decision, y' know."

Christian opened the storeroom door and urged Marty inside; they had spent so much time there rehearsing at the piano that it didn't seem uncommon to be there. Marty watched as Christian gathered the garments he had picked out earlier.

"Why did Clay invite Roscoe?"

"This is Roscoe's last night here," Christian replied. "Clay invited him to supper before he knew about the party." He offered Marty the shirt and tie. "Put these on."

"Sometimes I wonder about Clay," Marty said as he slipped out of his old shirt and into the new. "Roscoe has told me a little about him, but he seems so mysterious to me... like he's hiding his past."

Christian looked Marty in the eyes. "I've come to know him quite well, and although it's true that Clay has some dark days in his past, he's not trying to hide anything. He's a Southern gentleman by instinct, of exceptionally good manners, and mild-tempered until provoked... and then, for God's sake, *look out*. He's absolutely fearless, but he's not a trouble hunter. Clay has a lot of natural ability and practices good common sense. No matter what you're thinking, there is nothing low about Clay Edwards. He's high-toned, broad-minded, cool-headed, and brave. And as you *should* know from recent experience, he's a good guy to have on your side."

He helped straighten the tie, handed over the vest, and then held the jacket open for Marty to slip his arms into the sleeves.

When they returned to the dining hall, the table had been laden with a feast, and the pianist had transformed from a boy in ill-fitting street clothes to a dapper young man fit for a formal ball in long-tailed burgundy coat with satin lapels, matching vest, white shirt and black bowtie. He and Christian ushered themselves to the two vacant chairs next to Clay as the others' eyes followed the new lad, evaluating his appearance, although they knew the suit of clothes came from the theater's wardrobe. Marty felt a little uncomfortable at first, knowing all eyes were fixed on him.

"Everyone!" Simon announced. "Let us welcome our guests... Marty Mason, whom most of you have met, and Clay's friend, Roscoe."

Roscoe's cheeks reddened a little as he looked down into the tablecloth. He *was* out of place among this group and he knew it; the thought had crossed his mind to ask to be excused, but now everyone greeted him as though he belonged there, and the succulent roast pork, baked yams, and vegetable soup looked and smelled too good to walk away from, so he decided he would stay. Although he was clearly not interested in any of them beyond sharing a social supper table, the elite group made him feel welcome.

Marty's comfort level abruptly raised as he scanned all the faces around the table that were no longer staring, but seemed warm and friendly toward him and Roscoe, even though Roscoe had no real purpose there. Marty had to measure his capacity for self-discipline. Now it seemed apparent that he could turn his back on the circus, but he could not allow himself to be entangled in cheap competition for importance. He had to embrace this opportunity with exceeding intelligence.

"I've been told you're a splendid piano man," Charlotte Van Horn said, batting her eyes just enough to suggest she might be interested in the new arrival. She was one from the group Marty had not met, although Christian had informed him that she was an actress, dancer, and singer. That would account for her concern of his musical ability.

Before Marty had a chance to reply to Charlotte's remark, Henry Holland and Clyde Cameron chimed in: "We must get together sometime soon for a practice session."

Among all the other welcoming comments and greetings, it seemed to Marty that everyone there had reached the assumption that he was already a member of the troupe, and he wasn't quite sure how to react. But he was certain that he felt more thoroughly aware, now, of how the world worked—of who fit where, of what was grand and genuine, and what was shoddy and fake. He had joined the circus a year ago for the excitement and adventure. But the circus was filled with illusions, like the ferocious lions that weren't really ferocious at all—they were as tame as kittens—but they were well-trained to make the audience *believe* they were ferocious. The Fat Lady really weighed only 400 pounds, but to an unsuspecting circus audience, she was the world's fattest woman at 698. People believed they would witness the five-legged calf and the two-headed goat walking around in a pen inside the closed tent, when in reality they found on display deformed unborn fetuses preserved in formaldehyde and sealed in large glass jars. It all made for good entertainment, perhaps, but illusions, just the same.

There was nothing that appeared fake or dishonest about this group; Christian and Clay had been straightforward right from the beginning; Simon Bordeaux had laid his cards on the table along with his rules and honest expectations; and so far, nothing had aroused any suspicions about the others. Deep in reflective thought, Marty stirred his soup. He felt his true ambitions coming into focus as he envisioned himself as the majestic musician. He decided instinctively to accept Simon's offer, right there at the supper table, among the white linens, walnut, and silver, and the polite whispers and nods of the others.

"Ladies and gentlemen," Marty spoke up. He peered at all the faces; when it seemed he had their attention, he went on. "A couple of days ago, Mr. Bordeaux asked me to join your theater group as a pianist. I didn't give him an answer then, and I haven't yet. As you probably know by now, I traveled with the Ringling Circus last summer, so I'm not exactly a stranger to show business."

The others followed this unwinding of the new guy, carefully gauging his attitude and measured him according to their own rather critical yardsticks.

"None of you know me," Marty went on. "And I know none of you... well... except for Christian and Clay; they're the reason I'm here. They have chosen to have faith in me, and if the rest of you will share that sentiment, I can be the best piano man this troupe has ever known."

A few eyebrows lifted; Christian and Clay noticed. Simon Bordeaux noticed. Had Marty overstepped the boundaries of his welcome?

"What he means to say," Christian added, in an attempt to appease the ill feelings that may have been incubated by Marty's address, "is that he's willing to try to give us his best."

A few nods and half-smiles gave Christian the impression that that had been an acceptable revision of Marty's statement, but it was hard to totally assess the reaction as everyone had begun to enjoy the meal, paying more attention to the food rather than conversation.

When the meal was finished, the ladies of the group—Claudia and Vivian Moon, and Charlotte van Horn—excused themselves and delicately meandered across the room toward the exit. Clyde Cameron and Henry Holland soon followed, while Simon and Victor quietly discussed the selection of a new play. Nothing more had been said about Marty's boastful remark and he had been included in several discussions; Christian hoped that it would be soon forgotten.

Clay and Christian excused themselves, as did Marty; Roscoe just nodded his gratitude to Simon for the wonderful supper and followed the others out into the damp April night, around the corner where lights streamed warmly from cozy hotel room windows.

"So, Marty," Christian said. "Now it's official... you've been adopted. Will I see you for some rehearsal tomorrow? I can give you the sheet music for some of Charlotte's numbers."

"Yeah, okay..."

"Well, g'night," said Clay, as though he were passively bidding a "call" during a dull poker game.

"See you in the morning," Christian added as he and Clay headed for their room, leaving Marty and Roscoe to go their way.

Roscoe raised his open palm in a little wave, and then he turned to Marty. "Mason," he said. "I don't know about you, but I'm gonna get some sleep. I wanna get in some early morning fishing before I hafta leave tomorrow."

Marty just nodded as they started walking. He didn't know how he should feel; now that he was officially a member of Simon's theater troupe, he thought he should be celebrating, but instead, he was going to bed early. At least he wasn't climbing the dark stairway to the lonely little room stuck up under the eaves at his mother's house. "What time you goin' back tomorrow?"

"Thought I'd catch the two o'clock train."

"I'm goin' with you. Ma's prob'ly worried sick."

"You could take the morning train," Roscoe suggested.

"No... I wanna go with you."

TEN

After the fog lifted, clouds still painted the morning heavens in a dreary, somber gray with only a hint here and there that a blue sky did really exist. Roscoe kept hoping for a little sunshine on his last day at the lake; the fish might be biting a little better. Even though he had five nice Northerns waiting for him at the ice house, one more wouldn't hurt.

In the piano room, Marty seemed eager enough to begin rehearsals with the other singers and actors, but a trip to Baraboo seemed important to him, too. "I really need to go see my ma," he told Christian. "She's prob'ly worried by now... and besides... I'm still wearing the clothes I borrowed from Connor."

"When are you leaving?"

"This afternoon... I'm goin' on the train with Connor."

"So, when will you be back?" Christian asked.

"Monday. I'll come back Monday. First afternoon train."

"Why do you two always call each other by your last names?"

"Don't know... always have."

By one forty-five Roscoe Connor had retrieved his five chilled Northerns from the ice house and was waiting at the depot for the two o'clock train. "Great!" he said to himself. "*Now* the clouds start clearing." But it was too late to go back out fishing; he had his ticket in hand. He just marveled at the wonderfully pleasant afternoon as it unfurled before him, the sun patches growing and spreading as the clouds rolled away over the hills. He didn't feel disappointment, for he'd had a good week in spite of the interruptions. One day lost to a hunting excursion for his best friend, Mason, and a few late nights spent with new friends that hindered early morning rising was probably all worth the new friend he had made in Clay Edwards. Even though he might have little opportunity to ever spend more time with him, Clay had taught him the art of poker, and how to be a gentleman in Southern style that would surely astound his peers. Roscoe was eager to spend some of his savings for a new suit and shirts and ties like Clay wore. Perhaps he would still have time that afternoon... if the train wasn't late.

With only a few minutes to spare, Christian and Clay escorted Marty Mason to the depot platform.

"Hey, Mason," Roscoe greeted his friend. "I was beginning to wonder if you'd make it."

"Hey, Connor. Christian and I were going over some of the music for the show. If Clay hadn't come around to remind us, we'd prob'ly still be there."

"Hi, Clay," Roscoe smiled. "What would these guys do without you?"

Clay laughed. "They'd miss a lot of trains."

Marty turned to Christian. "Y' know... at first I was a little skeptical about leaving the circus and joining your troupe..."

"A little?" Christian grinned. "You were like trying to move the Rock of Gibraltar with a wheelbarrow."

"Well, I know I was a little difficult then, but I'm glad to be with you now... and I'm really anxious to start rehearsals."

"We're glad to have you... and you have no idea how anxious we are to get started again. Monday won't come too soon."

The big, black, smoking, engine rumbled slowly past them, steam hissing, bell clanging, and brakes squealing, delivering the passenger coaches to a stop at the platform. The foursome watched what seemed to be the entire population of Chicago disembarking the train. They made their parting handshakes, and as Marty and Roscoe stepped aboard the coach, Roscoe turned with a sorrowful expression and waved to Clay. "Come and see me at the store sometime," he called out.

Settled into their seats, Marty and Roscoe gazed at the familiar scenery in silence for the first few minutes of the short ride back to Baraboo. The week had ended much differently than either of them had expected; Marty had officially left the circus to become a theater musician, and Roscoe had gained the confidence to lead a more social life, thanks to his mentor, Clay Edwards.

"I s'pose you're wondering," said Marty after the long silence.

"Wondering about what?" Roscoe asked.

"Why I wanted to go back with you this afternoon instead of leaving on the morning train."

"I hadn't given it much thought, but now that you mention it... no, I wasn't wondering. I knew you had business with your new job this morning, so—"

"That's not why."

Roscoe appeared a little mystified. "Okay... so... why?"

"I... I... I guess 'cause I'm a chicken. I didn't want to get back to town alone and find Jasper waiting for me."

"Hey! If you're afraid of Jasper, that doesn't make you a chicken. Half the people in this town are afraid of Jasper. He's dangerous."

"I know... but I don't want anything to happen now... to ruin my chance to be a theater performer, and Jasper could wreck everything for me."

"So you think I can protect you from him?"

Marty looked at his friend. "Well, two of us together stand a better chance. Me, alone? Hardly."

Marty wasn't a fighter. There was little doubt that he could defend himself against someone like Jasper. He might be adventurous and daring, but he wasn't a fighter.

They both held their breath as the train slowly rolled to a stop at the Baraboo station. It seemed ridiculous to think they would see Jasper and his gang anywhere near, but they scanned the area through the coach windows, just the same. Marty offered to carry Roscoe's satchel while Roscoe grasped the box containing the iced fish.

"We'll go to the store first," Roscoe suggested. "I can get rid of this stuff, and then we'll go to your place."

Marty gave a half-smile. "Thanks, Connor."

The walk from the depot across the river bridge, up the hill to Oak Street and the Mercantile had never seemed so far. Roscoe had imagined his return would feel good after a week's absence, that viewing the brick buildings lined up, the Court House towering above all, the smells and the sounds of the city would be welcoming, but somehow, Marty's circumstances changed all that. Stepping briskly along the sidewalk, keeping one eye on the street ahead and one eye on the sidewalk across the street, a half-block from his father's store Roscoe suddenly reminded himself of the new confidence that Clay Edwards had given him. Scrambling down a busy street in broad daylight scared half out of his wits didn't seem the right way to be managing his self-confidence. He slowed his pace, stretched out his arm to slow Marty's pace as well.

"What?" Marty said. "Do you see him?"

"No," Roscoe replied. "This is crazy. It's broad daylight. There's a hundred Saturday shoppers on this street. We're acting rather foolish. If Jasper did see us, he'd know we're scared, and that's the last thing we want him to think."

"Well," Marty said. "I *am* scared."

"Can't let him see that."

Marty gave one last frantic look up and down the street before they pushed through the Mercantile front door, jangling the little bell above it. Once inside he finally calmed down. A few people mulled around the store; a couple of elderly women greeted Roscoe.

"Hello, Mrs. Anderson. Hello, Mrs. Waldorf," he replied. They were loyal customers of the store for as long as he could remember.

"Hello, Mr. Connor," Marty said with a smile when Roscoe's father greeted them.

"Hello, Mason," came the reply, somewhat surprised to see Roscoe back so early. Long ago, Mr. Connor had picked up on the habit of calling Marty by his last name, just like his son did. "Were you out fishing with Roscoe?"

"Oh... um, no, sir. I... um... just happened to be out at the lake, and we came back together."

Mr. Connor eyed the wooden box that Roscoe carried. "Welcome home, Son. Did you get some good ones?" he asked.

"Sure did." Roscoe lifted the box lid to expose the five Northerns.

"Well, that'll make a couple of fine suppers. Better get them into the icebox upstairs."

"Okay, Pop, and then I'm going with Mason over to his house, and then I've got some things to do."

"What things?"

"Shopping… it's time for some new summer clothes."

Mr. Connor studied Marty's attire. "Aren't those your clothes that Mason's wearing?"

"Oh… yeah."

"Why is he wearing your clothes?"

"Well, Mason ended up at the lake kinda unexpected… he didn't have any extra clothes along, so he borrowed some of mine."

Mr. Connor sensed that his son and Marty were trying to hide something, obviously on edge about something they weren't eager to divulge. "Okay… you boys want to explain what's going on?"

The boys squirmed. "Well, Pop," Roscoe said. "Marty had a little confrontation with Jasper a few days ago… that's why he ended up at the lake… to get away. He stayed with me at the hotel until things cooled down."

"Jasper? What kind of confrontation? Did he hurt you?"

"No," Marty said. "He didn't get the chance. A new friend of ours kinda saved me."

"So, what was the confrontation about?"

"I sorta suggested to Jasper that he could get a job as a clown in the circus… but I was just trying to be helpful. He didn't take too kindly to it, though."

Mr. Connor's face beamed with delight, and then he laughed. "A clown! How entertaining! I'll bet he'd make a charming clown!"

"But he was serious, Mr. Connor. He wanted to kill me!"

"And that's why I'm walking with him to his house," Roscoe added.

"I wouldn't worry too much, Mason. He's probably already forgotten about it."

ELEVEN

"What a relief!" Eleanor Mason said to Marty on the front porch steps. "I thought you'd run off with those circus people again without even saying good-bye."

"Ma… you know I wouldn't do that."

"So, where have you been?"

"Well, for starters, Toby broke his arm, and I stayed at his house and helped his mom with chores."

"Good heavens! How'd he break his arm?"

Marty chuckled. "Fell out of a tree."

"What was he doing in a tree?"

"Trying to get their cat down… but he should've just left her, 'cause she eventually came down on her own."

"Is he gonna be alright?"

"He'll be fine… he just won't be playing the trombone for a while."

"Here it is Saturday! Roscoe Connor came by last Monday looking for you." She locked her arm around his and together they stepped through the front door of their modest little house.

"Yeah, I know… he found me, and I've been out at the lake with him since then."

Eleanor looked Marty up and down. "Whose clothes are you wearing? They certainly aren't yours."

"No, Ma. They're Connor's. I borrowed them."

"Aren't the clothes I make for you good enough anymore?"

"Yeah, Ma... they're just fine. But my favorite yellow shirt and brown trousers got dirty, so I borrowed some clothes from Connor."

"Well, where are the dirty clothes? I'll have to wash them."

"I guess I forgot to get them out of Connor's satchel when we came back."

"Just like you... oh, well. I'll get them from his mother Tuesday after work. But right now I need you to help me move the sofa."

Eleanor Mason spent most of her week as a seamstress in a shop downtown. Saturday and Monday were her days off, and the shop wasn't open on Sunday, so she made the most of the three days with all the chores at home. This weekend had been designated for spring cleaning.

"I'm not going back to the circus this year," Marty said as they shoved the heavy Victorian sofa across the sitting room.

Eleanor stood upright, her eyes wide, not sure if she should be happy because her baby was not running away with the circus again, or upset because he had apparently quit his job. "Well... what *are* you going to do?"

"I have a new job as a theater pianist. I joined up with a theater troupe this week at the lake."

"What theater troupe?"

"They're new here... you wouldn't know them?"

"But you were doing so well with the Ringlings."

"I know, Ma... but I don't want to chase all over the country living in a train car for the next six months." Marty took his mother's hand and they sat on the displaced sofa. "I met these people at the Cliff House. I gave some auditions... and they like me. Mr. Bordeaux wants me to come back on Monday to start rehearsals."

"You mean... you'll be living at home?"

"Some of the time. I guess we'll be traveling some, too, but staying in hotels with regular beds, and not in some stinky old train car bunk."

"Sounds like vaudeville, and it sounds like your mind is made up."

"It's what I wanna do, Ma. It's my chance to become a real performer."

Eleanor grinned. "Well, then... we'll have to make you some new clothes! Theodore at the shop will fit you with a new suit, and—"

"Ma! They have a wardrobe. They'll dress me the way *they* want me dressed."

"Well, you'll still need some nice traveling clothes." There was no stopping Eleanor Mason when it came to making new clothes for her only son. He was going to get them whether he wanted them or not.

Safe at his mother's house—the only place he'd ever known as home—Marty tried to put the Jasper incident out of his thoughts. Now he needed to focus on a grander life; yes, even grander than the circus. Instead of stuffing himself into a hot, uncomfortable band uniform for ten hours a day, he'd be donned in silk shirts and tuxedos. He would be living a normal life, spending his time with people he enjoyed being with. Oh, it would be a lot of hard work, too, practicing and preparing for shows. But he was up to it, ready and eager to meet the challenge.

Sitting there on the back porch steps, Marty realized that he had nearly forgotten the beauty when the earth emerged and once again faced the spring sun. Tiny leaves of green sprouted from the gray branches of the skeleton trees, birds trilled their spring songs, and all the spring scents took to the air. He just sat there, breathing it all in until his mother called him to supper.

That night he climbed the dark stairway to his attic bedroom, but somehow, now it didn't seem so lonely. His life seemed changed with the season; he felt an odd sense of freedom that could take him anywhere he wanted to go.

His bedroom window that had been stuck closed all winter opened freely allowing the fresh spring air to flow in. The wintery dryness of his little room drifted away as the tantalizing breeze whipped across his bed and then danced on to the other rooms. He undressed and lay on his bed, the coolness washing over him until he settled into a restful sleep.

Marty awoke the next morning sweating under a heap of quilts and blankets that had protected him from the cold night air freely pouring in through the open window. He couldn't remember getting under the blankets; now they were smothering him. He threw them aside and abruptly sat up, rubbing the sleep from his eyes. He yawned and stretched the stiffness from his legs; the chilly morning air shocked him fully awake. He planted both feet on the cold floor, stood, and then strode contentedly to the open window. Gradually, the memories of yesterday crept into his thoughts as he felt the warmth of the sunlight on his face. It was going to be a great summer.

TWELVE

"MA! I can only find one white shirt. Where's my other white shirt?" Marty's Monday morning anxiety was building; he wanted to be ready to leave in a half-hour, giving him plenty of time to visit with Roscoe at the store before he boarded the train to the lake. He'd promised that he would.

"Why do you need *two* white shirts?" Eleanor replied from the bottom of the stairway.

"'Cause I'm gonna be staying out there for a few days. I need an extra shirt."

"Can't you take something else? Your other white shirt is down at the shop... I was mending a seam and I forgot to bring it home. Take the blue one."

Marty closed his eyes and shook his head, but then he admitted to himself that he shouldn't be taking out his frustrations on his mother; after all, she had his best interests at heart. A blue shirt was better than no shirt. He carefully folded it and put it in his satchel. One last inspection in the mirror: white shirt, black bowtie, charcoal gray coat and trousers—even though they weren't the most fashionable— shined shoes. He was ready to meet the day!

He could smell the bacon frying downstairs, and when he reached the kitchen after putting his satchel by the front door, a plate with the bacon, two hard-boiled eggs and a glass of milk were already on the table waiting for him.

"My, my, look at you," Eleanor said. "Are you preaching or playing the piano?"

"I just want to look good," Marty replied. "The fellows I will be rehearsing with always look good... especially Clay. He always looks like he just stepped out of a custom tailor shop."

"And so will you when Theodore finishes your new suit. What color would you prefer? Black, blue, or gray?"

"Burgundy," Marty said. "I need to be..." He hesitated,

searching for the right word.

"Different?" Eleanor suggested.

"Yeah... different," Marty agreed. He sat down to devour the bacon and eggs. "And tell Theodore I will be in for the final fitting when I come back from the lake."

"Final fitting! He's made suits for you before... he has your measurements."

"But this one has to fit perfect. Tell him I'll pay extra."

"But I can pay for—"

"No, you can't. I'll pay for the new suit myself. You can make some fancy shirts to go with it. Okay?"

Marty finished the bacon and eggs, got up from the table and started for the front door with Eleanor right on his heels. "Thanks for the breakfast, Ma. I'm gonna stop and see Connor before I catch the train to the lake."

"When will you be back?" She gave Marty a motherly kiss on his cheek.

"Don't know... maybe Thursday or Friday." He picked up the satchel, donned his cap from the hall tree, and headed out the door. At the bottom of the porch steps he turned and blew her a kiss. "Love ya, Ma."

It had been a week since Jasper Blackburn had made his assault; Marty hoped that Mr. Connor was right in assuming that he'd forgotten by now. But it was difficult not to think about the possible threat waiting around any corner, amidst any shadow, behind any tree. He hadn't mentioned a word of this to his mother because he didn't want her to worry; in his absence, he hoped the bully wouldn't bother her.

He was nearly half-way to Oak Street when he heard the horses and a buckboard coming up on him from behind. He veered off to the side of the road to give the team a wide berth. But as the wagon was even with him, it slowed down and kept pace with Marty's step.

"Hey! Mason!" a voice called to him.

Marty looked up at the driver and his passenger aboard the wagon. "Hey, Dobbs. What you doin' here?"

"Been waitin' for ya."

"Why?"

"Thought y' might like t' go for a little ride with me 'n Frank."

"Can't. I'm going to see my friend, Connor, 'n then I gotta catch a train."

"Well, then… hop on. I'll give y' a ride there."

"It's just down to Oak Street."

Dobbs reined the horses to the right and then to a stop, cutting off Marty's path. Dobbs and Frank were on the ground almost instantly, one on either side of Marty. With firm grips, they hoisted him up on the buckboard seat, and then sat themselves again, sandwiching Marty between them. Dobbs slapped the reins on the horses' backs, and in a flurry they rode off toward the river.

THIRTEEN

It was decided; *Oliver Twist* had been such an overwhelming success the previous season in Montana; Simon couldn't think of any good reason not to keep it as their opening play here in Wisconsin. Less time would be involved than preparing for a new production. They had all the props, scenery backdrops, and costumes. Only the new piano man needed to learn the music and his cues. Of course, there would still be all the vaudeville acts, too—the songs, comedy, dance routines—that filled in on the nights they didn't perform a play.

"I hate waiting for trains," Christian told Clay. "Especially when they're late."

Clay nonchalantly gazed up and down the tracks. The train was late, but only by fifteen minutes, so far. "If I remember correctly," he said, "Y'all used to spend a lot of time waiting for trains to arrive at Silver Spring."

"That was different."

"How?"

"Then it was my job... getting people to the hotel."

"Well, then," Clay replied. "This isn't any different; y'all are here to get Marty Mason to the hotel. It's just not the same hotel."

Clay's attempt didn't ease Christian's impatience. He had spent all weekend rearranging and cleaning the piano room so they had some space for rehearsals, and he was anxious to get started. Marty's arrival would put everything in motion.

The whistle echoing among the Baraboo Hills gave Christian a little relief; finally, the train was arriving, and with it their new piano man. In his mind, Christian could hear the applauding audiences; he could smell the grease paint; he could feel the heat from the footlights.

The engine chuffed by with its usual clouds of smoke and steam nearly smothering everything in its wake. When the coaches finally came to rest, the conductor stepped off onto the platform, ushering a number of passengers from the train while porters scrambled about with luggage. Christian paced back and forth on the platform in a space no bigger than a closet. He hadn't seen Marty.

The conductor was calling all aboard, but Marty still hadn't stepped out of the coach.

"Are y'all sure this is the right train?" Clay asked.

"Monday... first afternoon train," Christian replied. "Yeah, I'm sure this is the right train."

"Maybe he just got mixed up on the time... or maybe he just forgot."

"Anxious as he was, I don't think he forgot."

"What'll we tell Simon?"

"I don't know. Let's check the telegraph office... see if there's any message from him."

There was just enough room for them to get on the little steamboat back to the Cliff House. It might have been quicker to walk, but now there didn't seem to be any reason to hurry. When they arrived at the north end of the lake, they didn't waste any time getting to the Cliff House telegraph office; the agent checked all the undelivered incoming messages he had received that day. "Sorry boys... there's nothing from a Marty Mason."

"Will you let us know right away if anything comes in?"

The operator nodded and then abruptly directed his attention to the clackety-clack-clack of the telegraph key. Christian and Clay left.

Simon eyed the two young actors as they entered the room that had become a rehearsal stage. He kept watching the doorway, expecting Marty. "So where's our new piano man?"

"Marty wasn't on this train," Christian replied. "Maybe the next one."

But Marty wasn't on the next train, either, and for two more days, rehearsals went on with Clyde providing the musical effects on violin as best he could. By Wednesday, everyone was getting impatient; Simon was on edge; good, talented pianists were hard to find. "Christian... why isn't our piano man here? How can we expect the Silver Spring Players to get a show ready without our piano man?"

"We can't, Simon."

"I expected Mr. Mason to be more dependable than this," Simon uttered.

"And as well as I got to know him last week, I'm sure he is."

"But we agreed that he would start rehearsing with us on Monday. In case you haven't noticed, it is now Wednesday."

"Yes, Simon," Christian said. "I'm getting worried that something bad has happened to him."

"What could have possibly happened?" Simon asked. "He was only going to his home in Baraboo."

"Well," Christian hesitated. "Marty's been known to get himself into compromising situations."

"Oh?"

"Yes... that's how we actually met him."

"I thought his friend, Roscoe introduced you."

"He did, but when we went to Baraboo to find him, he was... um..."

Clay stepped in. "Marty was engaged in a personal dispute that was about to become rather unfavorable to his well-being."

Simon stared questioningly.

"You see," Christian tried again. "There was this gang of roughnecks..."

"Oh, great!" Simon blurted. "We've signed on a ruffian—"

"On the contrary," Clay corrected him. "The roughnecks Christian is talking about... well... there was five of 'em... they intended to offer Marty a little unfriendly guidance down to the ground. He was at an unfair advantage... so me 'n Christian 'n Roscoe sorta stepped in with a little assistance."

Simon quickly evaluated Clay's explanation that clearly described the beginnings of a brawl. "Well that's just what we need... my star performers getting involved in a public display of violence in the street!"

"Oh! No!" Christian said. "It wasn't public at all... we were in an alley where nobody saw us."

"Violence, just the same," Simon said.

By this time, Charlotte, Victor, Clyde, and Vivian had gathered around, quite amused with the developing account.

"Contrary to your assumption," Clay explained, "We did not engage in any violent acts. Our intervention caused a far more suitable outcome."

"But you two aren't much bigger than knee-high to a bumblebee... how could you dare stand up to a gang like that?"

Clay extended his right arm toward Simon and patted the cuff of his coat sleeve with his left hand. "My shiny little friend persuaded them to pursue other endeavors."

Simon and the others were acquainted with the actor's personal background, and quite aware of his habitual practice to conceal a derringer in his coat sleeve. "Clay!" Simon exclaimed. "You attacked them with a gun?"

"Not attacked... defended," Clay rebutted. "And in a quiet and dignified manner."

"That's when we brought Marty here on the train," Christian added. "We had to get him out of town for a while... for his own safety."

Simon stared some more, shocked, stern. "I thought we left such vicious conduct back in Montana."

"Doesn't matter if y'all are in Montana or Wisconsin," Clay offered in his calm Southern drawl. "If a man is fixin' to bash your head in with a lead pipe, then I'd think y'all would have the right to defend yourself."

Now their audience—the rest of the troupe—sided with Clay; Clyde put a hand on Clay's shoulder. "I agree," he confided. "You did the right thing."

"Bully for you!" Victor chimed in.

"We're so lucky to have you here with us," Vivian Moon cooed. "That was brave and honorable."

Simon had no choice but to concede; his unfavorable view of the alley incident seemed to be the unpopular one among the group. But nevertheless, he was still upset with the premature loss of the new piano player.

Charlotte Van Horne, who had clearly thrown numerous lustful glances in Marty's direction the night of the welcoming dinner party, openly expressed her conjecture: "So, when are you two heroes gonna go find him and bring him back here again?"

Christian and Clay exchanged brief but thoughtful glimpses.

"Perhaps we should," Clay said.

"We could take the next train," Christian added. He had been considering that option all morning.

"Then go," Simon demanded. "Find Marty... or *another* piano man. Just bring somebody back here who can play our music."

FOURTEEN

Clay and Christian stepped off the train at the Baraboo station. They had no baggage, as they didn't intend to stay any longer than it required locating Marty, and if time allowed a cordial visit with Roscoe at the Mercantile. Roscoe had taken them to Marty's house once before; they could find it again, hopeful that the search would end there, and they could all get on the next train back to the lake.

"D'ya think this will turn into another rescue mission?" Christian asked as they crossed the bridge over the Baraboo River.

"Well, if it does, I packed a little extra ammunition."

"And I couldn't help notice... by the bulge under your coat... you also packed the forty-five."

"I did. Y'all never know these days."

They walked along Water Street to where they turned away from the river and up the hill towards the neighborhood where Marty and his mother lived. At the top of the hill, Clay shaded his eyes from the bright sun. "Okay... which one is it? I know we're close."

Christian pointed. "That one. Down towards the end of the block. The one with the two maples in the front yard."

They were just about to knock on the front door when a voice called to them from the next yard. "Ain't nobody home at the Mason's."

Christian looked toward the woman who had her hands full with fallen twigs and leaves. "We're friends of Marty's," he responded. "Have you seen him?"

"Not since the weekend," the woman said.

"How 'bout Marty's mum?"

"Eleanor's a seamstress at the tailor shop over on Oak Street."

"Thank y'all, Ma'am," said Clay. He tipped his hat. "We'll talk to her there."

They knew Oak Street; it was on Oak Street where Connor's Mercantile occupied space in the middle of a block—the block they had avoided when searching for Marty the first time. But now there was no need to skirt around it, and they wanted to stop in for a visit with Roscoe, anyway.

Although they had not seen it before, large red and white letters spelling the name on the big plate glass windows made it quite easy to find. Across the street and down a few doors they spotted a tailor shop, perhaps the one where Mrs. Mason worked. "Let's go there first," suggested Christian.

"Good idea," Clay replied. "I could use a new suit." He stood back a step or two from Christian and examined his friend's attire. "And so could y'all."

"Yeah, well, we don't have time for that right now."

"We can look, can't we?"

Just inside the front door, a big green parrot on a high perch squawked a greeting: "NEW SUIT! NEW SUIT!" A few seconds later, from a doorway draped with only a curtain a bald-headed man emerged, shirt sleeves rolled up to the elbows and a bright yellow tape measure dangled around his neck. "Aaaaaa! Gentlemen... welcome. I am Theodore Baskin, proprietor."

Clay scanned the room, its walls lined with dozens of bolts of fabric of all colors and textures. Above them on one side of the studio hung artists' renderings of men, young and old, clad in various fashionable suits, and on the other side, the wall was adorned with pictures of women in elegant gowns and dresses.

Theodore continued his pitch: "As you can see, we have a wide assortment of only the finest fabrics... and a good variety of colors and patterns. Would you be looking for everyday or formal apparel?"

Clay was captivated by the quality surrounding him. "We both need new suits," he said as he gazed at the rolls of fine cloth.

"But not today," Christian interrupted. "Actually, we're looking for someone."

"NEW SUIT! NEW SUIT!" the bird squawked again.

Theodore turned to the parrot. "Napoleon... that's quite enough!" Then he turned to Christian again. "And who would you be looking for?"

"Is this where Eleanor Mason works?"

"It is."

"Could we please talk to her? It's kinda important."

When Christian noticed the woman that came from behind the

curtain covering the work room doorway, he immediately recognized her as the woman he had seen at the Mason's house more than a week ago.

"I heard someone mention my name," she said.

"These gentlemen are here to see you, Ellie," Theodore said.

"Mrs. Mason," Christian said. "I don't know if you remember us. Roscoe brought us to your house Monday before last... we were looking for Marty."

"Yes..." she said, showing a little reluctance. "I remember your faces, but I don't believe we were properly introduced."

"Oh, yes... well, I'm Christian Parker, and this is Clay Edwards."

Clay took Eleanor's hand, bowed from the waist and kissed her fingers. "Pleased to meet you, Ma'am," he said in his gentlemanly southern intonation.

Eleanor's face beamed with pleasure. She wasn't used to such behavior. "What is it that I can do for you gentlemen?"

"Clay and I are part of the theater troupe staying out at the Cliff House..."

"Oh, yes," Eleanor said. "Marty was so thrilled to join your group. He talked about you all weekend."

"He was s'posed to come out on the train to start rehearsing with us on Monday," Clay explained.

"Yes, he packed a suitcase and left our house Monday just before noon... said that he'd be at the lake for a few days."

"Well..." Christian hesitated. "He wasn't on that train or any train since."

Eleanor's beaming smile faded. "You mean... he's not..."

"No, he's not with us at the hotel. We thought we should come here to see if he'd changed his mind."

Now Eleanor's faded smile gradually melted into a frown. "I doubt that he would have changed his mind. Once he decides to do something, there's no changing him... like the circus last year. I couldn't talk him out of that for all the coconuts in Brazil."

"Are y'all sure he left on the noon train?" Clay asked.

Eleanor thought a moment. "Well... he said... he said he would... but..."

"But what, Mrs. Mason?"

"I think he said he was going to stop in and see Connor before he boarded the train... yes... I'm sure of that."

"Okay... we'll check with him next."

"Please," Eleanor begged. "Do let me know what you find out."

"Don't worry, Ma'am. We'll find Marty."

As they headed for the door, Theodore called out to them: "When you see Marty, tell him I have his new suit ready for the final fitting."

Napoleon got in the last word: "NEW SUIT. NEW SUIT."

FIFTEEN

The little bell jangled profoundly as Christian pushed open the front door of the Mercantile. It startled him just slightly as he paused and stared up at the bell. Clay pushed him inside and closed the door behind them. The bell jangled some more. They were standing in the spacious store amidst an array of goods varying from pots and pans to picture frames and everything else imaginable. It was no wonder that the store was busy with customers browsing about and considering their choices for purchase.

A young man whom Christian barely recognized came from behind a counter to greet them. Roscoe beamed a broad smile when he saw them, glad that his new friends from the lake had come to pay him a visit.

Christian stared at Roscoe for a few moments; he had always seen him dressed in casual and somewhat drab clothing, appropriate for informal outdoor activities such as fishing and hiking in the woods. But today, he was gazing at a gentleman in garments that reminded him of a larger version of Clay! The bold black coat, open in front to reveal the matching vest, fit like it was custom-tailored, crisp white shirt and black string tie, shined boots—Christian couldn't help but wonder if there was a derringer up his sleeve, too.

"Well..." Clay said as he looked the store clerk up and down. "So this is the Roscoe when he's not out fishing. He certainly has a fine taste in clothes... don't y'all think so, Christian?"

"I'm so glad you're here," said Roscoe. His face reddened just a little knowing his visitors noticed his new suit. "What brings you two into Baraboo?"

"We came to see y'all... of course," Clay smiled. He was definitely impressed by Roscoe's appearance.

"And to find Marty Mason," Christian added. "But it's really good to see you again, too."

Roscoe gave Christian a curious gaze. "Lookin' for Mason?"

Just then, another man richly attired in a dark green suit joined them.

"Hey, Pop," Roscoe said. "I want you to meet my friends from the lake. This is Clay Edwards and Christian Parker."

Mr. Connor smoothed his mustache with his fingertips and then removed his wire-rimmed reading spectacles, peering at the two. "I'm Jacob Connor, Roscoe's father," he said as he offered his firm handshake. "I've heard much about you from my son, Mr. Edwards, and I can now see that you've had a bit more influence on him than I first suspected."

"I hope y'all don't mean that in a bad way, sir," Clay said.

"Not at all. Roscoe seems to have gained a little fortitude since his week at the lake."

"Yeah, well, a week of fishing could do that."

"He said he learned from *you*, Mr. Edwards. And now I see how his altered preference in garments has come about."

Clay quickly glanced down at his own suit, and then briefly scanned Roscoe's, confirming the remarkable resemblance. "Oh, well, I really didn't mean to suggest that he should—"

"Tut-tut," said Mr. Connor. "You should be flattered. Now, if you will kindly excuse me, I think those ladies over there by the sewing notions may need some assistance. I'll leave you three gents to continue your conversation."

Clay tipped his hat, nodded, and watched Mr. Connor stroll away. "Your father is certainly an honorable man," he said to Roscoe.

"Sure he is..." Roscoe said in a low tone. "...now that he thinks I'm dressed more appropriately... for him and his store. I just wish he'd understand that I don't really want to be here. I want to go out and see the world."

"And just how d' y'all propose to do that?"

"Well, I figure you will be moving on someday, and when you do, maybe I'll go with you."

"Us? Move on?"

"Sure. All entertainers move on... sooner or later."

It was true; neither Clay nor Christian intended to stay here in Wisconsin for the rest of their lives. Although they felt a certain degree of loyalty and gratitude to Simon Bordeaux, and intended to stay with him—at least for the rest of this season —they both had bigger dreams. Christian had visions of performing on the stages of the magnificent theaters in New York; and Clay... well... he wasn't sure that he would continue his career as an actor, but he knew that he wanted to see London, Paris, Madrid, Rome, and maybe Hong Kong.

Roscoe saw that distant look in Christian's and Clay's eyes at the mention of a common trait in show people. "It's true, ain't it?" Roscoe said. "Now, what's this about you lookin' for Mason? I thought he was with you at the lake already."

"Yeah," Clay said. "He was s'posed to come on the first afternoon train on Monday... but he never showed up."

"We talked to his mum over at the tailor shop... said he packed a bag and left Monday before noon... that he was coming to see you first."

"Yeah," Roscoe said. "I was plenty pissed off when he didn't come like he promised. I picked up this new suit from the tailor that morning... just in time so Mason could see it."

"And a splendid suit it is," Clay affirmed. He ran his fingers along the edge of the lapel, and then gently grasped Roscoe's wrist, feeling and patting the sleeve from the cuff to the elbow.

"What are you doing?" Roscoe asked.

"Just checking to see if Theodore installed a pocket for some light artillery."

"No... but he said he would..."

Clay grinned.

"Any idea where Marty went?" Christian pleaded.

Roscoe contemplated for just a moment. "No... and I don't care... now that he's run out on *you*, and never told *me* where he was going."

"But maybe he never left town," Clay said. "Maybe he's still here. How 'bout other friends... maybe he's with them."

"Me and Mason don't have many friends."

"Well, Connor, would y'all at least help us look for him? Y'all know this town better than us."

It suddenly occurred to Roscoe that Clay had just called him *Connor*, like Mason always did. Even though he was still upset about his best friend brushing him off, he felt a little distress, too. "I have to work," he said, trying to hide his uneasiness.

"But aren't y'all just a little concerned about Mason?"

Roscoe started to cave in. "Well, I can ask Pop if I can leave for a while."

Mr. Connor didn't see the urgency in Mason's desertion. "You know, Roscoe, he's vanished before... and he always turns up again, just like a bad penny."

"He's not a bad penny, Pop."

"He ran off last summer to join the circus... remember?"

"But he didn't leave then without saying good-bye."

"He'll turn up, Roscoe."

"But, Pop. Clay and Christian are part of a theater group, and Mason's s'posed to be practicing with them... they're depending on him."

"Mason will eventually turn up," Mr. Connor insisted. "Now, there's someone at the cash register waiting to pay. Go take care of her and stop worrying about Mason."

Roscoe obeyed his father's orders and returned to the counter. He dispatched a frown to Clay and Christian. They understood his message, waved, and headed to the door.

"We'll just have to look around on our own," Christian suggested. "He's gotta be here somewhere."

"Let's try the circus grounds," Clay said. "Maybe a chance..."

SIXTEEN

Christian shuddered to think that Marty might have changed his mind and had returned to the circus. But the only way to know for sure was to go there and ask a few questions. They crossed the river bridge again and turned toward the circus lot along the river with no idea of who they should approach, but somebody would certainly guide them in the right direction. As they got closer, they could hear brassy music that was definitely being produced by a Big Top band.

"Hear that?" Christian said. "The band is here somewhere practicing."

"Yeah," Clay replied. "We find that band and we prob'ly find Marty."

"As much as I want to find Marty, I hope we *don't* find him *there*."

They found the band on a large wooden platform under an open tent. The musicians sat on wooden chairs in a semi-circle around the band leader at a podium, feverishly waving his arms in direction as the band played a lively Sousa march.

"He certainly isn't lacking in enthusiasm, is he?" Clay commented.

Christian agreed, but kept inching around the tent, until he spotted a piano partially hidden from his view by a bass drum and a tuba. When he finally got in position to clearly see the pianist, he let out a sigh of relief. It *wasn't* Marty.

When the march ended, the band leader noticed Christian attempting to get the attention of one of the drummers in the back row. "Either speak up so we can hear you, or kindly stop interrupting our practice."

"I'm sorry," Christian spoke up. "We're looking for Marty Mason."

"Mr. Mason isn't with us this year."

"I know that... but we were wondering if anyone here might have seen him recently?"

Christian could tell by the murmurs and whispers circulating among the musicians that nearly everyone there probably knew Marty, and he hoped for something positive.

A trumpet player spoke up: "You might try Toby Atwood's house."

"Who's Toby Atwood?"

"He's a trombone player... but he's out with a broken arm. Toby and Marty chummed a lot."

"And where do we find Toby Atwood's house?"

"It's the brown house behind the big white church... over there on the hill." The trumpet player pointed across the river.

"Okay... thank you," said Christian. He nodded and waved to the conductor. "Thank you," he said again.

The conductor rapped his baton on the podium a few times to get the attention of his band again. "Okay... let's do that one again... and this time we'll slow the tempo..."

Christian and Clay were already on their way back to the bridge. "D'ya think we'll find this Toby Atwood?" Christian asked.

"Don't know. Did Marty every mention him to y'all?"

"Not that I remember."

As they hustled along the river after they had crossed the bridge, they could still hear the circus band playing the same tune with a few variations from the first time they heard it. Clay noticed something that didn't look quite natural among some weeds and bushes still clinging to their brown leaves from last fall.

"What is it?" Christian asked when Clay detoured to the dry foliage.

"Looks like... maybe..." Clay mumbled as he dug his way through the dry branches and weeds. He pulled up a brown canvas satchel, noticing by its weight and firmness that it contained something... perhaps clothes. "It hasn't been here long," he said. "It's too clean and dry to have been here a long time." Then, after flipping it over to examine all sides he turned to Christian with a somber stare.

"What's wrong?" Christian asked.

Clay stepped out of the bushes to where Christian was standing and held the satchel so he could see the stenciled name on the bag next to the handle.

Christian read the name: "M. Mason. My God… this is Marty's!"

"Yeah… but how'd it get in those bushes? And why?"

Christian thought a long moment. "There has to be a good explanation for this." He thought some more. "Perhaps Toby Atwood has the answer."

They climbed the hill, found the little brown house behind the church and when they knocked, a woman opened the door.

"What're ya peddling?" she said before the young men could even say hello. "Whatever it is, I don't want any."

"Oh, we're not peddling anything, Ma'am," Clay charmed. "We're looking for Toby Atwood. Are we at the right house?"

The woman wiped her hands on her apron, all the while her eyes fixed on the two Dandies in their attractive suits. "What ya want with Toby? He in some kinda trouble?"

"Oh, no, Ma'am. We have a mutual friend… Marty Mason… and Marty's gone missing… wondered if Toby knows of his whereabouts."

"I ain't seen hide nor hair of Marty for over a week," the woman said. Her words were sharp.

"But if we could talk to Toby…"

Another voice sounded from inside the house. "It's okay, Ma, I'll talk to 'em." A young man appeared behind the woman; his right arm bent in a cast and supported by a sling.

"Are y'all Toby?" Clay asked.

"Yeah… who are you?"

"I'm Clay Edwards… and this is Christian Parker. We're friends of Marty's."

Toby stepped out of the shadows, now crowding his mother out of the doorway. "Go back to your baking, Ma," he said. "I'll handle this."

Mrs. Atwood backed away, and then disappeared into the interior of the house.

"Friends of Marty's," Toby said with certain suspicion in his words. "Never saw you around before."

"No, y'all prob'ly haven't. We just met Marty a week ago Monday."

"Why did ya come here looking for me?"

"A trumpet player in the circus band told us y'all might know where to find Marty."

"When did you last see him?" Christian asked.

"Well, let's see..." Toby scratched his head with his left hand. "Broke my arm Friday. Mason came over, stayed here Saturday and Sunday, and then when we woke up Monday morning, he said he had to go up town, but he didn't go right away."

"And y'all haven't seen him since?"

Toby shook his head thoughtfully. "No... said he was coming back, but I never saw him all last week."

"Because he was with us at the lake all last week."

"The lake! What was he doin' there? He should've been at band practice."

"Yes... well... Marty's not in the circus band anymore," Christian explained. "He joined our theater troupe. He's our piano man now."

Toby shook his head in a slow, indecisive manner. "Well, I guess I'm not in the band anymore, either."

"Why do y'all say that?"

"Kinda hard to play the trombone with your right arm in a cast."

"But your arm will heal."

"Doc says I'll have this cast for eight weeks... the circus train will be a thousand miles from here by then."

"I'm sorry," Clay consoled.

"It's okay... there's always next year."

"What do y'all know about a fellow named Jasper?"

"Jasper Blackburn? Yeah, I know him. He's not someone you'd want to marry your sister. Why do you ask?"

"Did y'all know that Mason and Jasper had a little confrontation after he left here?"

"No, I didn't," Toby said. "But it doesn't surprise me."

"Oh? Why?"

"They've been enemies for as long as I can remember."

The jangling door bell at the Mercantile didn't startle Christian and Clay this time, but the urgency in their arrival made Roscoe take notice. By the expression on Christian's face, he sensed that something had gone wrong. "Hi Clay," he said. "Did you find Mason?"

"No, but we had a good chat with his friend, Toby Atwood."

"Toby! You talked to Toby? I heard he broke his arm. Did he know anything about Mason?"

"Marty had been there... just before we rescued him in the alley, but Toby hasn't seen him since. And we found this... in some bushes down by the river." Clay held up the brown canvas satchel, turned so Roscoe could see the name.

Roscoe stared at the bag. "That's Mason's all right. Did you open it?"

"No, not yet."

They put the satchel on a counter. Roscoe undid the buckles, flipped back the top, and then pulled out a blue coat and trousers, blue shirt, ties, socks. "These are definitely his clothes. Looks like he planned to stay at the lake for a while."

"But why would he toss it in the bushes?" Christian asked.

"And that isn't even on his way to the depot," Clay added, "unless he was going to see Toby again before he left."

"I guess that's possible," Roscoe admitted. "They did chum together a lot after Mason joined the circus band."

"Well, he never made it back to Toby's. Y'all got any other ideas where he might've gone?"

"What's this all about?" Mr. Connor asked when he eyed the open satchel and Marty's clothes on the counter.

"Mason's disappeared, Pop... I mean... *really* disappeared. They found his bag down by the river in some weeds. It just don't seem right... d' ya think?"

"Hello, gentlemen," Mr. Connor greeted Christian and Clay. "Nice to see you again," and then he contemplated for a long moment. "You know... Mason's been known to run off for a spell now and then."

"Yeah, I know... but why would he leave his clothes behind in some weeds? It just don't make any sense."

"Tell ya what, Son... why don't you go with these gentlemen and ask around town... see if anybody knows of Mason's whereabouts."

When Christian and Clay returned to the Cliff House late that night, they were too tired to do anything but to get to their room and go to bed. Their search for Marty with Roscoe guiding them for four hours had rendered no results. No one they talked to had seen Marty for over a week. It was discouraging to say the least.

Next morning at breakfast, Simon found them in the hotel dining hall.

"By the long faces I would guess that you didn't locate our missing piano player?"

"Um... we found a trail," Christian started to explain.

Simon stared with expectation.

Then Clay continued. "We found where he'd been and who he'd been with... a week ago... but..."

"But what? Where is he now?"

"We don't know for sure." Clay stared into the tablecloth. "We sorta lost him."

"Well," Simon said. "I'm sure he'll turn up soon."

"We're going back into town today," Christian added. "To look some more."

A waitress brought Simon's plate of pancakes.

Simon lowered his voice and leaned in. "I have something important to tell you. I haven't told the others yet."

Christian and Clay leaned in, too, eyes wide.

"I've located a building for our new theater."

"Simon! That's great! Where is it?"

"It's an old storefront on Third Street. I'm going to the bank on Friday to sign the papers. We can take possession next week."

"Friday... that's tomorrow," Christian said. Then he turned to Clay. "We've gotta find Marty."

"It'll be several weeks until the carpenters have the place ready to use," Simon explained. "But I do wish you'd get our piano man back here for rehearsals. And then, perhaps, we should put him on a leash."

"We'll make this next trip to town a crusade," Christian vowed.

Clay laughed. "Does that mean we have to wear armor?"

Christian gave a hardly noticeable wink. "No... just the usual hardware."

SEVENTEEN

"We should make another visit to Toby Atwood," Clay suggested as they walked from the Baraboo station. "I think he knows more than he told us."

"What makes you think so?"

"Because he didn't hesitate when he said that Marty and Jasper had been enemies for as long as he could remember."

"Yeah? So?"

"So, that means he knows more about what's between those two. And of all the people we heard Roscoe talk to, did y'all hear anyone mention any other enemies that Marty might have?"

Christian thought a moment. "No, I guess you're right about that."

"So, we need to talk to Toby again."

"Okay... but let's go see Roscoe first. Maybe he's heard something... or at least we can let him know we're here. Maybe he'll go with us."

The walk to Oak Street was most pleasant; there were kids and birds and pretty ladies in their new spring dresses fussing about in their gardens of budding flowers. The smell and the feel of summertime filled the day.

For Clay and Christian, a new opera house would soon be a part of their lives. It didn't seem right that they should be wasting precious time hunting for a missing piano player; they should be preparing for the shows. But Marty had become a good friend, too, and if he had found trouble, they should help.

As usual, they found Roscoe Connor at the Mercantile strutting among the customers in his spiffy new suit. The jangling bell averted his attention to the door.

"Clay. Christian. Good to see you again. Any new developments?" He shook their hands.

"No, but we thought we would pay Toby Atwood another visit. Can y'all join us?"

"I'd like to, but I'm afraid I'm stuck here for a time while Pop tends to a few business errands."

"Well, okay… we don't want to keep y'all from your customers. We'll see y'all later, then."

Mrs. Atwood said nothing when she opened the door and discovered Clay and Christian standing on the porch. Leaving the door wide open, she disappeared into another room, and then they heard her call Toby's name. A few seconds later, Toby was there at the door, stepped out onto the porch and closed the door behind him.

"Hi, Toby."

"What are you doing back here again?"

"Wanted to see if y'all might've heard from Mason…"

"No, I ain't heard from him."

"Okay… so what is it with Mason and Jasper? What's their feud about?"

"Started over a girl. But that's a long time ago."

"Who won the girl?"

"Neither… she moved away… to Reedsburg."

"Where's Reedsburg?"

"West of here on the Chicago and Northwestern… 'bout an hour with all the stops."

"Do ya'll think Mason could've gone to find her?"

"Don't think so. He gave up on her when she left."

Clay wasn't ready to give up on this, though, quite so easily. He still believed that Toby was holding something back. "Can y'all think of anything else that might help us find him?"

"Look… I told ya before… I don't know any more. But you might wanna spend some time at the Red Brick Inn… a tavern over on Fourth Street."

"Why there?"

"The crowd that hangs out there usually knows all the gossip… what's going on around town."

"Alright, Toby… we'll go there. But if you hear anything, we're staying at the Cliff House at the lake."

They left Toby's house and headed back to downtown. Being a county seat, Baraboo was a fair-sized town, and its several blocks of two-story brick and limestone business district surrounding the courthouse square always seemed busy. During the day, buggies of all types and sizes lined the streets, and scores of people scurried about. Cops in khaki summer uniforms strolled the sidewalks with Colts hanging from their hips. But they were a pleasant lot, cordial, and the Montana lawmen that Clay and Christian knew would have them for breakfast.

Unlike Silver Spring, where the saloons and gambling joints howled nearly around the clock, Baraboo's taverns and saloons, including the Red Brick Inn on Fourth Street, were quiet this time of day. Nighttime, though, is when they came to life; the crusaders would just have to wait for a later hour when the place started to populate.

"You look lost," a voice said to them. Clay and Christian turned toward the man sidling up to them, his pork pie hat cocked at a comical angle, his weathered face nearly as wrinkled as his tan suit that smelled of stale beer and cigar smoke.

"Not lost, really... just looking for someone."

"Looking for someone," the man repeated. "Done my share o' that."

"What do y'all mean?" Clay wouldn't have chosen this creature out of a crowd to start a conversation, but during his time spent in saloons and gambling halls in the gold fields, he'd rubbed elbows with a lot worse.

"Fact is, when I was a youngun, I thought I wanted to be a preacher, but then the war come along and that all changed."

"War? Y'all mean between the States?"

"Certainly."

"Blue or gray?"

"Blue, o' course. Joined up with the Iron Brigade... Wisconsin's finest. Anyhow, when I come home after the war, I figured I'd had a part in too much killin' already, so instead of savin' souls I started trackin' the ones that couldn't be saved."

"Y'all mean... like criminals?"

"That's right... made my livin' as a bounty hunter."

"Did ya capture a lot of 'em?" Christian asked.

"My share. Had t' kill a few, too... the ones that weren't willin' to come in peaceable."

"Sounds like an interesting life."

"Was... but I give it up... started t' get too dangerous."

"I know what y'all mean by that."

"But just now, I thought you might be willin' to pay a silver dollar for a bit of information you need to know."

"What kind of information? And what makes y'all think I can just toss over a silver dollar to someone I don't know?"

"Oh... a southern gentleman like yourself paired up with this big city dandy? I seen ya play-actin' out at the Chateau by the lake... tellin' ever'body you was part of a theater troupe come here from Montana to entertain folks with vaudeville comedy and song. So, first off, I'd bet you could part with a silver dollar, and second, the information could save your life, but the only way you'll find out is to hand over the silver first."

"Y'all trying to fleece me?"

"No, sir. Not at all. John Helge is an honest man. I'm tryin' to be your friend. I gotta eat, too, ya know."

Clay dug in his pocket, pulled out the coin and held it up for John to see. "If this is some kind of trick, y'all will be sorry." He flipped the silver dollar in the air and John caught it as if he'd had a lot of practice. "Now, what's the information y'all have that will save me and my friend from an untimely end?"

"You're bein' followed."

Christian's face turned somber. "We are?" he mumbled.

Clay remained steadfast with his usual poker face.

"Don't turn around to look... just casually glance to your left. At the store entrance across the intersection you will notice a fellow of certain reputation in this town."

Clay glanced to his left, and then quickly looked back to John. "That's Jasper Blackburn."

"Yes, and he's been followin' you since you left the train depot this morning. You know him?"

"Sort of... we had a brief but disturbing encounter a couple of weeks ago. How do y'all know he's following us?"

"I was walkin' past the depot and I noticed him watchin' you in a peculiar fashion, and when he started followin' you at some distance, I followed him. Thought it was strange. Does he pose a threat to either of you?"

"Perhaps. What do y'all know about him?"

"Only that his father has had to bail him out of jail a few times, and has called in a favor now and then to keep the lad out of jail… too many fights and broken skulls, too many girls that didn't belong to him, and then there was the vandalism to the Catholic Church… I was raised Lutheran, mind you, but defacing *any* church doesn't sit good with me."

Clay and Christian suddenly realized that John Helge was, perhaps, more sincere with his friendship than they had first imagined. Jasper Blackburn *could* be a threat.

"I suspect," Clay said, "that Jasper Blackburn might be responsible for the odd disappearance of another friend of ours. Marty Mason was supposed to start as our piano man, but he has mysteriously vanished."

"I'll keep an ear to the gossip mill," John said. "I'll let you know if I turn somethin' up."

"I'm Clay Edwards, and this is Christian Parker. We're staying at—"

"The Cliff House," John finished. "I know."

EIGHTEEN

They watched John walk away and disappear into the next block to the west. He was truly an unusual person, but they were glad they had met him. As for Jasper Blackburn, they sensed his eyes still upon them; a brief glimpse toward Fourth and Oak found him, but now he had crossed the street, coming nearer. Clay winked at Christian and urged him to cross the street. "Let's see if Roscoe is interested in having something to eat with us... I'm hungry."

When they reached the opposite sidewalk another man fell in step with them. "I see you just met Mr. Helge... quite a character, isn't he?"

This man had a more distinguished look about him, brown felt bowler hat with a colorful pheasant feather tucked in the band, a strikingly squared jaw line that gave the three-piece brown suit, white collar and string tie an appearance of authority.

"Yes," Clay replied. "John is a very interesting man."

"And do you have business here in Baraboo, Mr. Edwards?"

Christian gave a startled stare.

Clay just smiled. "Y'all are the law."

"Yes, I am, but how could you tell?" The man didn't seem at all surprised that Clay had branded him a law officer, even though he didn't display any identifying badge; he didn't even carry a weapon, although Clay was certain there must be a revolver inside his coat.

"Perhaps the same informant that gave y'all my name."

"Ah, but Mr. Edwards, your reputation precedes you—

gambler, entertainer—and I guess it would be fitting that a man of your nature would have a nose for the law. Allow me to introduce myself." He offered his right hand as they continued around the corner. "I'm Chief of Police Daniel Rowley."

"Pleased to meet y'all, Chief. This is my friend and stage partner, Christian Parker."

They shook hands.

"We keep a respectable town here, gentlemen, so while you're here—"

"Oh, Chief, sir," Clay interrupted. "Don't worry about us. But we are concerned about a friend who seems to have disappeared."

"Oh? Someone missing?"

"Yes. His name is Marty Mason."

Chief Rowley stopped abruptly at the walkway to the courthouse steps. He gave a little chuckle. "Marty Mason? Ellie Mason's kid?"

Clay had to think a moment. "Eleanor... yes."

"Marty Mason has disappeared so many times, they should've made him a magician at the circus instead of a piano player. He always shows up again in a day or so."

"I guess, then, that y'all wouldn't be concerned that no one has seen him since Monday."

"Like I said, gentlemen. Marty Mason always shows up. Now if you'll excuse me, I have some business to attend to in the courthouse." And then he was gone.

When the chief was out of earshot, Christian said "Well, it doesn't look like we'll get any help from the police."

"Didn't expect to. And now we have to handle Jasper Blackburn."

It was Clay's intention to walk right up to Jasper and confront him out in the open, in plain sight of at least twenty people on the street. But just then was when the shooting started. Several gunshots in rapid succession echoed between the buildings; Clay spotted the man coming out of the bank with a gun in his hand and a black kerchief over his face, apparently the source of the commotion.

"So much for a respectable town," said Christian. He turned quickly to see Jasper retreating in haste. Then more shots came as the gunman scattered lead randomly in all directions, an effective means to clear the streets. Women screamed as the men folk grabbed them and hurried them off to take cover.

Two more masked bandits exited the bank, one firing shots into the bank, and the other firing over the heads of the screaming crowd trying to flee. Glass windows shattered and bullets ricocheted off brick walls. It sounded like a major battle. Then a masked rider emerged from the alley leading three more saddled horses. He fired several shots into the street with a Winchester to clear the way as the gunmen on foot kept shooting, running to the waiting mounts.

Police Chief Daniel Rowley ran from the courthouse toting a Winchester rifle, bravely taking up a position on the sidewalk across from the bank. He aimed and fired a couple of shots, wounding one of the riders.

Clay started toward the melee, but Christian grabbed his arm to stop him. "Are you crazy? They have Winchesters in case you didn't notice."

Clay easily wrestled away from Christian. "I have to help the chief" was all he said, and then turned to see Rowley take a bullet in the arm, knocking his rifle to the ground and slamming him against a wall. The gunman charged his horse toward the chief, Winchester pointed, ready to finish the job when Clay, only ten yards away, leveled his .45 and squeezed off a single shot. The rider toppled off his horse and landed on the dusty ground, never to move again. Clay aimed where the other riders had been, but by then they had fled southward and were headed out of town.

Blue gun smoke and dust hung in the still air as near silence engulfed the town. Pure shock was the general feeling as people began slowly creeping back into the street, curious of what had just happened.

Clay hurried to Chief Rowley. "How bad is it?" he asked.

Rowley already had a handkerchief wrapped around his bleeding arm. "Not too bad... just a flesh wound. A lot less damage than what you laid on him." He nodded toward the motionless bandit lying in the dirt, and then stood up. He and Clay slowly walked over to the body. Rowley reached down and slipped the kerchief mask from the dead man's face. A curious, mumbling crowd gathered around.

"Frank Corelli," someone said, and several hands were patting the chief's shoulder and Clay's.

Rowley solemnly stared at Clay. "Thanks."

Within a short time the grave silence was replaced by near chaos; crying and screaming and shouting erupted as the reality of the situation set in. The bank had been robbed, and people were injured and dead; the comfort of safety in the town had been compromised. Store owners stood outside their establishments with loaded weapons ready to defend but too late to do any good, watching confused and dazed citizens wondering what they should do next.

Clay picked up the Winchester that lay just inches from the dead man's outstretched arm, stepped back to the sidewalk; Chief Rowley, his sleeve red with his own blood, picked up his rifle and headed briskly to the bank.

As the disorder continued among the people on the street, Christian found Clay, and they watched as four men hoisted the body into a wagon. Clay stepped forward and laid the Winchester beside the body. "This was his," he said, and then stepped back to Christian's side.

"I saw what you did." Christian said. "You saved the chief's life. He should be grateful."

Clay stood there silently for a while, reflecting on the past few minutes. It had all happened so fast. The visions of the whole ordeal replayed over and over in his head, and he didn't like what he saw.

He snapped out of the reverie, and then he spoke to Christian without looking at him: "Let's go to Connor's store."

They started walking down Oak Street, the bank on the opposite side where a large crowd was gathering. A pathway opened up for a doctor and two nurses to get inside, and then abruptly closed in again behind them. Obviously, there were injured victims in the bank needing medical attention; Clay pushed onward to the next block, Christian following. There was no point in joining the mob, only to add to the confusion.

Men, women, and children were still running—some away from the scene, some toward it, some to reach a parked buggy or wagon. Up ahead, Clay saw Roscoe standing at the mercantile entrance, anxiously looking toward the bank area, a shotgun clenched in his right hand, just like many other storekeepers they had already passed.

"I don't think you need that anymore," Clay told Roscoe as he and Christian stood beside him. "They're gone now."

"I heard one of the bank robbers was shot dead."

"It was Clay," Christian said.

Roscoe's eyes widened as he turned his head to look at Clay. "You shot one of the robbers?"

"He was going to kill the Police Chief… I had to."

Roscoe's frown was traded for an admiring smile, for he was truly gazing upon his hero. He glanced down to see the slight bulge in Clay's coat. "The Smith and Wesson?" He had seen the remarkable weapon once when Clay showed it to him at the Cliff House, and now he was even more impressed.

Clay nodded. "Uh-huh."

Christian Parker had gotten used to Clay's practice of late to carry the .45 revolver under his coat. It was much like when he'd first met Clay back in Silver Spring, Montana; there it was common for most everyone to carry a sidearm—concealed or not—but here, it was rare. But he saw Clay in a different way than most people did. To him, Clay was like one of those dime novel outlaws that you like and admire, because that fictional character has that good side that doesn't hurt anyone undeserving of harm, and is the first to help out a poor soul in need. Clay was a gambler —or, ex-gambler—with his share of dark history. However, that was behind him now, and Christian saw him in this new light. Judging by Roscoe's expression at that moment, he knew that Roscoe saw him that way, too, even though he was aware of Clay's past.

Mr. Connor came walking briskly down the sidewalk.

"Pop!" Roscoe said. "I was worried. Were you at the bank?"

"Yes, I just came from there. Let's all go inside," Mr. Connor urged with a troubled look on his face.

The store was completely void of any customers, but that was no surprise considering the circumstances. Everyone in town was more drawn to the situation at the bank than browsing among flour sifters and bed linens.

Roscoe replaced the shotgun to its discreet perch under the front counter just below the cash register. Mr. Connor stood behind him, mopping his brow with a white handkerchief.

"So, what happened at the bank?" Roscoe asked.

Mr. Connor put the handkerchief back in his coat pocket. "I didn't see what was happening at first... I had my back to it all, and then I heard a woman scream and one of the robbers pointed a gun at the teller, demanding access to the safe. I was so frightened that I didn't hear what all was said. There were two more robbers each waving two pistols at everybody in there. Then... I don't know... maybe three minutes later the first robber came out carrying a bag... I suppose filled with money... and the next thing I knew, the shooting started."

"The robbers? Or somebody else?"

"I don't know for sure... the robbers, I guess." Mr. Connor wiped his forehead with the handkerchief again. "It all happened so fast. I ducked down on the floor... just like the other people in there did... and there were more shots fired during the next few seconds... and then it got quiet in there... I guess the robbers went out and jumped on horses. I could hear a lot of shooting from outside, but I didn't get up to look. No one did."

"Did y'all recognize any of them?" Clay asked.

"The robbers? No... they all had masks."

"One of the robbers was shot and killed," Roscoe informed his father, but he decided not to reveal the marksman just then. The word would get out soon enough.

"Yes, I heard someone say that afterward."

"Was anybody in the bank hurt?"

Mr. Connor grimaced at the question from his son. "Yes... I'm afraid so. Three seriously wounded... and two dead... that I know of... Sam Johnson and another man I didn't recognize."

Roscoe put an arm across his father's shoulders. "Sam Johnson? That's awful... but, Pop, I'm glad you're safe."

"Thank you, Son. Now if you don't mind watching the store for a while longer by yourself, I'm going upstairs to lie down for a while." He nodded to Clay and Christian. "Please, excuse me, gentlemen. It's been a dreadful morning."

"We're glad y'all are okay," Clay said.

"Get some rest," Christian added.

They heard heavy footfalls on the steps to the Connors' upstairs dwelling; a door opened and closed. Roscoe could imagine Pop hugging his wife, and then telling her the bad news.

"Your Pop is a lucky man," Christian told Roscoe.

"Yeah… I could've lost him."

A dark shadow passed over Clay's expression; both Roscoe and Christian noticed; could it be that he, too, just didn't feel well after his experience? Obviously, something was troubling him.

"Are you okay?" Roscoe asked. "Would you like to rest in my room upstairs?"

"No, I'm fine." Clay dug out his pocket watch to check the time. "We should be getting to the depot."

NINETEEN

Thunderous dynamite booms at the nearby quartzite mine rattled the dishes on the breakfast table. No matter how many times he heard and felt the blasts, Christian always flinched at the sound. The others had become accustomed to the noise and vibrations, only raising a few eyebrows, so Christian's reactions were usually amusing to them. They didn't realize, this particular time, that the prior day's experience had put him on an extra sharp edge.

News of the bank robbery had already circulated at Devil's Lake Village. So when the entire cast of the Silver Spring Players gathered on Saturday morning for breakfast in the hotel dining room, it seemed the only thing they didn't know was that Clay had been the one who'd saved Chief Rowley's life.

"Do you suppose they have any suspects," Victor wondered.

"Well, they have one," Henry replied. "The one that got shot by some hero on the street."

"But he's dead," Clyde said. "And dead men don't talk."

"It was Clay!" Christian blurted out. He couldn't hold it back any longer. "Clay was the hero on the street. We were right there when it happened."

Everyone at the table turned their heads and stared first at Christian, and then at Clay.

"Is that true?" Charlotte asked.

"I'm afraid it is," Clay responded.

"You had your forty-five?" Henry said.

"Yeah..."

"When did you start carrying a gun again?" Victor asked.

"Since we've been looking for Marty Mason."

"Why?"

"Because the scoundrel who's probably responsible for Marty's vanishing act doesn't play fair. The *equalizer* evens the odds."

Henry threw Clay a curious stare. "You suspect that our new piano man is involved in some foul play?"

"If y'all mean to say 'Is Marty the *victim* of foul play?' my answer to that is yes."

"And do you think this *scoundrel* you speak of is mixed up in the bank robbery?"

"No... Christian and I saw him on the street at the very moment the bank was getting held up."

"And he turned tail and ran when the shooting started," Christian added.

"And you shot one of the bank robbers," Henry said.

"He'd already wounded the Police Chief in the arm... and he fully intended to murder him next... I had to."

"It's true," Christian confirmed. "I saw it all."

"So," Victor said. "Now I suppose the newspaper reporters will be swarming in here next."

"Never know..." Henry said. "Could be good publicity for our new theater..." He raised his water glass as if to make a toast with a theatrical flair. "To the actor who gunned down a threat to society."

The wheels in Victor's head were definitely turning at a high rate of speed. "You know? This is beginning to sound like a good stage play. I should start writing..."

"Has anyone seen Simon this morning?" Christian asked.

"He said he was staying the night at a hotel in town," Vivian said. Then Claudia added: "He was meeting the carpenters at the theater early this morning. I do hope he arranges for some private dressing rooms."

Chatter continued during the rest of the meal, but now the

conversations were directed away from the bank robbery and toward the speculations of a successful new opera house. Not that they disliked living in the hotel at the lake, everyone—especially the ladies—seemed anxious to settle into more permanent quarters in town. Only Clay and Christian thought they might miss the lakeside atmosphere.

They all agreed that on such a lovely day, it would be a good time for them all to enjoy a cruise around the lake together on the little steamer *Capitola*, in celebration of the new theater.

"I'll arrange it with the captain," Henry offered, "so we all can board at the same time."

As they whiled away the time on the Cliff House veranda waiting for their turn to board the boat, Clay noticed a familiar face coming toward them. Police Chief Daniel Rowley could have been there for any number of reasons, but considering the recent events, Clay felt confident that the chief was looking for him. When Rowley spotted Clay and stepped closer, Clay stood up and offered his right hand. "Good morning, Chief," he said. "How's the arm?"

"Good morning, Mr. Edwards. The arm is a little sore today, but the Doc says there shouldn't be any complications."

"That's good. Glad to hear it." Clay directed the chief's attention to the others. "Chief Rowley… I'd like y'all to meet the rest of the Silver Spring Players." He introduced each one by name as they stood in a semi-circle and shook hands with Rowley.

"I'm pleased to meet all of you, and I'm glad that you're all here together."

"We're going for a cruise around the lake on the Capitola. Would you care to join us?"

"Oh… no… actually, I'm afraid my visit to you today isn't exactly pleasant; I'm sad to say that I am the bearer of some bad news."

All curious eyes were now on the chief.

In a sorrowful voice, Rowley went on. "I regret to tell you that Mr. Simon Bordeaux was one of the victims at the bank robbery yesterday. He is dead."

It only took a few seconds for the astonished expressions to appear, and then the sobs from Claudia and Vivian poured out; Charlotte fell back into her chair and covered her face with her hands. Clyde rushed to her, kneeled beside her and put his arms around her. Clay and Christian, Claudia and Vivian, all engaged in a comforting group embrace. Henry and Victor removed their hats and held them to their chests. No one spoke for several minutes.

Finally, Henry quietly said: "I'll go cancel our boat cruise," and he started his walk to the dock.

"Shall I walk you to your room?" Clyde asked Charlotte.

She only nodded her approval. He helped her up from the chair and they walked away.

"Let's go to our room, too," Vivian told her sister.

"We'll walk with you," Christian said, and he and Clay escorted the women toward the hotel entrance.

"Mr. Parker," Chief Rowley called out.

Christian stopped and turned.

"Please come back when you can… I'll wait. I need to talk to you."

Christian nodded, turned, and continued on with Claudia.

That left only Victor with Chief Rowley. "Do you have any suspects?" Victor asked.

"We do. They rode south out of town… one has a severe gunshot wound, and he probably won't make it too far. The county sheriff has a posse out. It's just a matter of time until they catch up with them."

Henry returned from the boat dock about the same time Christian and Clay came back from escorting Claudia and Vivian to their room.

"How 'bout a good stiff drink?" Henry said to Victor. "I have a bottle of Scotch in my room."

"Yes," Victor replied. "We can leave Christian to his business with Mr. Rowley."

The two of them wandered off.

"You said you wanted to see me," Christian said.

"Yes," Rowley replied. "If we could speak in private?"

"Anything you have to say to me, Chief, you can say in front of Clay."

"Alright, then. First of all, are you any kin to Mr. Bordeaux?"

"No… we've just been close… with the theater and all."

"Well, he must've considered you important."

"Why do you say that?"

"Because his last words to me were 'Give the key to Christian Parker.' Fortunately for me, because of our meeting yesterday, I knew who he meant. But the only key we found on his person—other than a hotel room key—was this." Rowley pulled from his coat pocket a gold key strung on a gold chain. "Do you recognize it?"

Christian stared at the key. "Yes. The chain was around his neck, wasn't it?"

"Yes, it was." Rowley put both keys and chain in Christian's open palm. "I'm terribly sorry for your loss."

Christian closed his fingers around keys. He was fighting back tears.

Clay put a hand on Christian's shoulder. "Where can we find Simon's body… for burial?"

"The body is at the undertaker's parlor on Second Street."

"Thanks, Chief. We'll make the necessary arrangements."

"Alright, then. I will let the undertaker know. Now, I must bid you farewell, as I have other matters to attend to in town." He shook their hands and left.

"What do we do now, Clay?"

"Now that you have the key, we go open Simon's lock box, and then I guess we have to go see the undertaker and arrange a funeral."

TWENTY

They buried Simon Bordeaux's body the next afternoon. The undertaker hired a minister to perform a simple graveside service in a hillside cemetery overlooking Baraboo. The Players decided to keep it a small, private affair since they or Simon didn't know too many people here. Roscoe Connor and Chief Rowley attended, mostly out of respect.

When the ceremony was finished, the women in their black dresses and the men in their black suits didn't linger long, as it had already been a painful ordeal. The teary-eyed and silent mourners boarded the carriages awaiting the procession back to the depot.

But they hadn't been entirely alone in the hilltop graveyard. Clay wondered what interest Anton Helge would have in Simon's funeral, watching from afar, but because Chief Rowley was there, he kept his distance; there would be other opportunities.

"Well, that's that, then," Victor said while they waited for the next train. "Guess I'll be going back to Saint Louis."

"Yes," Henry said. "I'll be heading back to New Orleans. What are your plans, Clyde?"

"Charlotte and I have been discussing the possibilities of San Francisco."

Christian couldn't believe what he was hearing. "But what about our new theater?"

Victor put his hand on Christian's shoulder. "Christian, my boy... without Simon, there *is* no new theater."

"He's right," said Henry. "Simon was the businessman... he knew how to make things happen. None of us have those skills that he had, and I doubt that we could attain even a fraction of the success that Simon could have achieved."

"But we could try."

"If you want to try, Christian, we can't stop you, but you'll be on your own."

Later that afternoon, Clay and Christian lounged in their room at the Cliff House, not in the mood for any outdoor activities, even on such a warm May day. The others had all split up, each to their separate ways; Christian assumed they might be packing their belongings in preparation for travel to their next destinations. It was easy to understand that everyone's spirits were low; Simon had provided bright expectations, and there had been little doubt that another successful season was on the threshold. Now, all that had suddenly changed, and emotions could be nothing more than sorrow and disappointment.

Christian sensed something different in Clay, however. Amidst the sorrow for Simon's death, there was something else that seemed just on the cusp of anger, difficult to define.

An unexpected knock sounded on the door. Thinking it must be one of the Players, Christian was astonished by the sight of the man he barely knew.

"Oh, I'm sorry. I thought this was Clay Edwards's room."

"It *is* Clay's room... and mine. What can we do for you, Mr.— I'm sorry... I don't remember your name."

"Helge... Anton Helge. I was hoping to have a chat with Clay."

Clay came to the door. "Anton. What a surprise. What brings y'all out here?"

"I heard 'bout your associate, Mr. Bordeaux... gettin' kilt at the bank."

"How did y'all know he was our associate?"

"Word gets 'round... y' know."

"I saw y'all watching us at the cemetery this afternoon."

"Yes... reckon you did... wanted to make sure the information was correct."

"What information?"

"That the deceased was a close associate of yours."

"Not only was he our associate... he was a dear friend... and the leader of our theatrical troupe."

"Yes, well, then maybe you'd be interested to see justice done. May I come in for a little more privacy?"

Clay gave Anton a curious stare and nodded.

"I mean... those robbers and murderers caught and brought in to get what they deserve," Anton said as he entered the room.

Christian watched and listened closely. With Clay's next words he began to see the anger coming out.

"I'd kill 'em myself if I got the chance. But I know that prob'ly won't happen. And besides... Rowley told us the county sheriff has a posse out huntin' 'em down."

"Only trouble is that posse's huntin' in the wrong direction."

"What d' y'all mean?"

"The posse is headed to Sauk... and maybe Lone Rock."

"Is that south?"

"Uh-huh."

"Well, that's the direction the robbers headed. I saw all three of 'em ride that way out of town... hell, everybody saw 'em."

"That's just what they wanted you and everybody else to see. Oldest trick in the book."

"So y'all are saying that they didn't go south."

"Nope. They surely didn't."

"So where'd they go?"

"Clay... I'm a bounty hunter. Bank's put up five thousand dollars reward money on them critters. I can't be spillin' out ever'thing I know quite so freely."

"But I thought y'all said ya gave it up."

"I did... but I thought I'd give it one last shot... providin' I had you for a partner. I heard 'bout you and the fourth robber."

Clay gave a look that could peel paint off a church. "What makes y'all think I wanna be a bounty hunter?"

"'Cause y' lost a good friend, and y' want justice. I can see it in your eyes, and I can hear it in your voice."

"Clay!" Christian said. "Don't—"

Then there was another knock at the door. Christian scowled at Clay; he clearly didn't approve of the risks Anton Helge was proposing. He stepped to the door and pulled it half open. "Toby!"

"I gotta talk to you," Toby said. "It's real important."

Christian swung the door open wider. "Come in."

Toby started to enter, but when he saw Anton, he stopped abruptly. "Oh... I didn't know someone else was here... I could come back—"

"Come in, Toby," Clay demanded. "I'm assuming y'all have some news about Marty?"

"Well... yeah... but if I'm interrupting something..."

"Not at all, Toby." Then Clay turned to Anton. "Excuse me, for a moment, but this is another pressing issue." Then he turned back to stare at Toby's cast. "How's the arm?"

"Okay... doesn't hurt so much anymore."

"That's good. Now, what d' y'all know about Marty Mason?"

"I heard about the bank robbery and your boss getting killed."

"Yeah..."

"And I heard about you shooting Frank Corelli after the hold-up."

"What does that have to do with Mason?"

"Frank Corelli worked for the Ringling Circus last season... on the canvas crew... him and Dobbs. They're from New York. Me 'n Mason chummed with 'em a lot during our off time."

Clay guided Toby to a chair. "Okay... so will y'all get to the point?"

"Frank 'n Dobbs came to see me about a week ago... had another pal from New York with 'em. They were real upset when they saw my arm in a cast, and when I told 'em that Mason wasn't around... that he'd joined up with your vaudeville act, they got real pissed off."

"So now we've identified at least one of the other bank robbers," Anton said.

"Why were they upset about Mason joining up with us?" Clay asked.

"Don't know," Toby replied. "But I'm afraid they might've done something bad to him."

Clay thought about the satchel he'd found in the bushes by the river; Toby's speculation was believable; and then the visions of the robbery replayed in his head again, and he saw the wild aggression in that desperado's eyes just before he squeezed the trigger of his forty-five. The sound of the blast jolted him back to the present.

He looked at Anton. "How far do we have to go?"

"An easy day's ride north."

"Clay," Christian pleaded. "Don't do this. Don't go chasing after bank robbers."

"This has gotten personal, Christian. They're not just bank robbers. They killed Simon. And they prob'ly kidnapped Marty. Don't y'all understand?"

"I understand that you'll be taking an incredible risk."

"It's a risk I'll have to take."

At that point, Christian realized there was no chance of convincing Clay to withdraw from Anton's proposal. His decision, right then and there, was final.

Yet another knock on the door.

"Who is it?" Clay called out.

"It's me... Roscoe," came from the other side.

Clay opened the door.

"I wanted to see how you're doing," Roscoe said.

"We're kinda busy right now, but come in. Did y'all arrive on the train?"

"No, on my horse." Roscoe, too, was surprised to see Anton Helge and Toby Atwood in the room. "Hello, Mr. Helge. Hi, Atwood." He looked at Clay as if to ask what they were doing there.

"Anton and I were just discussing some travel plans."

"Oh? Where are you going?"

"Anton seems to know where Simon's killers went, and we're going after them."

"Where?"

"A day's ride north, so says Mr. Helge. But he won't tell me any more."

Roscoe submerged himself in deep though. "Newport?" he said as he stared at Anton. "Of course... what a perfect hideout for thieves."

Judging by Anton's reaction, and his lack of response, Clay figured that Roscoe must be right. "Y'all know this place? What is Newport?"

"It's a ghost town... up on the Wisconsin River. I've gone fishing there a few times."

"Ghost town?"

"Yeah... it was a boomin' town at one time... the railroad promised to cross the river there, but it didn't... bypassed the town completely and built the bridge at Kilbourn. Now there's nothing left at Newport 'cept a few rickety old buildings and empty streets."

"We should leave at first light tomorrow," Anton suggested.

"No," Clay said. "We should leave now. They already have the advantage."

"There's not much daylight left."

"We'll camp along the way."

"I'm going, too," Roscoe announced.

Clay looked at Anton.

"Can y' use a gun?" Anton asked.

"Been shootin' rabbits since I was nine."

"Well... guess one more gun can't hurt. You two meet me at the livery stable in two hours. Bring a bedroll and some grub for breakfast... and wear a warm coat. It'll get chilly tonight."

TWENTY-ONE

When Anton and Toby had left, Christian, once again, tried to avert Clay and Roscoe from going on this manhunt for pestilent criminals. "It's a bad idea. Catching bank robbers and murderers is a matter for the police to handle," he declared. "These are some dangerous men you're going after... you could get killed."

But his pleading had as much affect as a stone tossed into a pond: it made a splash, and then disappeared.

Roscoe sat quietly, just listening and observing. He fully understood Christian's reservations, but he was determined to follow Clay's strong and bold perseverance, even if it was forbidding.

Clay continued to prepare for the trip, filling pockets with ammunition, rolling a couple of blankets, and finding his fleece-lined leather jacket. Then he turned to Roscoe. "Do y'all have a sidearm?"

"Just my hunting rifle... and this." He clumsily pulled a derringer from his coat sleeve.

Clay gave a little grin. "Christian... where do y'all keep your Colt thirty-eight?"

It was no use. Christian now knew there was no point in challenging Clay's objective; he would ride off to some unknown destination seeking Simon's killers, no matter what. "It's in the bottom of my trunk," he relented.

"Got any ammo for it?"

"There's a full box."

"Would y'all kindly get it and let Roscoe use it?"

Christian opened his personal belongings trunk and dug to the very bottom, bringing up the Frontier Colt .38, that Clay had convinced him to buy from a drifter needing cash. It was wrapped in an oil-stained white towel. He hadn't fired it since the day he acquired it—target shooting at bottles and tin cans propped up on a fence rail with Clay coaching him, and he hadn't carried it since he quit working at the Royal Hotel in Silver Spring.

He handed the pistol and box of cartridges to Roscoe. "Here... keep it... it's yours... it's in perfect working order... I don't want it anymore."

Roscoe stared at Christian questioningly, and then he glanced at Clay.

Clay shrugged his shoulders. "Go ahead. Take it. Doesn't do Christian much good buried in a trunk."

Roscoe took the gift in his hands, unfurled the towel and inspected the weapon that still looked like new. He looked at Christian again. "But it's yours... I really can't—"

"Sure you can. You need it right now more than I do. I want you to have it."

"Thank you. I don't know what to say."

"You've said enough."

Clay looked at his pocket watch. "We should go. By the time we get to town and y'all get your gear, it'll be time to meet Anton. Where's your horse?"

"At a hitching post back of the hotel." Roscoe slipped the box of shells into a coat pocket and then stuffed the revolver under his belt. To offer assistance, Clay adjusted the gun's position a little, and then buttoned Roscoe's coat. "There," he said. "No one will ever know it's there."

Clay gathered up the bedroll and his leather jacket, and as he followed Roscoe out the door, Christian caught him by the arm, spun him around and hugged him. "Be careful," he whispered.

On the way into town, riding double on the spirited chestnut stallion, Roscoe and Clay formulated a story to tell Mr. Connor as to the reason Roscoe wouldn't be at the store next morning. Roscoe felt a little uneasy about not telling the whole truth of his absence and the real nature of the trip, but Clay convinced him that their story wasn't entirely a lie. "I'll handle it if y'all get nervous."

The sun was low in the western sky, painting a bank of cottony clouds in glorious shades of crimson and gold; the temperature had risen considerably that day, and now it seemed more like a day for a picnic. But there wasn't time for picnics now.

On a Sunday evening, there were very few people out and about on the streets of Baraboo. Clay hoped Anton Helge wouldn't keep them waiting. As he followed Roscoe up the stairs to the Connors' apartment, he thought about the disappointment Christian must be feeling, the other Players, all with plans to travel to other parts of the country. He thought about Marty's fate, and what he would have to say to him if he ever saw him again. And he wondered about his own future, now that the Silver Spring Players were breaking up for the second, and more than likely, the last time.

Roscoe swung open the door; Mr. Connor sat at a dining table reading a folded-up newspaper. "Hi, Son... Clay," he greeted. On the table was a spread of roast beef, boiled potatoes, corn and place settings for three. Mrs. Connor came from the kitchen with a plateful of sliced bread. "Oh..." she said. "You brought a friend. I'll set another place at the table."

They weren't counting on this; they had overlooked that it was suppertime. Roscoe looked at Clay. Clay looked at his watch. It was a five minute ride to the livery stable; they had a half-hour. Clay nodded, and then said: "But we'll have to eat quickly... daylight's wasting."

They all sat down to the wonderful meal. As Mr. Connor passed the bowl of potatoes to Clay he asked: "Why are you in such a hurry?"

"I'm not going to be at the store tomorrow, Pop. I'm riding with Clay to Kilbourn. We have to leave tonight."

"Kilbourn! For heaven's sake... why are you going to Kilbourn?"

"Clay has some important business there, and he doesn't know the way."

"Oh? What kind of business?"

"Jacob!" Mrs. Connor scolded. "His business is none of your business."

"That's okay," Clay answered. "It's some personal matters

concerning Simon."

"Simon?"

"Mr. Bordeaux... the man who was killed at the bank. He was a close personal friend."

"Oh, yes... he was the proprietor of your vaudeville troupe, wasn't he?"

"Yes, sir."

"Well, then... I certainly hope Roscoe can be of service. He's been that way many times. When shall I expect your return?"

"No more than a couple of days, three at the longest, sir. Thank you."

"And Mom?" Roscoe said. "We'll be camping along the way, so could you put some food in a bag for us to take?"

When they had finished eating, Roscoe dashed into his bedroom, rolled up the heavy quilt from his bed and tied it with a couple of leather boot laces. He emerged toting the bedroll, his winter coat, and the hunting rifle.

"Why the gun?" Mr. Connor asked.

"Injuns and snakes. Y' never know."

Mrs. Connor came from the kitchen with a cloth bag. "There's some ham and bread and molasses cookies in here," she informed them. And here's a canteen of cold water."

Because Roscoe's hands were full, Clay took the flour sack with the food and the canteen. "Thank y'all, Ma'am," he said. "And thank y'all for the fine supper, too."

She smiled warmly. "You are quite welcome... anytime. And have a safe journey."

TWENTY-TWO

Anton Helge waited outside the livery stable with a third horse, saddled and ready to ride. "You fellas done dawdling?"

"Sorry if we're late," Roscoe said. "Mom insisted that we eat supper before we left."

"Was it worth it?"

"Absolutely," Clay testified.

"Got ever'thing y' need?"

"Warm coats, bedrolls, food."

"I see y' got one rifle... what is that?"

"Winchester Ninety-four Centennial, thirty-thirty," Roscoe replied.

"She's a beauty." Then Anton pointed to the horse he had ready for Clay. "There's a 'Seventy-three Winchester in the saddle holster for you, Clay. Oh... and by the way... you *do* know how to ride, don't you?"

"I'm from the south, I lived in Montana... what d' y'all think?"

"Just checking."

When all the gear was secured, they mounted the animals and rode to the north. They passed by the cemetery where Simon was buried just a matter of a few hours ago. The sight of the fresh grave made Clay even more determined.

Anton led the way as the three riders entered into the forested rolling hills; he seemed to know exactly where he was headed. The trails weren't difficult to see even in the half-light of dusk. Now and then, they came to wide clearings and open prairieland where farmers had tilled the ground, and then they plunged into deep forest again.

"What did y'all mean when you said 'Injuns' back at your father's house?" Clay asked Roscoe.

Roscoe chuckled. "The Injun wars ended long ago," he explained. "But now and again you might run into a few... they're mostly friendly, though... the Ojibwa and the Chippewa that are still around. I just needed an excuse for the Winchester."

"Oh," Clay said. He was still suspicious, but he hoped *Injuns* weren't likely to complicate matters. He went back to his thoughts about Christian, the Players, and his own future again. Certainly, he would be moving in some other direction now—that is, if he didn't get ambushed and killed by the desperados he was after. But Anton knew what he was doing. After all, he was an experienced bounty hunter, and his skills had kept him alive so far.

Nightfall was nearly complete; it was getting too dark to continue on. Anton brought them to a standstill at the edge of a small stream. "We'll camp here for the night."

"How much farther is it," Clay asked.

"We're about half-way, I'd guess."

"Maybe a little more," Roscoe commented.

They took the saddles and the gear off the horses and tied them with ropes long enough for the animals to reach the water and plenty of long, dry prairie grass. The night air now chilled without the warming sunlight. Night sounds began to fill the darkness. Owls hooted, coyotes yapped and howled, and a soft breeze whispered through the treetops. Clay and Roscoe gathered a few fallen tree branches while Anton kindled a small fire with twigs and dry leaves. In a little while, the campfire had produced a good, hot bed of glowing embers, and to the three sitting around it, the warmth felt really good.

Out of the night came another sound—one they hadn't expected. Horse's hooves against the trail came nearer; Anton and Clay drew pistols, ready for the worst.

"Clay! Connor! It's me, Toby Atwood. Don't shoot!"

Toby dismounted and stood back from the fire, but close enough for the light to fully show him.

Anton and Clay holstered their weapons.

"Toby! What are y'all doin' here?"

"I followed you."

"Why?"

"I want to help."

"Toby… you have a busted arm."

"My arm is broken, but I'm not helpless."

Anton looked Toby up and down. "You're the feller that was at the hotel this afternoon."

"Yeah."

"You shouldn't be here. You should go back home."

Clay got to his feet and stood beside Toby. "It's dark and cold out here, Anton. He can stay the night." He turned to Toby. "Do y'all have blankets?"

"Yeah."

"Okay. I'll take care of your horse. Y'all get warmed up by the fire."

"But in the morning," Anton growled, "You head for home."

"But I have a gun, and I can shoot. Why can't I go with you?"

"'Cause it's too dangerous for a feller with a busted arm."

Clay got the blanket from the horse and draped it over Toby's shoulders. Then he led the horse to where the others were tied.

Toby kneeled by the fire with the blanket wrapped tightly around him. A few minutes later, Clay returned and settled in beside Toby again.

Anton wrapped himself in his blanket, leaned back against his saddle, and within a short time, the others heard him snoring.

"Toby," Clay spoke in a low voice, not to disturb Anton. "Why in heaven's name did y'all follow us out here?"

"Truth is," Toby said, "I thought I might get part of the reward money they're offering for bringin' in the bank robbers. Ma is apt to lose our house now that I'm outa work for all summer. Don't know what we'll do."

"Toby… I'm sorry… I didn't know."

"How could you?"

"I'll give y'all my share when this is all over."

Toby's eyes widened. "I don't expect you to do that."

Clay put his hand on Toby's shoulder. "I'm not doing this for the money. I'll do that for y'all… but y'all have to promise me that you'll go back home in the morning."

"But I wanna help."

"Toby… y'all could get hurt even worse, and then what good would y'all be to your mother?"

The reality of the situation overwhelmed Toby. He just shook his head; he had no more to say.

"Now, y'all lay down and try to get some sleep."

Once Toby was settled down, Clay moved closer to Roscoe.

"What are you gonna do now?" Roscoe asked. "I mean, now that Simon is... gone... are the rest of you gonna keep on?"

"I doubt it. Christian thinks we should, but all the others are sayin' they're leaving... Saint Louis, New Orleans, San Francisco..."

"What about you?"

"Don't know yet... s'pose I'll have to go somewhere."

"Wherever you go..." Roscoe hesitated a long moment. "Wherever you go, can I go with you?"

"But... Connor. What about the mercantile and your father? Y'all have a future there."

"I hate that place. I don't wanna be there. I can't stand being cooped up all day, every day in that store."

"Connor... do y'all really know what I am?"

"I think so..."

"I'm not a natural-born stage actor. It worked out for a while when the gamblin' got a little too dangerous and Christian rescued me from a bad ending. But poker's what I do best. I don't know where I'm headed next, but I know I want to see the world... London, Paris, Madrid... maybe even Hong Kong. I don't plan to settle down anywhere... anytime soon."

"But you see... that's the life I want, too. I want to see the world. I have money saved up, so I can pay my own way, and I would gladly be your servant... your slave... anything to get away from here."

Clay pitched some more wood on the fire. "Y'all are serious, ain't ya?"

"Please... let me go with you."

"I'll sleep on it... and speaking of sleep..."

They settled into their blankets and quilts.

"G'night Connor."

"G'night Edwards."

TWENTY-THREE

Christian was at the depot to catch the early train into Baraboo. He hadn't slept well; the thought of Clay and Roscoe seeking a confrontation with hardened criminals had kept him in a sleepless, tossing and turning mode most of the night, and he'd been wide awake since before the birds started chirping their morning serenades. But there were things he had to do that day before the other Players left; if he could, somehow, take over the contract for the building that Simon had purchased, perhaps there was a chance that he could convince the others to stay.

The train was right on time; as usual, a lot of cheerful people got off, eager to begin their stay at Devil's Lake Village and many were boarding, starting their journeys home. While he stood in line to board the coach, Christian thought about Clay; he wondered—he hoped—that Clay was being cautious, and that he would return safely, with or without the success of the mission. Somehow, though, he sensed that he and Clay were drifting apart; Simon's death had changed Clay, as if his interest in the theater had diminished. If the other Players left, there would be little hope of keeping Clay there, either.

During the short ride to the Baraboo station, for those few minutes, Christian tried to enjoy the passing scenery as the train chugged its way through the hills. The forest was getting greener, and patches of white and blue and yellow wild flowers dotted the hillsides. Spring was in full bloom.

He stepped off the coach at the Baraboo depot among a dozen or more passengers. By the time he walked to downtown, it was just about time for the bank to open. Several other men were gathered around the entrance, dressed in various attires from farm work clothes to business suits, apparently waiting for the bank to open. The conversations among them were about the robbery that had taken place there; they wondered how it would affect the financial well-being of the community; they wondered if the sheriff had been successful yet in capturing the thieves; Christian even heard the name *Bordeaux* mentioned.

And then came the snap of the lock as someone from inside turned the key to unlock the door. The bank was open for business.

He waited his turn to talk with a teller. "Hello… my name is Christian Parker."

"How do you do, Mr. Parker. What can I do for you?"

"I would like to talk to somebody about the building that Simon Bordeaux purchased. He was here to sign some papers on Friday… and he was killed during the hold-up."

"Oh, yes… Mr. Bordeaux… most unfortunate… you should probably talk with Mr. Norman Landry. He handles all of the real estate business."

"Where can I find Mr. Landry?"

The teller pointed. "His office is right over there."

"Thank you."

Christian walked across the large room to a row of small offices along the far wall. Norman Landry's name was on one of the doors. He knocked.

"Come in," a voice said. It sounded pleasant enough.

"Hello, Mr. Landry. My name is Christian Parker."

Norman Landry offered his hand across his big shiny desk. "Hello, Mr. Parker. How can I be of assistance?"

"I'm here about the building that Simon Bordeaux purchased to be used as an opera house."

Upon hearing the name Bordeaux, Landry's face turned solemn. "And why might you be interested in that?"

"Well, you see, Mr. Bordeaux was the leader of our theatrical troupe…"

"I see. And you are a part of that troupe?"

"Yes, sir… actor and singer. Clay Edwards and I came here from Montana last fall with Simon, and the other performers came this spring."

"Yes... that's just exactly what Mr. Bordeaux told me."

"So now, all the other performers are talking about going other places, now that Simon is gone. But if I can assume the responsibility of the theater operation, maybe I can convince them to stay."

Mr. Landry leaned back in his chair. "Well, Mr. Parker, there's just one little problem."

Christian's heart sank. He had hoped that Simon's deal could still be executed, that he could assume the contract, and with a little effort on his part, he could learn how to run a theater. But now there was *one little problem.*

Landry continued. "Mr. Bordeaux never signed the papers. The robbery interrupted all business that day—as you can well imagine—and he died before the deal was completed."

"So... he doesn't own the building?"

"No. I'm afraid not."

"Well... can I buy it?"

"I'm afraid you're too late, Mr. Parker. Another interested party that had the next option signed the papers Friday afternoon. The building is no longer for sale."

TWENTY-FOUR

Anton had thought to bring coffee. He cooked it in a little pot that he dug out of a saddle bag along with a couple of tin cups. Clay and Roscoe shared a cup. Toby didn't want any. It wasn't the greatest coffee—strong and bitter—but it was coffee.

"Oh, I meant t' tell ya last night," Toby blurted out as they all sat around the campfire. "I heard in town that the sheriff's posse found the bank robber that Chief Rowley shot... out at Parfrey's Glen... dead as a barn pole."

"Well," Anton said. "Now we know it's only two left."

"Yeah... they're sure it's two guys from New York."

"Now that you brought us that news, you're gonna git on that horse o' yours and ride back to Baraboo."

"But Mr. Helge... are y' sure I can't—"

"I'm dead sure... I don't want your blood on my hands."

Toby lowered his head, disappointment oozing out.

"C'mon, Toby," Roscoe said. "I'll help you with your saddle."

They got up from the fireside and went to the horses.

"So we got about four hours to go?" Clay asked.

"A little less... more like two."

"Y'all got a plan for when we get there?"

"Never make a plan 'til I see the situation."

"Think we can take 'em alive?"

"Don't know that 'til we get there."

"Y'all ever been to this ghost town before?"

"'Fore it became a ghost town... when I was a kid."

"So y'all know the layout."

"All different now. Most of what I remember is all gone."

Roscoe and Toby came back with Toby's horse saddled.

"Y'all ready to head back?"

"Guess so..."

"Remember what I told y'all last night."

"Yeah... thanks."

"Okay. We'll see y'all back in Baraboo."

"Yeah... see ya." Toby mounted his horse and rode away.

The last mile crossing over the moraines was the toughest part of the ride. Anton had chosen to leave the regular trail for their final approach. "If they're in there," he said, "They could be watchin' the trail."

At the crest of the last hill, a glimpse of the Wisconsin River could be seen through the trees, its sheer yellow sandstone banks rising fifty feet above the water on the other side. Below the hill was a mill pond, but nothing remained of the mill but a few foundation rocks. Beyond that lay a dusty strip that Anton pointed out as Main Street, and the few relic structures that had once been part of the business district of Newport.

"There's no way to get in there without being seen," Roscoe said. "Once you get across the bridge over Dell Creek, there's no place for cover 'cept those trees down by the river."

"Looks deserted. Y'all sure they're in there?"

"They're there, alright," Anton assured. "See the horse tracks from the buildings to the creek? They're takin' the horses down there for water."

"Maybe we should wait for that."

"Prob'ly doin' it in the dead o' night. We'd never see 'em."

It was time to summon up every ounce of courage they had. Anton knew what they would have to do. "Best way to find out where they are... is for me to just walk down there like I own the place. If they see me and start shootin' you two can follow the gunfire 'n sneak 'round behind the building they're in. They'll be watchin' me and won't know you're there."

"And what if you get hit?" Roscoe asked.

"That'll be my problem to deal with. You just get in behind 'em and take 'em by surprise."

"Y' mean... shoot 'em?"

"Yeah, Connor... think y'all can do that?"

"I... I... I guess so."

"Mr. Connor," Anton said. "Just remember... these guys are killers. They've killed before, and they'll kill again. If you don't shoot them, they'll shoot you. Now, which would you prefer?"

"They killed Simon," Clay added. "Remember?"

"Yeah, I remember."

"Okay... I'm gonna cross the bridge and head for the first

building on the left. If there's no gunfire yet, it means they didn't spot me, 'n you two should be able to get across the bridge. I'll move up Main Street... try to draw some fire. You know what to do then."

Clay and Roscoe nodded. They all rode down the hillside to the edge of the tree line and dismounted. Anton tied the reins to a sapling and pulled his rifle from its scabbard. He took a deep breath. "You boys ready?"

They nodded, and Anton started walking. He was nearly to the bridge when Clay heard some leaves rustle behind him. He quickly turned to look. "Toby! What are y'all doing here?"

"I couldn't just leave... knowing that you might need another gun."

There wasn't time to argue. "Well, y'all are here now, so here's the plan." Clay explained the strategy, all the while keeping an eye on Anton's progress. "Y'all said y' have a gun?"

Toby pulled from a pocket a Baby Dragoon, a Colt designed for use by the cavalry during the Civil War, a small gun effective at close range but not much more. "It was my grandpa's."

Anton reached the first building on the left. There had been no shots fired. He waved and pointed to the building across Main Street. Then he saw Clay and Roscoe hustling from the tree line toward the bridge, followed by a third... with a cast on his right arm. Anton shook his head in disgust. "What the hell..."

When his backup men had reached their destination across the street, Anton stepped out from behind the wall and cautiously moved forward. Clay peeked around the corner to watch for any other activity. When the two shots sounded, he spotted a bluish puff of smoke at a dark window three buildings up. By the sound, the shots were from two guns, each with a different report. One bullet kicked up dirt and dust at least twenty feet short and to the right of Anton; the other struck directly behind him, apparently just missing its target. A third shot, however, did find its target, striking Anton in his left leg just above the knee.

Clay spoke softly to Roscoe. "They're in the third building on the left. Anton is hit." Roscoe instantly ran to the back of the building and turned the corner. Clay knew he was headed in the right direction. Before he could tell Toby to stay put, and then make a dash across the street to help Anton to cover, Toby was already on a dead run to Anton. Amidst bullets kicking up bursts of dust all around him, he helped Anton to his feet, and with his good arm around the wounded man, together they hobbled to the nearest alley between two buildings.

When Clay saw they were safely behind the wall, out of the line of fire, he turned and ran to the back of the building, heading the same direction that Roscoe had gone. As he ran, he heard more shots, this time from three different weapons; one of them had to be Roscoe's Winchester.

He stopped at the corner of the third building he passed, peering down the narrow alleyway. Roscoe wasn't there. The sun was hot and sweat trickled down his forehead into his eyes; he felt his heart pounding. Then three more shots echoed—a smaller caliber gun, perhaps the .38 or Toby's Baby Dragoon. It was nearly impossible to tell where the shots were coming from. The robbers had definitely been surprised by the intrusion, but the surprise was over; now they were using their cover, hidden inside one of the buildings to full advantage.

Clay knew he had to get across the street and to the rear of the building where the robbers were holed up; his best chance was to circle around far enough down the street where he wouldn't be noticed. But there were only two more buildings on his side, three on the other. And where was Connor? The silence for the next few minutes was almost eerie.

Clay darted across the alley to the rear of the next building, stopped and listened. He heard running footfalls and more rapid gunfire. Looking around the corner, he caught a glimpse of Connor sprinting to the other side of the street, and then he disappeared between two buildings there.

A minute later, Clay heard more shots, but they were somewhat muffled, as if they were coming from behind the building across the street. Connor had drawn the robbers away from the Main Street windows. Now was Clay's opportunity to get over there. With .45 extended, ready to fire at any moment, he dashed across, positioning himself flat against the front wall next to the doorway. He held his breath and listened. For the moment, there was no shooting, but he heard hastened footsteps on the wood floor inside. Sounding as if they were coming toward him, Clay pulled back the hammer of his .45. But then the footsteps seemed get more distant, and then came the crashing sound of another door opening. Clay quickly maneuvered to the window, the shattered glass panes strewn on the ground at his feet. Just as he looked inside he saw the back side of the dark gray coat and trousers scurrying out the side door. It was the same gray suit he'd seen on the rider bringing the horses out from the alley during the bank hold-up—not Simon's killer.

But the one left inside the building probably was, and right now he posed a deadly threat to Connor. Clay stepped back in front of the door and gave it a hard kick. As the door swung open he took three quick strides to get inside. In one instant he saw through the open side door another open doorway of the next building. In the next instant, he saw the man at the back window with the rifle. Startled by the front door crashing open, the man swung his rifle around and fired. Clay heard the bullet zing past his left ear. But before the man could lever another cartridge into the chamber of his Winchester, Clay squeezed off two shots. The force of the slugs knocked the man against the wall; a moment later, he was sprawled on the floor.

Clay walked cautiously to him. He kicked the Winchester away, and then he kicked the man in the ribs, checking for any reaction. There was none. Then he went to the open window. "Connor," he said in a barely audible tone. "Y'all okay?"

Roscoe recognized Clay's voice, and it seemed safe to raise his head up to the window to peer in. He gazed about the poorly-lit room. "Where's the other one?"

"Gone for now," Clay replied. He stepped closer to the window. "Anton and Toby are between the second and third buildings. Anton took a bullet in the leg. Go tell Toby to get his horse and ride as fast as he is able back to Baraboo and get Chief Rowley out here."

"What about the other one?"

"Don't worry 'bout him... just go tell Toby."

Reluctantly, Roscoe turned to go, and then he turned back to Clay. "Are you okay?" he said.

"Yeah, Connor... I'm fine."

Then Roscoe was gone.

TWENTY-FIVE

With his .45 still at the ready, Clay went to the open side door, looked both ways down the empty alleyway, and then studied the doorway across from him. Unlike the building he was in—all one big open room—the next one appeared to have been a saloon with a bar and a back room. He crossed the alley; trying not to make any noise, he stepped onto the threshold, glancing to the right and left. Large front windows facing Main Street let in a fair amount of light. To the left was a doorway into another room; to the right a staircase with a landing midway led to a second floor balcony. Straight ahead, a bar ran about half the length of the room. *Lots of places for him to hide,* Clay thought.

This is where they had set up camp for the time they had been there; on a table sat a box with a couple of cans of beans, a few slabs of beef jerky, some stale bread. A hunting knife was stabbed into the table top. Scattered on the floor were several empty bean cans and what appeared to be chicken bones. Two half-full bottles of liquor stood on the bar.

Clay thought first to check behind the bar. Someone could easily be crouched down out of sight back there. He was still quite certain there was only one more to find. Slowly he sidestepped around the table and chairs, frequently glancing to the upstairs balcony. As he inched his way to the end of the bar, he thought he heard a noise like a shoe scraping on a floor, a noise that he was sure he hadn't made himself. But he couldn't be sure where it had come from.

Nervous sweat rolled down his forehead and cheeks, and his shirt was soaked; he silently admitted to himself that this was, perhaps, the most precarious situation he had ever experienced, and he suspected the person he had cornered in this building shared similar feelings. Never in his wildest imagination did Clay ever expect to be in this position, but there he was, very near a showdown, and he hated the thought of what the outcome might be. He felt confident of his ability in this predicament; if his theory was correct, beyond doubt, he held the advantage—his opponent was not an expert gunman. But one fact couldn't be overlooked: even a novice can get off a lucky shot. He had to remain focused. The slightest distraction could mean life or death… for one of them.

He was just inches away from discovering what—if anything—was waiting for him behind the bar. An element of surprise would work to his advantage. With the Smith & Wesson cocked and pointed he took a deep breath and then one quick step to his right. He stood rigidly for a long moment staring at nothing but a bare, dusty floor.

A rush of air passed his lips as he released his held breath; his muscles relaxed just a little, but the tension remained. His eyes now focused on the doorway fifteen feet away at the other end of the bar leading into the back room. Then there was the sound of a squeaking floorboard, and Clay was certain that it had not come from overhead. The fourth member of the gang was in that back room, and by now, he had to be aware of Clay's presence.

Clay stepped gingerly toward the closed door, his pistol still poised. Stopping about six feet short of the wall, he listened again. Nothing. "I knew it was y'all," he said in a clam voice. "I don't want any more blood."

There was no response.

"If y'all have a gun… and I'm sure y' do… put it down and come out here where I can see you."

Still no response.

"Let's talk this out. No more shooting."

After a long wait, Clay heard a soft clunk that sounded like steel on wood. Then the door knob turned slowly and the door fell ajar. A Colt Peacemaker came sliding across the floorboards through the opening wide enough to let a dog through. "How did you know?" said a scared voice from beyond the door.

"I just did." Clay replied. He lowered the .45 to his side and sighed a breath of relief. "I recognized your cap."

The charcoal gray coat and trousers stepped timidly from out of the shadows and through the open door. It was the same suit Marty had put on the day he left to become the piano man for the Silver Spring Players. "I didn't want to do it," he said. His eyes were bloodshot and he looked like he hadn't slept for days.

"Why, then?"

"They kidnapped me on the way to the depot. Said they'd kill me *and* my mother if I didn't cooperate with 'em."

"But y'all knew them from the circus."

Marty nodded. "How'd you know that?"

"Toby Atwood. I was there on the street that day, Marty. I saw y'all bring the horses from the alley. And it was me who shot Frank."

Marty closed his eyes and lowered his head in shame. "I s'pose he talked."

"Frank was dead before he hit the ground."

Marty looked up again. "He's dead?"

"Yeah... and so's your other buddy... next door."

"Dobbs... I figured that much... when the shooting stopped. And he ain't my buddy."

"And the sheriff's posse found the other one south of town."

"Carmichael? Is he dead too?"

"Yeah... he was dead. But the worst part is... so is Simon Bordeaux."

Marty's eyes widened. "What... how?"

"Simon was in the bank to sign papers on our new theater. He got shot. We buried him yesterday."

Tears came to Marty's eyes. "I... I... didn't know..."

"Marty... only because I know y'all didn't have anything to do with the killing... and I believe y'all were forced into this mess, I'm willing to turn my back if y'all want to walk out of here."

"But they'll hunt me down sooner or later."

"No they won't. Police and Sheriff are convinced it was three guys from New York they were after."

"The others... they *were* from New York."

"And they're certain that the fourth man is from New York, too."

"Fourth man... meaning me."

"Yes. And everybody... including your best friends and your mother and the police figure y'all are off on one of your sprees... not concerned... that y'all are gonna just turn up again one day like y'all usually do."

"How do you know that?"

"'Cause we've been looking for y'all, Marty. Remember? Y'all were supposed to be our piano man. Or has your new occupation blurred your memory? Christian and I spent days looking and talking to a lot of people. And in case you don't know... Connor and Toby were along on this hunt today."

"Connor and Atwood are here?"

"Yeah, but they don't know it's y'all we're looking for. Toby went back to fetch Chief Rowley"

"But Connor is here?"

"He's tending to Anton Helge just down the street a ways."

"Anton?"

"Yeah... your buddy Dobbs shot him."

"I need to talk to Connor."

"No, Marty... y'all can't do that."

"Why not?"

"He doesn't know y'all are mixed up in this. Y'all should clear out o' here before he does know."

"But where would I go?"

"Y'all got any money?"

"Yeah..."

"Bank robbery money?"

"No... my own... the bank money is hid under the bar." He pointed. "It's all there."

"Then get on your horse and ride to Kilbourn. They say it's not far from here. Get yourself a hotel room and lay low for a couple nights, buy some new clothes and burn that suit and cap y'all are wearing. And get rid of that horse, too. Then come back to Baraboo in a couple of days after this blows over, and y'all will be just fine."

"I don't know if I can do it."

"Sure y' can. It's that or be here when Chief Rowley arrives in a few hours... and he saw that gray suit, too."

"Clay? Does this mean we're still friends?"

"No, Marty... not like we were before."

"Then, why are you helping me?"

"'Cause I think it's the right thing to do. Now, get on your horse and ride."

TWENTY-SIX

When he was sure that Marty was well on his way, Clay went behind the bar to search for the bank loot. When he found it, he tossed the canvas bag on the table with the box of stale food. He looked around to make sure there was nothing left behind that could identify Marty. It would probably be the next day when Chief Rowley arrived from Baraboo; that would give Marty plenty of time to make himself scarce.

Clay felt justified in what he had done. Even though two innocent bystanders had died during the bank robbery that Marty had taken part in, he'd had no part in what happened inside. A jury, however, would probably not see it in that same light and Marty would suffer the consequences of the others' actions. Marty didn't deserve that. And now that all the money from the robbery was recovered, there was less chance that a full-scale manhunt would continue. Anyway, they were seeking a hardened criminal from New York, not a freckle-faced kid from their own town.

Now he had to contend with Roscoe Connor and Anton Helge. But he had already figured out what to tell them. He stepped out into the sunlight; the fresh, cool breeze felt good.

"Did y' git 'em?" was Anton's first words when he saw Clay.

"One got away."

"Sure he's not hidin' somewhere right here?"

"Yeah... one horse is missing... he's long gone."

"We should go after him. Could y' tell which way he went?"

"Too many tracks in all directions... but we don't have to."

"Why not?"

"'Cause I found the bag of bank money."

Roscoe's eyes widened. "You found it?"

"Yeah... the bag's pretty plump... doubt if there's much

missing."

Anton tried to stand up. His face twisted in a grimace from the pain in his leg. "We gotta try t' pick up his trail." But the wounded leg collapsed under him as soon as he tried to take a step. He let out a mournful groan as he tumbled to the ground.

"The only place y'all are going, Anton, is to a doctor."

"Toby and the chief won't be back for a long time," Roscoe said. "If we can get Anton on his horse... we could start back to Baraboo. Let's go get the horses."

Clay recognized Roscoe's eagerness, and his sudden willingness to abort the manhunt. "I s'pose we could."

They helped Anton to get comfortable again leaning against the wall. "Will y'all be okay if we go to bring the horses down here?"

"Yeah, yeah, yeah... but if I can ride to Baraboo, I could ride after that bank robber."

"Anton... that leg needs tending to..."

" Yeah, yeah, yeah... go get th' horses."

Roscoe was on his feet immediately, urging Clay along. They walked in silence to the bridge, and there Roscoe stopped.

"That was a pretty nice thing you did."

"What do y'all mean?"

"For Marty."

Clay's poker face remained. "Don't know what y'all are talking about."

"I heard you talking to him."

Clay stared at the ground, scraped the dirt with his boot.

"I came back to help you... that's when I heard you and Marty talking."

Clay gazed off into the distance.

"Were you gonna tell me?"

"No... I wasn't."

"Why not?"

"'Cause he's your best friend."

"How long have you known that Marty was involved?"

"Since the day of the robbery... I knew it was him on that horse coming out of the alley."

"Why didn't you say something?"

"'Cause I didn't really want to believe it myself... and if I had been wrong..."

"So are we gonna go on keeping it a secret?"

"Marty was forced into helping them... to keep his mother safe... didn't have anything to do with Simon getting killed, and I don't think he deserves to go to jail over it."

"So what are we gonna do?"

"Don't know 'bout y'all, but I'll be leaving here soon. I guess it'll be up to Marty."

They started for the horses again.

"What about Christian and the others?"

"The others are already planning to go back to where they came from. Christian? Don't know what he'll do."

With a lot of help from Clay and Roscoe, Anton managed to get on his horse. "We should be goin' after that bank robber," he grumbled. Clearly, he was getting weak from blood loss.

"We should be getting y'all to a doctor," Clay replied, and then he marched back to the saloon building. He came out toting the bank money, stuffed it into his saddle bag.

They were at the top of the last moraine when they saw two riders and the doctor's buggy coming across the flat prairie toward them. Clay spotted the cast on Toby's arm; the second rider was Chief Rowley, and Roscoe recognized Doc Hammond in the buggy.

"How'd y'all make it here so fast?" Clay asked when they met.

"We started out at dawn," Rowley explained. "I saw you and Helge leaving town last night... figured Helge was after the bounty and he knew something the sheriff's posse didn't."

Anton could barely keep himself in the saddle.

"He took a bullet in the leg," Roscoe said as he reached over to help steady the wounded bounty hunter.

Doc Hammond rushed to Anton. "Help me get him down," he ordered the others. "We'll put him in the back of my buggy." When Anton was in the buggy, Doc immediately went to work on his leg.

Clay took Chief Rowley aside. "Y'all will find a body in the fourth building on the left side of the street," he said. "His horse is between the next two buildings. I'm sorry... but I had to shoot him. He didn't leave me a choice."

"There should've been two," Rowley said.

"There was… but the second one got away."

"See which way he went?"

"No… I was inside the building… just saw him head for his horse."

"What'd he look like?"

Clay thought a moment. "Big guy… black hair, real mean-lookin' and he was wearing a blue shirt and a big black cowboy hat."

TWENTY-SEVEN

Toby and Doc Hammond had gone on ahead with Anton while the others returned to Newport to retrieve the dead bank robber. It was quite late that night when Clay, Roscoe and Chief Rowley made it back to Baraboo with the body slung over the saddle of his horse.

At the end of the long, tiring ride, Chief Rowley turned to Clay. "I've been watching how you handle yourself, Mr. Edwards. I think I could use someone like you on my police force."

"Are y'all offering me a job as a lawman?" Clay said.

"I'm prepared to pay you a good salary."

"Well, Chief, I'm flattered... but I don't think this is the place for me."

"Why not?"

"It's kind of personal, and besides... I've made other plans."

"I see. And do your plans involve staying in Baraboo?"

"I don't think so, Chief... and thanks for the offer."

"Okay, but if you do change your mind, you know where to find me." The chief started to the undertaker's parlor with the body.

"Chief," Clay called out to him. He unbuckled the saddle bag and pulled out the bank loot. "Don't you want this?"

"Oh, yes... I'll get it back to them in the morning."

Clay and Roscoe got their horses back into the stable, and then they walked back to the Oak Street mercantile.

"There aren't any more trains back to the lake until morning," Roscoe said. "You might as well stay here tonight."

Clay didn't voice any objections; it had been an extremely long day. He was tired.

At the breakfast table the next morning, Mr. Connor was pleased that Roscoe and Clay had returned. "You must've concluded your business in Kilbourn quickly."

"Yes, sir."

"Actually, Pop," Roscoe said, "Clay shot another one of the bank robbers... and he got back the bank's money."

Jacob Connor nearly choked on a piece of bacon. "What? How did that happen?"

"Well, in all honesty, sir," Clay said. "That was the business I had to attend to."

"How did you know where to find him?"

"Anton Helge… he invited me to accompany him… said he knew where they might've gone."

"You shoulda seen it, Pop! Anton got shot in the leg and so he couldn't do any more… so Clay 'n me cornered 'em in one of the old buildings at Newport… that's where Clay shot him dead."

"He didn't leave me any choice, sir… just want y'all to know that."

Even though Mr. Connor seemed a little disturbed about his son exposed to such danger, he couldn't help but congratulate Clay's actions. "Well, he was a thief and a murderer… I guess he got what he deserved."

"I'm glad y'all see it that way, sir."

Chief Rowley know about it yet?"

"Yeah, Pop. The chief and Doc Hammond followed us there, and a good thing, too… 'cause of Anton getting shot… and the chief brought back the body."

"I heard the bank is offering a sizeable reward."

"Yes," Clay replied. "But it was Anton who tracked 'em down… the reward will probably go to him."

Roscoe was back to work in the store; Clay was free to roam about for a while, as the next train to the lake wasn't due for a couple of hours. He decided his first stop should be at Theodore's Tailor Shop.

"NEW SUIT… NEW SUIT," the big colorful bird squawked as he entered.

Theodore appeared from the back work room. "Aaaaah, Mr. Edwards, isn't it? So nice to see you again."

"NEW SUIT! NEW SUIT!"

"Napoleon!" Theodore scolded. "That's quite enough!" Then he turned to Clay again, eyeing his clothes that had recently become a bit tattered and frayed. "I see you are in need of some new garments."

"Yes, Theodore, I am… y'all can take my measurements

today... but I would really like to talk to Ellie Mason, too."

Eleanor Mason flipped the curtain aside. "Did I hear someone mention my name?"

"Hello, Mrs. Mason," Clay greeted. "I have some good news for y'all... I found Marty."

"Where has he been this time?"

"He's in Kilbourn..."

"Kilbourn! What on earth is he doing there?"

"I... I... don't really know... but I'm sure he'll be home in a couple of days or so."

"That's a relief... I sure wish he'd tell me where he's going."

Theodore measured Clay for the new suit and assured him he could have it ready by the end of the week, derringer pocket in the sleeve and all.

"Good, Clay replied. "I shall stop in again on Friday."

As he left the tailor shop, Chief Rowley fell in step with him.

"G' morning, Chief."

"G' morning, Mr. Edwards. Would you have a few moments to accompany me to the bank?"

"Well, I must get to the depot to catch the next train to the lake."

"This will only take a moment... it's very important."

Clay hadn't stopped thinking that Rowley would eventually figure out Marty's connection with the bank robbers. Rowley hadn't mentioned it yet, but now he was dragging Clay to the scene of the crime. "Okay... if it's absolutely necessary."

They walked to the next block and entered the bank; splintered recesses still showed in the walls where the bank robbers' bullets had struck, but business seemed to be back to normal. Rowley ushered Clay to a large office near the back of the lobby and knocked on the closed door.

"Come in," came a voice from inside.

Rowley opened the door; he and Clay stepped in.

"Well, Chief Rowley! I didn't expect you back so soon."

"I didn't have to go to the lake to find Mr. Edwards," the chief said. "He was right here in town."

The big, gray-haired man rose from behind his desk. He eyed Clay. "This must be Mr. Edwards."

"Clay Edwards." Clay offered his hand.

"I'm George Peterson, president of this bank." He shook Clay's hand firmly.

"Pleased to me y'all, Mr. Peterson."

"Chief Rowley tells me that you are responsible for recovering the bank's money... and gunning down those thieves."

Clay's face turned slightly red. "Well... yes... I guess I am. I'm sorry I had to kill them."

"You did what you had to do," Peterson said, reassuring Clay with justification. He picked up a thick brown envelope from his desk. "On behalf of the Bank of Baraboo, I present you this reward... five thousand dollars... as promised." He held the envelope within Clay's reach.

"But we didn't catch the last one... he's still out there somewhere."

"I'm sure that other critter will get caught sooner or later. We got all our money back from the robbery... that's the important thing, Mr. Edwards."

Clay gracefully accepted the envelope. "There were others involved in this, y' know... I'll share it with them."

"You do as you see fit, Mr. Edwards."

"Thank you, sir."

With five thousand dollars cash in his coat pocket, Clay walked calmly down the street. He had abandoned the plan to get to the depot for now; he had more important things to do. He turned the corner and headed to Toby Atwood's house.

Mrs. Atwood opened the front door. A look of disgust covered her face. "How dare you come 'round here... after gettin' Toby almost kilt?"

"I'm sorry, Ma'am... but I think y'all should be very proud of your son's bravery. He saved Anton's life."

Toby came to the door. His cast wasn't white anymore, stained and smudged with dust and dirt. "Hi, Clay."

"Hi, Toby. I have something for y'all and your mother."

"What?" Toby asked curiously.

"Hold out your hand." Clay counted out two thousand dollars into Toby's upturned palm. "There. That's your share of the reward money." No other explanation was necessary.

Toby stared in disbelief.

Awestruck, Mrs. Atwood couldn't say another word.

Clay closed Toby's fingers around the cash. "Don't let the wind blow it away."

Toby finally regained his composure. "See, Ma? I told you Clay was a good person. And didn't I tell you that I'd find a way to get us some money." He turned to Clay with tears welling up in his eyes. "Thank you. I don't know what to say."

"Won't you come in?" Mrs. Atwood said. She was smiling now. "I just made a pitcher of cold lemonade."

"Thank you, Ma'am... but I really must be going. I have to catch a train."

He left Toby and his stammering mother on the front porch. Now they could survive nicely until Toby's arm healed and he could get back to work.

A pair of crutches leaned against one arm of a big wicker chair where Anton sat on the front porch of his shabby little house, a yellow tabby cat curled up in his lap. His right leg was wrapped in white bandages, propped up on a stool. He shaded his eyes with one hand when he saw Clay coming across the tiny yard.

"Hello, Anton. How's the leg?"

"Mornin' Clay. Doc says I won't lose it... but it came close."

"I didn't know where to find y'all, so I asked Chief Rowley. Hope y'all don't mind."

"I hope you don't mind that I don't get up to shake your hand."

"Of course not. Does it hurt?"

"Only when I move."

"Well, I came over to see how y'all are... and to give y'all this." Clay pulled one thousand dollars from his coat pocket and handed it to Anton.

"What's this?"

"Your share of the reward."

"But you did all the dirty work. I didn't—"

"I want y'all to have it," Clay insisted. "Y'all gotta eat."

"But you 'n Roscoe should—"

"There's enough for all of us."

"And what 'bout that kid... Toby?"

"He got his share, too."

"Okay... good... 'cause if it wasn't for him, I might not be here."

The bell jangled as Clay entered the Mercantile. Out of habit, Roscoe turned to see the arriving customer. Clay always warranted his immediate attention.

"I thought you were going back to the lake on the next train."

"Well, something came up. Can y'all get away for just a minute? I need to talk to y'all in private."

"Sure. I'll tell Pop." He zigzagged across the room among several customers, whispered something to his father, and then motioned to Clay to join him at the rear of the store. They slipped out through the back room and into the alley.

"Why all the secrecy?" Roscoe asked.

"I wanted this to be just between us. Hold out your hand."

TWENTY-EIGHT

It had been nearly a week since they buried Simon. The pleasant May weather helped ease the sorrow, but his tragic loss was still painful. To add to the grief, now, once again, the Silver Spring Players were going their separate ways without having performed a single show together in Wisconsin. Claudia and Vivian were on their way to Chicago; Clyde and Charlotte were headed to San Francisco; Victor was returning to St. Louis and Henry to New Orleans. Christian and Clay saw them all off at the Devil's Lake Depot.

Clay returned to the lake Friday afternoon wearing the new Theodore-tailored suit. He and Christian sat at the Chateau overlooking the water, sipping ale and not discussing much of anything that had to do with either of their plans. Christian had been sulking for many days; Clay knew it was because of the theater building slipping out of his reach; he had wanted it more than anything, but now he, too, would have to plan a new strategy.

"Where do you suppose Marty disappeared to?" Christian asked.

It occurred to Clay that Marty's disappearance was part of Christian's low spirits. "I am quite confident that he's okay… that he'll just show up… like everybody says he will." Even though he had told Christian about the reward money and his harrowing experience with the third bank robber, he couldn't tell the whole story about what had happened at Newport; the last thing Christian needed was to form some negative feelings toward Marty. Marty could still be useful to Christian, and for Marty's sake, he hoped Christian would get him away from Baraboo.

Nor did he tell Christian that he had seen Marty in town earlier that day when he picked up his new suit at the tailor shop, or that he had invited Marty and Roscoe to join them for supper at the hotel.

They had just settled down at their supper table in the Cliff House dining room when two familiar faces appeared beside them. Christian's lower jaw practically bounced off the tablecloth.

Marty Mason was wearing his stunning new burgundy suit

from Theodore's Tailor Shop. Roscoe Connor looked more like a gentleman gambler every day in his classy black three-piece, shiny boots and black hat.

"Mind if we join you?" Roscoe asked.

Clay motioned to the two empty chairs; his eyes fired a couple of warning shots in Marty's direction.

Christian beamed a grin. "I'm glad you're here," he said. "But where have you been?"

Marty glanced toward Clay for only a moment, and then fixed his eyes on Christian. "I... I... ran into a little difficulty last week... and I... I... couldn't make it to the lake. But I'll tell you about that another time."

"Y' see, Christian?" Clay said. "Told y'all he'd show up."

Just as Clay had instructed, Marty acted as if he were unaware of the past week's events. "I'm terribly sorry for not making it to the rehearsals..."

"Everything's different now," Christian said, a little sorrow tainting his words. Then he went on to explain to Marty about Simon's death, and about the rest of the Players leaving.

In reality, Marty knew about Simon, but he didn't know about the total breakup of the troupe. He stared questioningly at Christian, and then at Clay. "So... what do we do now?"

Clay gazed a long moment into Christian's eyes. Christian was a dear friend, and he meant a lot to Clay. But Clay had different desires now, and Christian was already aware that continuing in show business wasn't among them.

"My acting career is over," Clay told Marty.

"But... but... what will you do?"

"I'm going to London."

"London!"

"And from there, prob'ly Madrid... maybe Morocco. It's time for me to see the world. And Connor is going to see it with me."

Roscoe Connor grinned.

Marty stared at each one, bewildered. Then he turned his gaze to Christian.

"And I'm going to New York," Christian said. "To perform in the theaters there. How 'bout it, Mason? I could use a good piano man."

ABOUT THE AUTHOR

J.L. Fredrick lived his youth in rural Western Wisconsin, a modest but comfortable life not far from the Mississippi River. His father was a farmer, and his mother, an elementary school teacher. He attended a one-room country school for his first seven years of education.

Wisconsin has been home all his life, with exception of a few years in Minnesota and Florida. After college in La Crosse, Wisconsin and a stint with Uncle Sam during the Viet Nam era, the next few years were unsettled as he explored and experimented with life's options. He entered into the transportation industry in 1975 where he remained until retirement in 2012. He is a long-time member of the Wisconsin State Historical Society.

Since 2001 he has fourteen published novels to his credit, and two non-fiction history volumes, *Rivers, Roads, & Rails,* and *Ghostville.* He was a featured author during Grand Excursion 2004.

J.L. Fredrick is currently exploring the U.S. in an RV.